I0732020

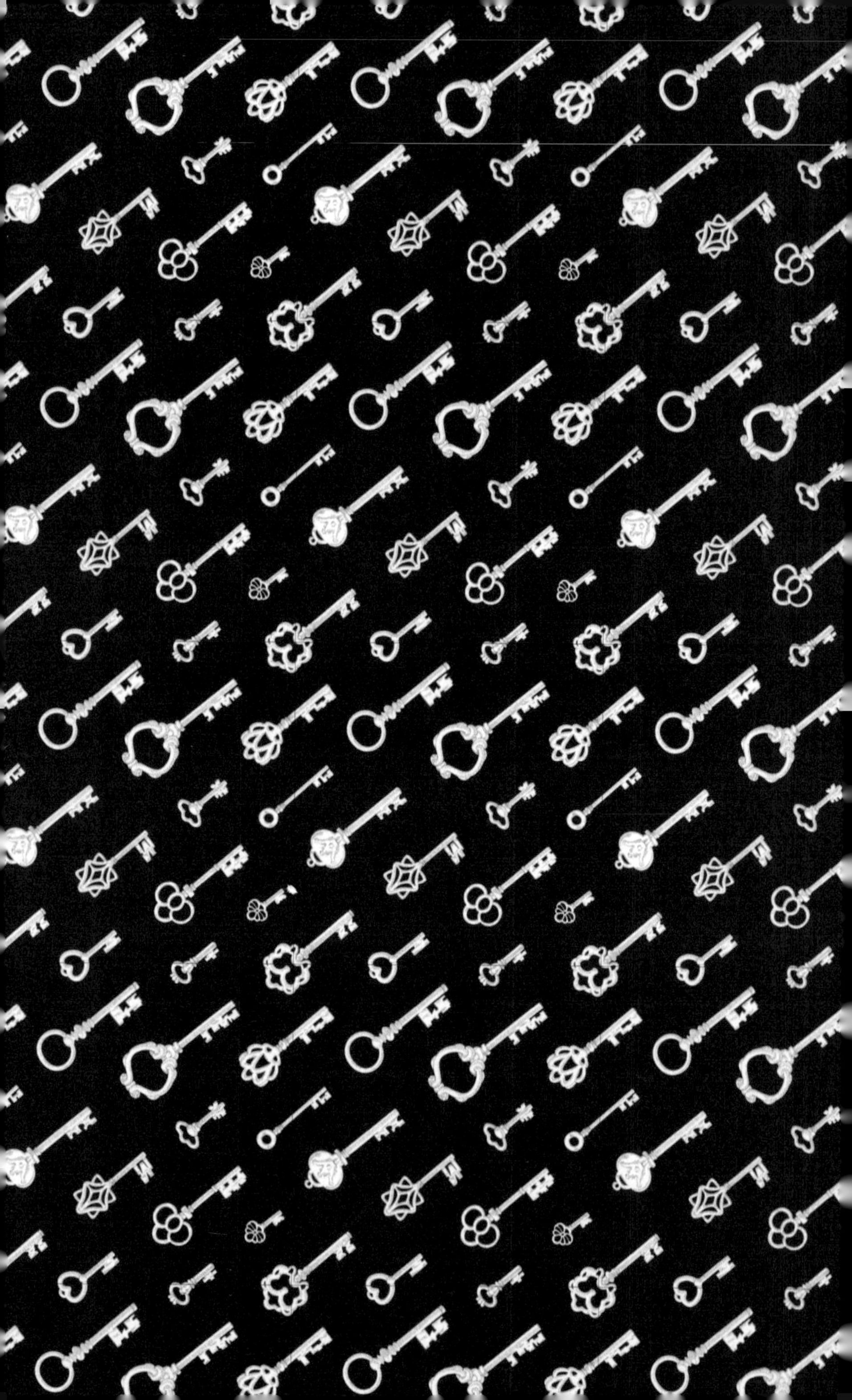

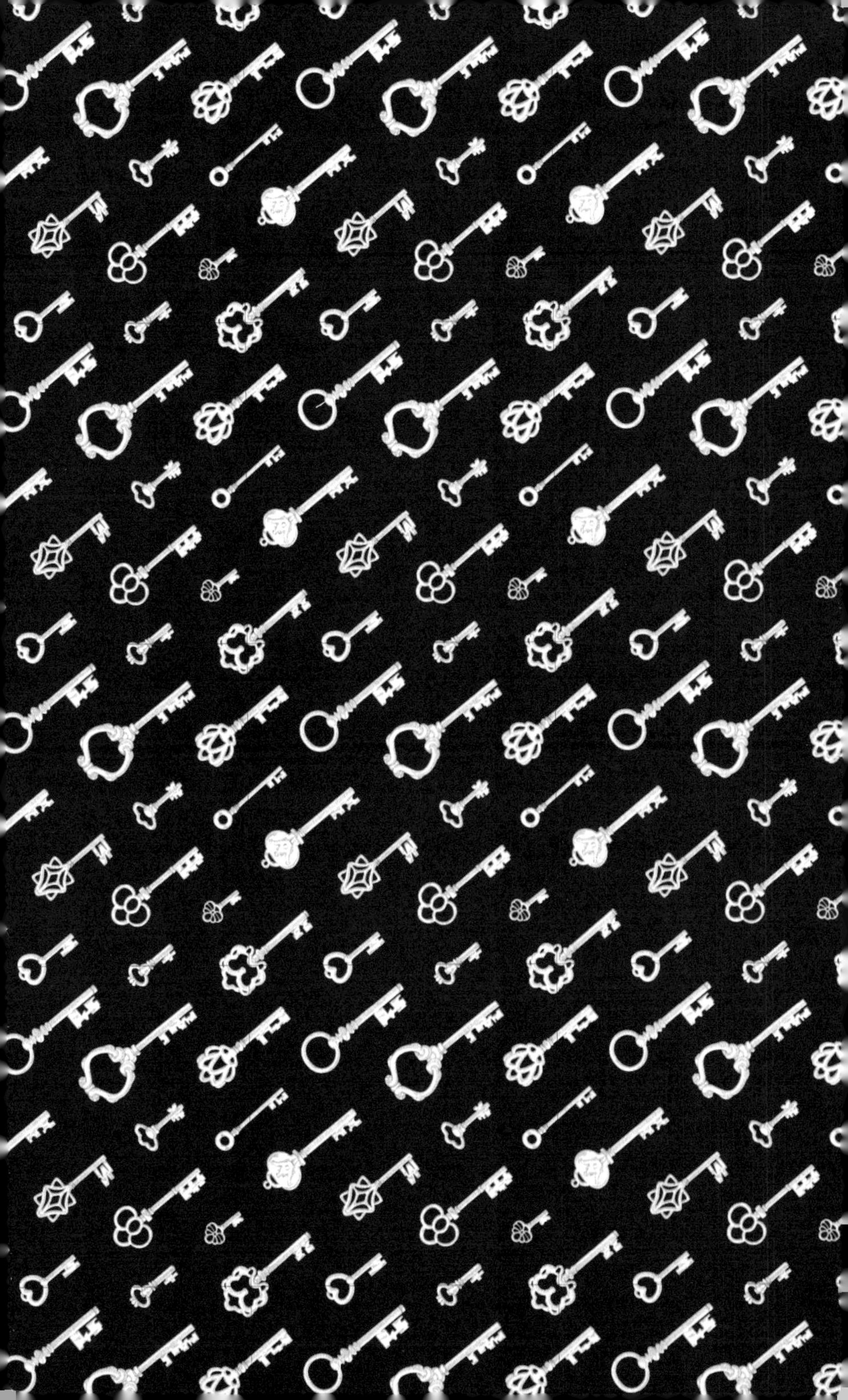

ZELDA FRENCH

4

COLETTE INTERNATIONAL

The International Edition

ISBN: 9781739686499

COVER DESIGNED BY MIBLART
COVER PORTRAITS BY KOMIKLY
INTERIOR GRAPHICS: GOODSTUDIOS AND VECTORTRADITION
INTERIOR ILLUSTRATIONS: JESSYM.

SUBSCRIBE TO ZELDA'S MAILING LIST AT:
WWW.ZELDAFRENCH.COM

.

BEFORE YOU READ

Content warnings:

This book still isn't intended for readers under the age of 18.
It unfolds at a slow pace and contains several dark and emotionally intense
scenes that you may find difficult to read.

The **updated** list of possibly triggering content is on page 471.
(Be careful as the list contains spoilers.)

Proceed at your own discretion.

Language:

The different languages spoken throughout the book have been
adapted/stylised to ease the reader's experience.
You will find **footnotes** where needed.

Alberto learned English in the U.K,
whereas Mathias was taught American English.
Their chapters reflect that.

♀

FICTION IS NOT REALITY.
THE CHARACTERS IN THIS SERIES SOMETIMES ACT IN AN OVER-THE-TOP
FASHION THAT WOULDN'T BE APPROPRIATE IN THE REAL WORLD.
YOU ARE **NOT** ENCOURAGED TO REPRODUCE
SOME OF THE THINGS YOU'LL READ HERE.

"Is love even enough?"

You're about to read arcs 4 to 7 and the final chapters concluding Alberto and Mathias's story.

It is recommended to take a short break between each arc.

"My heart, what have you done?"

Book of Sun.

Winter

"After years of stillness, the first tremor
will feel earth-shattering."

Dreamers

TOMORROW

TOMORROW WAS ALBERTO'S BIRTHDAY. On Monday night, it was on everybody's lips. "Look at him." "Look at the birthday boy." "Turning eighteen at last?"

How old are you, Alberto?

"Third time's the charm," he told a faded agent, and she said, "Wonderful, wonderful." No one ever listened.

Of course, now that he'd turn eighteen, a new chapter of his life was to begin. Adulthood, at last. Now, he'd get to look forward to that long, empty rail track stretching ahead of him. Him and Mamma against the world, as always.

Alberto snuck away from the cocktail party occurring in his living room and took refuge in the kitchen with Dina.

"I got you a gift," she said, putting a small package in his hand. They exchanged a brief hug.

Dina wasn't very talkative, but she was really kind. Sometimes, she would let Alberto sit at the kitchen island to do his homework. They would watch hoity-toity period dramas together, and Stasia could do nothing about it because Dina always kept an eye on her knives.

He opened the box, his lip curling. "Is this what we talked about two weeks ago?"

She nodded. "I was glad when you finally asked. It was about time. You know what I always say: you never know what can happen tomorrow."

"True." Alberto clutched the small USB device in his hand. The label on it said 2GB. It wasn't much, but it should be enough.

Dina gently put her hand on his shoulder. "Be careful, angel."

Alberto murmured his thanks and turned to leave, but she added, "That boyfriend of yours… he's very nice-looking."

"He's not my boyfriend," he protested, but his cheeks burned at the thought.

It did not surprise Alberto that Dina knew he liked men. After all, you couldn't watch the same programs together without showing a little preference for one type or another. Alberto's tastes probably amused Dina. She once said a sign of emotional maturity was when one stopped drooling over the bad boy type. Clearly, Alberto wasn't there yet; Mathias was exactly his thing.

Alas, after yesterday… Alberto felt nothing but regret over what happened at the museum. The first time Mathias knelt down before him, looking even more striking than Belmondo's sculptures, and Alberto couldn't even get it up. Indeed, he never got over the shock of seeing him here, of finding him at his worst. Every word Alberto uttered yesterday had been at gunpoint, the weapon held at his temple by his very own hand.

If only Mathias hadn't attempted to look into his eyes, that time after Xavier's brunch. If only he'd turned him over like he always did, then Alberto wouldn't have fallen apart like a fragile house of cards. Too many things had happened in one afternoon, too many memories itching to resurface, too many doors to keep watch over and ensure they remained locked. An impossible endeavour with Mathias's burning eyes peering straight into his soul.

When Alberto woke up the next morning, he was eighteen years old, and when he returned from his shower, his outfit for the day was missing. Stasia was standing in the doorway, holding his clothes and laughing at his clueless expression. He chased after her around the first floor in his bathrobe. She ran into her former bedroom and stood in front of the closet.

"Happy birthday, Albertino."

He waved his hand impatiently. "Give it back."

"I will, if you kiss me."

He hesitated. If he did, she'd let him go faster, but if he gave in again, he'd feel bad about it all day. He did it anyway. Smacking his lips against her cold cheek, he either missed or was tricked, and he ended up kissing the corner of her mouth. She gave his clothes back with a laugh at his disgruntled face. Alberto returned to his bedroom and fell back on his bed with all his weight. "I swear, you're the worst thing that's ever happened to me."

"Don't lie, Britney," Stasia said in a falsely concerned tone. "What would your daddy say?"

Alberto clenched his fists until his nails pierced the skin of his palms. "Will you get out now?"

She folded her arms over her chest. "No."

"Stasia," he warned, and the steadiness of his voice surprised him.

"Uh-uh."

"Get out!"

Her pale-blue eyes turned as black as her soul. "You're raising your voice now?"

Alberto leaned as far away as he could. "Please… I'm going to be late."

"Uh, I know, silly. And I'm not moving. Your choice."

That harpy. Alberto shrugged his bathrobe off and quickly got dressed while she watched with a little smile. He held her gaze with as much contempt as he could muster; she giggled, and when he was struggling to jump into his trousers, she landed a slap on his arse that resounded throughout the bedroom.

"Oops!" She pouted. "Sorry."

She'd been on his case the entire week. Without a boyfriend to suffer her antics, it all fell on him. She had sensed him weaker than usual after he returned from Mathias's, and she immediately burrowed her way in and launched enough attacks that he became too tired to move. She'd been so relentless, he had to revert to his old habits, even giving up the thought of getting out of bed.

Because of her, he didn't get to see Mathias. Because of her, he even turned into a limp-dick idiot who let the best thing that ever happened to him slip between his fingers. It was all because of her.

His throat burning, his body shaking, Alberto forced himself to draw a deep breath. He had money, he had an escape plan, and he had a future, somewhere, waiting for him. He wouldn't surrender to the darkest thoughts he sometimes had in his heart. He was eighteen now, and he was no longer a child for people to torment at will. Soon, he would be free…

"What are you doing?"

Alberto and Stasia both spun around with a start. Mamma stood in the doorway, holding a garment bag, looking impeccable in her white Prada dress. Her steely eyes, often cold to the world — but never to him — were fixed on Stasia.

"Wishing him a happy birthday." The Devil always reacted fast. Wrapping her arms around Alberto, she held him tight.

"You're sweet," Mamma said, her lip twitching.

Now that Stasia was satisfied she had ruined Alberto's morning, she quickly left for her Pilates lesson in her little Porsche, and Alberto was left to sit awkwardly next to Mamma on his bed.

"You worry me sometimes…" she said in a tired voice.

Alberto feigned innocence. "Why?"

"You and her. I feel like something is going on that I'm not aware of."

"No." Alberto shook his head. "We're just friends."

Mamma smelled divine; her floral perfume transported him back to the gilded mirror in the villa in Napoli, to the polished tiles, to the costume parties, their favourite dance…

Mamma caressed his cheek, breaking the spell. "You used to tell me things, once."

"I don't have anything to say."

It wasn't even a lie. Even if Alberto wanted to speak, he wouldn't know how to begin. Mamma waited for him to add something, and when he didn't, she opened the garment bag with a sigh.

"It's just an Armani."

Mamma cut the label from the fancy boutique the suit came from with her brand new pair of scissors — gifted by Dimitri. The glint of the silver almost blinded him. Alberto blinked at the suit and admitted it was stunning. Obsidian black and perfectly tailored, he knew already how good he'd look in it, and he would have loved to flaunt it before Mathias. *Look at me, am I not a vision in this?* Something must have flickered in his eyes, because Mamma's expression turned mournful. She put the suit down and scooted to the edge of the bed, and with her long fingers, she brushed Alberto's hair back, the way she used to when he was little.

"Don't you like it?"

"I do. It's perfect."

"*You're* perfect."

Shame coiled around Alberto's stomach like a snake. He shook his head.

"You are so beautiful," Mamma insisted.

"You're beautiful, too."

She smiled. "Beauty is all the more striking when it's also coming from the inside."

Alberto wouldn't hear this. He sunk his teeth into his lip and turned away from her.

"*Tesoro*," she said softly, "do you like modelling?"

"It's okay."

"Do you understand what it means for people like us?"

He glanced back, but he didn't answer.

"Freedom," Mamma said, and there was life in her eyes. "When they found me, they liberated me. That's what this job can mean to you, too. Independence, travel, money, connections… Fame and glory, if you want them. All of this and more. You must understand that right now, you are living your best years."

"Your career was over at my age."

"Yes, but you… if you play your cards right…"

"I'll do it, Mamma, I'll do it. I'm doing it right now."

Alberto's mother gave him a searching look. "I can see you're doing it, but you seem to take no pleasure in it."

"It's just a job."

"*Just a job?*" Pain flashed in her eyes, making Alberto regret his words.

Mamma never concealed from him she grew up very poor on

the outskirts of Parma. Her family dealt in blows, not embraces, and she spent her childhood in abject terror, avoiding hits not only from her parents but also her brothers. She only survived by playing her old VHS tape of *An Impudent Girl* over and over until it fell apart and dreaming, like its heroine, of leaving her dreary village behind and moving to Rome — or even better, Paris.

Accidentally named after a goddess, it soon became clear she also had the appearance of one. When a scout discovered her at the country fair, he took her away from her horrible life and propelled her to stardom just as she reached puberty. Her career was stellar, but it was to be a short one. Before her nineteenth birthday, with a newborn son to raise, she was removed from public life, her career never to start again.

"This job, as you call it, saved my life, and it gave me everything I could dream of." Mamma's voice was trembling. "And all I ever wanted was the same… for you."

"I know…"

"That's why I wanted you to start early—"

"I know."

"And I know I've made a mistake—"

"Mamma…"

"And I don't want to make that same mistake again." Her eyes shone with grief but also determination. "If you don't like it, if you don't want it, just tell me, and you won't have to do it again. You don't have to…" She ran her hand through his hair. "… to do such things, you don't have to go so far."

"I want to do it." He wanted the money, the independence. Fame and glory, he would leave those to the others. "For now."

"In that case…" Mamma brought him close and hugged him tight to her chest. "Happy birthday, my love."

He held her back. When he'd be free from Stasia, Mamma would hopefully follow him, and it would be just the two of them for the first time ever. He didn't need anybody else.

"I'm going to be late," he muttered, breaking away.

Mamma released him reluctantly. "You used to love it when we hugged."

"I was a child."

"You're still my baby."

Alberto looked away. "I know."

He took the suit and hung it in the walk-in closet. Mamma remained on the bed. "Alberto..." she called. "Where were you during the holidays?"

The fact that she used his name gave him pause. He pretended to adjust some hangers in the closet to avoid looking at her.

"With a friend."

"With a friend..." Mamma didn't sound convinced. "*Tesoro*, talk to me."

Alberto turned around and faced her. "There really isn't anything to say. Only that I had fun, and that I was safe. *Very* safe," he added at the sight of her narrowed eyes.

"And when am I going to meet your friend? At your birthday party, maybe?"

He let out a dry laugh. "That thing next week isn't my birthday party. It's another excuse for Dimitri to show off. It has nothing to do with me."

"You're being unfair." Mamma got up and handed him his backpack. "If you'd invite your friends, it would be about you."

He thanked her with a half-smile. "I'll think about it."

There it was. The first lie of the rest of his life.

Alberto glimpsed him when he walked past the school gates: Mathias in football gear. He appeared to be in a bad mood, very nice, very sexy. And his arse in those shorts... Alberto stared a little too long, only to meet Eric's incredulous frown. *It's my birthday, Lassie. Give me a break.*

When he took his seat in Paquin's class, Zak expressed his best wishes, grinning from ear to ear.

Alberto frowned at him. "How do you know it's my birthday?"

The grin vanished, replaced by a deep flush. "You must have told me?"

I told you nothing, Alberto thought with bitterness, but he forced a small smile. It was Zak, after all.

"Stalker," he said.

His jest wasn't interpreted as such. Zak seemed embarrassed, and he didn't look his way until Paquin kicked Alberto out for falling asleep again.

It seemed he was to make a habit of this after all. Alberto accepted his teacher's note for Van Bergen without a word and dragged himself to his office one slow step after another to stall for time. When he got there, he came upon Mathias's sister closing the door with a grimace.

"You don't want to go in there," she said.

"Not really, no," Alberto replied honestly.

If she was afraid to go in, then he wouldn't last a second. Everyone knew Van Bergen considered Elisa Rodin to be his favourite. Why else would he have given her carte blanche as well as her own office — seriously — to write and publish her paper?

"No, I mean, you don't…" She waved both her hands. "Never mind. Do you need him?"

"Sort of. Paquin kicked me out again."

"Oh yeah, I heard she does that." She pointed to the empty detention room next door. "You better wait for him in here."

"Thanks." He entered the classroom, dropped his backpack onto a table, then turned back to Elisa with a frown. "What the hell is this?"

Notes from some horrible song were coming from a portable CD player encased in a clear box on the lone teacher's desk. Elisa perched herself next to it and knocked on the case with a smile. "That's Cher!"

"I can hear that, but why?"

She flung her thumb over her shoulder. "His idea of torture, I assume? Those who end up in detention must listen to 'Believe' by Cher. On repeat."

Alberto gave a resigned sigh. "Save yourself, then. Shouldn't you be in class?"

"Nope. I'm on paper business."

"Of course." He awkwardly sat down on an opposite table, so he wouldn't tower over her so much, while Elisa watched him, her feet swinging back and forth.

"Haven't seen you in a while."

And after yesterday, you probably won't see me outside of school again, Alberto thought with a sinking heart. But he didn't want to make a big deal out of it in front of Elisa. She was press, after all. He was about to give her a dumb excuse, but his group of fangirls walked by the classroom and got excited at the sight of him.

"Hi, Alberto!" "You look nice today!" "Hope you had a nice Christmas!"

Elisa waited for them to be gone and turned to Alberto, her mouth agape. "Do they…"

"Every day."

"They don't mean anything bad, you know. They just find you irresistible."

Gorgeous enough to bring the world to its feet.

Alberto clung to the edges of the table. "I don't like that word."

"Why?"

"It makes it sound like… like it's my fault, somehow."

Elisa winced at the chorus of "Believe" before asking, "Why don't you put your foot down, tell them they make you uncomfortable? Kindly, of course, but——"

Alberto scoffed. "I did! It didn't work. And that's not really the problem."

"Then, what's the problem?"

"How is it on me to make them better people? Why does everyone assume it's my duty to tell all the crazies not to act on their urges? I'm not their parents or their therapists. Even if they can't take a hint from how uncomfortable I look, I shouldn't have to stop whatever I'm doing to teach them basic decency."

They'd never attempted to put themselves in his shoes, not even for a second. Or else why would they keep at it? Alberto had even resorted to hiding in the infirmary just to avoid feeling their eyes on him. How could he not resent them?

Elisa reflected on his words with a thoughtful expression. "It's weird. Everyone wants to be as good-looking as you, but you act like you don't like it, like it's a burden. It doesn't make any sense to most people. In fact, it makes us feel like you're faking it. And we… I mean, *people* don't like that false modesty stuff."

"Whatever," Alberto mumbled. "I don't need them to like me."

Except that was a lie. He did want one person to like him. Only one. The rest could get lost, along with all the others who made the simple act of looking at his own face a challenge.

"Bull… shit," Elisa said, in a perfect imitation of her brother. "Everybody needs people. You do, too. Why did you date Zak if you didn't need him?"

"You—"

"I've noticed," she added haughtily. "Zak has the most kissable face in the entire school, and I've never seen you do so much as pecking him on the cheek. So, either you wanted to hurt Eric, or…"

Alberto's eyes narrowed. "I wanted to hurt Eric."

"And this! This thing you do!"

"What?"

"I'm never sure whether you're telling the truth or you're just fucking with me."

Alberto couldn't help but laugh. "You are very foul-mouthed for a fifteen-year-old girl."

Elisa smirked. "You should have heard my mother. She even had a Sailor Moon outfit that said *Sailor Mouth*. It was a whole thing." She checked the time on the clock behind her and slid down the desk. "Alberto Gazza, I'm sorry I called you a sexist pig. I can see why you would feel a bit… harassed."

"Thanks…" Alberto blinked at her, at a loss for words. He tried to find something equally meaningful to say. "I'm sorry I said you were objectifying Zak. You're actually… nice."

"Yeah?" She beamed. "Nice?"

"Too bad Zak is in love with that *guy*, or he would have liked you."

"Pff!" Elisa pranced toward the exit. "I gave Eric a hard time in my paper, and he reacted like a champ! He's great. And since he's great, I'm happy for Zak."

"I know," Alberto said. "Me too."

She stopped as she reached the doorway. "Should I send my brother to rescue you?"

Alberto's shoulders dropped. He wondered what would be worse: Mathias never giving him another chance — as he feared right now — or him charging into the classroom, renewing his offer to go down on him, only for Alberto to get all limp on him again.

"I'll be okay," he muttered, but when she was gone, he looked around the room at all the empty tables, and his heart felt heavy in his chest. "I'm eighteen now."

2

BAD IDEAS

"Balls?" Mathias asked. "Balls?!"

"Yeah," Eric said.

Mathias had not been listening at first; his mind had been focused on other things—*better things*—like full lips leaving a trail of incendiary kisses down his chest, the sound of a broken moan in his ear, but Eric really went too far this time and tore him even from that daydream.

He glared at his friend. "That's your idea of romance? Balls?"

"Yeah?" Eric replied, loudly chewing his gum. He didn't sound so sure anymore. "No? Maybe?"

"Balls, really?"

"Yes, balls! Why?"

Mathias shook his head. *What an absolute idiot.* If Eric weren't his best friend, Mathias would have run away in embarrassment. They had just arrived at practice, and since Kayvin was barking orders at Xavier in the middle of the frozen football pitch, they stepped farther back toward Mathias's goal to avoid getting overheard.

"Let me make this clear: you want to invite Zak on a date?"

"Yes."

"To your place?"

"Yeah."

"And you want to impress him?"

Eric popped his gum. "Yup."

"You want to make him dinner?"

"*Yes.*" That asshole started to sound impatient.

"And as for the atmosphere... you're thinking... balls?"

Eric shrugged. "Sure, what's wrong with balls?"

Mathias wanted to grab him by his jersey and shout, *What's wrong with you?!* But he managed to stop himself. "Let's see... Have you ever seen a romantic movie where the girl is showing up to the venue for, I don't know, her wedding, and she enters the place, and she goes 'Oooh, nice balls'?"

Eric's smile faltered. "... No?"

"No? Are you sure?"

"No?"

"Then why the fuck are you going with balls?!"

"Because they're round!" Eric excitedly jumped in place. "Round shapes are, like, relaxing and... and nice to the eye! People like balls. They're funny! They're balls!"

"Okay..."

"Listen, I found this shop that sells like... these *massive* balls. You can sit on them, and they're super bouncy. Nice, nice stuff."

"Like a yoga ball?"

"Yeah, exactly that! But if I bought a lot of them in different sizes and colors, it would look really cute, I think." He spread out his hands. "*Magical.*"

"Yeah, so magical! Poor Zak."

"Why 'poor Zak'? Why? What do you know about these things, anyway? You're not a wedding planner, as far as I know."

"There's a whole universe between wedding planning and balls!"

"Okay, okay, calm down." Eric chewed on his gum fiercely. "It seems I got it wrong. Help me, best buddy. What do I do?"

Mathias slipped Kayvin a quick glance. He was now shouting at Charles-Henry, and he wasn't paying attention to them.

"First, forget about yoga balls."

"How about beach balls?"

"No! How does Zak deal with you, honestly?"

"Fine. No beach balls. What, then?"

"I don't know, but like... lights?"

"Lights?" Eric asked with a frown. "Light... balls?"

"Just lights!" Mathias clenched his fists. "The lighting does everything, not balls or whatever."

"Or..." Eric said, scratching his chin. "... I could also use balloons. Lovely pastel balloons!"

"I've never ever heard of anything romantic being associated with having balloons everywhere. Balloons are for birthdays and elections. I think you— Hey, listen! I know that face. I think you just like balloons, and you convinced yourself somehow that they're perfect for every occasion. Because you're crazy."

He saw he was right from the way Eric's ears turned pink. "So, no balls, then? Not even one or two?"

"The only set of balls you're allowed to bring to your date are the ones attached to your dick. And they should also stay in your pants—if you're a gentleman."

Eric grinned. "What do you know about being a gentleman?"

Mathias ignored his jab. "I was forced to watch a lot of rom-coms, okay? The sort of movie where no dork ever shows up with balloons like a circus clown freak."

"All right, I get it. But don't call me a dork. It reminds me of Alberto."

Mathias's heart jolted, and he momentarily forgot how to breathe. "Lights," he croaked. "Fairy lights. You want to make your boy feel special? You get the fucking lights. You get the mood right. And you get what he likes."

"Zak likes balls. He said it. It's not the first time I've thrown him a party."

Mathias clicked his tongue. "I bet your ass he lied because he likes you."

Eric giggled. "He does. I *hope* he does."

There was no doubt about that. Mathias had seen them together. With the way it was going, even Eric's transfer wouldn't be a problem. And of course, his thoughts flew back to the other freak. He wondered what would happen if he put together a romantic date for Alberto—tell him to dress nice, that they had the entire apartment to themselves—and he sighed. Alberto would probably show up in the same weird clothes, smirk at the fairy lights, and toss his cigarette butt in the Champagne right before he'd sweep the dishes aside with one hand, lay his ass on the table, curl his finger at him, and purr out some shit like, *You know where to put it.*

Mathias sighed ostensibly, not knowing if something was wrong with him, because that sounded like a really nice date, actually. But he also... he also would like...

What the hell was he thinking now? Last Sunday, Alberto clearly demonstrated he wasn't attracted to him anymore. And good riddance. Mathias had never liked him, anyway.

Unfortunately for him, despite how many times he told himself he wouldn't waste any more time on Alberto, the latter wouldn't leave his thoughts alone. Mathias kept thinking about the first morning he got this hands on him, all warm and soft, about his face when he sat among the trash, about his mocking smirk when he confessed he'd made out with Xavier, and Mathias hadn't understood at the time why he was so angry. These unwanted thoughts constantly plagued Mathias, and practice was the last thing on his mind. In fact, he didn't even notice when the ball was kicked his way and rolled to a stop at his feet.

"Shoot it back!" Kayvin sputtered from the halfway line.

Mathias stared at it without seeing it, his forehead creasing.

"Matt..." Eric was trotting toward him; he came at a stop a few feet away from him. "Matt?"

"I didn't see it coming," Mathias muttered.

Kayvin stomped his foot. "Shoot, *putain**!" His tone forced Mathias to look up.

If you insist.

Mathias shot, aiming right at the back of Kayvin's head. He didn't miss. He loved the dumb sound it made upon colliding with Kayvin's skull and had to try hard not to snicker. *How do you like being pushed around, asshole?* Because of him, Xavier had had his way with Alberto.

---

* French slur meaning about anything depending on the context. Here, Kayvin says: "Fucking shoot!"

Mathias turned to Eric with a smile. "You were right!"

"About what?" his friend asked, looking tense.

"Balls. They *are* funny."

Kayvin recovered fast enough, and he galloped back to Mathias's goal, his face purple with rage. Mathias leaned on his goalpost and slowly started to remove his gloves. *Come on, jerkface. Give me the pleasure.*

"What's your fucking problem?" Kayvin went off, jabbing his finger in his chest.

"Sorry," Mathias said in his most innocent voice. "It was an accident. I warned you my aim isn't very good."

"I'm your fucking captain."

"I know, I know."

"You better watch out before I get you kicked out." Kayvin spun on his heel and pointed at Eric. "And you, too. Your job isn't to chat with your new boyfriend, as far as I know."

Comforted by Eric's lack of reaction, Kayvin walked away. Mathias didn't like the way his friend helplessly stared after him.

"You're gonna get in trouble with him," Eric said. "I don't like it. You saw what he did to Alberto the other day."

"I'm not Alberto, am I?" Mathias gritted his teeth. "I can take care of myself."

"I'm aware." Eric gave a haughty shrug, one he had learned from Zak. "But it's all very unnecessary, as my baby would say."

Mathias turned his back to him. His *baby*. His traitorous *baby* also had had his way with Alberto. In fact, everyone but Eric seemed to have gotten to know him intimately. Okay, fine, and perhaps Kayvin, too. But it sure felt like the entire world was getting a piece of Alberto nowadays, except Mathias, of course. And without Alberto to vent his frustrations, all Mathias had was football and the privilege to shoot his ball straight at that Kayvin's enormous head.

So, the next time he cleared the ball, he aimed at him again and hit the mark beautifully, and that's how he ended up in detention at nine on a Tuesday morning. Even he had to admit he had surpassed himself.

V.B. himself went to get him, and he tossed him in the detention room, mumbling he didn't have time for him right now—his favorite dog had diarrhea, and for some reason, he was waiting in his office—and when Mathias turned around, he came face-to-face with Alberto. He was sitting with his cheek pressed to a table littered with empty coffee cups at the back of the room, his eyelids heavy with sleep.

"What are you doing here?" he asked in a raspy voice.

It took a second for Mathias to swallow his heart that had just jumped up his throat. "Kicked a ball at Kayvin's face. Twice." He appreciated the hint of a smile on Alberto's face. "You? Did you fall asleep?"

"*And* got interrogated. *And* didn't know the answers."

"Which book?"

"Rousseau, I think?"

"Rousseau? In English Lit?"

"Mmm…" Alberto laid his head on his hands. "Wrong book, wrong class… I really deserved to be kicked out this time."

Mathias studied him from a distance. Asleep or awake, he was always beautiful, but when he was between the two like now, he was simply adorable. Mathias cautiously approached him and sat in a nearby chair. "Yeah, me too."

"Kicking Kayvin in the face qualifies as a public service. That's probably why Van Bergen just sent you here and not straight to his office."

Mathias looked away. "I don't know. His dog is repainting his office at the moment, so…"

"Oh." Alberto straightened up, his expression mildly confused. "Right."

"Do you need me to get you some more coffee? Vitamins, maybe?" Mathias offered with an awkward laugh.

To his surprise, Alberto himself didn't look too assured today. He kept averting his eyes, preferring to cast them on his lap. If Mathias didn't know him to be a cold fish, he would have thought he was nervous to see him.

He helplessly racked his brain for something casual to say, but all he could think of was how terrible he was at blowjobs and how Alberto would probably never kiss him again with his decadent lips.

Then, he finally noticed a horrible noise, and he craned his neck around the room in search of the culprit.

"What's that sound? Do you hear this?"

Alberto pointed at the CD player on the desk. "Van Bergen's idea of torture."

"How can you stand it? It sounds like a herd of goats murdering each other in a nineties nightclub."

"I can tune it out by making myself disappear."

"Sorry, what?"

Alberto shrugged.

"In any case, I can't do anything like that." Mathias got up to unplug the thing and found the machine was actually locked inside some protective case. Even worse, the wire went through the wall, emerging straight into V.B.'s office. That lunatic had thought of everything.

With a click of his tongue, Mathias scanned around the room, grabbed the closest chair and slammed it on top of the case.

Alberto jumped to his feet. "Mathias!"

That was a promising result. Humming at his success, Mathias repeated the gesture until the lock—as well as the case—cracked open. Slamming his fist on top of the player, he sighed when the horrible music came to a stop. "Isn't this better?"

"Van Bergen is definitely going to kill you." Alberto sounded as excited as he sounded worried.

Feeling quite proud of himself, Mathias picked up the CD player and walked over to the window to open it. He threw the machine outside with a sneer. "I'm not afraid of oversized maniacs carrying riding crops."

He really wasn't, but when Alberto's eyes lit up, he lost a bit of his composure and shoved his hands in his pockets.

"You're so cool," Alberto said, his voice so quiet, Mathias could have almost missed it.

Those three words froze Mathias on the spot. It suddenly felt like the world was full of opportunities, if one could only live long enough. A part of him briefly pondered the possibility of offering Alberto to have sex with him on one of these tables, but he realized he'd have to be a proper basket case to do that. He dropped his arms to his sides with a sigh.

He clearly still wanted him. That was problematic, because Alberto seemed done with him the other day, didn't he? He met the creature's eyes, who lowered them in a weirdly timid way. His cheeks burning, Mathias seized his backpack. "Let's get out of here."

"What?"

"Come on." He jerked his chin toward the window. "Let's do it."

Alberto didn't move. "Are you sure? What if Van Bergen notices? You've already destroyed his torture device."

"So?" Mathias let out a dry laugh. "What's the worst that can happen? My mom dies again?"

The silence that followed made him worry he said something stupid again. But just when he was about to take it back and apologize, Alberto murmured, "Did she fight?"

Mathias nodded. "Until the very end."

"That's good," Alberto said in a sad tone.

Perhaps he cared a bit after all. Mathias believed in that enough that he found the resolve to ask, "Do you wanna see her?"

"See… her?"

"Her tomb. You wanna see it?"

Though Alberto opened his mouth, no sound came out of it for a few seconds, until he went, "Yeah, okay."

They gathered their stuff, and they did climb out of the window, but they were on the ground floor, or Mathias wouldn't have let Alberto do it, because though he sometimes reminded him of a cat, he had none of the agility.

They grazed along the side of the building until they could make a run for the gate. When they were safely onto the street, Alberto caught up to him, lost his balance, and accidentally bumped into him. Mathias leaned into the touch without saying a word and thought that if he'd moved his fingers a bit to the right, he could have caught his hand.

3

GRAVE DIGGERS

After his failure to visit last year, Mathias was almost expecting to see the place untidy, littered with dead flowers and leaves and dirt, but his mother's tomb was, as always, immaculate, and adorned with so many fresh blossoms, it looked like the windowfront of a flower shop.

Alberto stood before it with a look of surprise. "Do you come here often?"

"No. Actually... I haven't visited in a long time."

"Why not?"

"I don't know." Mathias forced out a smile. "Maybe because I'm a coward."

He wished he hadn't said that, and yet, it was exactly how he felt, so he was grateful when Alberto broke the silence. "Was your mum someone important?"

Mathias shook his head. "Nope." He noticed his incredulous frown and asked, "Why?"

"She has a spot at the Montparnasse Cemetery, and it looks like someone is buying flowers for her every day."

"Not every day..." Mathias bent down and rearranged the enormous bunch of sunflowers at his feet to avoid meeting his eyes. "But she had friends. Good friends."

"Friends who could afford a spot here?" Alberto clearly didn't believe him. "You always act like your family has no money and like you despise rich people, but… look. The tombstones in this spot all bear the family name Reyes. So, your mother was rich, or she wouldn't have secured a place here."

"Her family was rich, okay?" Mathias said in a sharp tone. Seeing Alberto's expression, regret churned his stomach, and he sat in front of his mother's grave with a sigh. "My mom had nothing. And she couldn't afford to be here. No chance."

Alberto looked at him, his lips pressed tightly together.

"All they cared about was appearances," Mathias confessed. "So, Mom ended up here. They knew Dad didn't have enough money to… do better, and that's what they did. They never lifted a finger when she was sick, never spared a penny to help with her treatment, they just sent some lawyer after her death to make all the arrangements." He forced himself to take a deep breath to push down the anger still simmering inside of him. "They didn't want her buried back in Venezuela, but that was fine with us, because she didn't want to leave Paris. She wanted to be here with her friends. These people, her so-called family, they didn't even bother coming to see her off. Only one cousin showed up from over there. The rest, they thought she was dirty."

Alberto took a seat next to him. Mathias was about to warn him about his coat, but he didn't seem to care. "Why did they think she was dirty?"

"It's complicated," Mathias said, hanging his head. "They didn't really accept her in the first place. Her mother wasn't the matriarch, you see. And it showed. She looked different from the others; she stood out. When it became too obvious, with her red hair and all, they sent her away here to live with her aunt, and she never wanted to come back. Years later, when they heard about her engagement to my dad, they threatened to cut her off, and she sent them packing and married him anyway. They disowned her, as promised. In the end, she was a simple dance teacher married to a math teacher, and they probably thought she was a big loser." He let out a dry laugh. "I don't understand how they could not have loved her. I don't get it. In fact, I hate them so much for… for… letting her down like that."

Alberto slowly bowed his head. "That's why you don't like rich people."

"I don't..." Mathias resisted the powerful urge to swing his arm around his long neck, biting his tongue instead. "Fine. Maybe... maybe it looks like I don't like rich people, but I just don't like selfish... shits."

They didn't speak for a minute, both of them seemingly lost in their thoughts, then Alberto said, his voice soft, "Tell me about her."

"About Mom?"

"Yes."

"I don't even know where to start..." Mathias took a moment to think about it, seeing her figure in his mind, laughing and waving at him. "Mom had so much energy... like a tornado. She liked playing sports. She was proficient at Taekwondo and taught it to kids, but what she liked the best was dancing. She danced all the time."

Mathias noted the corners of Alberto's lip had slightly turned up. He continued with a smile of his own. "She had electric guitars in her veins; she was always twitchy. She got me into Garbage, and she's the only reason I even know Bloodhound Gang. Mom went to concerts until the day she couldn't, you know? The only thing she was useless at was cooking. I've never seen anything like it. Maybe that's how I got into it: to save us all from whatever shit she was making."

"Were you close?"

Mathias glanced up at the headstone. *Beloved mother, wife, and friend*, it said. So unremarkable, compared to the woman she was, and yet, these words were nothing but the truth.

"We were *too* close, maybe. She had me at nineteen. We basically did everything together. I even brought out the rings at her wedding," he added proudly.

Alberto drew his legs up. "Like a dog."

"No, not like a dog!" Mathias was about to bite his head off, but he looked too cute, with his chin on his knees.

"My mother had me at nineteen, too. Imagine... that's just a year older than us."

Less than six months away from his nineteenth birthday, Mathias chose not to comment. "Wasn't she a famous supermodel? Why did she have you so early?"

"She fell in love. You know how it is for some. It changes everything."

Mathias cast his eyes down. He was so close to Alberto, he had to be careful not to move, or their arms would brush together. He wanted that very much, but here, in this cemetery, it would feel inappropriate, wouldn't it?

"Your mum had beautiful hair," Alberto said, unaware of Mathias's turmoil.

"You've noticed."

"Hard to miss the picture on your nightstand."

Mathias conceded with a smile. During the holidays, Alberto had woken facing that photograph of him and his mom at Disneyland more than a few times. She was laughing and holding him so tight, he could barely breathe, and her curly hair was so enormous that it obstructed that asshole Mickey Mouse standing beside them. Mathias was scowling, but his eyes, so alike hers, shone bright with all of his unspoken joy.

"That fucking hair," he grumbled. "You found it everywhere. On the floor, inside the sofa, even in the kitchen where she never set foot! It was driving me insane! Until, one day…" His voice grew weak. "No more hair. No matter how long I looked…" Feeling Alberto's eyes on him, Mathias carefully averted them. "Weeks later, when it was all done, I went searching for her hair in her bedroom—between the sheets, under the mattress—but it was all gone. I don't know what I was hoping for… She'd lost it all during treatment, anyway. But in her wardrobe, I managed to find one."

Mathias knew his eyes were filled to the brim and if he dared blink, a fat tear would drop and crash like a meteorite on his lap. He willed himself not to. Not in front of him.

"I knew it," Alberto said, his voice like a whisper.

"Knew what?"

"That's why you went for the buzzcut. Or else you'd look like a crazy poodle, just like your mum."

Mathias burst out a laugh, the tears tumbling and crashing down his lap. "I will never admit it."

"You don't need to." Alberto arched his eyebrow. "I know it. You've got crazy curly hair like your mother, and you're trying to hide it."

"You—"

"I know, I know. I talk too much."

With a long sigh, Alberto leaned back and made himself comfortable. Stretching his long legs, he pretended to be reading the letters on the headstone long enough for Mathias to collect himself.

"She requested one song," he said when his eyes were dry. "One song and twelve lesbians."

Alberto blinked several times. "Pardon me, what?"

"Her funeral. She asked for "Las Ketchup" to play as they lowered her down."

"She did?"

"She knew how much I hated it. It was our private joke. I think she did it to make me laugh."

"Did it work?"

"No. I cried the whole time."

Alberto's face contorted in a grimace. "And the twelve lesbians?"

"Ah… Forget them. There were only ten anyway."

Now he looked perplexed, like he wasn't certain he hadn't imagined this conversation. "So, she made that playlist, didn't she?"

His expression was enough to bring a smile back to Mathias's face. "Yes. For our last road trip."

"Now, that makes sense…" he mumbled. "How fast did it— I mean, was she sick for a long time?"

Of course he would want to know the gloomy stuff. Mathias tried to imagine an Alberto who would be joyous and bright, like his mom, and he couldn't even conjure an image. All he could see was that sweet, innocent smile from the portraits hidden in the basement. Perhaps his joyous nature had been buried underground like those pictures, like Mathias's mom.

"Not really. She was gone in a year, you know. She seemed fine, and then she was really sick, and then… and then…" Mathias's throat tightened.

"Then she was really dead."

Mathias blinked at him, stunned. Alberto gazed back at him with a childish pout. A weight lifted off his shoulders; he flicked Alberto's lower lip with his index finger. "Yes, *pollito*. Then she was really dead."

Such a weird thing to say, and yet, his mom once made a similar joke, a feeble attempt to distract him from her impending death. She was trying to lighten up the room, but he was angry and hurt, and he couldn't bear her upbeat mood there, in that place, in that hospital bed. He told her not to joke about death, and she asked, "Only dead people can joke about death, then?" He said, "Yes," and she laughed even though she was close to the end. Then, she slid down the bed, her tongue stuck out, playing dead, and when he got mad, she said, "Can I get an advance? I'll be really dead, really soon."

God, she was so annoying. He'd never met anyone so annoying and wonderful in his entire life. He kept telling her how annoying she was, and she kept messing with him, telling him, "You don't know every time you call me annoying, I hear wonderful. Every time you tell me I'm the worst, I hear I'm the best. Every time you say you can't stand me, I hear you love me the most." And he did. He loved her the most.

It's a really bitchy move to make people love you so much and then fucking die on them.

There it was… the anger. The hurt.

How could he still go around pretending it was all her fault, when, in fact, she had tried her best until the very end? And what did he ever give in return? He had been useless the entire process, and all he was now was mad. Mad at not being as good as her at making light of the whole thing. Mad at not being able to get over it the way others could. Mad at wondering what sort of good person he could have become if she'd stuck around, instead of the wreck he was now. He was consumed by darkness—the void she left behind her had swallowed him whole. No one could understand, and he couldn't ask anyone to keep him company. Who would want to wander these dark corridors with him, anyway?

He slipped a look at the person on his right. Alberto didn't just wander dark corridors, he'd probably designed them. Passageways with endless doors leading to haunted places… Behind each of these doors, there was probably another poor chump trapped between his lips. That's what Alberto was: just another void waiting to consume Mathias.

"The thing about Eric," he said, forcing his gaze away, "is that he reminds me of her. He's so… sunny. He's so…" He puffed out a laugh. "Sometimes, I feel bad around him because he's so bright, and I have this darkness inside of me. It's like we don't match at all."

"You shouldn't feel bad," Alberto said, and his tone was cooler now. "Eric is only like that because he hasn't had any hardships. He hasn't lost anything or anyone yet. When that happens, his light will get—" He snapped his fingers together. "—snuffed out. Just like that."

Mathias frowned. "I can't let that happen now, can I?"

"In any case…" Alberto lowered his gaze. "… Isn't there beauty in darkness, too?"

There is, Mathias said to himself. *I'm staring at it right now.*

What happened to you? He wanted to ask. *Why do you never speak about your dad? Did you lose him, or did he lose you?*

He was well aware now that Alberto didn't want to talk about him. Mathias was curious, but he didn't want to pry and risk Alberto slipping away again. Still, he couldn't help wondering… how ironic would it be if Alberto's dad was homophobic, as opposed to Mathias's own upbringing? Alberto didn't ask himself many questions about what he liked or how that came to be. Mathias was born under a rainbow, and yet he… had no understanding of such things. All he ever felt was confusion.

Even now.

"Is it true that Gwen and your stepsister threw you into the pool when you were a kid?" he asked, for lack of a better thing to say.

Alberto snorted. "Yes, a few times."

"Why?"

"They thought it was funny, I guess."

"But why?"

"I don't know, Mathias. They just couldn't resist."

"And why didn't you defend yourself?"

Alberto glanced up at the sky with a shake of his head. "Who knows? Why did people watch and do nothing when Kayvin did the same thing the other day?"

The blood drained out of Mathias's cheeks. About that day—that damn waste of a day that had started off so well—he had had enough time to regret his inaction. "I wasn't fast enough…" he said, embarrassed. "And then it was too late."

"Well, maybe it was the same for me." Alberto sounded tired now. "Once you let things happen the first time, there isn't much you can do about the others."

Despite Mathias's fears that he might be—rightfully—furious at him, Alberto didn't look upset. He was picking lint off his jacket, his lower lip stuck between his teeth. His face burning, Mathias wasn't sure what to say. Now that they were sitting here in front of his mom, he felt at a loss.

Usually, Mathias felt uneasy telling others about his mother. He really missed her, missed talking to her. But not today. Today, he felt if only he could have seen her one more time and asked her about demons and all, maybe he would have been all right. "I wonder what she would have said about you," he muttered.

"About me?"

Mathias realized he'd spoken aloud and gave a nervous laugh. "Yeah, whatever."

"Oh, but I know." Alberto nudged him with his elbow. "She would have said… *Fuck me, he's very handsome.*" And without warning, he leaned in and caught his lips.

Mathias tried to jerk away. "Fuck! We're in a *mph*—!"

He gave in at the first slide of his demonic tongue. Surrendering so nicely, it was he who gripped Alberto by his neck to bring him closer, and he was the one who sighed into his mouth when he felt the weight of his arms on his shoulders.

They made out in front of his mother's last resting place, the displayed flowers painting a fragrant rainbow over their heads. Mathias kissed him like their stage wasn't a cemetery, like he had never lost what was most important to him. A kiss like that might have resurrected the dead, in a perfect world.

"You're crazy," he whispered when they broke apart. "This is a mourning space. Don't make fun of the dead." Still, he held his face between his hands and had no desire to release it.

"I'm not making fun of the dead, I'm making fun of death. Not the same." Alberto puckered his lips, and Mathias kissed them again. "What do people know about the dead, anyway? Nothing at all. Maybe they are actually watching over us, especially in a place like this, and they're bored out of their mind to see ugly crying faces all day, and watching us just now made everybody's day. Maybe your mum was proud. Maybe she really was thinking, *Fuck me!*"

He's very handsome… Mathias ran his fingers through Alberto's hair then gave it a tug. "Screw it. You're right. My mom was fun, she didn't play by the rules, and she was a rock star."

"If anything, we honoured her."

"Yes… yes! I like that."

Alberto's lip curled. "What should we do now?"

Mathias stared avidly at his mouth, then said four memorable words in his ear, making him chuckle. They hadn't played *the game* in a while.

"This one's too hard to remember."

"That's okay." Mathias got to his feet and helped Alberto up. "I'll let you look the lyrics up on my computer while I rip off your clothes."

"Lovely." Alberto froze mid-movement, an adorable frown on his face, then he reached out to poke Mathias's shoulder and pressed himself into his space. He spoke a few words, his voice barely audible in his ear.

Mathias leaned back. "I haven't removed your clothes yet."

"No, those are the lyrics."

"Oh, fuck!"

"Exactly."

They burst into a laugh. Mathias stared at Alberto, who looked back with round eyes, in disbelief. They turned away from each other, and Alberto tore toward the exit without a look back.

After a few parting words against the cold headstone and a promise to return soon, Mathias hurried after him. There was a spring in their steps when they walked out of there. Mathias was so febrile, he almost fell flat on his nose outside the metro station.

Back home, they were already all over each other before they even made it to the elevator. Mathias would have gladly had him in here if there was a possibility. He blindly slammed his hand against the button panel, so they had to stop at pretty much every floor, but none of that mattered; he had him in his grasp again. They crashed and bounced against the walls of the shaft, Mathias's deft fingers already pushing Alberto's coat off his shoulders. When the doors opened, they stumbled out of the elevator and smashed into Mathias's front door. He never understood how he managed to open it with Alberto's tongue in his ear and his hand in his pants. His fingers were shaking something crazy.

In Mathias's bedroom, they battled for who would be the fastest at removing the other's clothes. Mathias won; he always won. But none of that mattered. He undressed them both more or less accurately—one of Alberto's feet was still caught in the leg of his pants, causing him to laugh in his ear. They were so frantic, they slid off the bed and ended up on the carpeted floor. When Mathias felt Alberto's erection digging into his abdomen, this time, he didn't hesitate. He put the whole thing into his mouth. Alberto yelped like his dick had never been sucked before, so Mathias must not have been so bad at it after all. He flung his hands over his eyes and instinctively tried to close his legs, but Mathias dealt with them easily.

Yes, sex was messy, and Mathias honestly used to think it was a lot of effort for not much reward. It just never felt right. Gay sex was even messier, and it wasn't for the faintest of people. Good thing he wasn't the faintest of people. He always did what he had to do in the least amount of time, knowing they were always at their best when they didn't give a damn.

Twice before, Mathias had attempted to take Alberto from the front. Twice before, he was severely rebutted. Not just with glares, but with a sharp *Don't!* uttered through gritted teeth. Maybe Mathias was the boring kind, but missionary allowed a view few could boast they'd seen before. But today, there was no rebuttal. Alberto said nothing, and Mathias didn't tease him either; he kept his head down the entire time. No way he would fuck things up like before. He wouldn't look into his eyes, even though he wanted to.

It was just as they liked it. Fast. Intense. Sweaty. Alberto moaned, writhed, and hissed nonsense in two different languages, his legs pressed against his sides. Mathias believed his heart, thundering uncontrollably, was definitely going to explode, until he heard something that made it stop altogether.

"What was that?" He panted. "What did you say?"

Alberto wrapped his long legs around Mathias's waist. "I love it, I love it."

For a moment, Mathias thought he'd heard something else. He kissed him—or more precisely slammed their lips together—drawing another interesting sound out of Alberto, who hid his face back into his neck. Something was rising and swelling in his chest, blocking up his throat, and his thrusts intensified; he didn't know how else to say it.

When it was Alberto's time, Mathias rose abruptly. He saw his face, his eyes, his tears. Pleasure erupted, and his vision turned white.

4

HANDPRINTS

ALBERTO'S LEGS were shaking like a foal's. Lying on his back atop Mathias's carpet, he felt both wrung out and mysteriously full at the same time. Above him, Mathias had thrown all pretence out the window and was licking his cum off his stomach and chest, and he was *humming* as he did. That was all too surreal to him, so much that Alberto wasn't sure he was awake after all. He didn't dare move. He hid his face behind his hands. "So? How do I taste?"

Mathias briefly paused, but he didn't stop. He swiped his tongue over his sternum first then raised his head to kiss him. Alberto tasted himself on his tongue.

"Weird," Mathias said between two kisses. "Hot. Bitter."

Alberto snorted. "Sounds about right."

Mathias answered in kind, puffing out a laugh right into the crook of his neck, where he found another drop to clean off him, making Alberto bite down a whimper.

And then, he held him.

He held him in an embrace that made Alberto shake even more. Dumbstruck, he wondered if this moment was really happening right now, and if it would be okay to never want it to stop. Mathias held him for a long time, heart beating against heart. Then, he whispered in his ear, "Thank you."

Alberto had lost his voice. "F-For what?"

"For coming with me today."

To his consternation, Mathias lifted his head, and suddenly, he was gazing into his wide-open eyes. *No, no, nope.* Alberto tried to turn away, but Mathias didn't let him retreat. He would usually get pushed away when he got like that. This time, Alberto didn't have the strength to fight him. He squeezed his eyes shut and let him join their lips together, his nails buried into the low pile carpet. Alberto wanted to groan, to curse; he hated that kiss as much as he loved it. Mathias's gentleness had always felt more brutal than his fiercest thrusts.

After a moment, he couldn't help himself and started squirming in an effort to escape him, to escape hope, and that's when he felt the pain. His faint hiss caught Mathias's attention, who immediately rolled off him, his wonderful heat replaced by a cruel chill.

"What's wrong?"

Alberto didn't want to make a fuss. "Nothing."

"What is it?" Mathias asked more firmly, seizing his wrist.

"Nothing! The carpet chafed my back a little."

Mathias flipped him to the side and muttered under his breath, "Why didn't you say something?"

Alberto internally rolled his eyes. "I couldn't feel it at the time."

"Come on, get up."

Alberto was still too weak to battle with him, so he let him pull him up without a word. Mathias took him to the bathroom without releasing his hand.

"Go on, let's clean it up."

Alberto liked the idea of taking a shower with Mathias, so he kept his mouth shut. He stood in a corner while Mathias checked the water temperature and led him inside, following after him. His breath on his neck felt much hotter than the water pouring from the sprinklers, making him twitch everywhere, including below.

Feeling naughty, Alberto was about to warn him he would soon be ready for another round, but when he threw a look over his shoulder, he noted Mathias's painful expression.

"What?" He twisted his neck to check his back. "Is it really bad?"

Mathias glanced up. "Why are you covered in bruises?"

"I'm not."

"You are."

"Must be you, then." Alberto spun around when he saw the alarm in his eyes. "Don't make that face. We've talked about this."

They had, ever since the first time Alberto had asked him to hold him a little tighter, then a little tighter, then a little more. Mathias always acted like he expected Alberto to call the evil spawn's name — the *safe* word — but that would never happen, so he always worried and grumbled under his breath. He was the only one.

"I haven't touched you in days." Mathias's tone turned sombre.

"Oh." Alberto turned his face away. "I mark really quickly. It's probably from just now."

"You don't have to lie. There's a red handprint on your ass."

Alberto didn't answer. Eventually, Mathias got closer. Alberto glimpsed at his face, and his heart stammered in his chest. There was sadness in his eyes. Sadness, concern, and a hint of pity.

Stasia really was the bane of his existence. The handprint had to be her, from this morning. The bruises, half and half. Alberto had bumped against every piece of furniture at home last week, but Stasia did push him down the stairs on New Year's Eve when she found out about the key. Alberto didn't hurt himself, but he really bruised easily, and the marks on his back right now may have made it look like he took a wild tumble.

Then, gentle fingertips lightly grazed his spine so softly, the hair on the back of Alberto's neck prickled at the touch. He couldn't help shaking. The sensation of warm water drizzling over his face and shoulders and Mathias's soapy fingers dancing across his skin… it felt so good, Alberto had to press his hands against the tiles to steady himself.

"Does it hurt?" Mathias asked in a whisper.

Alberto could only shake his head; his throat was blocked up. He meant it: none of these things could ever hurt more than the pain he had felt in the museum's lavatories, when Mathias glanced up from between his legs, disappointment so clear in his eyes. If Alberto couldn't have sex with him, then what was he good for?

Today, he had experienced firsthand the depth of Mathias's grief. He was already a problem because he was a guy and because he was *Alberto*; he refused to add to Mathias's burden. He'd rather hurt in silence instead.

"Look at you…" Mathias spoke against his neck, and Alberto felt weak in the knees. "I'm barely touching you, and you're, like…"

"Sorry," he breathed.

But Mathias didn't seem to mind. On the contrary, he nipped at his neck and trailed his fingers over Alberto's back, his arms, and his thighs, until his hands settled on his arse cheeks and he got greedier. Alberto said nothing and shut his eyes, afraid one word from him would make the pleasure stop.

"I…" Mathias began, pressing their bodies together.

"Yes?" Alberto felt his lips against his nape then his breath when he exhaled a sigh.

"Nothing, forget it."

Mathias started kissing his way down his neck, down his spine, down to his tailbone. Every hair on Alberto's body now stood to attention. When Mathias squatted behind him and softly nudged him against the wall, Alberto had to wonder: did he know it was his birthday today? He was acting so strange…

Then Mathias's tongue skimmed across an unexpected spot and Alberto couldn't repress the sound that broke from his throat. Huffing a quiet laugh, Mathias did it again, more intently this time, forcing Alberto to flatten himself against the wall, fingers clawing at the tiles for purchase. *Someone should barge in and tell him what he's doing is pretty gay,* Alberto thought briefly before Mathias's tongue moved again and he couldn't think anymore.

Before long, he was reduced to a mess of pathetic gasps and moans. They sounded silly to Alberto, but they drove Mathias wild enough that he suddenly sprung up, swinging him around without a word. They used their hands on each other until they both came, their faces buried in each other's necks.

His heart racing and his head swimming, Alberto recalled when their eyes had met earlier. The green ring around Mathias's pupils had caught the light, making them appear on fire, and in their reflection, Alberto had witnessed his own surrender.

Mathias still wasn't done with him. He kept touching Alberto's face, his hair… His breath was uneven, yet Alberto wasn't afraid. He knew he should tell him to stop touching him, that he wasn't the cuddling type — or the loving type, as a matter of fact. But again, Alberto said nothing. He leaned into Mathias's touch, ran his fingers over his scalp, and listened to his breathing every time he kissed back… His thoughts turned mellow, and he closed his eyes a moment.

The truth was… Mathias was so hot, not just attractive — and that he was — with his lean muscles as hard as iron and his shade-shifting eyes that always seemed to burn into his own. His skin felt warm against his, and his heart beat fast while Alberto's was slow. The two of them combined could almost make one normal human being. Mathias was so good to him, so good… Alberto opened his eyes just in time to see him bringing a hand to his face. He brushed a finger against Alberto's mouth.

"Shh… Stop biting."

Alberto released his bullied lip and pressed a kiss to the pad of Mathias's thumb. In an instant, he was pushed against the wall again and pulled into another kiss. A distant voice in his head told him to stop, to stop that nonsense. Soft was not what he wanted. When one gets his hands on the big bad wolf, it's not to watch him go soft. He wanted — he *needed* — Mathias to leave him no escape, to hold him so tight that he could barely breathe. That's when he felt the safest: choking on his own tears, thinking if these arms were to never let go, he'd never have to worry again.

And yet, he kissed back the way he was kissed, too soft, too kind, too much. *Stop that now*, he wanted to say, his hands feebly gripping Mathias's shoulders.

Mathias was devouring him kiss by kiss. His chin, his neck, his collarbones, no place was safe. When his lips settled over his heart and his kiss turned into a bite, Alberto had no will to even hiss in feigned anger. He cried out and slammed his hands against the sides of the shower. Trouble, like a spark on dry kindle, had ignited in the depths of Mathias's eyes. It had propagated like a wildfire when their mouths had met, had ravaged the place Alberto didn't even recall had any other use than pumping blood throughout his body.

"I can't stop," Mathias said, his eyes still burning.

"I don't want you to stop." Alberto swung his arms around his neck.

While they kissed, the water drowning any other noises, he faintly remembered a time when he thought it would be hilarious to mess around with Angry Buzzcut, press his buttons, get what he deserved. Alberto had wanted to bewitch Mathias, and now he had; Mathias couldn't stop, even if he wanted to. He was done for, hooked like a flailing fish at the end of his line.

"Don't stop," he murmured against his helpless prey's lips. "Please, don't stop."

For the next ten days, Alberto and Mathias barely saw each other. Paquin had called Mamma and told her he had skipped school to avoid facing the headmaster, which resulted in a week of added detention. His mother was absolutely shocked. Alberto listened vaguely while she gave him an earful of stuff that she'd probably just printed off the internet, rolling the chain around his neck between his fingers and thinking of Mathias.

Dimitri weirdly took his defence again, saying, "That's what boys do!"

"What do you mean?" Mamma asked, looking wretched. "What do boys do?"

Each other, Alberto thought.

He felt invincible, but despite all of that, he was grounded for a week. Oh, he understood why. Mamma just wanted to keep an eye on him. After two days of not letting him out of her sight, she noticed not only that he was fine, but that he was even better than usual, and the punishment was lifted. Dimitri, amused by her weakness, commented on it, to which she reacted by narrowing her eyes at his back. That lightened the weight on Alberto's shoulders. Once Mamma started squinting at one of her men, that meant she didn't care so much for their opinion anymore.

Alas, Mathias was busy with his mock exams, so the only time they found was at the infirmary between two tests. There, with only a few minutes to spare, they kissed more than they talked. In fact, the entire time, they said little more than *Hey* and *See you later*. And yet, Alberto was the least worried he'd ever been. The kisses were intense enough that Zak couldn't be said to have the monopoly of limp legs anymore. As for the silences in between, they were golden. In all this time, Mathias had not once told Alberto to shut up. All he did was laugh— *yes, laugh* — when Alberto murmured *More* each time they parted.

More. He always wanted more.

Alberto spent ten days in a daze on a different sort of cloud — one he was riding for once. He couldn't stop thinking about their reunion, imagining where Mathias would kiss him first, how fast they'd remove each other's clothes, and how Alberto would get him to do it face to face again without looking too keen.

On Friday evening, to his infinite surprise, Alberto heard from Michael again. The short film the Drama Club had shot back in July was nominated for some awards, and Michael, the unofficial director of the film, called to offer Alberto his seat at the ceremony because he was touring France with his boyfriend and his cousins' rock band and couldn't make it on time.

Mathias wasn't free tonight, on account of attending Zak's birthday celebration, but any opportunity to get out of his own so-called party sounded good to Alberto. He was already dressed in his new Armani and catching dust in a corner, while guests he'd never met shuffled from room to room wishing him a happy birth-day. He found his mother and asked — no, begged — for her to let him leave the party.

Mamma played annoyed, but she was struggling not to smile when he clung to her neck.

"You can go," she said. "But I want you to return home tonight, you hear me? No more sleeping God-knows-where for a while. I haven't forgotten your little adventure of last week."

Too happy to get away from that dreadful place, Alberto promised and went up to swap his uncomfortable shoes for his favourite Converse. On his way down, he came across Stasia with that look in her eye, the one that said she'd just talked to his mother and she needed to hurt someone before she exploded. She blocked his way down the steps, caught him as he was trying to squeeze past her, and once she grabbed him, there was not much he could do. She then followed him to the mirror in the hallway where he re-tucked his — now wrinkled — shirt into this trousers and hand-combed his hair back into place.

"Don't look at me like that," she said with a sigh. "I'm doing this for you, Albertino, for your own good. You need to toughen up. You'll thank me for this later in life, for sure."

Alberto turned to face her. "I hope one day you get a new boyfriend and he dumps you into a vat of acid like you deserve. And I hope I can watch."

Stasia sniggered. "That's oddly specific. Do you have anyone in mind?"

"I don't know… Satan, maybe?"

"Satan? So unoriginal."

He pushed past her to put his coat on. She knocked into him with a grimace.

"Also, if you're there to watch, does that mean… you'll be in Hell as well?"

Alberto ignored her and buttoned his coat while humming lyrics from a certain band. Yesterday, he and Mathias played their game, and then Mathias helped him sit on top of Sana's desk. He stood between Alberto's knees, pulled his arms around his neck, and they kissed for a long, long time. His skin was so hot, it felt like he, too, was on fire, and they'd burn together.

Together.

Alberto's new favourite word.

"Hell? Burn?" Stasia looked upset. "What are you mumbling about?" She followed him to the front door. "Is it me, or are you getting even weirder?"

"Yes." He flashed her a fake smile.

She stared back in confusion. "You absolutely suck today. No fun at all!"

He slammed the door on her mean face. That cloud he was riding was too high, even for winged harpies. Still, he exhaled a sigh of relief when she was out of sight.

5

THREE CHEERS FOR THE DEBAUCHED

MATHIAS ARRIVED at Eric's a bit late, but not too late, just enough that he wouldn't be the first to arrive. He entered the two-level apartment to the sound of cheers and found the whole gang crammed into the living room with Eric in the middle, some award proudly lifted over his head.

"Matt, look!" his friend said when he spotted him. "We won!"

Zak's best friend Camille, all flouncy skirt, baby hair, and sparkly eyes, seized Mathias by the shoulders and pushed another award into his hands. Her lanky boyfriend Arthur took it back with a smile. "Sorry, we're just drunk on success."

Drunk on success. Mathias had no idea what that felt like. He pushed past Joy, Melissa, Elodie, Xavier, and Charles-Henry and went to salute a few of Eric's footballer colleagues from his club, nodded at their girlfriends, and soon, he was in a corner sipping a beer and wondering if it would be appropriate to go home as soon as he'd finished it.

Now that the mock exams were over, Mathias wanted to see Alberto. After doing reasonably well this week—and even starting preparations for his entrance examination to his first choice of culinary schools—he logically felt he deserved a reward.

There was no chance of Alberto being invited to this party, not with Eric as a host, so he figured if he went home early, he might be able to convince him to spend the night together. Dad would be sleeping already, and in any case, he never cared about who stayed over, not even when he was an innocent kid and Daphnée shared his bed. Dad never even said a word about Christmas Eve, only nodding faintly at Alberto when he walked out of Mathias's room.

As for Elisa, she had long stopped mentioning Alberto, which was a bit suspicious, but she was busy wrapping up the *Colette Candy Guide*, and Mathias wasn't the kind to look a gift horse in the mouth.

Eric spotted Mathias hanging in a corner with his empty beer in one hand and his phone in the other, and he rushed over, his hands filled with little plastic cups. He nudged him with his foot.

"Matt, did you wish Zak a happy birthday?"

Zak, standing behind Eric, was all dressed-up tonight, clad in an elegant buttoned-up shirt and a pair of tight jeans that were probably the reason Eric's face was scarlet.

"Happy birthday," Mathias said.

Zak shook his head with a smile. "It's not midnight yet. My birthday's at midnight." He lowered his voice. "Everything will be different at midnight."

"Different how?"

His cheeks darkened. "Just different."

"Zak's really excited to turn seventeen!" Eric said, his hands shaking.

Yeah, must be that, Mathias thought vaguely, stepping back to avoid getting splattered by whatever red liquid was in these cups. He glanced up toward the corridor, only for his heart to stop.

Alberto.

He was here… awkwardly standing in the doorway, his thumb scratching his brow.

As tall as a baby giraffe and twice as cute.

"Give me that," Mathias told Eric. He emptied one of the cups and grimaced. "What the fuck is that?"

"Punch!" Eric cried, seizing the cup back. "And it was Zak's!"

"I don't care!" Zak squeaked. "Look!" He whirled his boyfriend around. "He really came!"

Eric's mouth fell open. "Christ on a cracker… He really did."

Mathias willed his heart to stop beating like a war drum and asked in a hoarse voice, "You invited him? How come? Don't you hate the guy?"

"He did!" Zak's eyes shone like two giant marbles. "Out of nowhere, he invited him at the ceremony!"

Eric looked as if a harmless prank had turned into a national disaster. "It's Zak's birthday. I wanted to make an effort." His boyfriend gawked at him, too shocked to comprehend. "I'm too fucking nice," Eric added with a bitter grin, before emptying a cup of punch.

Mathias glared at Zak suspiciously. To his knowledge, that kid was the only one beside Alberto's mother who didn't inspire a snigger or a condescending word out of him. Mathias was certain Alberto liked Zak more than he let on. It's the way his gaze softened when he talked about him. It wasn't much, but it was there. Did Alberto's gaze ever soften at the sound of *his* name? It did not. Mathias would know; he spent a whole lot of time staring at that face.

Alberto eventually noticed them and approached, unaware of the longing looks half of the girls—and Xavier—threw his way.

"Happy birthday, Zak."

His tone was soft as morning dew when he was talking to that little bastard. Mathias bit into his cheek until he drew blood. Zak warmly thanked Alberto, and Eric grabbed his hand and shook it hard enough to tear it from his wrist.

"You're late!"

"I got lost."

"How can you get lost on the metro?" Seeing him shrug, Eric did his best to conceal his animosity and let out a forced laugh. "I'm so glad you came."

Alberto replied in a voice so quiet, he was barely audible. "Thank you for having me."

"Get yourself a drink, don't hesitate!"

Eric pushed him out of the way. With a quick look at Mathias, who pretended to look elsewhere, Alberto disappeared around the corner. Zak immediately opened his eyes wide.

"Were you really serious about what you said earlier? You want to be friends with him?"

"Yes, yes!" Eric laughed. "I'm serious."

Zak gave him a doubtful look. "Why?"

"Oh, water under the bridge, that's all."

"Water under the bridge?" Zak turned to Mathias for support.

"Two weeks ago, he was still good old *Shovel Face*," Mathias muttered. "What happened?"

"I've had a lot of time to think," Eric said in a disinterested tone.

Was it special treatment because Kayvin shoved Alberto into the pool? It was entirely possible… And Mathias sincerely hoped it was because of that, and not to submit him to more humiliation at the hands of the football team tonight.

Eric wasn't in the mood for talking about his nemesis anymore; he waved his hands dismissively. "Zak, baby, did I remind you that I love you today?"

"Only three times," Zak said, faking outrage.

"Only three? Guess there's still time for a fourth, then."

"Great. I'll put the kettle on."

Before Mathias could even ask, they left hand in hand. When they were a safe distance away, Alberto reappeared magically by his side. Mathias nearly jumped ~~him~~. "You weren't getting a drink?"

"I was just hiding around the corner." His fingers brushed against Mathias's waist, who pushed his hands deeper into his pockets.

"What do you think the kettle's for?" he asked, to distract himself.

"I don't know." Alberto sighed a puff of hot air onto his neck, and one of Mathias's pockets tore. "I don't like not knowing. I'm not usually like that."

Mathias didn't like the way Alberto stared after Zak. He liked even less knowing that Alberto would brave dozens of people, bad music, and junk food just to wish him a happy birthday. "They, ahem… They're happy with each other."

"They sure are…"

So are we, Mathias wanted to add. In their own way, so were they. Weren't they? Good sex was nothing short of a miracle, wasn't it? And they were really good at it. Mathias yearned to plunge his hand in the pocket of his suit, graze a certain part of him with his thumb, and press his lips to his neck.

"Look…" He sucked in the last breath of air left in the room, forcing himself to be smart. "We can't—"

"I know." Alberto's fingers, instead of touching his wrist as they apparently intended, disappeared into his pocket. "I know. I'll just be on my side of the flat, and you'll be on yours. It will be like I'm not even here." He stepped back and shuffled toward the snacks, where he got immediately hounded by Xavier.

During the next hour, all thoughts of going home out of the window, Mathias wandered about Eric's apartment. He exchanged a few words here and there with Zak's friends and pretended not to be bothered by Xavier's insistence on introducing Alberto to everyone at the party, by his hands all over him, by his toothy grins and little complicit nudges. It only served to remind him of his stupid brunch, of when Mathias saw him leaving Alberto's room, smugly wiping his lips with the back of his hand.

Eric and Zak had long re-emerged, and they were circulating from group to group. Mathias was burning to tell Alberto the kettle had to be a dirty thing because they'd both returned with their hair a hot mess. But he could only stay on his side and watch from the corner of his eye as Xavier entertained the *girafon**.

Mathias gnashed his teeth in his corner, full of conflicting thoughts and even worse ideas. He didn't want to say the wrong things and have a repeat of the other day at the museum. But while staring at Xavier, he reminisced about the last time he and Alberto slept together, when Mathias was on fire and had fucked Alberto so well, he lost his English and had to revert to calling out his gods in Italian. He'd like to see Xavier try that!

"Good party, am I right?"

Mathias swung around with a start. Eric had returned and was offering him a fresh beer. "Yeah, sure."

"Then, why are you standing here all alone?"

----

* Alternate name for 'baby giraffe.' (French)

Mathias scowled. "I always say the wrong things."

"No, you don't."

"Fuck off."

"Okay, maybe you do."

"… Sorry." Mathias took the beer and patted Eric's shoulder. "Did you lose Zak?"

Eric pouted. "I have to give him space to enjoy the company of his friends."

"Christ, you sound like you're reading forums on dating."

"I do! If I had my way, I'd be clinging to him all the time. *How to Be a Good Boyfriend and Make Your Girl Happy* says I should definitely not do that."

"Hang on. Your *girl*? Aren't you reading the wrong book? I thought Zak was a guy."

"So?" Eric shrugged. "He's also like a girl."

Mathias blinked at him, bewildered. "How?"

"Like, you know, being a human being and all. I don't think there's a big difference between boys and girls." Faced with Mathias's incredulous expression, he grinned and explained, "For example, the book says if you wanna know how the girl you're dating feels, then you should ask, and chances are, she'll tell you. You just gotta ask."

"Okay."

"I don't see the difference between girls and guys about that. We all feel and think things. We all want to say things we're afraid to say. The more we wait, the worse it gets, whether you're a boy or a girl."

Mathias furrowed his brow. "Fine. Sounds good and all, but your book is also suggesting you shouldn't be yourself."

"How so?"

"You're naturally clingy."

Eric burst into a laugh. "That's right! But even I know I can be a bit much sometimes. I don't want him to get tired of me too quickly."

Amused, Mathias poked him in the shoulder. "What about you? Aren't you tired of seeing him all the time?"

"No! In fact, I don't see enough of him. Hell, I even became an actor to pursue him. I'd do all sorts of crazy things just to see him. I'd even…"

Mathias tuned him out and slipped a furtive look in Alberto's direction. Xavier, Joy, Melissa, and a bunch of other people surrounded him, and were laughing gaily while he clung to the food table—his own idea of personal hell. Was Zak really worth it?

And then he saw it: the quick glances, clearly addressed to him, full of knowledge and desire.

Wait. Was it possible? Alberto came here tonight not for Zak, but for him? The thought filled him with blinding light. *Now*, he felt drunk. His heart thumping, he dipped his head and couldn't help a smile from spreading across his face, but when he looked up, Eric was staring at him through narrowed eyes.

"Stop looking at me."

Eric drew his face unbearably close to his own, like he was trying to read into his soul. It was very uncomfortable.

"Back off! Are you making a pass at me?"

Eric quickly threw up his hands. "No, no."

"You should look after your boyfriend. He's flaunting his ass over there. It's…" Mathias searched for the word most likely to trigger him "… indecent."

Eric almost tore his head from his neck to check on Zak who, tipsy, had fallen face-first on Camille's lap, and his ass in its tight jeans was in full view of everyone. To Mathias's astonishment, Eric managed to gasp, yelp, blush, and break into a sweat at the same time, rubbing his face with his palms until his eyes turned bloodshot.

"Oooh, that ass!" He let out a sob. "I can't take it anymore! I'm gonna have to take a cold shower. Now!"

Mathias sighed. "I take it you haven't slept together yet?"

Eric shook his head gravely. "Zak's an angelic being and won't let himself be debauched so easily."

Angelic? Really? Mathias had rarely seen him without a frown. The rest of the time, he was usually wrapped around Eric and looked most certainly like he could be debauched easily.

For fuck's sake. Soon, Mathias would have to give sex-ed tips to a guy like Eric. "Wait. How long have you been together again?"

Mathias hadn't even spent one minute on a date with Alberto, but he never had any trouble debauching him. But of course, there was nothing angelic about Alberto—he was a dark creature—and it was probably the other way around: Alberto had debauched him, using his vast array of demonic tricks, and Mathias was the innocent one. Or something like that.

Beside him, Eric was counting diligently on his fingers. "About three and a half months." He forced a smile. "There's time. I don't care. I'll wait until marriage if that's what he wants."

"Ugh." Mathias shivered. "Seriously…?"

"No, no! That's not what he wants. But I'll wait. I'll wait almost forever, just not forever."

Mathias didn't exactly enjoy watching him look so helpless, but he kinda did, too, especially since he was always showing his boyfriend off, so he was tempted to make fun of him. But in the end, the question that passed his lips was nothing but serious, and it was something he'd wondered for a while.

"How do you do it?"

"Do what?" Eric wrinkled his nose. "You're not listening to me! We're not doing anything, that's the problem, that—"

"Shh, shh, shut up. I meant how do you control yourself?"

"Oh." Eric's expression turned sly. "So, you wanna know what your best buddy's up to, after all?"

"Who's that? Best buddy? I don't know him."

Eric gasped. "Don't be like that! I'll tell you!" He lunged at him, but Mathias shoved him aside. He couldn't help but think his friend was totally gullible and easily bullied. Smothering down his urge to laugh, he forced his face to look serious.

"I'm listening."

"We do— We do other stuff, that's all."

"Like what?"

"We kiss."

Mathias snorted. "Nerds."

"Stop!" Eric pursed his lips, vexed. "Meanie."

"Fine, fine. I'm joking anyway. Of course I've seen you two kiss." In fact, he'd seen too much of it. And not only him, but the entire school also had witnessed their… passion. And now that he mentioned it, the first time he'd talked to Alberto, that pervert had been staring at them while they were making out. "But no way," he said, pushing the memory away. "There's no way you two stop at kissing."

Eric jerked his chin. "It just requires a bit of practice and a lot of determination." He was sweating just talking about it. "And a bike."

"Oh…" Mathias really struggled not to snigger this time. "That's why you got the bike?"

"Maybe?"

"So… you just take him for a ride every time you want to… take him for a ride?"

Eric's mouth fell open. "Nice!" They shared a fist bump. "Listen. It keeps me in shape. Isn't that great? My coach is *very* happy."

Mathias threw his head back and laughed. "Yeah, you definitely need to release some of that tension."

"Right…" Eric gave him one of his brightest smiles and pulled him close. "Hey… I don't think I've ever seen you laugh like this before."

Mathias huffed and wrenched away. Eric was annoyingly tactile and had trouble understanding that some people weren't. Mathias didn't want to hug other men, squeeze their shoulders, slap them on the back, or other stupid shit like that. Strangely enough, he was fine pressing them into the mattress and doing all sorts of other stuff to them… Hold on. That couldn't be right.

"Of course you have," he said gruffly. "I laugh, like everyone else. It's just that your jokes aren't funny."

Eric cocked his head with an enigmatic smile. "I know."

In truth, Mathias felt particularly light tonight, and definitely luckier than some. *And* Alberto was wearing a suit with a tie; it was hanging loose around his long neck right now. Mathias was feeling creative about that tie. Now, to think of a decent excuse to isolate that demon from the rest of the crowd without people noticing… It would be difficult, but it wouldn't be the first time.

6

COME CLEAN

ALBERTO STOOD for a long time by the large table facing a long wall, hoping Mathias would take a hint to join him by using the excuse of wanting a cocktail sausage or some other disgusting-looking thing people like to eat at parties. He stood for so long even Eric came to talk to him at some point, asking him all sorts of weird and nonsensical questions before he huffed and dragged Zak out of the room, no doubt to tell him how much he regretted inviting Alberto.

Finally, Mathias left his corner by the lamp and came to his side. Despite the pounding music, Alberto had struggled so much to remain standing without falling asleep, but now he found he still had some energy after all.

"Sausage?" he asked.

"Don't start." Mathias opened a beer and stood next to him against the wall where they could see everyone coming and going. Eric was following his guests, mopping up any accidental spillage after them. On the other side of the room, Zak was watching him while sipping beer, looking so horny, Alberto worried Eric would have to mop him off the floor next.

"Xavier finally left you alone for a minute," Mathias said, raising his voice a little.

"Oh…" Alberto glanced at him. "Have you been watching us?"

"No." He took a large swig of beer. "I'm just… I'm observant."

"If you're so observant…" Alberto checked no one was looking in their direction before he leaned into his space. "Have you seen my arse in these trousers?"

This time, Mathias let out a laugh. His hazel eyes brightened, and his cheekbones took on a glow.

People don't have a clue what real beauty is, Alberto thought. That… *that* was beautiful. Not half-dead-looking faces on glossy magazines, those so photoshopped, their own mother couldn't recognise them. No. True beauty was a rare bloom on a desecrated field; or in this case, an unexpected smile on a usually dour face. Alberto stared, transfixed, burning the image in his memory for later, and he eventually flinched when Mathias snapped his fingers under his nose.

"Where the hell were you this time?"

"What?"

Mathias shook his head. "Michael and his boyfriend just arrived."

Alberto followed his gaze toward the opposite side of the room, where, leaning against the fridge, some hot guy was poorly pretending not to throw anxious looks at him. And next to him stood Michael, who was doing his best to resist the onslaughts of Joy and Melissa.

"You know them?" Alberto asked in a wheezy voice.

"I met them once. Eric's fond of Michael."

"Oh, right."

Alberto recalled the first time he and Mathias kissed, how he said Eric had told him about Michael, and his throat tightened. And, just as he feared, after some hesitation, Mathias asked, "If I ask you, will you tell me the truth?"

"The truth…?"

"What really happened between you and Michael? Why is Louis staring at you like that?"

Alberto didn't want to answer. These days, guilt rarely seized him, but in that instance, it really did, both for what he'd done and for the way Michael had reacted: with kindness. Decency. *Pity*.

He chuckled darkly. "Maybe because I forced myself on his boyfriend once."

Mathias sprayed beer all over the place, earning looks of surprise from those standing close by. He glanced at Alberto's serious face and turned white.

"Are you… are you serious right now?"

Alberto wiped beer droplets off his cheek with his sleeve. "No."

But close enough anyway.

"Christ!" Mathias shook his head. "Stop fucking with me like that. I almost died."

"Sorry, couldn't resist. You always make the best faces, no matter what I say."

Grabbing a pile of paper napkins, Mathias mopped up his shirt with a disgruntled expression that brought inexplicable flutters to Alberto's stomach. "What happened, anyway?"

"I did something bad. Every time I see him, I'm reminded of it." *You're not a good person, are you?* "And I don't like it."

"Wait…" Mathias frowned. "Maybe you did something bad, but you know… it doesn't mean you're a bad person."

Alberto met his eyes with confusion. "But you already think I'm a bad person. You tell me all the time. So, why are you defending me now?"

Mathias's expression turned sour. "I'm not," he grumbled. "W-What did you do to him, exactly?"

"I'd rather not say."

"Come on, since I already think you're a bad person, what's the worst that can happen?"

"I don't know, but it can always get worse."

"God." Mathias took a sip of beer. "Lighten up a little."

"Look at you after one drink. Suddenly, you're the life of the party."

Mathias turned red. "Fine! Shut the fuck up if you're not gonna tell me."

"Now that you ask so nicely, how can I refuse?"

They were both raising their voices, and some footballers were still staring from Mathias's earlier display. With a sigh, Alberto relented. Knowing the truth wouldn't make Mathias like him more, but he felt compelled to tell him. It had to be done.

"I jumped him once," he said. "I knew he had a boyfriend, and I knew he didn't like me, yet I cornered him and kissed him anyway." Alberto screwed his eyes shut. "It was awful."

Mathias was silent for a spell. He finished his beer before he spoke again. "What did Michael say?"

"He was paralysed," Alberto recalled with anguish. "It was really awkward. Afterwards, he tried to… to talk to me. It made things even worse. I left the room, and since then, I try not to think about it, but every time I see him…"

Mathias turned and turned the empty bottle between his fingers. "Why…? Why did you do that? You liked him that much?"

"*Like*?" Alberto frowned. "What *like*?"

Michael was picked because he was a perfect candidate… for Alberto's mother. Tall and handsome, he had it all: dark curly hair and deep-green eyes, he was sweet but not nauseating, cultured but not arrogant. He and Alberto shared an affinity for history, violent Korean films, and songs without lyrics. With Michael, Alberto saw an opportunity to kill two birds with one stone; not only was he good enough for him, but he was like a much better version of himself. Between a stick figure or the live model of the perfect son, what mother wouldn't choose the latter?

At the time, Alberto imagined very well locking himself into a relationship with Michael to make up for everything he could never be. So what if he didn't feel anything for him? He didn't feel anything ever, so what was the difference, exactly? It was lucky Michael didn't care for him. What a waste of both of their times it would have been otherwise.

Mathias huffed and opened another beer. He seemed pissed off. It was understandable. After all, he said it himself: he hated selfish shits. Alberto saw Michael, heard he was gay, purposefully ignored the fact that he had a boyfriend and didn't seem interested in him, and selfishly cornered him. It was really messed up of him to believe that it would only take one kiss to make Michael his. One kiss… Isn't that all it takes? In his experience, that was the case. When the idea came to him, it came violently, like every other impulse. *If I kiss him now, then I'll feel a great thrill. If I kiss him now, everything will be all right.* He had given in to his fear, just for a second, and he would feel guilty about it for the rest of his life.

It happened after Zak had confessed his adoration for him, of which Alberto was well aware. At the time, Alberto cared nothing for Zak; he was just another fanboy who couldn't see past his looks. To be honest, it even surprised him how collected Zak appeared when he declared himself after weeks of watching his every move with starry eyes. In any case, his declaration triggered something.

It occurred one stuffy afternoon, while Michael and Alberto were watching dailies alone in the dingy little back room. Michael — after calling it a day — stood and stretched in that way he did. He looked attractive enough, and Alberto had the feeling he would kiss back if given a little push. Wasn't he irresistible, after all? Before Michael's arms were back to his sides, Alberto was in front of him.

Michael had seen the look on his face and had swallowed. "Alberto…"

They were about the same height. All Alberto had to do was close the gap between their faces. He did so without hesitation and without emotion. When lips met lips, Michael froze against the wall. Then, he curled his hands around his arms and gently pushed him away. Alberto stood back, at first unsure whether he was frustrated or simply relieved.

"Nothing?"

Michael shook his head vigorously. When Alberto stepped away, he gave an audible sigh, and Michael's expression softened, his eyes taking on a glint of pity. "Are you all right?"

Now, Alberto knew what he felt was frustration. He shut his eyes and pinched his lips. "*I* should be asking you this."

"I'm fine, but you, you look—"

"Sorry," Alberto cut in. "Am I going to get in trouble for this?"

"No…" Michael hesitated. "Am I?"

"Of course not."

When Michael began extending his hand toward him, Alberto backtracked into the desk.

"I'm sorry," he said.

Before he knew it, he was out the door, and he never allowed himself to be alone in the same room with Michael again.

Tonight, he was forced to relive the scene, forced to witness the tension on Mathias's face. He was forced to take a ride on the same carousel of unpleasant memories, the one that always ended up breaking down at the worst possible times.

"I misread the room that time..." Alberto said in a whisper. "I misread things a lot."

His forehead creased, Mathias asked, "Do you regret it?"

Alberto nodded. He couldn't tell him how much he regretted it, that he would do such a thing... He was afraid his voice would crack if he tried to say it. Sometimes he asked himself, *Why did you do this?* It made no sense as all. Sometimes he knew the answer: he was bad; *rotten to the core.*

Mathias was silent for a moment, staring down at his beer like it was its fault. Alberto was getting frightened he would just tell him to sod off and that he never wanted to see him again, that he really was a bad person, a demon, or worse. He was frightened Mathias would ask him what else he'd done. He was frightened he would have to tell him the truth, because he couldn't help wanting to tell him things about him, and this mistake with Michael wasn't even close to the worst thing he'd done.

But what actually came out of his mouth wasn't at all what Alberto had expected.

"He doesn't trust it," Mathias said, his voice low. "Louis. He doesn't believe his guy rejected you."

Alberto's eyebrows drew together. "What do you mean?"

Mathias turned his head to the side, as though he'd rather not say. "He probably thinks his boyfriend is bullshitting him. That he kissed you back and then made it sound like it was all your fault."

"Why would he think that?"

"Because..." Mathias scowled at his beer. "No one in their right mind can reject you when you get all sexy, Alberto. Trust me. I wish I could."

Alberto dipped his head. "I know you do." Seeing Mathias's expression grow helpless, he boldly seized the moment and added, "Can I put this theory to the test?"

Mathias drew in a sharp breath. "Just lead the way."

"No, you go. Find us a place. But I promise… I'll be real good once I get there."

Mathias never graced him with another look. Clenching his jaw and his beer, he walked away in search of a secluded location. Alberto stared after him, puzzled.

Yes, he really was feeling bad for Mathias for falling into his trap, but that's not all he felt for him anymore. It was too late on all counts.

The clocks struck midnight shortly after, and the tipsy — or full-on drunk, in the case of some football players — guests gathered in the dining room to cut the cake. Alberto admired from a distance how Eric managed to convince Zak the cake on display was not, in fact, a wedding cake, but a "super special three-tier birthday cake," despite being clearly, from the snowy colour to the little bows to the outlandish size of it, a wedding cake. Zak, himself intoxicated and obviously smitten, went for the lie or pretended to believe him. He was, after all, a good actor.

They sang — Alberto didn't — the classic birthday song. Eric had a horrible voice, but Melissa didn't, so it worked out pretty well. Xavier popped open a bottle of Champagne, and the cork flew straight toward Michael's handsome boyfriend and would have given him a proper black eye if Michael hadn't caught it right before the impact, as though he were prepared for it. Before long, Champagne glasses were passed around, and Camille was cutting the cake with what appeared to be a giant butcher knife, while Zak was busy opening a large pile of birthday presents. His friend Arthur kept urging him to tear the paper open instead of carefully unwrapping each one and driving everyone insane with impatience.

Then, suddenly, Eric was standing near Alberto, holding a plastic cup under his nose. "Champagne?"

"No, thank you."

Eric flung the cup at one of his friends like he hadn't ever expected Alberto to accept it. "So… still doing all right over here?"

Alberto avoided meeting Louis's eyes for the tenth time tonight and nodded sheepishly. "Yep."

"Good. Good, good, good." Eric watched Zak open his next present with relish and refused the portion Camille offered him with a smile. "Thanks, but I don't touch that stuff."

"I don't touch that stuff either," Alberto said.

Eric gave him a sideways glance. "That— that can't be the only thing we have in common, can it?"

"That, and… we both put our tongues in Zak's mouth."

Eric gripped the edge of the table behind him with both hands. "I will fucking kill you one day."

"Mm." Alberto nodded. "I'm looking forward to it."

Eric opened his mouth to say something, but some burly footballer interrupted them, insisting Alberto take a glass of Champagne. Despite his polite refusal, the guy wouldn't take no for an answer, even when Eric told him to stop with a nervous laugh, but it was too late. His friends had heard them, and now Alberto was surrounded by drunk football players.

"You don't drink?" one of them asked. "Ever?"

"Ever," Alberto said.

"But why?!"

Everyone looked at him in shock. Alberto realised with some consternation he was the only one not drinking. "I don't know… it seems to make people stupid sometimes."

His comment was met with resentful looks. The next second, he was fending off remarks about how harmless drinking was and how weird he was for not wanting to join in the fun.

"You can have fun without getting drunk," Alberto said.

"But are you having fun right now?" Joy asked, smirking.

Alberto hesitated and glanced around the room, but he didn't find Mathias. "Not right now, no."

"Then, come on, have a drink!"

Resigned, Alberto reached toward the plastic cup when Xavier appeared out of nowhere and swung his arm around his neck, almost putting him in a headlock. "If he doesn't want to drink, then he doesn't want to drink!" With an exaggerated laugh, he pulled him away from the others and into the quieter corridor.

"Don't let them bully you," he said, releasing him.

"Okay." Alberto leaned against the wall. "Thanks."

"No problem. Hey, were you serious? About not having a good time?" The way he was looking at him, Alberto felt Xavier was about to ask him to kiss him again. He must have looked smug, because Xavier came closer, so close, Alberto felt his breath on his neck, and he couldn't help feeling amused. "Can I help in any way?"

Alberto twisted his neck to check out his eyes. They were eager and bright — and utterly confusing. Glancing over Xavier's shoulder, he made eye contact with Mathias, who was just about to go upstairs, and his expression was murderous. Naturally, with the way Alberto had been flirting with him, Mathias had every right to consider his arse was his for the night. After the other day, he'd better stay clear of Xavier, however amusing his behaviour was.

"I'm having a moderate amount of fun," he replied prudently, while Mathias made his way upstairs. "Thank you."

He slipped away then, but Xavier followed, still bent on hugging him back to the dining room, where a group of people were watching intently.

"Xavier and Alberto!" Joy exploded, making Arthur jump in fright. "Are you a couple?"

Xavier burst out laughing. "You wish! I mean, I could have him anytime…" He met Alberto's disapproving stare and gulped. "No, that's not what I mean! I'm not gay!"

"Yeah, we know that." Joy narrowed her eyes impatiently. "But the question everybody wants to know tonight is… are you?" She was looking at Alberto. "Are you gay or not?" She added under her breath, "Is Zak a liar or what…?"

Zak's mouth fell open in outrage. "At my party, really? You're gonna be like that?"

"Zak isn't a liar," Alberto said, and his cold tone actually made Joy's friend Melissa shiver. "Not that it's any of your business."

With this revelation, half of the girls in the room let out a sound of disappointment under the bewildered gaze of their boyfriends. Joy sneered, clearly still mad at Alberto for the other night, while Elodie spread out her hands, muttering, "Seriously? Why always the hot ones?"

Satisfied with his answer, the crowd moved on, except for Zak, who hovered by Alberto with a wounded expression. "So, what was it?" he asked. "You didn't find me attractive?"

Caught off guard, Alberto blinked stupidly at him. "What? No, not true. I always thought you were cute."

"Cute? Like a little boy?"

"No. Cute, like, cute. *Cute.*"

"But you didn't want to touch me. Didn't even want to kiss me."

What a dangerous conversation to have. Alberto had to get out of this, and quick. He looked around for a way out, but Zak was blocking his path.

"Does it matter?" he asked. "Your boyfriend wants you so much, he's practically foaming at the mouth, and he's hotter than me, so why are you even talking to me?" He chortled at Zak's shocked expression. "What? You both want it. Why not get it over with?"

"Because!" Zak stomped his foot. "I had— I mean, I *have* principles. I wanted to wait." He gave him a long, shrewd look. "And I always thought you were… you know…" He lowered his voice to a whisper, "like me."

"Like you?"

"Waiting… you know… for the right one?"

Alberto chuckled. "I'm probably the biggest slut in this room."

Zak's formidable brows shot up. "What?"

"Probably. Xavier is also here, so I don't know." Alberto carefully omitted Eric from the list, not just because he wanted a truce, but also because Eric had an unfair slutty reputation. Contrary to Xavier, who did bed more than half the girls in his year, Eric only had flings with a few. Eric was, in fact, possibly like Alberto, a monogamous slut, who dedicated themselves to one person enough to wear them out. That's what Alberto intended to do with Mathias, anyway.

"I really know nothing about you, do I?" Zak mumbled, wringing his hands together. "It's just… I've always wondered what was so wrong about me, why you didn't like me that way. Whatever it was… what if Eric thinks the same once he… sees me…"

Alberto reacted fast and poked Zak in the shoulder. "He won't. It's not the same."

"Then, tell me why—"

"Take off your clothes, see if his first reaction is not to try to destroy you. I'm willing to bet my favourite pair of shoes that he'll turn into an animal."

Zak blushed. "Alberto…"

"I'm just saying…" Alberto leaned forward and whispered something in his ear.

"Alberto!"

You're welcome, Alberto thought. One day, he would tell him the truth, but today was not the day, so he left that cute little thing looking smug as hell and not worried anymore.

Since when was he giving away advice to people? And rooting for them, too? He was turning into a strange person indeed.

And speaking of strange, Mathias hadn't returned; Alberto was missing him already. He left Zak to go in search of him, but he'd only taken a few steps before a hand closed around his wrist and pulled him away into the darkness.

7

DANCE FOR ME

HE HELD his hand in a vice-like grip. They took a staircase, Mathias leading in the dark — Mathias *always* leading in the dark — and Alberto advanced into the deepest black, a shadow among shadows, but with a faint smile on his face. He knew. He knew he wasn't alone, and he knew what awaited him atop these stairs was nothing to be afraid of.

Once again, he couldn't have been more wrong.

Mathias led him into an office. Small strings of fairy lights hanging over the desk bathed the room in a faint but warm glow. Alberto accidentally squeezed Mathias's hand, and he felt it twitch back. His heart lurched in his chest.

"I like this song," he blurted out. He'd almost said something stupid.

Not letting go of his hand, Mathias turned his ear toward the door to listen. "Dance for me," he said.

Alberto shook his head. "I don't know how."

"Lies. I know you can move."

Alberto couldn't recall when he'd seen him dance, unless he'd somehow travelled back in time and spied on him and his mother, seen them dancing in their elaborate costumes in front of the gilded mirror, trapped in the ever-spinning carousel.

"Plus," Mathias added, lips hot against his ear, "you said you'd be good once I got you up here."

Alberto didn't know how to answer that, so he said nothing, but he did dance. He moved under the burning gaze of Mathias and didn't break eye contact once, hoping he'd get a proper reward, a reward in words, perhaps—or better, in empty promises.

He danced for a short amount of time until Mathias closed in on him, and he had to stop. His back met with a bookshelf. Shivering slightly, he bent his head just a little. Mathias, quiet as a breath, softly kissed his offered lips. His fist tightened around his tie and pulled until what was a soft caress turned into something more... familiar.

"I like the suit." Still hanging onto the tie, he spoke against Alberto's lips. "You look good tonight."

"Don't I always look good?"

"Particularly tonight," he whispered, making Alberto's lips tingle. "Was that for me?"

Alberto was anxious not to say the wrong thing; it was an unfamiliar feeling. He was used to playing this or that role to get Mathias to do him the way he wanted. Now, he couldn't ignore how nervous he was not to mess things up, and it wasn't because of sex. He did want Mathias to like him, to stop calling him a bad person. He wanted to be good. His *good boy*, like when they were wrestling under the sheets and Mathias lost himself to his lust and whispered praises in his ear. He wanted that feeling outside of bed, too.

Huh. He wanted way too much, for someone whose only quality was to look like his mother.

"What would you like me to say?" His helplessness never translated. His voice was like a whisper, barely audible.

Mathias took some time before whispering back, "Say nothing."

He kissed him again. Alberto felt himself turn liquid, and he thought of Zak slumping into Eric's arms, legless. He wondered out of nowhere what sort of sex Zak and Eric would have tonight, and suddenly, he felt the urge to laugh.

"What's so funny?" Mathias asked, sounding vexed.

A burst of feminine laughter downstairs made Alberto flinch. "There are too many people around. If we don't watch it, we're gonna get caught."

"I know. You're right."

Mathias released the tie and, using his palm, pushed him away for good measure. Now, Alberto panicked. He didn't want to let go. "Wait."

Slinging his long arms around his neck, he brought their mouths together again. Mathias laughed against his lips. Tipsy, tipsy Mathias. Whatever he drank, he tasted the same: rich, sweet, and exquisite. He suddenly caught Alberto's arm, whirled him around, and pushed him against the bookcase.

When he cupped him, Alberto gasped. "Hang on… do you know where we are?"

"I'm pretty sure I don't care right now."

"But it's—"

"The safest place, now *shh*."

Alberto closed his mouth. If Mathias wanted to get naughty, he wouldn't be the one to stop him. He allowed himself to get trapped between his burning body and the bookcase, full of titles he couldn't be bothered to decipher right now. Mathias never wasted time, and in seconds, he held him in his fist, his grip firm and soft at the same time. Alberto wanted to tell him not to go too far, and he also wanted to tell him to go beyond every limit. In the end, he said nothing. Closing his eyes, he flung a hand back to stroke Mathias's scalp, enjoying the possessive feel of his greedy lips on his neck.

"Am I your best fuck?" Mathias asked suddenly. His voice was hot and smooth in his ear. Knowing better than to interrupt good sex with useless words, Alberto said, "Sure," thinking, *why not*, and Mathias seemed satisfied.

"Am I?" Alberto couldn't resist asking in return.

Mathias grunted like he was annoyed — that beast — even though he started it. "You are," he muttered, plunging his nose back into his neck.

And instead of making things awkward, it just made everything better.

Working him closer to his climax, Mathias was pushing his hips into him and smothering small noises into the flesh of his nape. For a moment, Alberto thought he'd lose control and actually fuck him against the shelf — in Eric's home — which drove him a little wild with guilt but also with trepidation. In the midst of all this passion, he decided he should wear ties more often. One thing was certain: he was past the point of caring whether Mathias would ever admit to being gay.

Alberto tried to keep quiet the whole time, only allowing the quietest sounds to escape, but gradually, sighs turned into moans which turned into pleas, and Mathias kept urging him to *go on and go on and come for him*… Suddenly, he questioned whether the music downstairs could cover their voices, and when he found his release, a strangled cry broke its way free. His whole body shaking, he gripped the edge of a shelf and held on tight, his mind so blank he couldn't recall his own name.

"Alberto…"

There it was. Alberto exhaled a shuddering breath. Tonight, something was in the air, something powerful, frightening, and exhilarating. Alberto desired to give all his goodness to Mathias — every little pathetic shred of it — watch him smile, and witness that glint of desire in his eye. His chest constricted, full of all the words he couldn't say.

He understood the shift in his heart as it occurred, with a clarity he had never experienced before. *After years of stillness, the first tremor will feel earth-shattering.*

"Did you hear me?" Mathias whispered in his ear before kissing it.

Alberto shivered, stunned by the sudden realisation. "W-What?"

"You'll stay over at mine tonight, right?"

"Yes," he replied immediately. Then, as Mathias's lips trailed down his cheek, he recalled and said, "No!"

"Hm?"

"No, sorry, I can't stay over."

"What?"

Mathias finally stopped rutting against him. Alberto slowly faced him.

"I've got to go home. I've avoided another one of my stepfather's parties, but I had to promise my mother I'd sleep at home."

Mathias pretended not to be annoyed, but Alberto knew him too well now. He pressed his body against Mathias's. "Hang on, I'll get you off."

"No, I'm good." He sounded blocked up.

"I'll get you off," Alberto repeated gently, and he gave him a light kiss.

He sunk to his knees and did something with his lips that had Mathias rub his scalp with both hands and glance toward the ceiling with a pained expression.

"No?" Alberto asked when their eyes met again.

Mathias gripped his hair with both hands, a crude gesture which couldn't be misinterpreted.

He would never be proud of what happened in that room then, but Alberto really was. It took less than thirty seconds that time, and when Alberto rose again — licking his own lips for added effect — a vulnerable Mathias, cheeks flushed and legs unsteady, suddenly spoke up. And though Alberto knew better than to believe the words of a guy who'd just got off, he couldn't help having a faint smile curl his lip.

"You're amazing," Mathias had said.

The party was at a lull when Alberto returned downstairs. To his relief, both Michael and his boyfriend seemed to have left already, and Alberto congratulated himself on not having exchanged a single word with any of them, despite Michael gifting him his spot at the award ceremony. In his mind, and he was sure Louis would agree, a polite *Thank you* text would suffice.

Zak had gone from adorably tipsy to only drinking pint after pint of water under the confused gaze of Eric. Arthur was explaining the overall plot of the movie they were about to watch to Eric's mother, who had just returned from her *Ladies night* and looked just as overexcited as Camille next to her. The movie in question was the one they shot last summer, *My Summer of Love and Woe.*

Alberto had no desire to watch it again. He checked the time, knowing he should go, but Mathias was sitting miserably at the kitchen table surrounded by Eric's friends, so he dragged his feet over, and Xavier immediately pulled him close.

"What's up?" Alberto asked faintly, the taste of Mathias still lingering on his tongue.

Charles-Henry replied with a grin, "Xavier has a crush on Camille."

"I can't help it!" Xavier whined. "I love it when they hate me."

Alberto tossed her a look over his shoulder. "She's too smart for you, let it go."

Xavier sighed in defeat. "What can I say? Alberto's always right."

"You can add that to the list of the dumbest things you've said," Alberto said without thinking, slumping on a chair. A little burst of laughter coming from Mathias attracted everybody's attention.

"What's up with you tonight?" Elodie asked, sounding amazed.

"Matt's in a good mood," Xavier said, teasing. He attempted to squeeze Mathias's shoulder but was discouraged by his warning glare.

When Camille started playing the movie, most people got closer to the TV. But Xavier and Charles-Henry stayed put, and Alberto noticed with some pride that it was testing Mathias's patience.

"Not going to watch?" he asked them in a sarcastic tone.

Xavier laughed. "Nope, watched it so many times already." He chugged down a shot of tequila and passed one to Charles-Henry, who asked if he had brandy instead. Xavier ignored him, and, leaning on the table, he flashed Alberto a wink. "We can chat instead."

"Chat?" Mathias looked repulsed at the notion, causing Alberto to bite down his lip to repress a laugh. "About what?"

"I don't know. Anything." He glanced at each of his friends with a slight frown, then offered, "Let's do celebrity crushes!"

Charles-Henry giggled nervously. "Isn't that a bit private?"

"What? No! We're at a party, loosen up a little."

Never vexed by anything, Charles-Henry humoured him with a smile. "Fine, you go first, then."

"Hmm…" Xavier took some time to answer. "Charlize Theron, obviously!"

Alberto rolled his eyes. "So out of your league."

Mathias acknowledged his statement with a subtle nod.

"Matt, who's yours?" Xavier pushed a shot of tequila toward him. To Alberto's surprise, Mathias drank it without question.

"Dunno."

"Come on, everyone has one. C. H., what's yours?"

"Uh… Charlize Theron's great."

"See? Another one, maybe?"

"Maybe… Eva Green?"

"Who?"

"She's beautiful," Alberto agreed.

"Never mind." Xavier drank another shot. "Who's yours, Matt?"

Mathias looked bored. "I don't know. Stop asking me."

"Xavier!" Eric shouted from the living room. "You're about to get whacked! Come on!"

"Oh, it's my scene with Camille!" Xavier sprung to his feet and left them to watch the moment Camille, playing the kitchen wench, beat the crap out of him for spying on their lord. Officially, it was Alberto's favourite scene in the movie. Unofficially, Alberto preferred the ultimate kiss between Eric and Zak's characters. He wouldn't admit it out loud, but the way Eric pushed Zak against that writing desk suggested he had some skills in the laying waste department.

"I'm going to watch, too. I love the way she hit his head with that prop spoon." With an eerie smile, Charles-Henry trotted away. Only Mathias and Alberto remained, and the former looked sombre as he helped himself to a glass of wine.

"Is everything okay?" Alberto asked.

Mathias drank without meeting his eyes. "What's yours?"

"My…?"

"Who's your celebrity crush?"

"Oh…" Alberto rested his chin on his hand. "I don't have celebrity crushes."

Mathias glanced up. "You don't?"

Alberto flashed him a wicked smirk. "I have fictional character crushes."

Mathias's eyes narrowed. "Always so fucking weird…" He forcefully cleared his throat. "Anyway. Who's your fictional character crush, then?"

"Easy. Omar Little."

"Who?"

"Omar Little from *The Wire?*"

"No idea who that is."

Alberto explained to him who he was. Mathias looked disgusted. "You see yourself with some old guy carrying a shotgun? Why?"

"Omar's not that old… and so what? I like the idea of doing crime with my hot duster-wearing boyfriend. What's wrong with that?"

Mathias glowered at him and helped himself to some more wine. "Nothing, I guess."

"Omar can kick ass." Alberto stretched his arms over his head, making sure Mathias didn't miss it. "I'm sure he'd give me a nice pounding, too. He's super fit."

Mathias's face darkened. He was so handsome; it was worth staring at his disgruntled expressions for hours. His hand was shaking a little when he chugged down his wine.

"Who's your crush, then?" Alberto asked. "Of course, you couldn't tell them, but you can tell me."

"What do you mean?" Mathias put his glass down. "Why do you think I couldn't tell them?"

Because your crush is probably proof that you're as gay as I am, Alberto thought. He knew he couldn't say it, or Mathias would start breathing fire again. They held each other's gaze in silence until Mathias's lip curled, and he poured himself another glass of wine.

"So?" Alberto pushed forward. "Your crush?"

"Don't have one."

"Come on—"

"I don't!" Mathias drank deeply from his glass. "Didn't have much time to think about this stuff while Mom was sick, did I? I don't even turn on my TV. I think the last show I watched was *Prison Break,* so—"

"Nice!" Alberto chuckled. "A prison show with countless guys to drool over."

"You're obsessed, you know that?" Mathias said in a gruff tone. "I'm not like you. I don't look at people that way. I have other things to think about."

Worried he went too far, Alberto cast his eyes down. He only looked up when Mathias spoke again.

"In any case…" he was muttering, "I can give you one, if that's what you want."

"Give me what?"

"A good pounding."

Alberto's heart thumped; his blood rushed to his face. Mathias didn't notice, too busy drinking his wine as fast as possible. Suddenly, Alberto wanted nothing more than what he was just offered, and he resented the promise he made to his mother.

"I have to go home…" he mumbled.

Mathias wiped his mouth with the back of his hand. "Why? Do you always do what your mom tells you?"

"Well… yes. She's my mother. She only wants the best for me."

Only twice ever had he disobeyed Mamma. Once was when she insisted he finish that photoshoot, and he raised hell instead. Her reaction was to dump her husband, jump onto the next train, and move them both to yet another country, and he ended up with Stasia for a stepsister.

Alberto tried his best not to disobey or disappoint her, but sometimes, he had to. That's why he did feel bad about deliberately failing his Drama Club audition last summer, but not bad enough to prevent him from sleeping. Alberto did not like the spotlight as much as his mother did, but he'd rather she didn't know that. Every time they moved, it got worse. What would happen next time? So, he'd long decided there would be no next time. He simply told her Eric got the part because he was better than him, which he was, hands down, and despite Mamma's disappointment, he felt no regret.

"I get it," Mathias said. "But my mom's the one who told me I should disobey while I was still young."

"I'm sure she was fun," Alberto conceded.

"She was." Mathias shifted in his seat. "Is yours…? Is your mom fun?"

"I don't…" Alberto frowned. "I don't think so."

He really had no clue. Mamma could be butchering people in the basement *Dexter*-style, and he would still think the world of her. He was like that. Once he loved, he loved blindly and unconditionally. And he loved her more than he loved life. But was she really fun? She may have been, once, or maybe she'd always been either on the lookout or too tired to move. Perhaps she and Alberto shared more than their looks, perhaps they were one and the same: The brittle and empty shell of a once-promising child.

If his mother wasn't so beautiful, she'd have no one and nothing. And Alberto would go down the same road if he wasn't careful. He used to not care at all about this, but lately, he found himself wanting a little more from life. It had happened so gradually, he didn't notice at first, but if he'd been told he'd meet someone who would make him jump out of bed in the morning with the simple memory of their scent, he wouldn't have believed a word of it. And yet… Alberto closed his eyes and inhaled deeply to get a whiff of Mathias's cologne and hummed when he caught it. When he opened his eyes again, Mathias was watching him curiously.

A loud yelp interrupted them. It was Eric, who looked like he'd just learned some mind-blowing news. "Thank you all for coming!" he bellowed, a fierce look in his eye. "Stay as long as you want. You can find your own way out!" He caught Zak by the hand, and they flew down the corridor. Shortly after, a door slammed shut.

"More things than a few glasses will get broken tonight, it seems," Alberto said. His words forced another laugh out of Mathias.

"You're so bad. *So bad.*"

Alberto swept a ravenous gaze over him. "Next time you see Zak, ask him about his butthole."

"Christ." Mathias coughed in his fist. "You're not… not even a bit jealous?"

"Huh? Why?"

"You and Zak…"

Alberto shook his head. "I'm really happy for Zak."

Mathias sighed. "I don't understand you."

"I'm aware." Alberto flattened his palms on the surface of the table and began to rise. "I'm going home."

"No!" Mathias said, half-rising himself. He threw a quick look around. Everyone else was in the next room watching the movie. "Wait. Stay a bit longer."

His palms flat on the table, Alberto hesitated.

"Come on," Mathias said. "Have a drink with me."

Alberto glanced toward the living room, at all those tipsy people, who were having the time of their lives, and he realised, tonight, he wasn't so different. In fact, he felt pretty normal. Just a normal guy having a normal glass of wine with his normal — but super-hot — hook-up. He could do this. He *would* do this.

"Okay."

Mathias's eyes brightened, and before long, Alberto was taking his first sip of wine in a very long time. It took no time at all for him to feel flustered and strange, his lips stretching at a mere word from *him*. His glass soon became empty, and he didn't protest when Mathias filled it again. In fact, he would have given everything for this night never to be over. Time became meaningless, and it felt like only seconds had passed when the drink really got to his head and he was starting to think mushy, unspeakable things, like how he wanted to be held by Mathias, even by force — and *especially* by force — so that he'd have the excuse to tell the world, *Look, I didn't have a choice, he held me so tight, I didn't have a choice but to feel warm and safe.* He knew how wrong it sounded, and yet he couldn't allow himself to see things any other way. When his fingers stretched, itching to touch him, to link themselves between Mathias's own, even to press a kiss to the back of his hand, a shudder rocked his

body from head to toe. Alberto stared at the wine in his glass in
stupor.

8

SILENT SHADOWS

WHEN MATHIAS HAD PROPOSED Alberto drink with him, the latter hesitated, his gaze sweeping across the room. Something was going on in his head. Pros and cons, probably, wondering what sort of reward was in it for him if he stayed.

He then said, "Okay." Such a small, sober word, yet it lit a roaring fire in Mathias's chest.

Alberto sat back down and contemplated his glass for a while before drinking, pulling a grimace when his tongue met the liquor. Mathias slipped his foot between his legs under the table, and he snorted in his drink, his cheeks reddening. It took all Mathias's willpower not to grab that tie and pull it to bring their mouths together.

God, he was beautiful. Mathias would never understand how he could resent someone so much, grow ulcers at the sound of their name, yet feel weirdly ecstatic at the mere sight of their flushed face. He realized there was so much about himself he didn't understand. He felt no one but his mother could help him shine a light on whatever was going on. His mother… and maybe the one in front of him.

Halfway through his first glass, Alberto swirled the wine around, his demon eyes glinting curiously. On the other side of the table, Mathias felt reckless. "I want to ask you something."

"Ask me what?"

"Something I've wanted to ask you for some time."

If— If I asked you to…

As if to brace himself for whatever Mathias was about to ask, Alberto gulped his wine down too fast and chortled. Mathias waited with bated breath, but in the end, Alberto didn't smile. It was a thing of his, like his way of pronouncing *p's* like they were intended to sound dirty, or that he never felt pain—whereas Mathias could *only* feel pain.

They couldn't be more opposite, yet Mathias had grown to feel they were weirdly similar. Once, Mathias would have turned up his nose at Alberto's earlier words, his admission of never liking Michael despite pursuing him so aggressively. Now, Mathias only felt helpless, and a little doomed, too. Whether or not he'd find the courage to ask, he already knew his answer, didn't he?

"Why do you never smile?" Mathias changed directions abruptly, deciding to ask the other question later. After another drink, maybe.

Alberto shifted in his seat. "Smiling gives you wrinkles."

Mathias thought he heard wrong at first, but Alberto repeated the same sentence and took a sip of wine as if to toast the words.

"What the fuck? Who told you that?"

Alberto put his glass down. "My mum."

"You really believe that stuff?"

He shrugged.

"Your mother doesn't want you to smile? She doesn't want you to be happy?"

Alberto's brows knitted together. "My mother wants me to be safe. If I become happy on the way, then it's all the better, isn't it? If not…" He waved his hand dismissively, then gasped. "Am I talking too much?"

"What? No." Mathias stared at him, confused. Alberto met his eyes in kind. Mathias refilled his glass. They gave up talking, but kept drinking until some of the other guests called it a night. Soon, the fact that they were sitting together in the kitchen would start to look suspicious, yet Mathias's feet were glued to the floor.

Alberto made the first move. He excused himself to use the

bathroom, and Mathias noticed how badly he was swaying. Remarkable, considering he'd only drank three small glasses of wine. If Mathias knew one thing about rich kids, it's that they could hold their liquor.

Disproving his point, Xavier, completely smashed, returned from the corridor with one girl under each arm. "I just saw Alberto. He threw me out of the bathroom. He's really drunk!"

"So are you," one of the girls said, dropping him onto a chair. "Good night." They dumped him there and left.

Xavier slid down the chair with an anguished expression. "I really need to pee!"

"There's another toilet upstairs," Mathias said, getting up. He hurriedly went to the bathroom and recovered Alberto just as he exited, his hair damp and his shirt half-untucked. That bastard looked so good, Mathias had to wonder what Xavier had intended to do with him in the bathroom before he was kicked out.

"I can't leave you alone for a second," he muttered. Alberto gave a childish shrug, causing him to smile. "Come on, drunkard, let's get you home."

Mathias looked all around him. Everyone was pissed and having a good time. Back in the living room, Camille and Arthur were getting wrecked by Charles-Henry and Eric's mom at some dance video game; they weren't paying attention. Worried he'd stumble upon some other kind of wrecking, Mathias avoided checking on Eric to say goodbye, and, slipping his arm around Alberto's waist, he dragged him happily toward the exit.

"*Sei il ragazzo più bello del mondo**," Alberto slurred, stumbling forward. Mathias caught him just in time.

"I don't understand what you're saying."

Alberto leaned on him. "*Scusa†*."

Mathias scanned around for stray guests lingering in Eric's courtyard and saw none. He pressed Alberto closer. "That's okay. I like it when you speak Italian."

The creature got all curly against him. "What else do you like?"

---

* "You're the most beautiful man in the world." (Italian)
† "Sorry." (Italian)

"You know, that thing you do… when you don't talk."

Drunk-Alberto puffed out a laugh and threw his arm around his shoulder. He was acting the opposite of his sober self; tactile and clingy. Delighted, Mathias wondered what sort of things he could extract from him if he pushed a little, but he was aware this wouldn't be fair to him, so he decided to behave, until Alberto called out, "Mati…" so softly, Mathias's heart suddenly dropped to his stomach.

"What now?"

Alberto flinched at the harsh tone of his voice. Mathias held him tighter, his way of apologizing.

"I don't feel so good."

"You can't hold your liquor for shit!"

"Of course I can't. I never drink."

"What?" Mathias looked at him. "Never ever?"

"Never ever ever."

"Christ, *pollito*, why didn't you tell me?"

Alberto blew a raspberry. "Hey, *ascoltami. Per favore*[*]."

"Okay, I'll listen, but you have to speak English or French. Do you know any French?"

"Only *je t'aime*[†]."

Mathias almost dropped him. "Fantastic."

"And *voulez-vous coucher avec moi?*[‡]"

"Shut the fuck up, then. Do me a favor." A bead of sweat trickled down Mathias's temple. "I need to get you home." He couldn't carry him home if his knees didn't work.

"No, no." Alberto's legs, too, were like jelly. He hugged Mathias's neck for support. "Listen to me, listen to me."

"Yes?"

"I'm beautiful."

"I know, you're a demon."

"So, you must listen." Alberto's childish pout was too damn

---

[*] "Hey, listen to me. Please." (Italian)
[†] "I love you." (French)
[‡] "Do you want to sleep with me?" (And not in a sleepover sense) (French)

cute. Mathias opened the gate and hauled him out onto the street with a racing heart.

"Listen to what?"

"Me."

"I am!" Resisting the urge to laugh, Mathias attempted to prop him against the brick wall so he could use his phone, but he wouldn't let go of his neck.

"Kiss me."

"No, no, no." Mathias used his elbow to pin him against the wall. Alberto groaned, then seemed to realize he was on the street and yelped.

"Get me a car, would you? Take me home."

"That's the plan, so hold tight."

Mathias tried to find a number for a taxi online, but he had never needed one before. From the look of it, Paris had more taxi companies than inhabitants. Perhaps it would be best to just wait for one to drive by.

Alberto dropped his head onto his shoulder. "Where do you think we live?"

"We?"

"Where's my home?"

"I've been to your place, remember?" Mathias pinched, then stroked his cheek. "God, what a handful you are."

Alberto huffed. "My other home, my real home!"

"What the hell are you talking about? Italy?" When he started squirming, Mathias had to put his phone away to catch him.

"Why do you always call me a demon?"

"I don't know." Mathias's movements paused. "Because I'm a jerk. Does that bother you?"

Alberto blew another raspberry right in his ear. "You can call me whatever you want, but first, you have to kiss me."

"I can't," Mathias said, wiping spit off the side of his face. "I'm getting you a car."

"Are you coming with me? You have to come with me."

Mathias sighed. "I think I do. I can't abandon you in that state, anyway." He winced when Alberto tried to lick his cheek. "Stop it."

"Don't leave me. *Al buio tutti i ragazzi sono brutti.*[*]"

"Whatever you say."

A cab couldn't come fast enough, really. But of course, there was nothing in sight. Perhaps they were all too busy driving young Parisians home from the nightclubs.

"You must stay…" Alberto was saying, rubbing against him, oblivious to Mathias's despair. "My bed is big enough for two. For three, even."

"Good to know," Mathias mumbled, wondering if he had ever put that theory to the test. "But I don't think I should stay over."

"Why?"

Mathias snorted. "I don't want to get raped by your drunk ass."

Alberto turned rigid against him. "… What?"

"I was joking, Alberto. Like you? You do it all the time."

"What?" He repeated dumbly.

"Your dark jokes? To make people uncomfortable?"

"I make pupils uncomfortable? I make peepholes inflatable?" He groaned. "*Cazzo*[†]."

Mathias pinched his waist. "You know you do. You get off on this." Alberto started poking his chest while muttering in Italian. Mathias slapped his hand away. "Okay, stop. I'm not fighting you tonight."

"Let's have sex, then."

"Same fucking thing. Here!" Mathias spotted a taxi coming up the street and gestured wildly at it. He watched it slow down to a stop before them with relief. "Now, be good and get in the car."

Alberto tossed his wallet at him. "There, there. Take my money."

"Oh, thank you." Mathias waved it in front of his nose. "You're so generous. I should run off with it and ditch you."

Alberto clicked his tongue. "You'd take my money, but not me? I see, I see."

---

[*]   Alberto's personal twist on "At night, all cats are grey." Here he says, "At night, all guys are ugly." (Italian)

[†]   "Fuck." (Italian)

Mathias laughed despite himself. "I will remind you of this night every day for the rest of your life."

Alberto stumbled toward the car with a lot of attitude, but not much coordination. "Hey, open the door, would you? The back door, baby."

"Asshole."

"You said it. I said *back d*—"

"Shut the fuck up."

The entire ride, Alberto, though half-asleep, clung to Mathias and wouldn't stop chattering. Mathias had no clue what his mix of Italian and English—alternately slurred, whispered, then whined—meant, and he eventually tuned him out. But he did let him slump over his shoulder and hang on to his neck for the duration of the trip, stroking his hand to soothe him, and he tried his best to ignore the rude smirks from the taxi driver.

When they reached the gates of Alberto's mansion, Mathias felt ten years older. From the way he was acting, Mathias had a feeling the word *cazzo* he kept saying had nothing to do with "houses" or "hunting," but everything with what was between his legs. For once, Mathias was grateful for the biting cold, and he took a deep breath when he escaped the confines of the backseat.

"You're home, Alberto," he told him, gently spinning him toward his house.

Alberto looked at the gate in confusion, then his expression turned dark. "We have to be quiet."

"Okay."

"Really quiet." He gripped his sleeve tightly. "Don't let her catch you here."

"Sure." Mathias rolled his eyes. He wasn't afraid of Alberto's mom.

Alberto opened the gate, then pushed Mathias inside, asking him to check the lights. Everything was dark and quiet in the yard, with no lights coming from either the main house or the dependence. Only when Mathias swore did Alberto follow him in.

"She really can't see us," Alberto added.

Mathias's firm nod seemed enough to reassure him for now. They scuttled across the lawn and crept into the house, two silent shadows stalking the gleaming floors. Then, a light was turned on outside, and Alberto flattened them both against the wall. Mathias chuckled, all too amused by this ridiculous situation, triggering another avalanche of Italian.

Ignoring his rambling, he took Alberto's hand and led him up the staircase. "I'm taking you to your room. How can you be so drunk after three small glasses? I swear to God, you're not human."

Alberto replied something absolutely unintelligible, his knees giving way. Mathias had to half-carry him up the stairs.

"Okay, okay. We're almost there."

A few more steps. Funny how he could weigh so much tonight when he usually weighed so little in bed, Mathias reflected as he dragged him up the stairs.

"I was wrong," Alberto suddenly muttered in his ear.

"You were wrong? About what?"

"I said I was wronged!"

"Wronged?"

"Yes."

Mathias patted him gently on the shoulder. "Poor little demon."

Alberto abruptly turned his head. "Come on, kiss me a little."

"No."

"I want you…"

"I'm not touching you tonight."

"Why?" Alberto used his tricks, becoming as soft as a kitten against him. "Am I suddenly not good enough for you?" He staggered forward and covered his eyes. "Oh, I need to sleep."

"Yes, you do."

"Just fuck me a little before you go."

"No."

"Just a bit."

Mathias couldn't help laughing. "No!"

Alberto lost his patience when they reached the top of the stairs. "Come on! Grab my arse or something!"

"Shh…" Mathias kept his laughter quiet and gave him a stern look. "You'll wake your parents."

"That arsehole's not my dad." Alberto clicked his tongue with annoyance. "And no one can hear us in here, I swear. You could slaughter a whole flock of lambs, no one would hear a thing."

"Okay, okay, just calm down."

"I'm always calm." Alberto slumped into Mathias's arms just as they entered the bedroom. The latter got excited from relief at the sight of the bed, and he was about to bluntly—if not nicely—throw that drunkard on the mattress, but Alberto caught him by surprise and pushed him down first.

"One little kiss," he said, climbing on top of him.

Mathias burst out a laugh. "You're one slutty drunk, you know that?"

Alberto crushed their lips clumsily together. Mathias returned the kiss first with impatience, then with growing desire, and he finally pushed Alberto off him and rolled him to the side of the bed.

"Well played, but it's still no."

With a dramatic sigh, Alberto finally lay flat on the mattress. "What if I'm slutty? What are you like when you're drunk?"

"See for yourself." Mathias leaned over him and flicked his lower lip with a smile. "I'm pretty drunk right now."

"You don't look drunk."

"That's probably because you're seeing three of me right now, and they're all blurry. I'm used to drinking, and I had proper food at the party. Did you even eat anything?" Alberto lifted his head and whispered some words in his ear before he swiped his tongue over it. Mathias shuddered and pushed him down. "Bed. Now." He began removing Alberto's clothes, but Alberto suddenly became very still. Perhaps he thought he was about to get what he wanted. His eyes wandered drunkenly around the room and fell on the door Mathias had left ajar.

"Lock the door," he said.

"Yeah, in a minute."

"*Lookn'tshelf, inblulephant.*"

"What?"

"The blue elephant!"

Mathias tried his best not to laugh out loud, so much so, the corners of his eyes were prickling. At last, Alberto's clothes were removed, and Mathias was covering him with his plush comforter.

"Remember…?" Alberto whispered in the dark when Mathias's lips grazed his forehead.

"What?"

"Remember the holidays?"

"Yes, I remember what happened a few weeks ago. I'm not like you."

"Remember what we did?"

Mathias chuckled. "No. You tell me."

"We had sex. A lot of it."

"That's true."

Good sex, too, if he may be so bold. Fantastic sex, until that time he treated Alberto with the gentleness of a husband and got himself blacklisted for over a week.

"And also…" Alberto's eyelids were now half-closed. Mathias wanted to kiss them, but he knew he had to exert restraint.

"Tell me."

"We sang."

"We what?"

"We sang songs, remember?"

Mathias smiled. "I remember." They sang Bloodhound Gang songs in front of the mirror. They never got to the end of the last one; Mathias had never let him. He felt his heart grow heavy.

"I wish we…"

"You wish what, *pollito*?" Mathias bent down to kiss Alberto's lips, laughed, and drew back with a grimace. "You could use some mouthwash."

"Mm." Alberto sighed. "You too."

"Thanks, *bastardo*."

Alberto loosely pointed to the bathroom door. "Help yourself." But when Mathias tried to leave, Alberto caught his hand. "Don't go."

"I'm not. I'm not going anywhere."

"No?"

"I'll be here tomorrow."

"You will?"

"Mm-hm. I'll be right here, next to you."

"Can we have sex then?"

Mathias pretended to think long and hard about it. "Depends how stinky you are."

"I won't be stinky!" Outrage twisted Alberto's fine features, causing the corners of Mathias's lips to curl upward.

"That will be for me to judge."

Alberto giggled, and then he was out like a light, his hand falling back onto the mattress with a thump. Mathias blinked softly at him, his heart at rest for the first time in a long time, even if tonight, it was too late to ask him any more questions.

Earlier, he had almost found the courage, first by getting himself drunk, and then, despite failing to entice Alberto to come to his place, when he convinced him to stick around a while longer. The knowledge that he was his favorite lover had emboldened him; he felt, perhaps after a few drinks, he could ask the burning question that had been on his lips since the day they skipped school and he witnessed the depth of his eyes as he climaxed—when his heart had grown twice its size in his chest.

If I asked you to stop sleeping with other people, and to sleep only with me, if I asked you to be mine and only mine, in body at least, what would you say to me?

"What a prince," he muttered once he was back in Alberto's large and pristine bathroom. He opened the nearest drawer and found a spare head for the state-of-the-art electric toothbrush Alberto owned. When he was done washing up, he finally remembered Alberto asked him to lock the door. He returned to the bedroom, and, to his shock, he saw warm light pouring in from the corridor, and a man's silhouette blocking the light. Mathias nervously retreated into the bathroom. Was that Alberto's stepdad? Did they wake him by making too much noise?

Judging from Alberto's insistence, it was vital his mom didn't find out about Mathias's presence, so naturally, he had to avoid the stepdad, too. Mathias watched quietly as the man pushed open the door, came in, and sat on the edge of Alberto's bed, muttering some words. Alberto woke and groaned at first, then spoke back to him. Mathias couldn't hear what they were saying to each other.

He pressed his face into the opening until he felt his eyelashes brush against the doorframe.

The man put his hands on his fluffy comforter, his voice barely audible. Whatever he said forced Alberto to laboriously push himself to a sitting position while mumbling something. Considering how he was speaking in weird tongues two minutes ago, it was unlikely he'd recovered yet, and Mathias silently smirked at the thought of the nonsense he might be spewing. And then, his smile was wiped off his face, replaced with a look of pure shock.

Time came to a stop in the mansion, at least in Mathias's mind. He thought of stepping forward, of stepping back, but his legs wouldn't work, his mouth wouldn't open. His blood pounding in his ears, he screwed his eyes shut. When he dared take a peek again, it was already over. The man was staggering out of the bedroom, and Alberto was falling back into the mattress with a sigh.

Burning up, yet frozen to his core, Mathias waited until the stepfather was gone, then he rushed forward to close the door, and only then did he spot the sculpture of a blue elephant on the bookshelf. He caught it with shaky fingers, saw the opening on top, flipped the whole thing upside down, and felt a key fall into his palm. He whirled around with a curse; Alberto was still passed out on his bed. Mathias used the key to lock the door, then, as if this simple action had worn him out, he fell to his knees in front of the bed.

Alberto was sleeping peacefully, his lips parted, still moist. Mathias watched him for a long time, until he felt a pain in his forehead from too much frowning. Silently, he leaned forward and wiped his lips dry with the pad of his thumb.

Stalkers

9

MORNING AFTER

IT WAS EARLY when Alberto opened his eyes. The curtains were closed, plunging the room into a soft, cosy darkness. When he moved his legs, he felt Mathias's heat close by; his lip curled up. He twisted his neck and found him asleep, his brow knitted as though he was having a bad dream. Alberto slowly turned over and almost pressed his finger to his forehead, but in the end, he didn't want to wake him. Not yet.

About last night, he couldn't recall much. Only the feeling of sinking into a pleasant state, as if he were enveloped in a plush and warm blanket. Maybe that's what had happened after all. Alberto simply drank some wine and woke in his own bed with Mathias by his side, like he had jumped through a wormhole and ended right where he was supposed to. And even if he was feeling dehydrated, at least he had slept well. He checked the door, saw that it was locked, and praised himself for remembering to keep the Devil out of his safe space for the night.

Alberto was an expert at being quiet. He always had been. He slid from under the covers without stirring Mathias and tiptoed into his bathroom, closing the door behind him. After drinking three glasses of water, he brushed his teeth until his mouth didn't feel so dry anymore, and he scrubbed himself in the shower until his skin was raw.

Afterwards, he stood at the foot of his bed for a long time, dressed in new briefs and smelling of his favourite soap. Mathias hadn't moved at all. Perhaps he had fallen asleep really late because they had been up to no good. In any case, though he looked a little out of place under Alberto's comforter, the latter still felt a bizarre urge not to wake him. Alas, he would have to, sooner or later. Mathias couldn't stay here forever; there was danger in being here.

But for now, all these worries were meaningless. They were alone, the door was locked, and Alberto had other plans.

He slipped back under the covers and cosied up to Mathias's warm body. How do you wake the one you like? Should he whisper words like secret spells into his ear? *I like you. If only you knew how much I like you. If you wake up now, it means you like me, too.*

He'd never had to ask himself the question before. While at Mathias's, he usually woke first and escaped the bed as soon as possible, worried his bad breath or body smell might deter Mathias from ever touching him again. Even though he planned to return to bed immediately after cleaning up, his savage little werewolf inexplicably always woke the moment he sneaked away. That being said, when Mathias roused first, Alberto would feel his burning lips clamp on the back of his neck, so he thought he would be glad to find him all clean and ready to play this morning, but since he also liked to be in charge, Alberto didn't want to spook him by taking the lead.

Alberto studied his sleeping face while all these thoughts bounced around in his head, and he didn't dare make the first move. Scooting closer and closer until they were nose-to-nose in the middle of the gigantic bed, he admired Mathias's handsome features in silence, especially the thickness of his eyelashes. When, with a thumping heart, he discovered the previously unnoticed freckles on his nose, Alberto decided he'd cheat a little. He found Mathias's hand and positioned it on his buttock. Then, he waited.

Mathias's instinct took over before Alberto's eyes. His fingers twitched, then groped, then squeezed. He wasn't even awake before he was seeking Alberto's lips. Their kiss was soft yet possessive, with Mathias's arm coiling around Alberto's waist, drawing him closer like an enchanted vine. Alberto slid his hand up his neck, and when Mathias's eyelids fluttered open, he finally saw his eyes, as soothing as they were overpowering. Alberto's breath caught at the sight. Mathias gazed at him without seeing him at first, and then it was like someone had poked him with a fire iron: the warmth in his eyes turned to ice, and he jerked back.

"Hey." Mathias cleared his throat and rolled away from him.

Alberto thought he'd startled him. He chased after his warmth by pressing himself into his space. "Hey."

Come on, he'd even shampooed his hair with the product he knew Mathias loved — by the way he often woke to his nose buried in his hair. Now wasn't the time to get shy. But to his surprise, Mathias threw off the covers and immediately began dressing.

Alberto watched him with a sinking heart. He had left their bed the first half a dozen times and never once imagined that Mathias could feel as dejected as what he was experiencing right now. But to watch him jump into his jeans as though his life depended on it…

Alberto discreetly sniffed his own armpit and didn't find anything wanting.

"Everything okay?" His voice came out a little cold, but it was still better than sounding whiny.

"Everything's fine," Mathias said, both arms already in his sweater.

But Alberto was aware of when he was being lied to. "Was I very drunk?" he asked.

That was the only thing that came to mind. The only reason Mathias would be so eager to get away from him. And indeed, Mathias's movements finally paused, and he let out a thin laugh.

"Now I know why you never drink."

Alberto swallowed a lump. "What did I do?"

Mathias was all dressed up now. He briefly met Alberto's eyes, only to look away. "Can you get me out of here unnoticed, then?" he asked his window, burying his fists deep into his pockets.

Alberto observed his hoodie. It wasn't the one Mathias once lent him at the museum. No, that one was tucked away like a precious treasure in one of Alberto's drawers, to be worn only when he was safe in his room and in need of a reminder of the scent of his skin. This one was light grey, the same he wore when they first met and Mathias had cut the wind off him.

And now, Alberto felt just the same, like all the air had been sucked out of the room.

"Yes." His tone had dropped by a hundred degrees. "Of course."

What could he do now except deal with the current situation to the best of his abilities — lift his chin up and play it cool — and wait for Mathias to return to him, in need of his next fix? Alberto shook himself off and went to his dressing table, where Dina had laid his clothes for today. Mathias watched him get dressed with a knitted brow.

"What is it?" Alberto asked.

"Does your mother choose your clothes for you, too?"

"It's one less decision to make in the morning." Mathias's frown deepened, so he added, "Besides, she knows what's good for me."

"Does she, really?"

"Yes." Alberto buttoned his shirt with an air of aloofness. "What's wrong with that?"

"Nothing," Mathias said, but his tone was sour, and it was obvious he thought Alberto was just spoiled.

It's just clothes, Alberto wanted to say. *She wants to take care of me, and I love being taken care of. Don't overthink it.* But Mathias had already put his jacket over his hoodie and was hovering by the door. Alberto grabbed a cardigan and led him out into the corridor.

On a Saturday morning after one of their parties, it would be impossible to find Mamma awake, so they didn't have to worry about running into her. Dina would be downstairs preparing their next meal. But like his daughter, Dimitri was a machine and hardly ever slept; it would be best to avoid him altogether, and Alberto knew how. He silently led Mathias down and tucked him away in a corner, but when he heard Dimitri pacing in his office, he realised his plan to let Mathias out by the smaller exit at the back of the house would be impossible. His shoulders sagged; his only other option was the front door, and if Stasia was around, she would probably sniff them out like the harpy she was.

There was no other choice. Mathias looked so tense, Alberto

didn't want to antagonise him further. He quietly unlocked the door and feigned innocence when Mathias frowned at the security camera above the door. Alberto waved his hand dismissively; he knew unless they were burglarised, Dimitri would never check the footage.

This time, they got lucky. They flew over the lawn, keeping close to the edge of the property, and in no time, Alberto, breathless, was unlocking the gate.

"Unnoticed," he said. "As you wanted."

"Thanks," Mathias slipped out, his gaze locked on the pavement. "Have a nice weekend." He pulled his hood over his head and walked away.

He usually said, *See you later, I'll text you*, or whatever. But not today. Today was *Have a nice weekend*, something he'd never said before. Alberto stared after him until Mathias had turned the corner at the end of the street, then he shut the gate, his chest tight. What did that mean, *Have a nice weekend*, anyway? *Have a nice weekend, gorgeous, I'll miss you* wasn't the same as *Sure, have a nice time on your own, loser*. And Alberto immediately started thinking Mathias definitely meant something sinister. *Have a nice weekend, you vain, useless prick.*

Alberto stood in a chilly draft, wondering what he had done last night, when Stasia appeared out of nowhere, her arms folded over her chest.

"There he is again," she said in a smooth voice. "Your *boy* friend. What's his name again?"

Alberto ignored her and trudged back toward the house. Naturally, she followed, remaining one or two steps behind.

"You were so noisy last night. You think I wouldn't hear?"

"Sorry," Alberto muttered, uncertain what she meant by that.

"Sneaking in drunk in the middle of the night." She trotted up to his side. "I didn't think you had it in you, to be honest."

When he didn't answer, she quickened her pace and knocked into him. "I haven't said anything to Daddy yet. He doesn't know you're a homo."

Alberto snorted. "Everyone knows I'm a 'homo'. *Including* your daddy."

For heaven's sake, it's not like he wanted it to be a secret like Mathias. Alberto wasn't in the metaphorical closet everyone always talked about. He wasn't ashamed; he just thought his sexuality, just like everything else about him, was his business until he decided otherwise. And possibly... until he found himself a boyfriend whom he would feel safe walking the streets hand in hand with.

"You're right," Stasia said. "He always suspected you, anyway." She gripped his arm. "What about your friend? Does he know? He's sort of hot, isn't he? He sure doesn't look unnatural to me."

"Unnatural..." Alberto shook his head. "You want to see something unnatural? Look in the mirror."

He stretched his hand out to open the front door, but Stasia blocked it with her body, her eyes glinting. "Did you do something to him last night? Is that why he was so eager to run away this morning?"

Alberto's hand froze mid-air. Was that it? He went too far when he was drunk and tried to force Mathias into doing something he didn't want to? God knows he was capable of it. And in his state last night... Why couldn't he recall a thing? What if, what if... Was he really that far gone?

Stasia burst out a laugh, yanking him back to reality. "Oh god, I'm right, aren't I? You put your gay hands on him in the middle of the night and scared him away?" Her face split into a wide toothy grin. "Or... did he search through your room and find your—"

"Shut up!"

Alberto whirled around and started off toward the other side of the house. Stasia didn't follow him but called after him, her voice full of glee, "Remember, Albertino. *I'm* the only friend you've got!"

Once he was back in his room, the key safely hidden in the elephant, Alberto finally released a breath. His heart was throbbing in his chest; he put his hand over it and dug his fingers into his skin.

It wasn't possible. He was different; he wouldn't have taken advantage of Mathias. Even if he were that vicious, there was no chance Mathias would ever let himself be victimised. Not him. He wouldn't.

But there was that other possibility... Fearing Stasia's assumption was true, Alberto scanned around his room for anything out of place. Nothing appeared to have moved. In the bathroom, Alberto discovered Mathias had used a toothbrush head and a washcloth. Alberto pounced open the drawers under the sink and found everything where it should be. He returned to his room and fell back on his bed with a sigh of relief.

He was overthinking it. Stasia had only meant to hurt him; it didn't mean she was right. Mathias was the strangest being Alberto had ever met. He probably felt awkward waking up in Alberto's bed, in this unfamiliar house. He probably felt nervous about coming across people who'd assume they had spent the night together. *Rich, selfish shits.* That was it. It had to be.

There was nothing to fear. Tomorrow, everything would be back to normal.

10

UNWELCOME

THROUGH THE LEAFLESS and gnarly branches of the trees, the wind blew, uncaring and unrelenting. A full head smaller than her friends, Elisa strolled across the playground, her chin held high. Mathias watched his sister through the windows of the cafeteria with a faint smile. She'd never succumbed to misery, even after their mom died. She was the only tough cookie in this family. Dad had checked out and withdrawn into himself, and though Mathias couldn't deny their recent change of scenery had definitely bene-fited him, he was far from being the laid-back, dorky father he was before he lost his wife.

As for Mathias, he simply couldn't remember who he was before. A part of him was still walking down that long corridor, his shoes squeaking across the linoleum, the dreaded door drawing closer and closer…

Lifting his fork to his mouth, Mathias bit into his french fries and grimaced. Soggy, tasteless, inedible. He looked down at his plate with a frown.

"Hang on a second… something's different." He turned to Eric and froze. His friend looked like he was about to explode. "Hey, have you—"

"I had sex! With *Zak*!" Eric grabbed the edge of their table and shook it, sending pieces of food flying everywhere.

Xavier dropped his fork into his pasta. "Woah!"

"That's right!"

After letting it all out, Eric finally seemed at ease. His cheeks glowing, he propped his chin in his hand with a contented sigh. Slowly closing his eyes, Mathias also sighed, but it was an expression of lassitude.

"I was talking about the food. The food's different."

"Ah." Eric glanced down at his plate, then immediately back up. "But—"

"No."

"Matt."

"Uh-uh. I don't want to know."

Xavier leaned forward. "I'd like to know!"

What a surprise. Mathias threw him a dark look and thought he should consider himself lucky he didn't throw him his fist instead.

"What?" Xavier met his hostility with a dumb smile. "I was there, remember?"

Mathias blinked. "What?"

"Can you not remind me of that?" Eric asked, wrinkling his nose.

"I wasn't in the room! I didn't hear or see anything!"

"Anyway…" He gave Xavier a warning look. "It happened at Zak's birthday party. And I tried to keep it to myself for as long as possible, but…"

"You've managed to keep silent for more than a week," Mathias grumbled. "I guess it's impressive enough—"

"Nine days! And I almost died! Zak told me I could tell someone before my blood pressure gets out of control."

Mathias thought Eric looked a bit pent up last week, that's true. He also didn't spend more than two minutes with Mathias outside of class, who then had plenty of time to be trapped with his own thoughts. Now, he understood why: they had probably found a hiding place somewhere at school where they could… do to each other what Mathias and Alberto used to do. What a disheartening thought.

"So… what happened?" Xavier asked, his eyes bright. "How does it work? Did you do butt things to his butt?"

"Hey!" Eric took on airs. "That's obviously classified." He winked at Mathias in a way that hinted he'd tell him all about it later.

Mathias grimaced and crushed his french fries under his fork. Why the fuck would *he* want to know?

"Why did you bring up the subject if you don't want to tell?" Xavier whined, pushing his plate away.

"Don't," Mathias said. "Stop indulging his little gay fantasy."

"What?" Xavier looked shocked. "I don't have a gay fantasy."

"You don't? Really?" His clueless expression was an insult to him. "Just go suck a dick, okay? You'll do us all a favor."

Eric's mouth fell open. "Mathias!"

Xavier tut-tutted. "My dude, you are *very* aggressive."

"So leave, please! Piss off! Go hang out with someone else!"

"Why?" He took on a wounded expression. "Why can't I hang out with you?"

Eric poked Mathias. "Yeah, why?"

The looks on their faces finally got through to him. Noting his french fries had turned into mashed potatoes, he gave in with a sigh. "I'm sorry. Forget it."

By all means, they should let Xavier take notes on whatever Eric and Zak did together. Then, the next time he'd feel like it, he could just grab Alberto and practice with him and then pretend he wasn't into guys at all. *Hypocrite.*

Claiming he felt unappreciated, Xavier left anyway. Eric turned on Mathias the moment he was gone. "Stop stabbing your food. Look at me."

"No. I hate looking at you."

"No one hates looking at me. I'm too cute. What's going on? How come you're not even happy for me?"

Mathias glanced at his friend and realized he was being a dick. "I guess… I mean, *of course* I'm happy for you."

"Good!" Eric stole his hotdog, removed the sausage from the bun, and shoved it straight into his mouth. "You know, I feel like all my problems have been solved now. Like I'm at peace with the world." He returned the empty bun to Mathias's plate.

Lucky bastard, the latter thought with envy. If having sex was the key to solving problems, then all his troubles should have vanished the moment he first slammed Alberto against that wall, but it seemed, to him, it was the opposite.

"You know jerking off does exactly the same thing to you, right?" he said in a bitter tone.

One eyebrow quirked, Eric briefly pondered his words, then burst out laughing. "Sure. You almost had me there for a second." He poked Mathias again. "Anyway, now that I solved my problems, I'll have more time to fix yours."

"Bitch, I don't have any problems, okay?"

"*Bitch*, you *are* a walking problem. If you don't get help now, you're gonna turn into Kayvin."

Mathias didn't know whether he should laugh or shout.

"Maybe *you* should go and suck a dick," Eric said. "Might help you! Just sayin'." He broke into another laugh, then caught sight of Mathias's face and immediately turned serious. "I'm sorry, I'm sorry. You don't have to… ahem… *suck* anything unless you want to. It's just, I'm your best buddy, and I couldn't help but notice… You see, you looked sad after the holidays, then you looked sort of happy—you did, really—but now you look sad again. What's going on?"

"I… I have mood swings."

Eric's eyes widened; he lowered his voice. "Like a girl…?"

Mathias threw his fork to the side. "I need a new friend."

His last remark wasn't too well received, and he had to apologize and even hug his friend in the middle of the cafeteria. Only then did Eric's tears magically disappear.

"*Who* are you?" Mathias grumbled, feeling used.

"Come on now." Eric slipped his arm around his shoulder. "I'm here for you, if you need to talk."

What was there to talk about? Mathias was so thoroughly confused by everything that happened since the day he transferred to this school. He couldn't make sense of anything anymore. The whole weekend, he paced in his room, trying to understand what he saw—if he even saw right, because it was dark, and late, and he was intoxicated—but it was what it was. He saw Alberto and his stepdad kissing. Even drunk, he couldn't have made that up because it was, in fact, unimaginable.

"Ah, Mathias…" Eric sighed as they were leaving the cafeteria. "Today's the best day of my life."

"*Today*?" Mathias took out his pack of smokes and his lighter. "*Today*'s the best day of your life?"

"Yeah…"

He struggled to light his cigarette, to no avail. "Today, really?"

"Yeah, why?"

"The day you tell me you've slept with Zak is better than the day you actually slept with him?" Mathias tossed away his lighter with a curse.

Eric watched it fly over his head with a perplexed expression. "Oh, wait… maybe not."

"You're a dumbass, you know that?"

Eric, giggling, was about to say something, but Zak appeared just at that moment. If Mathias didn't know before, he would for sure now. Zak and Eric were staring at each other like they had discovered the cure for cancer. It was unbearable. And Mathias kept hearing Alberto's voice in his head, whispering in his devil's tongue, "Ask him about his butthole."

"Goddamn it!"

Deciding he should remain inside after all, Mathias shoved the door open with both hands, leaving the shocked pair behind. He heard Zak ask, "What the hell?"

"Mood swings," Eric replied as the door shut.

After repeating Alberto was *the definition of arrogance* to himself so many times, it surprised Mathias how easy it had been to get rid of him. It took two and a half days of not answering his text messages, two more days of avoiding meeting his eyes when they crossed paths in the school's corridors, and only one embarrassing occasion where he abruptly turned around and fled at the sight of him, and the job was done. Alberto didn't whine, nor did he send a string of insulting messages, as Mathias half-expected. Though it was entirely possible that he simply didn't care enough—and in a way, that was a relief, because Mathias simply couldn't look at him anymore. He just couldn't.

Mathias could only hope Alberto would never find out about his cowardice and simply move on with his life. He had probably already found another hook-up—hopefully not Xavier, there were limits—or returned to his other ones, who knew? Mathias had once stood on the edge of the pool as Kayvin pushed Alberto in the water, paralyzed for some reason. The second time he fucked up was worse: if Alberto's stepfather was some sort of molesting pervert and Mathias just stood there and watched, he had no right to ever look at Alberto in the eye again, never mind putting his hands on him.

If I told you, you wouldn't believe me. Christ, how could he forget Alberto's words now? If he had meant that day that his first lover was his mother's husband, Mathias would never recover. *He wouldn't.* Guilt would eat at him until he would have nowhere to hide. It wouldn't just ruin his relationship with Alberto, it would ruin everything else.

And what about the bruises he'd seen that time they showered together? Were they a result of sex with another lover, or worse? Only now did Mathias realize how sheltered he was growing up. As a kid, he had been vaguely aware of the sharp glint in his mother's eye when she let him and Ella play in the park. She was never not watching them. He had seen movies going on and on about how little girls and women were constantly in danger. They felt like pure fantasy to him—horror stories, really—because he couldn't fully understand what these monsters wanted from them, but at least he got the idea. This was different: the thought of a boy being abused hadn't occurred to him until last weekend; he had genuinely never thought about it. Now, he couldn't think of anything else.

Mathias's only hope for salvation was that Alberto wasn't molested at all and that their kiss was consensual. His memory was blurry, but he recalled Alberto's arms were hooked around the man's neck, not unlike what he did when he and Mathias kissed. In that case, Mathias was well rid of him, and he should even congratulate himself on dodging a bullet. After all, that night, he *was* about to ask him the impossible. Since then, he learned confusion was like a bottomless well, and the more he tried to claw his way out, the deeper he was doomed to fall.

After his terrible lunch at the cafeteria, he spent two hours of economics grappling with his own disturbing thoughts, and Xavier's return after class did nothing to ease his mood. Xavier wasn't supposed to be here; he wasn't even in their class, but he'd turned into sticky rice lately, always glued to them for no reason. *So annoying*.

He and Eric walked along the corridors, chattering on about their next football game against the American High School of Paris, while Mathias followed Eric with his head down. His heart sunk when he recalled they had math class, and so did Zak. For this period, their classrooms were right next to each other, which meant that if Mathias and Camille stood in front of them and acted like a shield, Eric could kiss Zak without anyone noticing, right before embarking for two hours of geometry.

On their good days, Mathias used that time to share secret glances with Alberto and build up some tension that they usually released in the infirmary after class. Today, he tried his hardest to ignore both his friends making out and Camille's relentless attempts to convince him to star in her next movie. Alberto was standing just behind her, and Mathias had to keep his eyes fixed on a distant point down the corridor to avoid laying eyes on him.

An unwelcome sight as usual, Kayvin strolled by with his friend Steph and stopped to shake Xavier's hand. Zak immediately pushed Eric away, and an awkward silence ensued. Kayvin didn't know how to exist without having an *f* joke to throw around, but perhaps because of the look Mathias gave him the last time he insulted Eric on the pitch, he opted to go for another victim.

Oblivious to the world, Alberto had dozed off against the wall. He was a professional sleeper, after all, and like those in the military, he could catch some z's pretty much anywhere and in any position. Mathias knew that, just like he knew the little faces he could pull when he was worn out after a good tumble. But this time, Kayvin spotted him before Mathias could understand his intentions, and he didn't waste a second blowing into his whistle right by his ear. The shrill sound had Alberto and half of the students in the corridor jump out of their skin in fright.

"Wake up!" Kayvin shook the whistle before Alberto's eyes.

Mathias had seen his demon in all sorts of states, but never afraid. And no matter how fast he schooled his expression and even somehow managed to smirk at Kayvin, Mathias saw how pale he'd become. Mathias turned to Kayvin, his own fists shaking.

"What the fuck is wrong with you?!"

To his shock, someone had spoken before him. Xavier was in Kayvin's face before Mathias had even opened his mouth. Kayvin stared back at his friend, his eyes wide with disbelief. Alberto ignored them both, pushed past them with a barely audible "Excuse me," and was immediately absorbed by the throng of students. Without thinking, Mathias followed him, but when he was about to barge into the men's room after him, he found Xavier right at his heel.

"What do you want?" Mathias barked, blocking his way.

"I'm going to check on him!" Xavier furrowed his brow. "What are *you* doing here?"

"I... uh... I need to take a piss."

Xavier shrugged like that didn't concern him at all and rushed to Alberto's side, who looked displeased to see them both. Despite the tempest of emotions raging within him, Mathias had to pretend to take a leak, so he stomped toward the urinals. Xavier hugged Alberto and spoke to him in a hushed tone.

"Are you all right?"

Mathias witnessed the scene in the mirror with gritted teeth. In his opinion, Xavier's concern was out of this world. He never contradicted Kayvin about anything, never even batted an eyelid whenever his friend was acting out, but now he was rushing to Alberto's side like he gave a shit.

"I'm fine," Alberto said. He did sound fine. He sounded bored even.

No one would like to be woken up by having a whistle blown into their ear, fair enough, but it's not like it was the end of the world either. Xavier didn't need to fuss over him like this, and he clearly didn't need to touch him so much.

"Are you sure?" Xavier lifted his hand toward Alberto's face, who lurched to the side.

"Leave me alone."

When he was absolutely certain Alberto wasn't dying, Xavier left with reluctant steps, and Mathias could stop pretending to pee. When Alberto noticed his gaze on his trembling hands, he slowly hid them in his pockets. Mathias felt the garment looked familiar and realized it was his black hoodie, the one he gave him at the museum. His determination fell to pieces.

The next second, their lips were locked together, and Alberto was pulling him into a stall, using his foot to shut the door.

There was desperation in that kiss, coming from either or both of them; Mathias wasn't sure who, but he could taste it. He thought the desperate one was definitely him; his guilt rushed back and stole a groan from his chest. He pushed Alberto away. "Stop, stop."

Alberto pressed himself against him. "For a second, I thought you didn't find me hot anymore."

Shut the fuck up pollito, you infernal freak. Did I ever tell you how much I hate you sometimes… How he wanted to tell him that!

"Zak and Eric finally had sex," he said instead, clenching his fists.

Alberto chuckled. "Tell me something I don't know." He tilted his head. "Did you ask Zak about his butthole?" His eyes widened when Mathias slapped his hands over his own face. "Hey, what's wrong?"

Why did he sound so soft? Was he always like this? Mathias always assimilated his voice to a demon's seductive whisper, but it sounded pretty gentle, actually. And now wasn't the right time to think about that.

"I'm fine," Mathias said gruffly.

"So, when are we meeting up?" Alberto ran his hands over Mathias's shoulders, down the length of his arms, and settled on his wrists. "You said you'd give me a good pounding, and then you disappeared."

"I don't…"

"What?" His hands left his wrists and caressed their way

upwards until he threw his arms around his neck to steal a kiss. Mathias couldn't hear anything over the sound of his blood pounding in his ears. When Alberto slipped his fingers into the band on his boxers, he abruptly pushed him away.

"I can't. I can't do this anymore."

Alberto gave Mathias an appraising, calculating look, like he was trying to determine how serious he really was. "Why? We're so good at it."

That was the problem with this bastard. He could never shut his mouth when he was asked to. Mathias growled under his breath like a threatened animal. "I just don't think we should see each other anymore."

"Sure…" Alberto rolled his eyes. "Or… you could tell me what I did wrong, and I'll make it up to you and save us both some time." Mathias felt his fingertips graze the zipper of his jeans, and he shuddered.

"You've done nothing wrong." He pushed Alberto's hand away. "I'm just… done with it all."

Alberto's eyes narrowed, but at least he drew back. "What is this? What happened at Eric's party, Mathias? What happened afterwards?"

Mathias gave a quick shake of the head. "Nothing."

They were alone in that stall, barely enough space between them. Mathias knew he had to say something to him, or Alberto wouldn't let him leave. It made sense: if their roles were reversed, Mathias would have wanted answers, too.

"Come on…" Alberto insisted. "What did you see?" Mathias cast his eyes down, his heart beating erratically in his chest. He couldn't say it, but strangely enough, Alberto reached a conclusion on his own and let out a joyless laugh. "I think I know what you saw now. Look, it's not as bad as it seems…"

"*Look,*" Mathias cut in, suddenly filled with irrepressible terror. "It seems to me your life is complicated as it is, so…"

Mathias wanted to say, *Ask me for help, ask me, and I'll help you*, but that would mean hearing Alberto's confession. His shame and his cowardice teamed up and won over his bad conscience, forcing his lips shut.

"Right," Alberto said, lifting his chin. "I get it, I get it." His voice fell to a whisper. "Kiss goodbye?"

Mathias accidentally met his eyes and found them unfeeling and cold. His lip was vaguely curled, as if the situation was amusing somehow.

"No," he croaked out, sick to his stomach.

Seemingly convinced Mathias was serious, Alberto cruelly dismissed him with a "*Pfft*," before sliding out of the stall.

11

ANSWER ME

ALBERTO WASN'T the sort to cry. The last time he wept was years ago, and since then, there had been no need for grand effusions. In any case, it's not like he could produce rivers of tears. Just like the rest of him, his lacrimal ducts were all dried out.

For days, he had waited patiently for Mathias to get himself together, to at least talk to him, but he received nothing but silence. Yet he remained master of himself, not even letting one sound out when what he truly wanted was to beg Mathias to let him know what he'd done wrong, at the very least so he could apologise and make it better.

But about what Mathias had seen the other night… Alberto could apologise for it a million times, but he surely couldn't make it better. He would have never thought that Mathias was the prying kind, the sort to go through his things the second he left him unattended. Despite years of practice, it seemed Alberto couldn't figure people out a hundred percent after all. It was impossible.

People were made of secrets and wouldn't boast about their least endearing traits. Mathias's rummaging tendencies at least had some charm to them. It beat being a bully like Kayvin or a wimp like Alberto. And it's not like Mathias wouldn't have found out Alberto's secret, anyway; it was bound to happen. Secrets, like ancient artefacts, were supposed to be dug up, excavated.

The silly part was that Alberto had begun thinking — no, hoping — that Mathias would just… accept it, take it in its stride. *Oh sure, Alberto's broken, but isn't he handsome? That's all that matters in the end.* That would have been better than this sordid little scene in the school lavatories.

And how could Alberto convince Mathias he wasn't so pathetic after all? If what he'd discovered last weekend wasn't enough, witnessing how easy it was for Kayvin to wipe the floor with him this afternoon wasn't about to do the trick.

No, Alberto wouldn't cry. He was past the point of crying, wasn't he? Except that now that he was alone in his bedroom, things appeared different. Little by little, the reality of what his future would be like closed in on him like the sides of a coffin, and if he couldn't cry, he found himself gasping for air, his fingers clawing at his chest.

He had no one, truly no one.

Months ago, the thought wouldn't even have made him pause, even less reflect on it. Today, he couldn't ignore it anymore. This, and those things people said about him, how soulless and uninteresting he was.

The truth was that Mathias had been way more than a hookup this entire time. For almost three months, they had been not only each other's secret, but also each other's companion. They had definitely been there for each other, in their own ways. Wasn't that the definition of friendship? To lose a lover wasn't such a bad thing, but to lose such a friend… Alberto feared that loss like he feared opening the secret drawers he kept shut in his mind.

Mathias had given him something to do, someone to be, a reason to get up, and a reason to be beautiful, for once. Mathias had made him interesting. Without Mathias, Alberto was nothing. Nothing, nothing, nothing.

"Oh god, what have I done…?" Fighting against the pain swelling in his chest, Alberto bit back his tears and slumped at the foot of his bed. The family pictures on the corkboard above the desk caught his eye, his gaze sweeping over the picture of his father before falling on the reassuring face of his mother.

There was no point running to Mamma. He couldn't seek comfort from her. First, she would worry so much, she'd make herself sick. Then, even if she were able to hear him, she wouldn't get it; she couldn't remember love. Dimitri was just another man she'd allowed to be close for comfort and protection. The latest one was always *bigger and badder* than the one before, with one exception: they couldn't be like Alberto's dad. They should be a better example to him, and with some luck, they might teach him how to be a good man.

There were no good men, Alberto was now convinced. Only honest and dishonest men. Alberto was dishonest, whereas Mathias was the opposite. Without him… what would happen to Alberto without him? Alberto wanted to swallow the lump in his throat, but it felt like concrete; he gave up and drew up his knees under his chin.

"Don't you look a picture…" a voice called softly from the open door.

No point looking up; Stasia always knew when he was at his lowest. Now that she had caught him already defeated on the floor, Alberto didn't even have the will to get up. He wrapped his arms around his knees and waited.

"What happened to you?" She drew closer when he didn't answer. "Is it about that friend, the one you were trying to hide the other day?"

At the memory of Mathias's earlier parting words, sobs rose up Alberto's throat.

Stasia fell on her knees in front of him. "He ditched you, didn't he?" Though he didn't confirm nor deny, Stasia could draw her own conclusions. Her eyes were burning with excitement. "Let me guess: I was right. You brought him home, like a fool, and now he knows how much of a loser you are." Alberto, hugging his knees, let out a shuddering breath. It only got her more excited. "Poor Albertino. Now you're all alone again."

Alberto buried his face between his knees. "Stop it."

She crawled a little closer. "It's kind of your fault, you know that, right? What did you think? That you'd have a little boyfriend?

You? In your state?" She laughed. "Oh dear, did you actually think he… liked you?"

The closer she got, the more stifling it felt in the room. Alberto struggled to fill his lungs with air. "I… I'll fix it. You'll see…" He met Stasia's eyes. "I'm going to be a model, and I'll leave, and—"

"Yes, yes, you're gonna be a model. You've been saying that for months now. modelling's all you can do, anyway. You and I both know you're too dumb to do anything else." Stasia leaned away from him with a thoughtful expression. "It was always going to be that or high-end escort services. Don't you glare at me, I said high-end. I personally know creepy old guys who'd pay good money for someone like you. And you wouldn't scare them away like your boyfriend, because they actually prefer their toys to be brainless."

A brief silence ensued where Alberto became painfully aware his chin was trembling and Stasia could definitely see it. He lifted his head in an effort to defy her, but one look at her face was enough to convince him he'd never win against her. He gripped his hair with both hands.

"I can't… I want to… I want to…"

"What? What do you want?"

"I want to change…" His voice sounded so small, especially drowned by Stasia's ensuing vicious laugh.

"Albertino, don't make me laugh!" She leaned forward and slapped his knee. "You don't have the guts to change. If you had any backbone, you wouldn't be sitting here weeping like a beat dog."

He slipped and let out a sob. A small, idiotic part of him forgot itself and even sought comfort from Stasia, searching into her face for a hint of softness, of regret. Her eyes were glistening, but there was no compassion in them.

"Poor lamb," she said. "Take my advice. You should stop worrying about school and photoshoots, and you better start getting ready to peddle your ass on the streets, because let me tell you something: modelling won't last forever. Sure, you'll do a few shoots here and there, but eventually, you know you'll screw up. You'll start acting up again, you'll become a bad sport, and they'll stop calling you. How could you be able to keep a job? Look at you, you couldn't even keep one friend."

By then, Alberto was shaking. He already knew all of this. That monster was always right. She knew him as though she were a festering disease, intimately acquainted with each of his cells. However much he hated himself for feeling the weight of her words, he was still powerless in avoiding their pain. He finally let out a cry of anguish as though she had stabbed him in the heart.

"I can't— I can't live like this anymore!"

Stabs of self-hatred rocked him like a ship in a storm. He hid his face between his knees, and soon after, he felt Stasia's hands on the back of his head.

"What's happening? Are you crying? Look at me."

She forced him to raise his head. Her smile waned at the sight of his tears, but the light in her eyes brightened. Her voice lowered to a gentle whisper. "Shh… that's okay. Think about it: you still have a few good years! You should make the most of it while you can. And I'll get you a number, right? I swear, it's a very clean business." He let out another sob. Her face was so close now, he could almost see into her black soul. "Oh no… does it seem unbearable? Does it?" The light in her eyes flickered. "Answer me."

He gave a weak nod.

Stasia let out an affected sigh. "Then… there's still the other option."

"What… what other option?"

"Haven't you ever thought about it?" Stasia asked, her voice soft. "I know you have. I saw you staring down at rail tracks, hoping the answer's down there."

Alberto shivered ostensibly. Stasia tut-tutted him.

"Don't look so shocked now. I'm not suggesting anything that drastic. I wouldn't want you to suffer." She glanced at something on their left. Alberto followed her gaze toward the bathroom sinks. "Think about it. It would be painless." She put her hand on his shoulder. "They say it's like falling asleep."

The room became quiet as the two of them stared in the same direction, contemplating exactly the same thing. Alberto grew numb as the idea took shape in his mind.

Stasia gently squeezed his shoulder, bringing her lips near his ear. "You wouldn't need to be afraid, I'd be with you all the way. I would hold your hand, even. Am I not your best friend after all? I'm the only one who cares. You wouldn't need to worry about the future, about disappointing your mother. What else are you going to do, anyway? Even looking like this doesn't make you happy. Imagine what will happen to you once your beauty fades. With the way you are, you've got five, maybe eight good years left, and then what? You'll just be a fading slut. Worn out like one of those tourist horses, dragging your tired limbs all over town and letting the worst kind of people ride you."

Forced to contemplate this image, Alberto gave in. Gushes of tears flooded down his cheeks, filling his mouth and his throat; the sobs he had pushed down for too long felt like painful kicks in his ribs. Stasia drew closer, held his face between her hands, and watched him with a ravenous expression. He thought at first she was about to kiss him, but her lips stopped at the corner of his eyelids.

She was drinking his tears.

Alberto recoiled in horror, cracking his head against the bed frame. Stasia didn't move. She licked her lips, an eery smile on her face.

"You're so cute when you're hurting… How can you blame me?"

His vision swimming, Alberto crawled away from her. "Get out," he gritted out. He could barely move; like every ounce of energy had been drained from his body. "Get out, get out, get out." Repeating the words to himself like a protection spell to ward off evil, he painfully dragged himself to his bathroom and locked himself in.

"Get out," he repeated weakly, resting his head against the door.

Through it, he heard Stasia's laughter as she walked herself out. She didn't believe in defeat. How could she? She was as confident as she was patient. And she was playing a long game, Alberto knew it now. She had always known when he was at his lowest. She had always known the words to say as well. He always thought she was… magical, almost. But she had just shown her hand.

With heavy steps, Alberto shuffled to the sinks and wiped his cheeks with the back of his hand. Ignoring the drawers, he stared at his own face in the mirror instead.

Stasia was right about many things. She was right about his flaws, she was right about his fears, and she was right about one last thing: just like his mother, he was beautiful even when he cried.

12

FRIENDSHIP GOALS

A WEEK or so had passed when Alberto woke up in class to Mrs Paquin shouting at him again. She asked him a question, then another. Were they still doing Rousseau?

Rousseau? In English Lit?

Alberto recalled the way Mathias's lip had curled…

"Did you even do your homework?" Paquin asked, relentless.

Alberto flicked open his notebook with a haggard expression. There was nothing in it but a few decent doodles of Mathias's hands and wrists, which she unfortunately noticed, resorting to shrieks. That's when he decided he'd had enough. He abruptly got up, sending his chair flying backwards and shocking the classroom into silence.

Unimpressed, Mrs Paquin scoffed at his tall figure. "What is it? What excuse are you going to give me this time?"

Alberto had never given any excuse; he usually accepted her wrath with indifference. But he recently went from sleeping too much to not sleeping at all, and the blood rushing in his veins felt like so many crawling vipers, rendering him fretful. "I've got a condition," he said coolly.

She gave a mocking laugh. "Listen to that, everyone, Alberto has a condition. How about this: prove it, and you can stay. Otherwise, get out of my class." She paused and added, "And for that little display, I'm calling your parents over for a visit. Today."

That last bit irritated Alberto enough that he held her stare until she threatened him with a month of detention.

Mrs Paquin never engaged in empty threats. While Alberto was finishing class in detention — mercifully free of Cher's company — she found two minutes to call home, and when the bells announced the second half of lunch break, Alberto could only watch as Mamma stormed Colette in her high heels with a dark expression he had rarely seen. He felt himself shrink at the sight, and he cast his eyes down and waited for her to scold him, but she only took his arm and said, "Let's go, *Tesoro*."

When they entered her classroom, Paquin rose from her chair and thanked Alberto's mother for coming so quickly. Mamma shook her hand impatiently. Judging from her simple attire — jeans and a soft cashmere jumper — and her hair hanging loosely on each side of her face in its most natural state, she had most likely been forced out of a nap by Paquin's phone call and wasn't happy in the least.

"I don't understand why I have to be here," she said coldly.

Alberto's teacher blanched a little. Despite her formidable appearance, Mamma had always been sort of shy when faced with the typical macho man, but she wasn't afraid to use her power over women she disliked. She towered over Paquin, all supermodel like, and didn't look at all friendly. On the other hand, Alberto's teacher was a veteran, and she couldn't afford to be intimidated by parents. She said her piece in a haughty tone, explaining in detail what had happened this morning, not forgetting to blame Alberto for a *pattern of abject rudeness and indifference to authority*.

"And when I asked him why he constantly falls asleep," she concluded, "he claimed he 'had a condition.'"

Mamma had listened without interruption, only slipping Alberto a quick glance, who turned his attention to his shoes.

"As a matter of fact…" she said, taking a seat in — coinciden-tally — Zak's chair. "… he does have a condition."

Her words made Alberto look up in surprise. Paquin also blinked, momentarily speechless.

"W-Well…" she said, "in that case… if I could see a doctor's certificate, then I might be willing to—"

Mamma's eyelashes fluttered angrily. "Excuse me? Are you suggesting I should share my son's medical history with you?"

Paquin turned ashen. "But I need to see proof he has a condition."

"Then I need to see the headmaster right away, to ask him since when it is legal for teachers to request private medical information about their pupils." Mamma crossed her legs and pointed at the door. "Go on, go get him. I'll be waiting right here."

Paquin was getting paler and paler. Alberto could understand why: nobody would want to spend more time than necessary with a man who was rumoured to have become a headmaster in order to torment students *and* staff indiscriminately.

"I see no need to bother Mr Van Bergen, Mrs Gazza."

Mamma's eyes narrowed. "Why? I'm sure he'd love to be bothered by me."

Paquin seemed to hate hearing those words just as much as she disliked Alberto, but it worked anyway: she readmitted Alberto into her class without Mamma having to divulge any kind of information.

Alberto and his mother walked back to the car together. Mamma had driven herself in the Jaguar. The sight of it reminded Alberto of Mathias, of how they'd met, of that silly story he had made up about their parents' affair. He affectionately brushed his fingers against the roof of the car.

Despite holding the key in her hand, Alberto's mother didn't open the door. She was gazing back at the school with a frown. "You'll be homeschooled from now on so I can keep an eye on you."

Alberto's heart lurched in his chest. "No! No, I don't want to." He took her hand. "What about Ma— my friends?"

"Fine, then. Let's meet these *friends*." Mamma tilted her head toward the gate. "Introduce me to them right now, and we'll see."

Alberto stared at her, dumbstruck. What should he do? He didn't have any friends, and he really didn't want to be home-schooled, or Stasia would likely be the end of him.

As they walked past the gate, Alberto scanned every corner of the yard for someone — *anyone* — who could pass as a friend. Xavier's face popped into his mind, but he was nowhere in sight, and with the risk of having that *bastardo* Kayvin creeping after his mother, Alberto would have never gone for it.

Then, a childlike laugh exploded throughout the schoolyard, catching his attention. Alberto's gaze fell on Eric, on Zak nestled into his arms, on Arthur and Camille standing arm in arm next to them, and on Mathias hovering behind them with his head down. He realised he had no other option. Between the idea of embarrassing himself in public or spending more time with Stasia, the choice was easily made.

"They're over there," he told Mamma.

When they saw them approach, the lot stared at Alberto as though he'd just come flying down on the back of some winged horse with glittery hooves.

"Hello, everyone!" he said, using every ounce of his acting skills, knowing he was probably red to his ears from cringing. "So, Mum, these are my *friends*."

Arthur let out a loud snort, prompting Camille to elbow him in the ribs. If Zak seemed shellshocked, Eric's lips were pressed together so tightly, they had disappeared altogether, and Mathias looked like a wooden toy with his hands buried in his pockets.

Mamma inspected each one of them carefully, then sort of smiled. "It's so nice to meet you all at last." She shook everyone's hands.

Alberto spoke before someone — Eric — could say anything stupid. "We did the movie together this summer."

"The movie?" Mamma's brow furrowed lightly. "You mean the part you didn't get?"

"Yes!" A weight lifted off Alberto's shoulders. "Eric got the part," — Mamma gazed at Eric as though he owed her son an apology — "and this is Zak. He was playing the leading role."

Zak looked petrified. "How are you, Madame?"

Mamma barely spared him a glance. She seemed perplexed, as though she could feel, deep down, that she was being strung along, but she couldn't be certain of it. When Alberto accidentally met

Eric's eyes, he helplessly blinked at him to urge him to play along and received a puzzled look back.

"I wrote the movie!" Camille said, helpful at last, "and Arthur here did the camera work. It was really fun!"

"And what did you do again?" Mamma asked, turning to Alberto.

"You know, this and that…" His cheeks grew hot when he recalled he mostly spent his time running after Michael, whom he didn't even like.

"Alberto was the director's assistant," Camille said. "He was very important."

"Assistant?" Mamma said, a note of disappointment in her voice. "What can I say? He's always been too shy."

There was a silence. It was clear no one here believed Alberto to be shy, but more like he was a great arsehole. Thankfully, Mamma didn't notice, being too heartbroken over her son's crippling timidity.

"There's just one thing I'd like to know," she said, breaking that heavy pause. "Which one of you slept over the other night, then?"

While the others all stared at her, wide-eyed, Alberto's stomach dropped like an anchor. How could she possibly know about Mathias staying over, if it weren't for Stasia? She really would be the death of him. Alberto's eyelids fluttered shut, because he couldn't get out of this, and even if he lied and said it was someone else, it was going to be impossible to prove. If only Xavier were here, but he wouldn't be able to cover for Mathias anyway, because that poor soul was thicker than a neglected sheep's fleece and… God! It really was the end, wasn't it? It was over. Alberto was done for.

"It was me," Eric said out of the blue.

Another awkward silence followed his statement. Mathias had turned as red as sin, and Alberto hoped he was the only one who'd noticed. Camille and Arthur's expression had turned completely blank, and Zak said nothing, but his eyebrows drew together in an ominous frown.

"Oh," Mamma said. She gave Eric a thorough once-over, including the hand he had wrapped around Zak's waist. "Next time, why don't you stay for dinner or… breakfast? Whatever's coming next."

Eric turned a perfect shade of pink, while Zak's face darkened and darkened. Mamma turned back to Alberto.

"Let's go, *Tesoro*."

Leaving Zak and the others behind, Alberto let out a sigh of relief and followed his mother toward the exit.

"Who is this Eric?" Mamma asked once out of earshot.

"He's a… he's a football player."

She wrinkled her nose. "A football player?"

"Yes. He's… nice." Alberto grimaced at his own lie.

"But why is he touching that little boy?"

"Little boy? Wh— Oh! No, Mamma, that's Zak! They're… they're a couple."

Mamma stopped right in front of the gates. "Excuse me, what?"

Alberto looked all around in fright. "What?"

"Why isn't he with you?"

"I… ahem… What?"

"Why would he pick that little boy over you?"

Alberto's mouth fell open. He shook his head so fervently, he almost unscrewed his head from his neck. "No, Mamma… I don't want him."

"You don't want him? Then why does he visit you in the middle of the night?"

"Huh…?"

"Stasia said someone came in the middle of the night, some handsome young man. It's him, isn't it?" She tilted her head. "I could have sworn she said his name was Alex…"

Alberto sucked in a breath. He didn't want to admit to drinking and having poor Mathias take him home. "It was him! Eric, Alex, sounds about the same, right? Stasia was probably confused."

Why did that sly, evil monster have such a good memory, when his own was like a malfunctioning old copier that would only start when kicked repeatedly?

"I brought him home because… he was drunk, and he didn't want his family to know because they're… they're American

Mormons! They don't believe in alcohol and... ahem... swearing and stuff."

Alberto's mother didn't seem convinced. "So, you were never a couple?"

"Mamma, I can promise you that. He left in the morning, and he was embarrassed. He still is! You saw how pink he was out there."

She nodded and brushed her hand against his cheek. "He *was* pink. Okay, my love, that was kind of you to help him. You're a good friend."

I'm really not, Alberto thought, now hating that he owed Eric a debt — Eric, of all people. Now, he would have to be called *best buddy* and have his hair ruffled and... God, no! He'd rather move to Iceland.

"I'm relieved, I'm relieved," Mamma said with a sigh. Before Alberto could ask, she added, "It was obvious he likes that little boy!"

"Please, stop calling him that. Zak's only a year younger than me."

"And you wouldn't be a good match, obviously." She lowered her voice. "A football player, it's already questionable... But a *Mormon*, really?"

"Come on, Mamma..." Alberto turned his face away. "Don't discriminate."

"And look how tall you are, compared to him."

He let out a nervous laugh. Did he really need to find someone taller now? It would be hard enough to find someone who liked him. Now size mattered? He only knew one man taller than him, and it was the freakish headmaster. Alberto's thoughts turned to Mathias, his 180 cm*, his rough hands, his aggressive lips, and the size of something else that arguably mattered. He let out an anguished groan, and Mamma put her hand on his arm.

"What is it? Are you embarrassed? Did you think I didn't know?"

"What? No. Though... am I really so obvious?"

---

* 5'11"

The words *predictably queer* rushed back to his head, forcing a grimace out of him.

"I'm your mother, *Tesoro*. I know you're not interested in girls, or we'd be swimming in them by now."

Alberto gave a dry laugh. "It's not like we're swimming in men either."

"And I like it just this way," Mamma said with a smile. "They're all so… *brutish* at this age. Just wait a little, don't be hasty. When a good man presents himself, we'll assess him together."

"Yes, Mamma."

But Alberto knew boys could be brutish, and they could also be worthy. Like Mathias, who wanted to snuggle during the night.

Mathias and his ceaseless kisses down his neck.

Mathias and his fingertips dancing, featherlike, across the skin of his back, causing even the smallest of his hairs to stand on end.

Ma-tyas.

No matter what it'd take, Alberto couldn't wait to be alone with him again.

"Alberto." Mamma held his face in her hands. "How fast you've grown… You're taller than me now." She stared into his eyes, but was probably faced with a reflection of herself; she looked unhappy when she released him.

13

BULLIES

FEBRUARY HAD ANNOUNCED its arrival with a thin layer of snow.

The not-so-friendly game between Colette International B.S. and the American Assholes of Paris was fast approaching. That morning, some, like Charles-Henry, had tried their best to have practice canceled because of the weather, but they were prevented by Eric. Mathias's friend—who preferred wearing shorts to anything else—stood proudly outside the changing rooms with his legs bare and his hands on his hips, and he let the whole team know a bit of snow would never be enough to stop them. That was enough for him to earn himself a reprimand from Kayvin, who reminded everyone for the thousandth time *he* was their captain, not Eric.

Mathias had discovered Kayvin's moods were actually easy to read. He was always unpleasant—whoever was at once sexist, racist, and homophobic even deserved to be called worse, honestly —but lately, his tantrums were related to how well or how poorly his new girlfriend Gwen, Xavier's cousin, was treating him. When adding the fact that he hated losing, he spent a whole lot of time yelling at his teammates. His favorite victims were usually Xavier, who always guffawed no matter how much abuse was hurled at him, and Eric, whose ongoing contract with the *** now apparently forbade him even to take notice of Kayvin.

Today, Eric was out of control. Everyone was struggling against the cold, whereas he was singing to himself while adjusting his woolen gloves, oblivious to their misery.

"Everyone's clattering their teeth out here," Mathias said, suspicious. "How come you're so warm?"

"Simple." Eric winked. "I'm in love!"

Mathias rolled his eyes. "Oh, Christ."

"What?"

"See?" He showed him his hands. "I'm not shaking either."

"Right, right…" Eric shrugged. "It's just that I had my special date with Zak last night."

"Your date…? Oh. I remember. So, how did it go?"

"It was great! No, it was *awesome.*"

"No balls, then?"

"*Hmmm,* yes." Eric nudged him with his elbow. "There were balls. There were—"

Mathias covered his ears. "No, I don't want to hear it—"

"Ice cream balls!"

Eric erupted in laughter then, loud enough to reach Kayvin's ears, who immediately started blowing into his stupid whistle.

"I hate you," Mathias muttered, wanting to shove Kayvin's whistle into a certain place and pushing his hands into his pockets instead.

Eric snorted. "No, you don't."

"I do, I swear. Piss off."

"Wait! I haven't told you about my date yet."

But then, Eric abruptly stopped laughing. Mathias turned around and saw the way Kayvin was glaring at them. There was pure, unfiltered cruelty in his eyes, just like when he humiliated Alberto the other day. Mathias instinctively stepped in front of Eric. He knew Kayvin hated him just the same, but was still on the fence whether to get physical with him. Mathias, who was desperate to get physical even on a good day, dared him to start trouble with a sharp look.

While Kayvin took next week's game seriously because he hated defeat, and Eric because he simply *couldn't* lose or it would look bad on his record—and in front of Zak—Mathias felt differently. He would do his job on the day because he'd never embarrass his other teammates, nor would he do anything to harm his best friend. Another reason, which he wouldn't admit to, is that he, too, hated losing. But as it turned out, watching Kayvin turn purple with rage every time he missed a save during practice had become his favorite pastime.

What else was there for him? Since Zak had given it up, Eric barely had a second to spare Mathias. He pretended he had to spend every possible moment "talking to" Zak before his transfer, but Mathias called bullshit. He knew what it was, not to be able to control oneself. How could he not?

After Mathias had received confirmation he'd passed his mock exams, all he had to distract himself from his problems were boxing and the entrance examination for his chosen culinary school that was scheduled at the end of the month. An insignificant football game wasn't enough to do the trick. He had to throw himself into his craft or into boxing practice like a desperate man, or risk remembering that awful night again, and the loss that ensued.

Meanwhile, the unshakable Alberto had already moved on. Despite Mathias knowing it was all for the best, it didn't change the way he felt about it: a little vexed, and a little hurt, maybe. Mathias should have taken comfort from the fact that he was Alberto's favorite lover for a time. *His best fuck.* But he couldn't take comfort from anything anymore, except one thing: they had never been good for each other, and he'd always known that.

Now, Mathias didn't have to worry about the things that used to keep him awake, such as Eric finding out, or the slow return of his recurring nightmare, the long white corridor… He didn't have to live in fear any longer… Mathias even knew what he had wanted to ask Alberto wouldn't have gotten him the answer he desired. Maybe Alberto wasn't capable of love. Now, Mathias could only imagine why, and he'd rather punch himself repeatedly in the face than risk opening that door again.

When Alberto's mother had shown up yesterday, Mathias felt like he had jumped into a precipice, certain that she would single him out. But she barely registered him, a clear sign Alberto had never mentioned him. And why would he have done such a thing? He'd never had a reason to.

As to why Eric helped Alberto yesterday, so promptly declaring himself the one who slept over at the mansion, Mathias was burning to ask, but he was afraid his curiosity would betray him. If he was patient enough, he might just hear it from Zak later; Xavier was having a party on Friday night, and Mathias had planned to use this opportunity to discover the truth. Zak was known to be *very* chatty after a beer or two.

Between the hostile weather and Kayvin's dictatorship, practice that day was a bleak affair. The team returned to the changing room shaking from head to toe, taking refuge in the showers.

Eric wouldn't admit defeat. As they were getting dressed, he started enumerating the benefits of exercising in the snow to inspire his teammates to look on the bright side, but all he got for his trouble was a loud "Shut up!" from his captain.

"When's *he* going to shut up?" Mathias asked through gritted teeth.

"Leave it." Eric shook his head. "It's not worth it."

The players returned to school in small groups. Kayvin walked ahead with Steph, Charles-Henry, and Xavier, while Mathias trailed behind with Eric, forced to listen to his detailed retelling of his date with Zak.

"After the starters, I wasn't sure how to make his favorite food, but it turns out Zak is really into instant ramen? Which is kind of adorable, if you think about it, because... Hey! Are you listening? How else are you going to learn to be a proper boyfriend?"

Mathias slid him a cold glance while holding the gate open for him. "Excuse me, who gave you the relationship expert mandate?"

"Well... I'm in a happy relationship, and you are..."

"Go on." Mathias quirked an eyebrow. "I'm what?"

"All alone, despite being... you know... super sexy?" Eric grinned sheepishly. "Listen, I'm not saying your *mood swings* have anything to do with it, but I know at least two girls who have a crush on you, and you——"

"Nope. Not interested."

"In *them*? Or in this conversation?" Eric asked eagerly, not even looking where he was going. "Because one of them is really nice, you know, top-notch. A bit like me, but a girl, so really good stuff. Not as good as Zak, but if you just t—"

Eric didn't finish that line. He knocked straight into Kayvin, who had made a sudden U-turn.

"For fuck's sake," Kayvin said, his mean eyes flashing, "if I have to listen to another word coming out of your mouth…"

Eric, who was all grins and giggles a second ago, transformed right before Mathias's eyes. "Good thing I wasn't talking to you, then," he said coldly. To Mathias's surprise, he surreptitiously stepped back and moved in front of him.

Kayvin ignored Xavier and Steph's pleas to drop it and get inside and pressed on Eric instead. "Everyone can hear you, you know that, right? *Zak, Zak, Zak, Zak, Zak!* Do you ever talk about anything else? I can't stand it anymore! The only times you're not blabbing on about him are the times you're parading yourselves together throughout the school like freaks!"

Eric met his rant with a defiant laugh. "If it bothers you so much, why don't you do something about it?"

"Trust me, I would have already, if it wasn't for the bulldog at your side."

"The what?" Eric went from badass to dumbfounded in less than a second. "Bulldog?" He glanced up at the one standing behind him. "You mean Matt? Come on, he wouldn't hurt a fly."

"Nope," Mathias said, "I would definitely hurt him."

"Such a good pal!" Kayvin sniggered. "How does it feel to be friends with a pervert?"

"Hey!" Eric angrily pointed his finger at him. "Matt's not a pervert!"

"I was talking about *you*!" Kayvin went into a crazed fit of laughter. "You disgust me," he said, his eyes red and glistening. "For years… for years I've allowed you to be around me… not knowing…" His voice started trembling. "I keep thinking of all the times we were together… I trusted you, while you… you must have really enjoyed yourself all this time, having those disgusting thoughts about me, about all of us! It turns my stomach just to think of it."

Eric stared at Kayvin without moving. He had been listening calmly the whole time and with no attempt to interrupt, despite the hurt visible in his eyes. Mathias didn't know what to do, but he noticed his hands had freed themselves from his pockets on their own.

Kayvin met Eric's eyes, and they locked themselves in a brief staring contest, until the latter gave in and looked away to the side. Kayvin snickered, his expression clearing. All he ever wanted was to watch Eric submit. Now that he got his heart's desire, he turned his back to them, grinning from ear to ear.

Eric started off toward the main building, then stopped, his shoulders slumping. Mathias could only stare at the expression on his friend's face helplessly. Alberto had told him once: one day, Eric's light would get snuffed out. Mathias wouldn't let that happen to him. Never, and especially not because of Kayvin. One of these days, Kayvin would have to be dealt with. Mathias had been hiding for too long, standing back while others got hurt, shaming his mother once again. He strangely recalled the pictures of Alberto down in the basement, and his chest tightened.

After a moment of silence, he finally extended a hand and gently put it on Eric's shoulder, who glanced at him, managing a smile.

"Can you believe we used to be best friends?" He let out a laugh, but it was joyless and small.

Mathias set aside his unease and patted him on the back. "I can't— Ah!" Encouraged by his gesture, Eric had pulled him into a hug. Mathias froze, momentarily speechless.

"Now, *you're* my best friend," Eric whispered. He tightened his grip around him. "Thank you."

Mathias tried to ignore the looks they were getting and tentatively hugged back, embarrassed. "Okay."

"You're my guy."

"All right, all right. Back off, now."

Eric released him but didn't break eye contact. "I'd do anything for you."

"Oh, really?" Mathias laughed awkwardly.

"Of course! I love you!"

Eric's eyes were a bit too eager for Mathias's liking. He wanted to retort with a joke, but he found there was a boulder stuck in his throat. Eric gave him a warm smile.

"There's nothing you could do that would make me think less of you, you know that, right?"

Suddenly feeling overheated, Mathias jumped to the side and landed straight into someone. To his dismay, it was yet again Kayvin, who was heading back toward the building.

"Careful!" Kayvin was still smirking from his empty victory over Eric. His brows rose to his hairline when he saw Mathias's face. "What's wrong with you? You look like you're about to shit your pants like Alberto the other d—"

Mathias moved fast, so fast, Kayvin lost balance and ended up ass down on the concrete. Mathias grabbed him by the front of his pastel sweater. "Do you— No, don't move, you're fine where you are. Do you ever shut the fuck up? I'm so tired of your constant yapping, that useless background noise… I'm asking you, do you ever shut up?"

Kayvin was so surprised, he didn't even have time to pretend not to be scared. "What the hell is wrong with you, man?" He threw a helpless look at Xavier, who lowered his eyes.

"What is it? What's your problem?" Mathias closed his other fist around his sweater and brought them close until Kayvin, his jaw slack, had no choice but to look into his eyes. "You get off on this or something?"

The sound of an air horn being blown to the max suddenly resounded across the schoolyard. Mathias ignored it. "Every day, we all have to make choices, and every day, you make the same decision to be an asshole." He tightened his grip around him. "The next time you mess with my friend, I'll do the choosing for you."

A grip like a vice seized him by the collar of his jacket. Van Bergen yanked him backward, forcing him to let go of Kayvin. "That's enough, kid."

Mathias pointed his finger at Kayvin. "There won't be a warning next time."

"Hey!" The headmaster shook him, almost lifting him from the ground. "Enough!"

But it was too late. Upon seeing Kayvin's smirk, Mathias's anger, frustration, rancor, and guilt engulfed him like wildfire. He whirled around and shoved Van Bergen away with both hands, shouting, "Eat shit!"

The entire schoolyard let out a horrified gasp before falling silent. One look at V.B.'s face was enough for Mathias to realize his mistake. But it was too late now; with an ominous expression, Van Bergen seized Mathias's neck as if he were a chicken on his way to the slaughter and led him toward the building and his punishment.

14

WINNER

WHEN VAN BERGEN'S horn resounded across the playground, everyone stopped in the middle of their conversations. Soon, a cluster of students agglutinated past the front gate to observe the scene, their necks stretched and their mouths agape.

Since he was taller than most, Alberto could clearly see Mathias hovering above Kayvin. His own mouth fell open, and his cigarette tumbled to the ground. Was he kicking his bigoted ass? That's what everyone around was suggesting, their voices full of hope. It seemed like there wasn't anyone Kayvin hadn't frightened or harassed in his three years at Colette. Alberto watched the scene unfold in quiet bewilderment until he heard a squeaky voice like a mouse near his elbow.

"Press! Press! Let me through! I'm press, *merde**!"

Alberto recognised Elisa's voice before she even slammed head-first into him. She glanced up in exasperation — good God, did she look like her brother at times — and her expression turned to shock when she recognised him.

"Alfred!" She gripped his arm. "Is it really Mathias?"

Alberto nodded. She stretched on her toes to get a better look, to no avail. Alberto pointed at his own back.

---

* Shit! (French)

"Do you want to…"

"Yes!" She didn't hesitate, and she jumped on his back with no consideration for his clothes or his backpack, letting out a squeal of triumph upon discovering what the world looked like from his height.

Cutting an impressive figure, Van Bergen was towering over Mathias in the middle of the schoolyard, and yet, the latter pushed him away — going as far as baring his teeth at him — and yelled, "Eat shit!"

Mathias's words had everyone gasping in horror — and awe. The colour drained from the headmaster's face, causing Mathias's expression to crumple as well. As Kayvin scrambled back to his feet with a wicked smile, Eric rushed toward Van Bergen, but the headmaster stopped him with a threatening glare.

Van Bergen seized Mathias by the neck and led him toward the building. When Mathias gave in, his arms falling limply at his sides, Alberto's stomach churned, and he almost let out a helpless sound.

Elisa's hand closed in a tight fist around his hair — that too, apparently, ran in the family. Using her other hand, she was filming the scene with her phone.

"What are you doing?" Alberto asked. Ignoring the burgeoning pain in his lower back, he readjusted her weight with a huff. "Taking pictures for the paper?"

"Nuh-uh. Personal archives."

Alberto frowned. "Mathias won't like being reminded of this."

"Who says it's for him?" Before Alberto could retort, Elisa added, "Let me down before I get murdered here." She slipped down from her perch with great agility. "Your fan club's watching, and they don't take kindly to our great familiarity."

Alberto glanced over her head and saw his three most resilient admirers. If looks could kill, Elisa would be in serious trouble right now.

"Oh, right."

"If they can't take this, wait until they find out about my brother," she added, straightening her oversized military jacket.

Alberto graced her with a faint smile and got pulled into a

yawn. "Sorry. I haven't seen them in so long, I had almost forgotten about their existence."

"You can thank me for that, too!" Elisa made her way toward the main building. "I told them to leave you alone after our little talk."

"Why… Wait!" Alberto trotted after her. "Why would you do that?"

Elisa gave him a pointed look. "You have every right to walk around in public spaces without being harassed. Did you expect me to do nothing? My principles could never allow it." She briefly paused, then mumbled, "What sort of friend would I be otherwise…?"

Upon hearing that, Alberto almost collided nose-first with the door he was holding open for her.

"We're… friends?"

Elisa sniggered at his clumsiness. "Of course we're friends. Didn't you say I was amazing the other day?"

Alberto took advantage of his height to open a path for them through the heaps of students making their way outside, some still commenting on the way Mathias got dragged into Van Bergen's office. "Hum… I said you were nice. If I recall, I didn't—"

"Here we are!" Elisa stopped in front of the *Colette Times*'s editor-in-chief's office and watched him struggle against another yawn. "Again? I know it's not my brother who's keeping you awake at night. What's up with that, by the way?"

Not too keen on talking about that, Alberto steered the conversation back to his fan club. "How did you convince those girls to leave me alone?" He thought of Mathias with alarm. "You didn't threaten to punch them in the face, did you?"

Elisa laughed as she opened the door. "My mentor—you know, the headmaster—*does* claim that the only way to deal with bullies is to punch them in the face." She mimicked a boxer hitting someone with their fist.

"Hang on…" Alberto followed her inside. "Van Bergen's your mentor?"

"He is!" She nodded excitedly. "He's *The Godfather,* you know?

And he's so tall, he's over half a meter taller than me. That's like…" She interrupted herself, her expression turning thoughtful. "Oh, never mind. Of course I didn't hurt those poor girls! Unlike my brother, I'm mostly nonviolent. On that note, Kayvin should watch out, or he's gonna get it."

Elisa elbowed her way past the piles of files, books, and magazines littering the already cramped space and dropped into the large swivel chair on the other side of an old desk. "No, I merely threatened to divulge their embarrassing secrets in my next paper. Mostly the nasty stuff they say behind each other's backs. It worked like a charm."

"Hm…" Alberto nodded absently. "You know… your brother really isn't that violent." He recalled it took a certain amount of convincing for Mathias to be rough enough with him. He was always worried about hurting him; it was quite endearing. Mathias *was* quite endearing. Alberto really couldn't wait to feel his lips upon his skin again.

"I know that!" Elisa said. "But he got suspended from our former school for punching someone. Considering Kayvin's behavior, it's a miracle Mathias hasn't lost his cool already." She whirled around and pointed at a small Tassimo machine on a crooked shelf behind her. "Coffee? You really look like you could use some."

Alberto waved the offer off. "I don't touch that stuff anymore." More importantly, he had seen Mathias keep his cool even as Kayvin pushed him into the pool. He wondered what could trigger him to show a little more… spirit. "Why did your brother punch that person?" he asked in an innocent tone.

"Oh, you know…" Elisa gestured him to sit down on a nearby rickety stool and flashed him a peace sign when he refused with a grimace. "Some dumb guy was making fun of Daphnée."

"Daphnée?"

"Matt's best friend, Daphnée, yes."

"His girlfriend, you mean?"

Elisa's face darkened. "Yeah, that one. Anyway, it wasn't his first offense, so they suspended him. That's part of the reason why my dad, who was teaching there at the time, even considered taking a position here. Mathias didn't want to go to a private school either, but, you know, he was lucky enough to even be offered a second chance."

Alberto felt a pang of jealousy at the thought of Mathias going to such lengths for Daphnée. "What happened the other time? Who did he punch?"

"There was this boy at school…" Elisa looked up and met his eyes with obvious reluctance. "He was the target of jokes. No one told me why, but it seems to me it was because he was gay. One day, Mathias was nearby when it happened, and he lost it."

Now, Alberto felt even more jealous; his expression turned morose. Elisa misinterpreted and hastily stood up.

"He's not usually like that! I mean… Mom was sick at the time, and he was on edge. And the second time, last summer, he had a lot on his mind… But he doesn't hurt the people he loves. He's not that type!"

Alberto cast his eyes down. Mathias was perfectly capable of hurting people… by abandoning them out of the blue. But of course, it was different: he didn't love Alberto.

"What's going to happen to Mathias?" he asked in a thin voice. "I heard Van Bergen literally suspends students from the ceiling."

"He'll be fine!" Elisa waved her hand dismissively. "Now leave, please, I have to proofread the *Guide* one more time. We will announce winners tomorrow." She winked at him. "Be prepared, Alberto Gazza!"

Alberto had no idea what she was talking about, but he took his leave, his heart full of worry for Mathias, but also bitterness. Since Mathias so readily defended other people, why wouldn't he come to his rescue at Xavier's? Not that Alberto thought he deserved that special treatment, but he'd been rewinding their time together during the Christmas holidays, and it seemed to him they were getting closer, and it seemed to him Mathias had no intention of leaving the bed that morning. Alberto shouldn't have gotten up; when they came back, something had changed, for certain. Alberto believed — no, he was certain — they should have never left that bed.

Stasia was right: Alberto was too pathetic to keep a friend, never mind a lover like Mathias. But since she showed her true face the other day, he'd decided he would do everything in his power to get him back. He'd already resorted to drastic measures, so he hoped their break would be of short duration. Without Mathias to hold him tight enough to bruise his bones, Alberto was constantly worried about falling to pieces.

Alas, the next day, Mathias didn't show up, and Alberto naturally grew so worried, he started picking at his fingernails, a habit he'd managed to lose years ago. In class, he was twitchy and unable to concentrate at all. If Mathias got himself expelled from Colette, it truly would be the end of the world.

Alberto left the history lesson with no recollection of what had happened in there. His mind poisoned with anxious thoughts, he didn't notice the figure coming at him at full speed: Eric swooped down on him just as he was exiting the building.

"Hi!" Grinning as always — his smile was so bright, Alberto almost took out his sunglasses to escape the glare — Eric whipped out Alberto's expired ID and held it before him. "Found this in class the other day. It's yours, isn't it? It has to be."

"Yes…" Alberto gingerly took the card. How the hell did it end up in Eric's hands, of all people? "My name's on it, after all."

"Your middle name's Gabriel!"

"Yes… it is."

Though Alberto expected Eric to walk away, he stood there with a bizarre smile plastered on his face, filling him with an inexplicable sense of dread. What if he came to settle the debt after what he did for him the other day? *I lied to your mother to cover your ass. Now, hand over the money, or the bunny gets it!* Or something like that. Alberto hoped he'd ask for money. He had literally nothing else to give. But that made no sense! Though Eric dressed like a Playmobil, he was probably richer than Alberto; he didn't need any money. So, what else could he possibly want?

"Anyway, now that I've got you…" Eric let out a quiet laugh, and Alberto held his breath. "Me and a few others, we're to announce the winners and all, so I must inform you that, as a consecutive winner yourself, you have access to VIP stuff, including taking part in some bets. Some of them are really dumb, but you should still do it, it's kinda fun."

Completely at a loss, Alberto blinked at him. "What are you talking about?"

"The *Colette Candy Guide*? The awards? The bets?"

"The what?"

Eric grew perplexed. "The *Colette Candy Guide* is an unofficial list published every year that rewards students for stuff like... *Best Student, Brightest Future*, et cetera..." He pulled a rolled-up booklet out of his pocket. "Like the Oscars, but dumb. You... you're not even aware that you got an award?"

"No."

"And last year?"

Alberto's eyes widened. "I got an award last year?"

His ignorance seemed to amuse Eric. "Yes! One of the best ones! That's why you're a VIP, and you can place bets—"

"Which award did I get?"

"*Best-Looking Guy*."

"Oh."

"And..." Eric leaned in conspiratorially. "*Best-Looking Gal*, too."

"Right..." Alberto briefly pondered the absurdity of his existence. "What about you? Which one did you get?"

That idiot flushed up to his ears with glee. "*Best Personality*."

Of course that bisexual *bastardo* would end up with the real prize.

"I also got *Best Body*," Eric added smugly.

"*Best... Body*?" Alberto repeated, incredulous.

"Why are you making that face? You thought *you* would get *Best Body*?" Eric's eyes swept over him suspiciously, causing Alberto to wrap his coat tighter around him. "What are you hiding under your weird clothes, anyway?"

"I never said I should get *Best Body*."

"But you made a face like I shouldn't have gotten it!"

No, he shouldn't have. Who the hell decided which award went to whom? Not only was Mathias built like a machine, but he was as powerful as one. People might not know much about him here other than his position as goalkeeper, but outside of school, Mathias was a rigorous boxer, lifter, jogger, and an insanely good fuck. Just thinking of his lean, hard muscles made Alberto's legs go weak. But was there any way Alberto could tell Eric how he felt about this gross error in judgment without betraying himself? No. He'd better ask Elisa the next time he came across her. After all, she was at least partly responsible for this debacle.

Eric, oblivious to Alberto's torment, was all flushed from anguish. "Who is it, then? Who's better than me? Is it Kayvin? No, it's Xavier, isn't it? I know you have this weird relationship going on…"

"Nothing like that," Alberto said, inwardly rolling his eyes. "It's all in your head."

"Then…?"

Alberto couldn't help feeling amused. He had never seen Eric like this. For once, he held power over him; he wasn't about to relinquish it just yet. "I just don't think you should have gotten *Best Body*, that's all. And judging from your reaction just now, I can't believe you got *Best Personality* either."

"Huh?" Eric suddenly looked like he'd been switched off. He gazed down at his booklet with a frown, letting an odd silence settle between them. "You know what? You're right. Maybe I shouldn't have gotten it after all."

Uncomfortable as he was, Alberto couldn't help using Eric's confusion to ask about Mathias. He lightly cleared his throat. "What happened to your friend yesterday?"

Eric looked up abruptly. "My friend?"

"The one who Van Bergen took away by the scruff of his neck?" Alberto haughtily jerked his head. "Did he get murdered by him or what?"

"Oh…" Eric gave his booklet a last glimpse, then rolled it back up and put it back in his pocket. "He injured himself, so he's staying home. He'll be back on Monday."

"He injured himself?" Alberto madly stepped forward and was about to seize Eric's arm, but he stopped himself at the last second. "He— What happened?"

"He flung his fist through a window."

Alberto's heart dropped to his stomach. "Is he… is he okay?"

"He's better than the window," Eric said, his eyes narrowing.

He wasn't as idiotic as he appeared. Soon, he would become suspicious. Alberto had better revert to his usual persona, as well as change the subject.

"Did… did Zak get an award?"

That was enough to make Eric's eyes glimmer again. "Of course he did! He got *Cutest Couple*."

"Ah. With me?"

Eric's jaw dropped. "You bastard…" He abruptly seized Alberto by the lapels of his coat. "With me!"

Alberto feigned surprise. "Oh?"

"*We* are cute. *You* were not cute. You were not cute at all!"

Take that, Best Body, Alberto thought with mischief. "I know, I know," he said. Enough with the games. At least Eric didn't appear suspicious anymore. "Could you please stop shaking me? Or I'll have a…" — Eric released him with a gasp of horror — "… headache."

"Sorry, sorry!" Eric even smoothed Alberto's coat, who feared he was about to hug him. "I kinda lost it there. Really, forgive me, I'm under a lot of pressure, I—"

"That's fine, no harm done," Alberto said truthfully. "Thanks for returning my card and for… I don't know why you did that, but thanks for covering for me the other day."

Eric laughed. "Of course! You looked like you definitely needed a way out! Who hasn't lied to their parents before? I can sympathize…" He checked the time on his phone and started. "I have to get to practice, so I'm gonna go, but I'll see you tonight?"

Alberto furrowed his brow. "Tonight?"

"Yes. Party at Neuilly?"

For the first time ever, Alberto didn't get invited to one of Xavier's parties. He schooled his expression to pretend he naturally did.

"You better come," Eric said, "or Xavier will whine all night." He turned around to leave before stopping in his tracks. "*My friend* Mathias will probably be there, so you can ask him about… about his hand."

Alberto watched him walk away with a racing heart. Now that his mind was clear of the usual fog, it wasn't too difficult to put two and two together: the invitation to Zak's birthday party, the forced kindness, his rescue the other day…

It became clear to Alberto that Eric knew about them. And even more shocking, he seemed to be on their side.

15

NOT CRAZY, JUST FOND OF YOU

ALBERTO WAS the best-looking guy at school. Someone even voted him *Best-Looking Girl*, too. It was enough to seduce Mathias, once. Hopefully tonight, he could do it again.

He stood in nothing but his underwear in front of his mirror, and he carefully stared at his own reflection for the first time in four years. His thighs and his forearms slightly shaking just like last time, he gave himself a serious inspection.

In his opinion, he looked too skinny. Frail, even. He had moles on his body he didn't care for, and dark circles under his eyes. And speaking of, they were a dull grey and not at all worth remembering. Nothing like the burning embers Mathias had been gifted with. His hair was fine, he supposed — smooth and black, like Mamma's. But his skin tone was too pale; he often looked sickly. However, tonight, his eyes were bloodshot from lack of sleep and his entire face was flushed with thoughts of retribution, yet he somehow looked even hotter.

That's because he knew how to dress. Growing up around models and designers had its benefits, after all. He had an eye for what looked good, especially *on him*. That and a mother who spent her allowance buying him the kind of clothes that would make anybody look like Prince Something.

After he got dressed, ready for battle, Alberto sat at his dressing table and lit a cigarette, perfectly aware he wasn't allowed to smoke in his room, or to smoke at all, for that matter. But he couldn't care less tonight. As he was pondering earlier how he could make himself not merely sexy but devastating, dressed to kill — or simply to remind a certain someone of what he was missing — he opted for the *I don't give a shit about clothes but still, I look like a rockstar* style, that *I'm not afraid of looks, in fact, please, do look at me* vibe that he often had to fake for the magazines. Alberto blew smoke at his reflection and smirked; he looked *insane* tonight. Reckless. Danger-ous. *Shut one drawer, open another; Pandora's box is filled with uppers and downers.*

The heady notes from Discobitch's hit single pounded through Xavier's speakers, making the walls of the villa shake and pulse in rhythm, like the bloated heart of a corrupt monster. Alberto made his entrance into the packed living room thinking *he* was the *baddest* bitch tonight, and he might as well have been right: the mere sight of him had such an effect, the other guests parted like sycophants to let him through. Alberto split the crowd feeling like Cleopa-tra — regal and doomed — and with a sweeping glance across the room, he easily spotted his Mark Antony.

Standing against the wall near the kitchen, Mathias was accom-panied by the inescapable Elodie. Alberto tried his best not to charge straight at him and scream, "Why won't you talk to me?!" It had been almost two weeks already — two weeks of this *torture*. Alberto couldn't accept the idea that Mathias had gotten hurt and he wasn't there to make it better. Nor could he accept Mathias might not miss ~~him~~ their games at all, so he came here to find out, and not just that: he came to make sure Mathias would not only leave with him tonight, but also renounce girls – and to hell with it, all others — for the rest of his life.

The rolling mass of dancers — which seemed to include half the bloody school — regurgitated people from all sides; Alberto did his best to go around it to get closer to Mathias, grimacing when a gesticulating guy accidentally shoved him into the wall. He found himself face-to-face with Eric, who was coming from the opposite side, and whose burst of laughter died in his throat at the sight of him.

Alberto tightened his lips. Should he say hello? But Eric, his expression unusually anxious, barely spared him a nod before slipping away. Alberto didn't know what to make of this. If Eric really knew or suspected something had happened between Mathias and him, and had invited him on purpose, didn't that count for something? Eric had always disliked Alberto, and Alberto later made sure to give him a reason why. If Eric was nice to him now, it had to be related to Mathias — it had to be. Everything was so much clearer now! So, why the long face? Had he been quietly encouraging a relationship between them, only to regret it at the last minute?

But Alberto didn't want to waste too much energy worrying about Eric. He tossed a look over his shoulder, hoping to find Mathias searching for him, but the latter was still talking to Elodie, and he wasn't paying attention to him *at all*, as opposed to the number of girls who couldn't help throwing him avid looks. Alberto could see every one of them tonight, and he decided he needed a drink. He elbowed his way to the bar, where he found Zak rearranging the snacks display while bobbing his head to Discobitch. His eyes doubled in size when he saw him.

"Alberto? Hi!"

Alberto briefly held up his hand in salute and returned his attention to the bar. Zak watched him read the labels on the bottles with a slight frown.

"You're… Are you drinking tonight?"

"Think so, yes." He pursed his lips. "Is there any Champagne?"

Zak's frowned deepened. "Champagne? Why?"

Alberto pointed at the speakers. "Bad bitches drink Champagne."

"Oh." Zak scratched his cheek. "No, I haven't seen any. Xavier's cousin Gwen probably drank all of it. She broke up with Kayvin, and he's in a terrible mood, even worse than usual. Xavier's been running around all night, making sure no one causes trouble…"

"So… no Champagne, then?"

"… No." Zak hesitated for a few seconds before he picked up something hidden behind half a dozen bottles of strong liquor. "But… could I perhaps interest you in a glass of red wine?"

Hearing the word *wine* and remembering the bottle he once shared with Mathias, Alberto first felt tempted, but here was the problem: he had no recollection of his behaviour once he got drunk, but he vividly recalled Mathias ditching him the morning after, so he still wasn't confident he hadn't done or said something repulsive.

"The thing is…" Zak added bashfully in the face of his hesitation, "I always bring a good bottle of wine to parties, thinking, one day, some other weirdo will want to drink it with me, and we'll talk about things no one else wants to talk about, like *adults*, and hahaha! I'm talking too much, aren't I?"

Alberto gave him a long look, then snatched the bottle from him. "I can do that. I'm a weirdo."

"Well, let me open it," Zak said, seizing the bottle back. "Because you're shaking — is it that cold outside? — and this is actually good wine, according to my sister, who gave it to me…"

A quick look at his hands told Alberto Zak was right, so he let him carry on without a word.

"… Because, *unlike you*, I'm still a minor," Zak went on, "and I'm not allowed to drink, technically, but I mean, live a little, right?" His lips stretched in a grimace. "Oh God, I really am talking too much."

Alberto felt like telling him that there were worse things a minor could do than having a glass of wine — he spoke from experience — but he swallowed back the urge and waited for Zak to pop open the bottle instead.

"So, what did you do for your birthday, anyway?" Zak asked, searching for glasses.

It took Alberto a few seconds, but he eventually recalled, even letting out a chuckle. "Cemetery stroll." Zak froze and almost dropped the two little plastic wine glasses he'd found. "Fancy," Alberto said, pointing at them.

"Right?" Zak appeared both confused and relieved by the change of conversation. "Xavier said Gwen broke most of the proper ones in a fit of rage, so the baronet got mad." He tasted the *Saint-Émilion* like a connoisseur, which Alberto found amusing since until six months ago, he had never had a drop of alcohol. "So, what should we talk about? Maybe not your birthday, then… What about—"

"I got one," Alberto cut in. "You know Xavier's father isn't a baronet, right?"

He took an enormous sip of wine, but Zak was too shocked to notice. He was looking at him as if he'd just announced the President was actually three children stacked on top of each other under a trench coat.

"No way…"

"Way. *Way, way.*"

"But why…"

Alberto giggled into his glass of wine. "That's not even the worst part. I don't think he's lying. I think he's clueless!"

Zak's magnificent eyebrows drew together. "W-What?"

"First, baronets are an English thing, and they don't even have them anymore. There are almost none left anywhere. Xavier's father is a *baron*, not a baronet. And the funny thing is that a baron is of a much higher rank, too, but for some reason, Xavier got his father's title wrong."

Zak finally noticed his mouth was wide open; he hastily cleared his throat and smiled. "How do you know all this?"

"My mother has an interest in those things. I looked Xavier's father up once. It was an easy find."

Before Zak could answer, Xavier emerged from the crowd and stopped before them, his face glistening with sweat. "Alberto! You… you came?"

To Alberto's surprise, Xavier looked more shocked than happy to see him. It brought the former an inexplicable feeling of vexation. He retorted, "Why do you call your father a baronet even though he's a baron?"

Xavier blinked several times. "I… uh… I just thought it sounded cuter. Less, you know… *threatening*." He briefly squeezed Alberto's shoulder. "Just stay close to Zak, okay? I'll be right back."

Mind your own business, Alberto thought, throwing back his drink.

"Oh, you like the wine, at least," Zak said with a nervous laugh.

"Yep." Alberto poured himself another glass and winked at his ex's dubious expression.

"You seem different tonight."

"Oh? Am I not handsome in your eyes anymore?"

Alberto instantly regretted saying that. It felt cruel, for some reason. But Zak merely lowered his eyes. "Don't play games with me," he mumbled. "You know you look handsome, even more so tonight. But still, you look… different."

Alberto should think so. After so many days, his head was buzzing, his jaw was aching, and his heart wouldn't stop beating madly in his chest, so fast that it made the rest of the world look and sound eerily slow — trapped, like him, in an ever-spinning carousel.

And Mathias still hadn't returned to him. On the contrary, he was flirting with blonde girls who looked exactly like that blasted Eric; that was enough to set his blood on fire. Speaking of, Alberto ignored the odd look of terror on Zak's face and asked, "What are you doing so far away from the boyfriend?"

Zak laughed, but not before his cheeks darkened, rendering him absolutely adorable. "We can spend some time apart, you know. Might as well get used to it," he added in a thin voice.

"Even if you're talking to *me*?"

"Huh? Oh, right. Yeah, even if we *dated*." The way he said the word gave Alberto pause.

"What? Are you denying that we were together now?"

Zak scoffed. "Were we? I mean… *were we* together? You…" He lowered his voice. "Let's be serious, here. You didn't even like me."

Alberto's shoulders sank. "Of course I liked you, Zak."

"Clearly, not enough."

"No… maybe not."

"Finally." Zak exhaled a sigh of relief. "You admit it. So, what was it in the end? Why did you ask me out? Was it out of pity?" He scowled. "Did you feel bad because you said these horrible things to me when I first asked you out? Is that it?"

"No…" Alberto pinched his brow. "What was it I said again?"

Zak let out a dry laugh. "You don't remember. Great. As a matter of fact, you said you couldn't throw yourself away—"

"—to the first one who asks. Right." His fingers tightly wound around the stem, Alberto studied the wine swirling around in his glass. "Did I ever tell you about my mum?"

Zak gave him a startled look. "No, never. You… you've never told me anything."

"You're right, I haven't," Alberto conceded with a half-smile. "She… My mother, she got married way too young. It's by far the biggest regret of her life. She jumped into that relationship, and it almost cost her… everything. For years, she told me to be careful, to not, well… *throw myself away to the first one who asks* as she herself did. She meant for me to be safe, but she drilled this into me over and over, and it's the first thing that popped into my head when you asked me out." Alberto let out a sigh. "I'm sorry, Zak. I didn't know what else to say. I didn't know you at the time… I thought you were like everybody else: just interested in my looks."

Zak's expression twisted. "You were right in the end. I'm just as shallow as you thought."

Alberto vehemently shook his head. "That's not true! After that party, I spent a lot of time watching you. I saw how hard you worked, and how devoted you were to that Drama Club project…"

"Oh…" Zak's voice fell to a whisper. "No, not so much, really…"

Alberto knew Zak was probably more devoted to flirting with Eric than to the film, but he pretended not to pick up on that. "And you were kind to me, always. No matter how many times people tried to tell you I was soulless and uninteresting, you never said a single bad thing about me." Alberto looked away from Zak's rising eyebrows. "In any case, my words at the time made it sound like I thought you were beneath me or something. But it wasn't like that."

"And this whole time, I've wondered if there was something wrong about me…"

"No!" Alberto held up his hands. "No. It wasn't your fault, Zak. It's me who did wrong. I knew you were attracted to me, and I used it against you. I also knew Eric liked you…"

Zak's expression turned bitter. "You knew?"

"He was clearly all over you; only an idiot wouldn't have noticed. So, of course I kn—"

"All right!" Zak balled his small fists. "Then why, why on earth did you ask me out if you didn't even like me?"

The hurt, the confusion flashing in his eyes… All of it was Alberto's fault. It was a sorry sight, one that churned his stomach with guilt.

"You were asking earlier if I pitied you. It's not you I pitied, Zak. It was me."

When Zak's expression softened, Alberto turned his face away. "I know what people say about me… I've known it since the start. My first week at Colette wasn't even over before Joy was asking me out. I rejected her, but she wouldn't get it. She kept coming back, so I told her to leave me alone, and she got vexed. She started telling everyone that I was soulless, boring, and dead inside…" His voice grew weak as he spoke. "I saw it become this thing, but what could I do…? It's not like I could make myself interesting all of a sudden… So, I said nothing."

Inside his glass, the wine looked like another dark pool he was on the verge of falling into. "You know… you hear something often enough, and eventually, you start believing it…"

"Oh…"

"Zak… the truth is, after observing you for so long in Aurons, I really wanted to be your friend."

"Oh," Zak repeated. "But… but we could have been friends! You could have just asked. You didn't need to ask me *out!*"

Alberto let out a joyless laugh. "Would you really have wanted to be my friend? Really? You know very well it's not my dazzling personality that attracted you in the first place. You liked my face, and I used it against you, and it was wrong. I *know* it was wrong. I feel so awful that I refuse to even think about it. It's just… I just thought it would be nice to be just like everyone else. To not be alone, for once…" He briefly shut his eyes, then faced Zak again. "Don't think I didn't try to make it work. I thought it'd be really nice if I could fall in love with you. It just didn't happen."

And when he realised there was no chance of it happening, he waited for the right time to send Zak off. Why else would he have told him about Kayvin and Eric's fight? When he understood Eric's feelings for Zak had grown way beyond the mere crush, Alberto knew he had to find a way to tell Zak, if only to feel better about himself about asking him out when he shouldn't have.

"You never really tried—" Zak slammed his glass of wine down. "You never told me anything about yourself!"

"Zak… Don't forget you were in love with Eric the entire time."

"I'm not likely to forget!" Zak jabbed a finger in his arm. "Y-You stood in the way of our true love!"

Alberto rolled his eyes. "*You* stood in the way of your true love."

He meant it. In this affair, they were both in the wrong. Alberto just happened to think he was the worst out of the two. Not only for snatching Zak from under Eric's nose in a sad attempt to curb his loneliness after the Michael debacle, but also because of his monstrous failure to feel anything when Zak ditched him after four weeks. Alberto had listened to Zak's breakup speech, numb and frightened, not at the thought of being alone again, but at how collected he was, faced with the inevitability. He had always been alone, anyway. Him and Mamma against the world… Or so he thought until…

"Anyway…" Zak abruptly interrupted his thoughts, changing his stance and taking on innocent airs. "It seems Eric wants to be your friend now. What a notion, right?"

Alberto bit his tongue to stop himself from laughing. "It appears so."

"He lied to your mother the other day. It was a lie, right?"

"It was. Eric never stayed at my place."

Zak opened his mouth, and Alberto suspected he wanted to ask who did but decided otherwise. "Why did you introduce us to your mother?"

"She wanted to meet my friends."

"Are we friends, then?"

"I think…" Alberto paused while a couple helped themselves to beers before jumping back into the crowd. "I think you and I should keep our distance."

"What the fuck?" Zak's eyebrows shot to his hairline. "Didn't you just say you wanted to be my friend?"

"I…" Alberto scratched his brow with the tip of his thumb. "I don't want Eric to worry about us."

"Why would he worry?"

"I just don't want to antagonise him anymore," he said, pretending to be absorbed by the snacks displayed on the table.

These past few days, Alberto had come to understand the depth of his resentment whenever he was faced with Zak and Eric's love. How comfortable they were around each other, how relaxed. Their evident devotion was a prickly, painful reminder of everything Alberto was denied: a friend, a companion, someone who'd love and care for him, motivated not by the bounds of blood, but by genuine affection.

I chose you, and you chose me. We chose each other.

Nobody would choose Alberto. Mathias obviously didn't, not that version of himself, anyway. Better luck with the next one.

Alberto grimaced at the food arranged in front of him. Looking at snacks was also like looking at couples: a display of delicacies he could merely gaze at, but never taste. Eventually, he found some olives. He could do olives. They were fine.

"I don't want Eric to have ideas, that's all," he said. "To worry… that I might be up to something…"

Zak cut in with a laugh. "I'm surprised you suddenly care so much about someone who keeps calling you a shovel."

"In all fairness…" Alberto stuffed an olive into his mouth. "My face is kind of shaped like a shovel."

Their talk ended up leaving Zak looking completely nonplussed. "I'll be damned…" he said. "You… you wouldn't have developed any ideas about him, would you?"

Alberto almost choked on his olive and went into a fit of coughing. "Not— not my type!"

Who would choose a golden retriever over a wolf? Not him, that was certain.

"Good!" Zak didn't bother to conceal his relief. "I wouldn't want to be in a competition against you." With these last words,

Zak put his — almost untouched — glass of wine down and walked away.

Plucking a cigarette from his case, Alberto used his height to keep an eye on him. Why would Zak say something like that? Alberto never got what he wanted.

Zak met Eric by the sofas at the other side of the room, and the latter immediately brought him close, pressing a kiss to his forehead, barely even pausing in his conversation with his friends. Alberto briefly met eyes with Mathias. Before his heart could leap hopefully in his chest, the other immediately looked away.

16

ALL EYES ON ME

ALBERTO WAS DRUNK, probably. He had no idea. But suddenly, the people dancing didn't seem so ridiculous or so repelling. They looked young and beautiful. *Carefree.*

He could spot them in a crowd, the ones who were truly loved. Confident, smiling with their teeth, their eyes brightened by the knowledge they were adored. Alberto wasn't like them; his eyes carried the shadows others had passed on to him. Tonight, it was okay, though. Tonight, he would laugh in their faces. An unstoppable force, just like his father.

Alberto puffed out a bitter laugh. He had to be drunk, or he wouldn't think of him. Good. He worried he wouldn't be able to get Mathias back in any other state.

Right as he was filling another glass of wine, Kayvin showed up, flanked by the inseparable Joy and Melissa, his expression overcast as usual. He cursed under his breath when he saw Alberto. "See?" he asked. "That's exactly what I'm talking about."

"Wait." Melissa poured her friend and herself a drink with a dubitative frown. "What are you saying, exactly?"

Kayvin leaned into her space, stealing a grimace from her. "I'm saying the world has already gone to shit compared to, I don't know, two years ago? Now, there are gays everywhere. What the hell happened to this country?"

Melissa giggled. "You should join the fray, Kayvin. Just be bi and be done with it."

He glared at her. "Do you want to get bitch-slapped or what?"

To Alberto's surprise, Melissa stretched on her toes, her eyes glinting with anger. "*Do I? Do I* want to get slapped in the face? Never mind the country, what the fuck happened to *you?*"

Joy let out a frightened noise and inadvertently backtracked into Alberto. Kayvin saw it and broke into a mean laugh. "You think he's gonna defend you? Look at him, he's practically a girl."

Noticing Alberto gazing at him, Kayvin pointed his finger at him. "You… I'm watching you."

Alberto scoffed. "That will be one thousand."

Kayvin lurched forward, looking as if he were about to hit him. Alberto's fingernails scraped against the edge of the table he hadn't realised he was gripping, but Kayvin only seized a six-pack of beer and left without a look back.

"What a dick," Melissa said, her hand on her chest.

"Stop provoking him!" Joy hissed.

"You're kidding, right? I haven't done anything wrong!" Melissa let out a groan of frustration as she followed her friend into the sea of people.

Now alone, Alberto resolvedly sipped his wine. Save the secret costume parties he had with Mamma, he had always dressed like a boy, then like a man. He talked like a man, styled his hair like a man, even stood taller than most men, and yet, he'd often been called delicate, weak, and feminine over the years. His mother always told loud mouths not to mock him for being shy and gentle, but they never got the message, because to some, *being gentle meant being pathetic, and being pathetic was a* feminine *thing.*

The first slap he received was because he looked too much like his mother, and the first time he met Stasia, she'd called him a helpless little girl. *Girl.* That bulletproof insult.

What was it about people, that they constantly came up with the word *girl* as a substitute for *weak?*

You're like a girl.

But in reality, girls and women were far from being weak. It takes a certain strength to keep going, especially when beaten, humiliated, ridiculed by others. Women tend to keep going. Alberto worked with young girls whose feet were crooked and bleeding from wearing thankless heels, and yet, they never uttered one word of complaint. His own mother quietly served as trophy-wife to one business man-child after another, despite being worth ten of them, if not more. Mathias's mother had cancer, and she died fighting, whereas Alberto could barely find the will to get himself out of bed.

And Stasia? She wasn't evil because she was a woman; she was evil in spite of it. But weak? No, she wasn't weak. And she was right about some things: women weren't fragile little creatures at all. Men just happened to be bigger.

Alberto would freely admit to being weak, but that had nothing to do with his sexuality. He would say being gay didn't somehow make you smaller. The horrible way others treated you for being different, on the other hand, certainly had a way of making one shrink.

Alberto wondered if it was the booze, but he was starting to make sense and was not too impressed by it. His thoughts returned to one person, and he cackled into his glass. Look at Mathias: whatever he was... *weak* would never be a word associated with him.

Mathias...

Alberto swept the room in search of him. He hadn't moved and was still leaning against the wall with his signature scowl as Eric happily chattered in his ear.

Mathias was the only one who saw Alberto, *really* saw him. Even at his worst, when they were together, and he was so stran-gled by shame that he held on to Alberto tightly enough to break his ribs, even then... Mathias loathed him because of how mascu-line he was. With Mathias, Alberto truly was a man. He might have been resented for it, but under the sheets, he was honoured for it.

Another song started playing, with a beat as urgent as Alberto's pulse. He blew away his distracting thoughts in a cloud of cigarette smoke and chugged down the rest of his wine. Then, he jumped in. The crowd was moving in waves, giving him the impression he was swimming again.

Alberto knew what to do. He stopped in front of Melissa and asked, like in the movies, "Do you want to dance?"

Her mouth fell open; she watched him with round eyes. Before he could say "Forget it," she gulped downed the shot she held and dumped it in Joy's hands.

"Fuck yes," she said, while next to her, her best friend's expression soured.

Alberto cast Melissa a faint smile. He felt like a character from a teenage romcom. *Hey, handsome, look at me, are you jealous yet?* But was it working? Over there, in the back, Mathias did look close to punching someone in the face, but again, he never looked any other way.

A voice whispered in Alberto's mind, *That's a lie. He looked quite sweet whenever they were alone. "Do you like this?"* Mathias would ask, his fingertips gliding along the sensitive skin of his inner thigh. *"Remember your safe word,"* he would grit out, always so concerned about his well-being. *"Are you tired yet?"* he liked to ask, teasing, when dawn broke through the curtains and they lay, still panting, in the middle of his bed. Alberto missed him so much, his skin was on fire tonight… No, he wasn't tired. Not anymore.

Alberto drew closer to Melissa, and she responded in kind, laughing. He threw Mathias a look back, and this time, their eyes met, and Mathias's jaw clenched.

Are you *tired yet?* Alberto thought. *No? Just* wait.

She was a good dancer, Melissa; that's why he picked her. She could make anything look sexy without even meaning to. And she was relaxed around him, as girls often can be around gay men. She was soon gleefully rubbing against his crotch, causing more than one head to turn. As for him, Alberto's gaze never left the corner of the room where Mathias, Zak, and the rest stood watching.

The song was so catchy, Alberto felt almost feverish. Melissa complimented him on his dancing, saying something like, *"Sweetie, you can move."* Alberto said she should thank his mother for that. She laughed and asked, *"Are you close to your mother, Alberto?"* And he replied, *"I guess,"* while his heart screamed, *"Mamma and I are one, forever and ever. No place for anyone else, unless…"*

He glanced back at Mathias, who wasn't paying attention to

him anymore. No, apparently, the football players on the side were way more important. That scowling brute would be the death of him.

Alberto took Melissa's hand and twirled her around. She beamed at him. She was a beautiful girl; he'd never noticed before how gorgeous she was. Between her and Mathias in the back, his attention was fully taken, so, naturally, when by the third chorus, everything exploded, he was caught by surprise.

In the blink of an eye, the crowd started shoving in every direction amidst cries of shock and protest. Kayvin's fist flew toward Alberto's face, who instinctively pushed Melissa out of the way, but someone slammed into Kayvin right before the impact. It turned out to be Mathias, whom Eric was unsuccessfully attempting to restrict with both arms.

In the chaos, Melissa lost her balance and fell into her friend's arms with a gasp, but Joy pushed her down with a snarl, and Melissa, holding on to Alberto, retorted by kicking her in the tibia. In less than five seconds, the dance floor had turned into an angry mosh pit, with football players punching the shit out of each other and girls screaming and pulling each other's hair.

Kayvin boldly swung his fist at Mathias, who dodged, only to hit Eric squarely in the jaw. When Zak saw his boyfriend struck down, he threw himself at Kayvin with a vengeful battle cry. Some burly fool hurried to grab him, only to be tackled by Zak's friend Camille.

With a fire burning in his chest, Alberto broke from the crowd and watched as hell broke loose all around him. A slow, twisted smile stretched his lips, and he shut his eyes. As he was basking in the chaos, a hand grabbed his, pulling him away. Xavier held on to him, his eyes wide.

"Run," he said. "Before they catch you."

"*The dead travel fast*," Alberto muttered, not remembering where he got that from.

They slipped outside through the patio doors, Alberto shivering from the unearned pleasure of it all. "Where are we going?" he asked, laughing.

Xavier held his hand in a tight grip. They advanced into the garden under the cover of darkness and took refuge under a large tree, the shrieks and shouts dying down with each step.

"I can't believe it!" Xavier whooped and clapped his hands while Alberto lit up a cigarette. "My dude, you just started a riot."

Alberto arched an eyebrow. "Did I?"

"Yes!"

"How so?"

"I think that suggestive little dance with Melissa had something to do with it."

Alberto tilted his head. "Then, Melissa deserves half the credit."

"Yeah." Xavier's smile turned soft. "She's a great girl."

"And…" Alberto let out a puff of smoke. "You're an idiot for letting her go."

"You said it. I *am* an idiot." He leaned toward Alberto's cigarette.

Alberto let him take a drag without a word. The other swung his arm over his shoulder and pulled him close.

It was quiet for a moment, the muffled sounds from inside all but stolen away by a wisp of wind. Out here, it might have been cold, but with how he was burning from the inside, Alberto couldn't feel it. He could, however, feel Xavier's fingers kneading his shoulder. He let him steal another drag from his smoke before he asked, "Why are you always touching me? You *know* how it looks."

"I know, I know," Xavier said. "I know how it looks. I don't care."

"But… why?"

Xavier released him. "You're so cool, Alberto, you're so cool! And… and you're smart. And I was just…" He burst into a nervous-sounding laugh.

"What?"

"I don't know… I was kind of hoping it would rub off on me."

Alberto scoffed and only brought his cigarette halfway to his mouth before he met Xavier's eyes and saw he had meant every word. He truly thought Alberto was cool. And smart. The same wave of gratitude from before washed over Alberto, sweeping away all other thoughts.

Barely taking the time to look around for bystanders, he abruptly seized Xavier's chin and brought their lips together. After a brief hesitation, Xavier hooked his hand around Alberto's neck. They kissed, tongues and all, against the tree, until Alberto gripped chunks of his hair with both hands and heard it tear at the scalp. When they parted, Xavier looked completely undone. He stumbled back against the trunk. "Wow…" He panted. "W-What was that for?"

Despite feeling aware enough of the old shards of pain rattling through him, Alberto did his best to show little emotion.

"You're sweet," he said.

"I'm sweet?"

He shrugged. "I was hoping it would rub off on me."

Xavier watched him through dim eyes. "I… I must be really drunk."

Alberto left him there to pull himself together, and he retraced his steps back toward the house. The drawn curtains didn't allow him to see clearly inside, but through the ajar door, he found out the scuffle was over.

Recalling what had just happened in there, Alberto let out a laugh. *That's what it feels like to walk away from an explosion*, he thought. *Let's see if Mathias wouldn't fuck him after that.*

A faint shuffling sound startled him, and the thin hair on his neck rose on its end. Turning his head toward the shadows, he spotted a thin ladder of smoke, and underneath, Mathias was smoking a cigarette. In the absence of light, how could he have seen him? Alberto steeled himself and walked over to him. He almost flashed him a smile, but the look on Mathias's face made it impossible.

"Hey," he said, breathless.

Mathias didn't speak.

I came for you, Alberto wanted to add. He pointed at the bandage around Mathias's hand instead.

"Are you all right? What happened?"

Mathias glanced down at it with a half-shrug. "I punched my fist through a window."

So it was true, then. Alberto wasn't sure Eric hadn't exaggerated the facts.

"Why did you do that?" he asked.

"I didn't plan on it."

"But… was it because of Kayvin?"

"No."

Alberto hesitated. "Was it because of me?"

"Goddamn it," Mathias said, lifting his gaze to the black sky. "It's not all about you, you know."

Tonight, as things were, Alberto couldn't miss the frost in his eyes. As if to confirm his worst fears, Mathias ground his cigarette in the nearest ashtray and quietly sneaked back into the house, clicking the door shut behind him. Once he was gone, Alberto's stomach suddenly lurched; he doubled over and forced down the bitter taste that had risen in his throat.

The taste of power from a moment ago had already turned to ashes in his mouth. Alberto turned on his heel, draped in bitter disappointment. When, eager to leave this place, he slipped into the dark passage on the side of the house, he ran straight into a moving wall, and his vision turned black.

KEEP STARING

"Dance for me," Mathias once said, lips brushing against Alberto's cheekbone and fingers curling around his arms, a storm raging in his chest. And boy, did he deliver.

Up and down he went, the dim glow of the fairy lights dancing in his eye. Alberto, who knew all the right moves… Not ten seconds had passed that Mathias had wanted to interrupt, and yet, he stood and watched a little longer. It was as it had always been: the temptation to spoil him, push him down, and turn him inside out, but also the urge to keep staring, to not ruin the moment just yet. He watched until he couldn't take it anymore, until his hands moved by themselves, seized him, and roughly whirled him around. But before he could sink his teeth into the tender flesh of his neck, he was torn from his memory with a start.

"Hellooo! Where are you?"

Mathias frowned at the hand waving in front of his face, and he only relaxed when he recognized Elodie. She said something else, but the music was always so loud at Xavier's, Mathias didn't hear her. He shook his head while pointing at his ear.

She drew closer with a smile. "I was asking where you were."

"I… uh…" His voice was drowned by the music, the cheers, the conversations, but he had no strength left to speak up. Not that he would have told the truth, since he was in Alberto Hell, of course. Locked in the memory of that night, the night he almost threw it all away for a chance at a smile…

When Alberto made his entrance ten minutes ago—looking more monstrous and dangerous than ever—all eyes fell on him, and Mathias was no exception. His wounded hand flexed in his pocket; his heart jolted before it recalled he and Alberto were over, then it sunk miserably to the bottom of his stomach.

"Sorry," he said, trying to think of a valid excuse for his inattention. "I've got a lot on my mind."

Elodie's pretty features twisted up in concern. "Your mock exams?"

"That's… that's done. But I have that entrance examination soon."

"What's that for?"

Mathias realized he had never told her about his plans post Colette. "Culinary school."

"You want to be a chef?" Elodie's face brightened. "That's amazing!"

"Is it, though?" Mathias couldn't associate his name with the word *amazing* any more than he could separate the words Alberto from *Hell*.

"Of course! Chefs are known badasses."

Mathias chuckled dryly at the thought. "Badasses…"

Searching for his eyes, Elodie added, "I know you'll look great in that white uniform." She nudged him with a bump of her hip. "Come on, give us a smile. You'll do just fine at the exam, I'm sure of it."

His lips stretched faintly, then he hung his head. When Mathias told Alberto he wanted to be a chef, the latter said he'd look hot in a black uniform. Not white, *black*. Since then, Mathias hadn't been able to see himself dressed any other way; he'd be a chef in a black jacket—the black sheep of the flock.

"I heard it's a very difficult job," Elodie said. "High-pressure, with lots of people to manage…"

"True," Mathias said, nodding. "But that's okay. I like keeping busy."

He would have to, if he didn't want to lose his sanity. With Eric gone to Lyon and Elisa busy with her own studies, he'd be alone with his thoughts practically all the time. He would do whatever he could not to think at all.

"There's also the waking up at crazy hours…" Elodie went on.

"I don't mind."

"Your girlfriend might." She said it in a playful tone. Mathias wasn't sure how to answer that.

"I already wake up early to exercise. I'm used to it."

Elodie let out a laugh. "Now that's something your girlfriend could never be mad about."

Mathias felt at a complete loss. "What are we talking about? I don't have a girlfriend, so no one is going to get mad about anything."

Her smile wavered. "Okay…" After an awkward pause, she said, "You don't have a girlfriend, really? A hundred percent sure?"

Mathias checked his surroundings in case there might have been a girlfriend hiding somewhere that he didn't know about. "No."

Elodie lowered her gaze, apparently in deep thought. Mathias was wondering what he had done wrong this time when she abruptly raised her head and set aside her drink on the console behind them. "Look, Matt." She sounded serious. "I'm not gonna beat around the bush. I like you, I'd like to go out with you. What do you think?"

Mathias's eyes briefly fell on the discarded cocktail leaving marks on the surface of Xavier's antique console before snapping up to meet Elodie's. "You… you like me?"

"Yeah! I mean, I was kind of obvious about it, but you never seemed to notice, so I kinda assumed you had a girlfriend outside of school…"

Mathias could only gawk at her. "Why?"

"Because if you were with someone from school, I'd have noticed…"

"No, I mean, why do you like me?"

Elodie laughed at his question, or the look on his face, or both. "Why not? You're hot, and you're nice…"

Mathias inspected himself to understand what was so hot about him in his baggy jeans and his old hoodie, when he clearly made no effort tonight—why bother, really—then he did a double take. "Nice? I'm nice?"

Elodie shrugged. "I don't mind the surly type."

Mathias couldn't help smiling. He liked her; he always did. "I thought Eric was your type."

"You can have more than one type." She grinned. "Ask Eric."

"Can you?"

Mathias wasn't so sure. He was acutely aware of Alberto standing by the bar on the other side of the room. His type. Tall, thin, with a high pain tolerance and a good set of lungs. Was there any other type?

"Eric's very cute," Elodie went on. "You're a different vibe, for sure, but I like it. Anyway, I'm starting to feel self-conscious here…" She briefly hid her face behind her hands. "… So, here it is. Have you ever thought about me that way?"

Mathias knew he hadn't. He wished he had, once again. They would have made a nice, maybe even healthy couple. Boy meets Girl, no *gay agenda*, no risk, and no heartbreak. But since he liked her, he owed her the same straight-forwardness she accorded him. "No," he said. "Not really."

"Oh, okay." Elodie exhaled a slow breath, and her cheeks took on a pink tinge, but she recovered quickly. "Any chance you might change your mind, or…"

"I…" Mathias's voice faltered. He couldn't help being distracted by the sight of Alberto and Zak sharing what seemed to be a deep conversation. What was that about? "I… I don't think so, no. Sorry."

"Is it because of Joy?"

"What?" His attention returned to Elodie. "Who?"

"Never mind, it's not that." She shook herself off as if she'd been through something unpleasant and extended her hand. "Anyway, it's done. Friends?"

"Sure. Friends."

They shook hands, and that was that. She left him, and when Mathias glanced up, he found Alberto's eyes weirdly fixed on him. His pulse quickening, Mathias turned his face away.

He wished he'd never gone to Alberto's place. He wished he had been blind that night, and never saw what he saw. And he wished… he wished he'd paid more attention to Alberto's cryptic sentences. He and his stepdad, they couldn't be lovers. Mathias couldn't recall a single nice thing Alberto said about the man; he had had enough time to go over their past conversations.

What was the point of thinking about that now? Mathias was trapped in some sort of limbo, unable to do anything. Alberto would never say what really happened, and Mathias didn't have any tangible evidence to speak up. He couldn't go around accusing ultra-wealthy businessmen of shady shit. Anything he'd say could have serious consequences, not only for him, but for Alberto's family.

All Mathias could do was reflect on how useless he was.

One thing was for certain: despite how he felt right now at the sight of him, he could never have Alberto again. If he forgot himself and got near him again, he truly wouldn't be any better than the girls from the *Oɔcult* video greedily throwing themselves at Alberto, unconcerned with his indifference. In all their time together, Mathias had never really tried to get to know him. He had only been good for stripping him of his clothes.

He should have kept staring. Mathias dipped his head, and his shame coiled around his heart, making it hard to breathe. Back then, at Eric's party, up in his mother's office… The place with the fairy lights, the bookshelf, and Alberto's quiet little moans. When Alberto was dancing just for him, his gaze softer than the lights, when Mathias's hands were shaking for want of touching him. He should have kept staring. But no, he had to move, ruining it all. This world was always in motion; no matter how desperately he wished so, Mathias would never have the ability to stop time.

By now, the loud music had all but melted away, drowned by the sound of Mathias's blood thrashing in his ears. Was Alberto, like him, haunted by nightmares? By his worst memory playing on repeat every time he made any sort of mistake? In Mathias's case, it was a never-ending hospital corridor with squeaky floors and flickering lights overhead, each inevitable step taking him closer to the door he didn't want to open…

A string of comments, spoken first, then laughed out loud, gradually tore Mathias away from his thoughts. He blinked his way back to the party, listening to people's jeers, and he realized with surprise that they were talking about Alberto. A quick look toward the dance floor told him everything he needed to know: Alberto and Melissa's dance moves were suggestive enough to make it look like they were one minute away from tearing each other's clothes. Mathias recognized the provocative glint in Alberto's eye, sharp as a blade, reminding him of that T-shirt he once wore that said *LOOK AWAY*, implying *I dare you.*

With great difficulty, Mathias did tear his gaze away… only for it to fall on Kayvin. A murderous rage darkened his face; Mathias realized Alberto was the source of his hatred, and he didn't even have time to think because Kayvin moved—and fast—with Steph at his heel.

Before even realizing it, Mathias was moving, too. He sprung forward into the mass of flailing limbs, his own hands extended toward Kayvin, his legs moving on their own as if they felt he was about to perform the greatest save of his career.

He got to him just as the other was flinging his fist right at Alberto's unknowing face, slamming into him and hearing his huff of surprise. Kayvin reacted as if his fists also had minds of their own and had been hoping for a chance to swing at Mathias, but with the latter's boxing training, ducking a drunken fist was no problem at all.

How Eric had flashed between them was a mystery—or not, considering his career choice—but Kayvin's fist landed straight in his face. It only enraged Mathias further, but despite his grunt of pain, Eric was determined to stand between them. His arms wound around Mathias's waist, and he shouted at them to knock it off, but the wave of chaos had swept over the inebriated crowd, and now several people were fighting, including Zak and his friend Camille. The two gave Kayvin's equally aggressive friend Steph such a hard time that he slumped to the floor and was never seen again.

Mathias struggled against Eric's grip. "Let me get to him! What the fuck are you doing?"

"Don't. Do. Anything. Stupid!" Eric snapped back. He did his best to drag Mathias away despite his protests, and Kayvin only lowered his fists when Elodie stepped between them, using her body as a shield. Her move was followed by a charged silence.

"Enough of this bullshit," she told Kayvin, her eyes flashing.

He let out a crazed laugh. "He started it!"

"And what were you rushing over there for?" Mathias retorted. "A picnic?" He turned to Eric. "Why did you stop me?"

His lip busted, giving him a sorry appearance, Eric forced Mathias to turn away from Kayvin. "Because... his father can make your family's life difficult, and you don't deserve that. Kayvin isn't worth losing everything, Matt."

"But he... but he—"

"He what? You think he's worth your dad losing his job? Or your sister not getting accepted into the school of her choice? Yeah, he knows Elisa's your sister, and he's capable of it."

Eric's words had the effect of a slap in the face; Mathias let his arms fall to the sides. The same hands had already caused enough trouble when they got him expelled from his former high school, putting his father in an impossible situation. They were the reason his former friends never kept in touch with him. They were the reason *everyone* he used to know was purposefully avoiding him.

"I don't want to cause trouble," he said in a thin voice.

"I know." Eric rubbed his face with both hands. "It's Kayvin's fault anyway. He's been super tense all evening, I saw him fight with Xavier earlier. I had a feeling something bad would happen. Why did you charge at him like that?"

"I thought he was about to hurt... Melissa."

"Melissa?"

Mathias didn't want to tell him what he really thought, but thankfully, a disheveled Zak stepped over Steph's body to jump into Eric's arms, removing any other thoughts from his friend's head.

"My love!" Zak clung to him with glistening eyes. "Oh, look how they massacred my boy!" His tone was way too dramatic for the occasion. Mathias quirked an eyebrow at him, and Zak pretended not to see him.

"Is Melissa okay?" Eric asked, suddenly sounding all dignified.

Camille—also stepping over Steph—came to stand by Mathias's side, her face flushed. "She's fine, but her friendship with Joy took a bigger hit than your face." Eric gave her a wounded look, which she answered with a sheepish smile.

"Never mind Melissa," Zak said, ever so charming. "Alberto got her out of harm's way. Come here." He took Eric's chin and inspected his lip.

"Ow, ow, ow!"

The noble look all but vanished as Eric's features twisted in pain, but he flashed Mathias a wink the moment Zak, barking for Xavier, turned his face away. The latter was nowhere to be seen, which was surprising, considering the scene erupted at his party.

"Kayvin's mental," Elodie said, looking shaken. "We need to do something about him."

"I agree," Mathias said grimly.

"Just—OW!" Eric howled when Zak gently pressed his own sleeve to his bloody lip, prompting Elodie and Mathias to exchange a look. "Someone should check on Alberto. I think Kayvin was going for him."

"Good point," Mathias said, immediately slipping away.

The crowd had exploded in smaller groups. Some, like Kayvin and his remaining friends, hurried to get their stuff and scram, others agglutinated near the bar, while the more hardcore ones hadn't even stopped dancing. Mathias pushed past them, his scowl powerful enough to discourage any complaints. After a quick but unfruitful inspection of the nearby rooms, he concluded Alberto probably just went home.

Noting one of the patio doors was ajar, Mathias slid it open and stepped outside into the garden for a smoke. It was quiet enough to hear the faint sound of the wind whisking through the branches of the trees, but the exterior lights were turned off, and the only light was coming from the inside. Mathias didn't notice anything unusual until he heard laughter in the distance and slowly approached to get a better look.

He only saw a vague silhouette at first, then his eyes adapted, and he recognized Alberto and Xavier standing together in the dark. They were talking in low voices that Mathias couldn't hear.

After a while, Alberto's long fingers lifted to Xavier's mouth, who took a drag of his cigarette. They looked at each other and laughed. Mathias's heart ripped open from jealousy, from self-loathing, but he remained standing there stupidly, despite his desire to leave. After all, Alberto was fine. He didn't appear hurt and was obviously having fun with Xavier and… and… oh? Yes. They were *kissing* now.

Wow.

It seemed their relationship really had already evolved into something else. How long had they been making out like that? Since Xavier's stupid brunch? And to think, Mathias had once thought himself special. *What a load of shit.*

In addition, it seemed Mathias wasn't the only one who knew about it. Tonight, Kayvin really was targeting Alberto when he charged into that crowd. At least Mathias did what he was supposed to: he helped Alberto out in the nick of time. Wasn't that good enough?

Mathias stood there long enough to watch them kiss then part. But when Alberto, retracing his steps toward the house, saw him standing there and started acting concerned for him, something compelled Mathias to return inside before he could say something stupid, something that'd benefit no one. "It's not all about you," he told Alberto when the latter asked him why he hurt his hand. But of course, it was all about him. When had it ever *not* been about him? From the very beginning, it had always been about Alberto.

Back in the living room, Eric was still sitting against the wall, looking as if he were close to breathing his last. Zak was kneeling by his side and dabbing his lip with a giant handkerchief. If he was aware of his boyfriend's overreaction, he didn't seem to mind in the slightest. "Look at you…" he said, his eyes soft. "What can I do?"

"I don't know," Eric said weakly. "It will never get better. I'll be scarred forever, probably… Maybe I'll even die…"

"Hey!" Mathias impatiently kicked his heel, interrupting their scene and receiving a scandalized look from both. "Are you going to be okay? At your club, I mean."

Eric wrinkled his nose. "Sure, I'll just tell them my lover bit me."

"Your lover will shatter your kneecaps if you ever throw yourself into a fight like this again!" Zak snarled, causing Eric to burst out laughing.

"Ow!" He winced, raising his hand to his lip. "Don't make me laugh! I'm dying, remember?" Zak gave him a reproachful look. Eric caught his sleeve with a hopeful pout. "Now, what were we saying about making it better?"

Mathias attempted to apologize to his friend for the whole debacle, but Eric wouldn't hear it. He did, however, tell him to take care of himself before Zak pulled him to his feet and led him—unjustifiably limping—out of the room.

Mathias left the party with a heavy heart and returned home to an empty house. He couldn't know for sure why his feet had moved on their own tonight, but weeks ago, he would have feared his actions would betray his feelings toward Alberto to the world. Now that he finally acted on them, no one had noticed anything weird. It was almost laughable…

Exhausted, Mathias took refuge in his bed. Not even an hour later, as he lay there awake, his gaze lost in the ceiling—*still staring*—he received a text. The light coming from his phone caught his eye, and the name of the sender flashing on the screen made him bolt upright in bed.

18

NIGHT SWIM

THE CLUB WASN'T a fancy affair. There wasn't even a line to get in, at least not at this hour. Alberto glanced at the bouncer, who gave him a once over — as he should — and let him in without a smile. *Fuck you, too,* Alberto thought. He could do better than an overweight thirty-something old man. He was irresistible, he'd been told; he could get *anyone* he wanted.

Inside, everything looked cheap and tacky, from the flashing strobe lights to the thin crowd of pickled men letting themselves loose at the end of the week — all of them, on parole until Monday. *Nothing sadder than this bunch,* Alberto lamented. *Himself included.*

Turning up his nose at the stench of sweat permeating the air, Alberto went to the bar, because that's what people did. He slid a sideways glance at a tragic patron who jumped clumsily to his feet at the sight of him.

"What?" Alberto sneered. "Do I look like jailbait?"

He was always rude when he was high, and his latest encounter with Kayvin had him popping Diazepam like they were effing Tic Tacs. He almost missed the stool when he heavily lowered himself on it and snorted.

The generous patron got the right idea and fled, but the young bartender with the stupid haircut laughed at Alberto's words.

"You kinda do, pretty boy," he said, pushing a pink shot toward him.

"Never stopped anyone before," Alberto grumbled, throwing back the shot. It tasted like strawberry cum. Or how he imagined it, anyway.

The bartender snapped his fingers playfully. "All right. Show me some ID." Alberto did so with a fake smile, and the young man returned his wallet with a seductive twinkle in his eye. "Freshly eighteen."

"Let me guess: suddenly not so pretty anymore."

"You're joking, right?" The young man leaned forward. "How's your night been so far?"

Let's see, "pretty boy." Alberto went to a party to seduce this were-wolf he was obsessed with, but that beast had no intention of returning to him, and he had to admit defeat. He did cause a bit of trouble at least, because *fuck everyone,* why should they be happy when he was so miserable? But as he was attempting to leave, this brutish football player ambushed him. He slammed into him and threatened him with all kinds of niceties if he ever approached his best friend again.

Alberto kept telling him, "Xavier's not gay, Kayvin, I promise you that, nothing ever happened between us," but that bully wasn't having it, his eyes all bloodshot like Papà's, his hand already snaking up his throat. If Joy hadn't showed up and asked what they were doing in a small voice, Alberto would probably have another scar on the back of his head. He bolted out of there as fast as he could, and he only realised some time later, he'd made it all the way back to Mathias's place. He only dragged himself to this club because it was nearby, and he felt he couldn't walk anymore. Rainbow lights usually meant it was safe from the Kayvins of the world, right?

So, yes, his night could have gone better, but at least he was still alive — for now. He asked the bartender, "Am I irresistible?"

The other smiled. "Irresistible? I don't know about that, but you're cute. Your ID says you're Italian?"

"*Sì.*"

"Cool! I'm actually Spanish."

Alberto's heart lurched hopefully. "Really? Do you speak Spanish?"

The bartender's confident grin turned bashful. "Uh… no. Actually, it was my grandparents who were Spa—"

"Yeah, okay," Alberto cut in, turning his head.

You're not Spanish, you liar. You know who wasn't either? Mathias. But *he* could jump start a sentence in English then finish it with a little *Pollito* this or *Pollito* that, and Alberto was aware that it meant *chicken* and that it was another insult — one day a demon, another day a coward, why the hell not — but he kind of liked being *Pollito* until he became nothing at all.

Alberto blinked and gave the bartender a thorough look. He was nothing special. In fact, he was barely cute. Alberto wasn't cute, he was deadly, and with any luck, by the time he was done tonight, everybody would lie at his feet, and he would be celebrated king of the world, of Hell, of *chickens…*

God, what was he thinking…

"Give me another," he said, pointing at the bottle in the bartender's hands.

"I'm gonna be honest with you." The young man turned serious as he poured him his drink. "I lied, earlier. You're definitely irresistible."

"Right." Alberto gave an exaggerated shrug. "What's in that thing, anyway?"

"Vodka." The bartender put his hand on top of his. "Hey, my break's in half an hour, do you—"

"Too late," Alberto said, and he walked away.

Sucker, a nasty voice added in the confines of his mind. Standing up so fast made him feel really strange, and he thought, with his luck, he'd probably get murdered tonight. He vaguely hoped not to be found in a dumpster or Mamma would have a proper heart attack.

One step after another, he found the dance floor, and he pushed his tired shape into the crowd. Imitating the others, he flung his arms in the air toward the pulsing strobe lights, thinking with a half-smile, *Drenched in sweat, no one can see you cry.*

And then, it all went dark.

He felt the heat of Mathias's body first, inching closer and closer until he pressed his hips into him, and his lips fluttered across his neck. Then, his hands, rough and tender at once, slid up his neck to grip his hair, and Alberto's mouth opened in delight…

"Did you just moan?"

Alberto forced his eyes to open. Under the lights, his feet moving in rhythm with the pounding music, a tall stranger was looking at him, standing so close, they could almost kiss. Alberto blinked at him indifferently.

"Maybe. I was thinking of something nice."

The man laughed, joined by the friend at his side. "Are you for real?"

"Yes…" Alberto swayed on his feet. "No?"

"Thirsty?"

"Yes!" He smirked, almost adding, "The first one to dare touch me will get me. How about that?"

"Here. Take my drink."

Alberto did so without hesitation. "What is it?"

"Gin and tonic."

"Whatever." He jerked his head back and emptied the glass in one gulp, enjoying the feeling of the ice cubes on his tongue. The two friends made an appreciative sound.

"You really were thirsty!" The tall one kept staring at his lips. Alberto wiped them with the back of his hand.

"Sorry. I'll buy you a new one."

"Don't worry about it. I'll get more. Just don't move, okay? Stay right here."

He was gone in a blink. Alberto hesitated. The guy dressed like a trader or a realtor; Alberto wasn't that desperate, was he?

But of course he was, or he wouldn't be here. He craned his neck in the dark, trying to find one of his peers. *Anyone here is a nine out of ten and feeling like a bag of soft shit? We should get together, we should, we should.* Funny how Alberto's dad had not even possessed one tenth of Mamma's beauty and yet he'd snatched her away with a few smiles. The key to the Gazzas' hearts might really be a punch in the gut after all.

In an instant, Gin and Tonic returned, slightly glaring at his friend, who'd been dancing glued to Alberto's back the whole time. They argued in each other's ears as Alberto gulped down his cocktail and complained to himself about the spirit/ice ratio.

"I think I'm pretty fucked," he mumbled.

Gin and Tonic pulled him close. "Don't worry, I'm here."

"What did you take?" his friend asked, his brow lightly furrowed.

"Huh… Vodka. Some wine."

"Did you take any drugs?"

"Some pills."

"You have pills?"

Honey, I have pills for days, Alberto thought, and he started spinning in place. One for the morning, one for the night. One for the good times, one for the bad times, and another for forgetting the good and the bad times alike. Pills? He was full of them. And he kept spinning and spinning, and the more he did, the more his brain started lying to him, showing him both pretty pictures and terrifying scenes. He bumped against familiar and monstrous faces among the crowd, covered his ears to muffle Stasia's laughter, avoided his father's jeers, and winced at the unrelenting flash of the camera.

When he saw his mother standing only a few feet away, he stretched out a hand toward her, fingers clawing at the leathery fabric of her top. She turned around; it wasn't her who stared back, but his own face instead. Frightened, Alberto wrenched his gaze away, only to be blinded by another flash.

Some of the men surrounding him were talking to him, but he couldn't hear their voices anymore. The floor under his feet turned black and tumultuous, pulling him down like a tidal wave. The camera kept flashing and flashing, and he kept sinking and sinking, until the water swallowed him whole.

When he reached the bottom of the pool, he mechanically performed the moves he and Mamma had come up with so many years before, and he felt vaguely that everyone around him, the entire dancefloor, was imitating him. He let out a chilling laugh. *Who else came here tonight, led by an irrepressible fear? Who here was better than him? Who was worse? What would they have done? Huh? What would* they *have done?*

Exhausted, Alberto waved his hands, hoping to resurface, to fill his lungs with air. He re-emerged sandwiched between the same two men in the heart of the dance floor.

Who else… in here… had made a terrible mistake…

He glimpsed them in the distance: two little boys who looked strangely like him. One really young, one not so much, watching him with eyes full of silent judgement. With a surge of panic, Alberto stumbled forward.

"Where are you going?" Gin and Tonic protested. "Stay!"

"*Al buio, tutti i ragazzi sono brutti!**"

"What? What did you say?"

"I need to go to the bathroom," Alberto said. Despite the friends' protests, he slipped away and laboriously trudged his way toward the creepy little neon light that said "Gents."

The club's lavatories were all red and black. Black tiles, black sinks, black stalls, and ominous red lights. A suffocating womb. A sensory nightmare.

What was happening to him? How come he was so destroyed? And where was his coat? He patted himself; at least he still had his phone and his wallet. He felt tempted to slump onto the floor and sleep it off, right there in the dirt, just like that time Mathias had pushed him into the trash and he just couldn't think of a reason to get up.

Alberto closed his eyes, only to reopen them with a start. Someone was standing behind him and talking to him. He met eyes with him in the mirror. "I don't speak French," he said in an unwelcoming tone.

The young man mimed drinking from a bottle, then switched to a clumsy English. "Too much drink?"

"Mm. Too much."

"That's okay! Me drunk, you drunk, everyone drunk."

---

* "At night, all guys are ugly." (Italian)

Alberto watched him with uncertainty long enough for this new guy to approach. There was someone else with them, but he quickly finished his business and flashed them an odd look on his way out, shaking his head as he left.

"You need help?" the stranger asked.

Heavens. If there was one guy on this planet who needed help, it was definitely him.

"Mathias," he mumbled.

"Hello Mathias, I'm Patrick. Put water on your face." He opened the faucet for him. Alberto bent over and shoved his entire head under the water jet. He felt a hand rubbing his waist, then his back. When he looked up, his hair and face dripping, the man was gazing at him with a smile. Instinctively, Alberto moved away from him and backed straight into the hand dryer.

The other burst into a laugh; Alberto now felt stupid, on top of feeling drunk.

"Better?"

"Mm."

"Come here, you are sick?" He stuck out his tongue and pretended to throw up.

"No, don't think so."

"Come here."

Alberto came closer, drawn by his cooing tone. He had to relax; not everyone was a creep. His new friend used a paper towel to dry his face, his movements careful and gentle. He was older than him, but still young. Midtwenties, maybe — maybe not — but he certainly was blurry. Not a nice face, but a nice body. He kept muttering about how handsome Alberto was as he wiped his face down, his hand gradually journeying down to his neck, to his chest, to his stomach. Alberto stared down blearily at him without paying attention, busy trying to swallow the lump stuck in his throat. Was it him? Was he the one he would sleep with tonight? This guy wore an awful shirt and even worse aftershave. But he was here, helping him, and he had already closed his fist around Alberto's wrist. So, you know.

"How old are you?" the stranger asked.

How old are you, Alberto?

"Fou—" He staggered backwards. "Eighteen."

"Good!" the stranger said. "You are alone?"

Do you like boys or do you like girls?

Alberto winced and held his own forehead. "I… I like Mathias."

"Woah, you don't make no sense." Laughing to himself, the other started leading him toward the back. "You're very, very beautiful."

Say thank you.

"Thank you." Alberto pouted, and the guy pressed a quick kiss to his lips. Okay then, they were doing this.

"You are nervous?" The other ushered him into a stall. "First time?"

Alberto's brain was nothing but mud at this point; all he could think was nonsense. *Third time's the charm,* the friendly voice last whispered in his ear. Panic rose within him; he called out, gripping the other guy's arms with both hands.

"My name's *Patrick*," the other said. "*Pa-trick*. You are trying to drive me crazy?"

"I really…" Alberto turned his face away. "I really don't care."

Patrick tilted his head. "*T'es un vilain, toi.**" He was smiling from ear to ear, but the unyielding grip around his wrist suggested he had another side to him as well. Drunk people usually did. Alberto's father was a warm family man who enjoyed endless parties, dances, and games with his friends. He was also the sort to bash his mum's head against the wall for wearing the wrong dress. You never knew with people.

Closing the door to the stall behind them, Patrick brought their lips together. Alberto didn't react at first. That was what he came for, right? To shag the first stranger who'd look good enough to pass for Mathias. This one didn't look that great, but he got the advantage of being here right now when Alberto was fucked up enough to no longer discern right from wrong. So, dazed but still resolute about getting what he came for, Alberto tentatively returned the kiss.

---

* "You're a naughty one." (French)

Proof of his perpetual bad luck, his sad hook-up wouldn't stop chattering, and he started to dirty-talk him like in a cheap porno. Alberto snorted as the other spun him around and pushed him against the wall, but his laughter stopped abruptly when he noticed how dirty the stall was up close. That didn't feel right. Alberto pushed away from the wall with his palms, and the guy grabbed him and swallowed half his face, his hands sliding under his shirt. And still, he wouldn't shut up.

"I can't believe it. You're so hot, I can't believe it," he kept repeating, while Alberto kissed back without enthusiasm, trying to force thoughts of Mathias out the secret door in his mind.

From the other side of the door came the sound of countless men coming in and out of the lavatories. Bursts of laughter, faucets opening and shutting, water gushing, hand dryers whooshing… Alberto started thinking he should be out there, too… Mercifully, the horrible kisses ended then. Patrick had a better idea, which he conveyed to Alberto by exerting strength over his shoulders.

Alberto's knees hit the red tiles hard enough for him to give a grunt of pain. That arsehole wasted no time and shoved his face into his crotch. Alberto always fantasised about being dominated like in the dirty movies he watched, but right now, with his knees stuck to pissed-stained tiles and an unfamiliar dick pushed into his face, he found he wasn't in the mood after all.

"Nope," he said, shaking his head for emphasis as he attempted to get up.

"You're something," Patrick said, frowning at him.

What he meant was *"You're annoying."* Alberto laughed. Oh, he knew. He had all the appearance of fun, and yet, he was nothing but trouble. But he was such a sight, rarely seen in this place — and he was drunk, or high, or both — and if he didn't want quick and dirty sex in the toilet, then maybe he'd want to go home with him, and that would be just the thing, wouldn't it? Going home with a *nine*. Once home and with enough tequila, there's no way he would say no — or no way he could. Alberto saw all of that and more in his eyes, or maybe he imagined it. And maybe *not*. From a young age, Alberto had taught himself how to read the intricacies of people's expressions, if only to accommodate the dangerous ones; he usually knew.

Patrick seemed perplexed by Alberto's sudden reluctance, and his subsequent silence. He hesitated before he asked, "What's wrong with you?"

His gaze unfocused, Alberto looked right through him. "I feel small..." he murmured.

"What?"

"I feel small." With a sigh on his lips, he lurched forward and leaned against the grimy wall, painstakingly pushing himself to his feet. "I've always felt small... Like a baby bird... people could crush within their fist." He even mimed the gesture, closing his fist under the other's nose.

"Oh yeah?" Patrick's laughter didn't reach his eyes. He snatched Alberto's hand and redirected it below his belt. "And that? That feels small?"

Alberto decided he didn't like this guy. "Go down on me," he said, his voice just the right amount of sultry.

"I don't do that," Patrick said. "I don't suck dicks."

"Excuse me?" Alberto hoped it was a power play move, otherwise he'd have to tell him he was in the wrong place. "Sure you do," he said instead, imagining it was Mathias he was talking to. Not only did he hold his gaze, but he swiped his tongue over his lip in the way that would usually make Mathias lose his last bit of self-control.

"*Merde,*[*]" the other said with a low chuckle. "You always get what you want?"

Shut up and suck my supermodel dick, Alberto thought cruelly. *I'm a nine. You're a six, and only because I'm drunk.* But even his guilt at acting so savagely couldn't make him like this guy more. In the end, this place felt too sordid, even for him.

"Forget it." Without warning, Alberto shoved that fool back with both hands and watched him fall on his arse with bewildered eyes. Not waiting for his reaction, he stormed out of the stall and past the sinks, earning some whooping and whistling from floating

---

[*] "Shit." (French)

faces along the way. He was panting now, thinking his brain really was foggy and nothing felt right. At least the thought of getting home was something to look forward to. Lesson learned: this experiment had been a failure. He wasn't ready to whore himself out just yet.

Alberto decided it wasn't even worth getting his coat back after all. He wished he could puke, but he'd settle for a cigarette instead. He felt so dirty, he was desperate to get some air. Even if he could barely make it out, the exit sign was a welcome sight. Alberto gritted his teeth and forced his legs to move forward. He would get out. He'd run to that door. If he couldn't run, he'd walk. If he couldn't walk, then he'd crawl. But he'd get there. Keeping his head down as he wobbled past dozens of faceless men, he eventually reached the door...

When he spilled out into the narrow side alley and the bitter cold whipped his face, he almost shed tears of relief. It was drizzling outside. The cobblestones were slick with rain, and the precious drops fell gently on his face, cleaning away the sweat and the spit sticking to his cheeks.

Unfortunately, Alberto's head was still spinning. He stumbled backwards and squinted at a shape in the distance that reminded him of Mathias. Pfft, he mocked himself. *Obsessed much*? Why would Mathias be here? That spineless prick. Why did he abandon him? Wasn't it clear he didn't know how to take care of himself?

A hand fell on his shoulder. Alberto whipped around, blurting out, "Mati?"

It wasn't Mathias, but Gin and Tonic from earlier. He looked older in this light, and even more like a realtor. Where were these bastard football players when you needed them? You could never turn on your TV without seeing them, but they were nowhere to be found when needed. Alberto groaned and shivered under the drizzle, now almost as pissed off as he was miserable.

"Why did you leave?" Gin and Tonic asked. "Don't you have a coat?" He pulled him to his chest. Alberto felt the heat of his skin through his shirt against his own sweat-soaked back. "Come on. Let's get you inside."

Swaying on his feet, Alberto jerked his head, wanting to push him away, but something caught his eye, and his knees gave way. He hadn't imagined the shape after all: Mathias was standing right in front of him, and his unusual eyes, unmistakable even in Alberto's state, were burning with rancor.

19

HOME

ALBERTO'S MOUTH FELL OPEN. "What are you doing here?" Mathias gave him a dark look, and Alberto pressed his lips shut.

Mathias withdrew one hand from his pockets to point a finger at Gin and Tonic — never mind that the former was still in high school, whereas the latter was in his thirties — and Alberto felt the guy's arm tense around his shoulder.

"Let go of him."

Gin and Tonic blinked at him. "He's your boyfriend?"

"I'm not his boyfriend," Alberto muttered.

"I don't need this shit," Mathias said.

Alberto's heart jumped in his throat and stayed up there. He was thankful to be under the influence, or the pain flaring throughout his chest might have consumed him on the spot.

Mathias's eyes caught the light from the neon sign above the door and seemed to glow in the dark. "You can either let him go, or I will make you."

Gin and Tonic didn't need this *shit* either, because he literally hurled Alberto at Mathias with a quick, "Sorry, man, I didn't know he was yours!" and teleported back into the club.

"I'm not…" Alberto mumbled. No one heard him.

When Mathias seized his elbow, Alberto flinched away. He'd

been pawed all over by different men tonight and didn't want to dirty him.

"Where's your coat now?" Mathias sounded really mad. "You're freezing."

Alberto realised he didn't feel hot or cold, just hazy and numb. He fumbled in his pockets and retrieved a crumpled piece of paper with a number on it.

"It's in there, I'll just..."

"You stay right here. Do *not* move."

Mathias took the ticket and walked up to the bouncer. "Can you let me in? I just want to get his coat back."

At the sight of his face, the burly man at the door lost his bored countenance and gave him an appreciative smile. "Come in, handsome."

An impatient soul who had been waiting in line saw that and lost his temper. "Seriously?"

The bouncer snorted. "Yeah, seriously. Is there a problem?"

Alberto felt the need to speak up. He needed to yell that there was, in fact, a problem. "Watch out!" he slurred, staggering toward the entrance. "He's a boxer. He'll punch you right in the gut without warning."

Unimpressed by his outburst, the bouncer held him up with one hand and advised him to calm down. "He's picking you up and getting your coat, but he's *not* your boyfriend?"

"No," Alberto said, almost snarling.

The man gave a low chuckle. "Too bad for you, I guess."

Fuck the lot of you. If Mathias wasn't gay for him, then he shouldn't be gay for anyone. Alberto would have gladly provoked this mountain into a fight he knew he'd lose over Mathias, but he tripped over his own foot and landed in the bouncer's arms, who gave a heavy sigh.

"Careful, kid, don't push your luck."

Alberto found himself soothed by the man's deep voice and his pleasant smell. He buried his face in his chest. "Where is home, Mister?"

The bouncer displayed a surprising amount of patience. "I don't know. Your *not* boyfriend will probably know."

"He thinks I'm a demon. Where do you think demons live?"

"In Hell, I guess."

"Precisely," Alberto mumbled, just as the bouncer, seeing Mathias, tossed him back into his arms.

"Take him home, he's barely lucid."

"All right."

Mathias looked angry. And gorgeous. Ah, the longing, even now. The unhealthy cocktail of booze and pills swirling around in Alberto's blood had every blood cell in his body marching to the chant of *Mathias, Mathias, Mathias!*

Mathias, I tripped up, I admit, I didn't plan any of it. I feel so dirty. Take me back, I'll be good. Mathias, I'm so sorry. I only want to do it with you.

Pathetic. Mathias wouldn't care for such words. Alberto better forget about it and shut up altogether. And he did. Wrapped up in his coat, he eventually stopped shivering and was silent on the way back. As for Mathias, he only spoke once.

"I see you waste no time. Or effort. That guy was seriously ugly."

Was he? Alberto had forgotten all about him already. He mumbled a few incoherent words that warranted no answer. They made it back to Mathias's building in what felt both like two minutes and two hours.

Once in the lift, Mathias spoke again without meeting his eyes. "I thought you didn't drink."

I thought so, too. I guess I've changed my mind. Too tired to speak the words, he shrugged instead.

For some reason, it seemed to make Mathias even angrier. He withdrew his keys from his pocket with a dark expression. When he opened the front door, he lifted a finger in front of his mouth. Alberto got the message and nodded. They removed their shoes in silence, and as they tiptoed their way to the bedroom, Alberto saw Cyril passed out on the sofa, and his chest tightened with guilt.

What was he doing here, intruding on Mathias's night like this? How did Mathias even find him, anyway? Was he a regular at that derelict club?

"What happened?" Alberto asked once sat on Mathias's bed, suddenly aware none of this made any sense. "Why am I here?"

Mathias hung by the door with a frown. "Check your text messages." He gave a quick sigh. "Don't move, I'll be right back."

Alberto searched his pockets for his phone, and after some fumbling, he found the text. *I'm awfully, awfully drunk at The Night Howl! Dancing, dancing, dancing around. You should come, too!* Followed by half a dozen of little *x's* like so many kisses.

Wasn't he chirpy when he was out of it? What a disgusting human being he turned out to be. Alberto had no recollection of even typing this message. It must have happened when he was hallucinating on the dance floor. He could only assume everything his mother had told him about mixing pills and alcohol was true. Basically, a terrible idea. He had only one wish now: to sleep this night off. God, waking up tomorrow would *suck*. If only there was no tomorrow.

Mathias returned with a large glass of water, and Alberto grabbed it with both hands. "Can I have more?" he asked once he'd finished it.

"Go take a shower first. You reek."

Alberto did as he was told. Scalding water and Mathias's soap flushed away the grime and some of the shame, at least for now. His hair damp and his face flushed by steam, Alberto returned to the bedroom ten minutes later and sat by Mathias's side on the bed. A bottle of water lay on the nightstand, obscuring the picture of his mother. Alberto averted his eyes and glanced at the pillows with longing. "Mathias…" he began, not knowing what would come next.

Mathias seized his chin with rough fingers and looked into his eyes. "Are you going to be okay?"

"I think so. I'm just sleepy now."

They gazed at each other. Alberto was close, so close to open up, lean his head on his shoulder, let it all out. *It went overboard,* he wanted to say. *The way I miss you. Want you. Your body. No, not just your body. All of it. All of you.*

Mathias was also staring at him like he wanted to say something, so Alberto waited, his heart thumping in his chest. After a harrowing length of time, he said, "Your mother called three times."

Alberto gasped. "Did you pick up?"

"No. You better tell her something."

Mathias watched as Alberto struggled to write a decent text to reassure his mother — knowing he'd get another earful tomorrow. "Why did you text me tonight?" he asked.

"I... uh..."

His jaw clenched as Alberto blinked cluelessly at him. "I told you we were done."

Alberto considered telling him how hurtful those words were, but he decided against it. He wouldn't grovel. At home, Stasia might be able to make him kneel, but free from her clutches, he would still cling to the remnants of his dignity.

"Listen," he murmured, finding Mathias's eyes. "I want to tell you something..."

"What?"

"You're... you're an... asshole."

The light flickered in Mathias's eyes, and his lip twitched. "Thanks."

"You're welcome."

Mathias said something, his brows knitting with each word. Alberto didn't listen, losing himself in the sight. He wished he could just... rest his face on his chest for like... one second... maybe two... Listen to his heart beat against his ear... Tell him, maybe... *What about me? I never said I was done with you.*

"Hey," Mathias said when he noticed Alberto had spaced out. "Hey! Look at me."

Alberto obeyed with difficulty, his eyelids heavy with sleep. "What...?"

"Did you get what I just said?" Mathias sounded serious. "Don't text me the next time you..."

"Huh..."

"... you see how close I was..."

"'Kay."

"... bastard..."

"Uh-huh..."

"... or I'll fucking kill you."

Alberto started. "Okay, yes, okay." His chest tightened.

Mathias had been consistently strange over the past few months, but he'd never threatened him before. Alberto had really done it this time. He sat stiffly at the edge of the bed, wondering how it was that he could make everyone around him so angry they wanted to hurt him.

"Okay," Mathias repeated. "Good."

As if he hadn't just threatened him, Mathias then obligingly helped Alberto into a long sleeve T-shirt and a pair of pyjama trousers, and, without a word, opened the comforter for him. Alberto almost whimpered when his head fell onto the cool pillow.

"I'm sorry…" were his last words. Then, the events of the night and the rest caught up with him, and he all but passed out.

That night, Alberto dreamt again. He was revisited by the stubborn old nightmare that used to plague him years ago. Mamma wept and coffins rattled, and soon enough, he fell into a deeper sleep and got sucked into a darker dream. He was being tortured in the fires of Hell, and his tormentor wore the face of Mathias. Three monstrous imps were handing him the weapons, cackling gleefully as they did. It didn't matter how much Alberto begged, Mathias's figure in the dream was unmoved. It said, *This is your home, this is where you belong.*

Alberto jolted awake, drenched in sweat. At once, terror struck him. The three imps were here, hunched over his bed, their talons scraping the frame. One had blond hair, one had black hair, and one had no hair at all. They were all watching him, their evil faces split into malevolent grins. Alberto screamed, or so he thought. His eyes opened to a different bed, in a different room. It had only been another dream.

He rose, shaking like a leaf. Though their bodies weren't touching, he could feel the heat off Mathias's skin, as though they were a mere inch apart. His presence by his side flooded him with relief.

"Are you all right?" Mathias asked.

"Yes." Alberto forced out a laugh. He felt drowsy and feverish at the same time. "It's just… for a second, I didn't know where I was…"

Willing himself to stop shaking before Mathias noticed anything, he seized the bottle of water on the nightstand. Only after he'd drank deeply from it did he exhale a slow breath. Afterwards, he lay back down and curled into a ball.

At no point had he dared to turn around and face Mathias. When he had settled at last, Alberto heard his voice again, low and quiet in the dark.

"Now, I know what you do at night." He sounded almost accusatory. "Why you're so tired all the time."

Alberto was too flustered to understand his meaning, so he glanced over his shoulder. Mathias was lying on his side, looking at him. "What? What do you think I do at night?"

Mathias arched his eyebrow meaningfully.

"Oh…" Alberto finally understood. "You mean my *other lovers?*"

Mathias gave a small nod. Alberto's brow furrowed. Why was he bringing that up again now? He was better placed than anyone to know the reason why he had no energy. But if there was a chance of making him jealous, then perhaps… Alberto rolled over and faced him, even managing a taunting smile.

"Does it turn you on, to think of me with other men?"

Mathias took the longest time to answer. He stared at him in silence while Alberto waited for him to break it, his anticipation slowly morphing into dread.

"Yes," he said at last. His tone was neither mocking nor upset. Like the thought of Alberto being a slut was just fact, and nothing to trouble himself over.

Here it was; Mathias had finally admitted it. And when he did, Alberto didn't find the resolve to tell him there never was anyone else.

20

NEVER BETTER

THE TEACHER WOKE Mathias in the middle of his philosophy class. His arms clasped behind his back, the man was peering at him from under his glasses with a stern expression. Mathias, who didn't care about presenting as a decent human being anymore, ignored the obvious kicks Eric gave him under the table and returned his look with a scowl.

"What's going on, Mathias?" Mr Lelong asked with a faint smile. "You haven't paid attention to the lesson at all. Have you given up?"

Yes. If only he could tell the truth, for once…

Oh, hang on.

"YES," he said, loud enough for the entire class to hear.

The teacher silenced the ensuing laughter with difficulty. "Mathias, how can you say that?" He went into a concerned tirade about youth, opportunity, becoming one's best self…

That self-help bullshit might have worked on some people, but Mathias wasn't like other people. At least, he didn't think so. He answered with a loud sigh.

Lelong shook his head, clearly disappointed. "Look at yourself… Is that really who you want to be? Think about our lesson. Look in the mirror tonight, and ask yourself the grown-up, mature questions."

Mathias sniggered. The last time he took a good look at his reflection was when V.B. had dragged him to his office to lecture him about bullies. Mathias saw his own face in the window and immediately hurled his fist at it. He should probably avoid mirrors entirely.

"Where do you think this attitude's going to lead you, hm?" his teacher asked, relentless.

"Nowhere."

"Don't say that in that tone. It sounds like you're enjoying it."

"What if I do?"

"Don't be ridiculous. What about your future? What do you want to do for the rest of your life?"

To his surprise, Mathias immediately thought of Alberto. His face flashed in his mind so clearly, his name almost slipped out. Mathias slammed his forehead against his desk, hoping the image would disintegrate, but it didn't, and now Alberto's face was smirking in his mind. *Asshole*, he was saying, his decadent lips curling.

His lack of answer made Lelong scan around the room for support. "Should I… should I expel him, you think?"

"Fine by me," Mathias muttered, unsticking his face from his open notebook.

"No, of course not!" Sounding scandalized, Eric intervened like the champ he always was. *Such a great, steady friend*, who, by some twisted joke, just happened to hate the only person Mathias had ever… liked, making him impossible to talk to.

A sharp pain jolted him out of his thoughts; he'd bitten his thumb so hard, he'd drawn blood. The bell rang at that moment, announcing break. Eric sprung up like a doe and threw his books into his bag.

"Break! Quick, quick, I have to meet Zak."

Mathias pulled a face. "Ugh. You didn't get enough of him last night?"

Eric dragged him out of class by his sleeve, laughing. "Mathias, Mathias…" He shot him a quick glance. "How's the hand?"

"The hand's fine." Mathias sighed. "You need to stop asking me about it."

"But the game is today—"

"I know! How could I forget? You won't shut up about it."

"Then let's talk about Zak instead. Last night was so freaking great—"

Mathias pretended to shoot himself in the head, which sent Eric into another fit of laughter. Once outside, he hooked his arm around Mathias's shoulders and led him toward their favorite bench, where Zak was waiting for him, accompanied by Xavier, Charles-Henry, and the girls. "You know my friend Cam, right? Camille? You know her, right?"

"Yes! I only see her every other day."

"Ah, good, so you *do* notice girls after all."

"What?"

"Anyway, she'd call you a blushing maid."

Mathias broke free from Eric's grip with a curse. "Screw you, I'm not a blushing maid."

"There you go!"

"I just don't want to hear about it."

"About… it?" Eric's eyes glinted mischievously. "*It?*"

As they were nearing the bench, Mathias spoke through gritted teeth to avoid being overheard by the others. "Your sex life!"

Eric stopped in his tracks. "Because we're guys?"

"Are you really asking me this?" Mathias retorted, fuming. "How long have we been friends?"

"That's right! For a second, I was surprised."

"Why? Why would you be surprised?"

Eric didn't reply, going to Zak instead. After taking a seat on the bench, he manhandled his boyfriend to stand in front of him so he could stare at his ass unnoticed.

Mathias lit up a cigarette, grumbling under his breath. He knew Zak couldn't be *that* great, because he already had the best under him, and it wasn't Zak. Zak may have been a cute piece of meat, but Alberto was filet mignon.

What? He didn't make the rules. If he did, how different his life would have turned out…

"How are you, Mathias?" Elodie asked kindly, ignoring Joy's knowing smile. "You look exhausted."

"Never better," he answered, which earned him a concerned look from both.

Mathias hadn't had a good night's sleep in a long time. And on Friday night, with an intoxicated demon under his sheets, he found it impossible to shut his eyes. The moment he saw Alberto's drunk text in the middle of the night, he knew he had to get up and check on him before things spun out of control. He was well aware of how vulnerable Alberto was when he was drunk, so to imagine him alone at a bar, a pickup club filled with horny men? Mathias was out the door in seconds.

The fear he'd felt at finding him obviously confused and frozen outside with an asshole groping him engulfed him with a rage he'd barely been able to contain. Mathias tried to convey his regrets at acting so aggressively later when they were back at his place, suggesting it was best they never spoke again because he was too close to telling that bastard outside the club to let Alberto go before he fucking killed him, but Alberto was so out of it, he probably didn't register shit.

He'd acted weird after his nightmare, alternately shivering from cold or pushing away the covers, his brow furrowed in his sleep, inching closer and closer to him. What was Mathias supposed to do? Little by little, his hands moved on their own, until the *girafon*, his forehead burning, was nestled safe and sound in his arms. Too worried something might happen to him, Mathias watched over him all night; he whispered words of apology in his ears, told him he was sorry about not being good—or strong—enough. But he wasn't like the other guys, at the club or elsewhere. Knowing what he knew, he couldn't just have mindless sex with him only to let him go.

In the early hours of the morning, exhausted, he'd finally surrendered to sleep, and when he woke not even an hour later, the bed was empty and cold. Mathias's chest felt even colder. He'd gone to the window and picked up the binoculars to peer out into the streets, but Alberto was long gone.

Mathias had pressed his forehead against the cold glass. Was the idea of Alberto sleeping with other men a turn on? Sure, as much as the thought of getting his nails ripped out. But he had to lie to him, to push him away, because he wouldn't be able to do this every weekend. The sight of him was torture, as was the sound of his voice… Mathias repeatedly knocked his head against the window. He thought of his mother. He thought of how Alberto's presence in his life had brought his bad dreams back, the ones he'd hoped never to have again. His shoulders sank under the weight of his feelings. In his distress, he imagined his mom was in the room with him, not laughing this time, but watching him silently.

She, too, knew he had done wrong.

"You didn't get hurt this weekend, did you?" Elodie asked, interrupting his thoughts.

Mathias glanced at her. "What do you mean?"

"The fight!" Charles-Henry said, uncharacteristically giddy. "Everybody's talking about how you went after Kayvin!"

"Oh…" Uncomfortable, Mathias looked away and saw that Xavier looked just as awkward as him. Elodie noticed too and furrowed her brow.

"Xavier," she said, "don't you think you've had enough of Kayvin? What does he add to your life, except trouble? You would be better off without him."

"I've known him for a long time," Xavier said. "He's still my friend."

Elodie clicked her tongue. "Not only does he treat you horribly, but you're much nicer without him. Is he really a friend? Not just to you, but to anyone here? It seems to me he's turned into a real jerk."

"I know…" Xavier looked at Eric for support, who patted him on the back. "School's over in about four months. I'm pretty sure I won't see him again afterwards. I mean, if my cousin Gwen breaks up with him for good." He sighed. "They're already back together."

Mathias doubted Xavier would ever be rid of Kayvin. That asshole was too happy to use his friend as a punching bag and wouldn't let go of him so easily. Mathias still dreaded to learn Alberto and Xavier were lovers—or worse—but he felt bad for Xavier and was about to tell him he deserved a better fate, when something else caught his attention. Behind Xavier, Melissa and

Joy were exchanging strange looks. Melissa seemed to be urging Joy to speak up, but her friend only hung her head, her cheeks flushed. She looked frightened, causing Mathias to feel strangely protective of her.

"Are you okay, Joy?"

She didn't reply, but she nodded, becoming even redder. Her expression reminded Mathias of someone. Of Clément, in fact.

… Clément?

Why was he suddenly thinking of Clément? Perhaps because he had once let him down, too. Like his mother. And like Alberto.

Eric let out a loud sigh, as if talking about Kayvin was the only thing that could drain him of his endless reserves of energy. He reached around Zak and pulled him close so that the side of his face was squished against his derriere.

Elodie and Melissa burst out laughing, causing even Mathias to smile. "What are you doing?" he asked, shaking his head.

"He's just being Eric, as usual," Zak said in an off-handed tone, but his eyes were filled with warmth.

Eric only hugged him tighter. "Just let me know if Van Bergen is around. I don't want to get in trouble with him. He's so scary!"

"He's so scary!" a mock-childlike voice said behind him.

Naturally, Van Bergen just happened to be passing by with his riding crop, causing a general gasp of terror among the group. Mathias ostensibly rolled his eyes. The headmaster pretended not to have seen it and gave everyone a haughty look, twirling the thing in his hand as he walked away.

Eric let out a breath. "That was a freebie!"

Relief startled everyone into laughter. Van Bergen had a weird "No touching" policy at Colette, and he was known to randomly tighten the rules of what was acceptable displays of affection in public. Eric burying his face into his boyfriend's ass probably wasn't an exception to those ridiculous rules.

His face still squeezed against Zak's generous cheeks, Eric sighed contentedly. "But seriously, how's your hand, Matt?"

"Right!" Xavier perked up. "We can't lose today, or Kayvin will blame you."

Mathias ignored that laughable notion. "My hand's fine."

"We really can't lose," Xavier insisted.

"My hand's *fine*."

"I sure can't embarrass myself when Zak is watching," Eric said snobbishly.

"Then score some fucking goals!" Mathias barked, sending Zak into a fit of laughter.

"Hey-oh!"

The headmaster had reappeared out of nowhere, freezing everyone to the spot. Eric was so terrified that he made no attempt to un-squish himself from his boyfriend's ass, only clinging tighter to it, his eyes screwed shut. As for Zak, he had become as white as him. To everyone's shock, Van Bergen ignored the blatant breaking of his rules and pointed his riding crop at Mathias.

"You reckless hormone bags better not be late to the game today. You can't lose this one." His riding crop whipped the air as he pointed it at Eric next. "Not like last time."

"I was heartbroken, sir…" Eric squeaked. "Surely even you know how it is…"

"Ha!" The headmaster smirked. "Good one."

"How does he move so fast…?" Melissa whispered to Joy, who nodded nervously.

Van Bergen heard her and straightened up. "I'm all magical." The riding crop whipped the air again. "Break's over. Everyone back inside. See you at the game."

"Break's not over," Zak said unhelpfully. "The bell hasn't r—"

The bell rang at this exact moment.

"How…?" Melissa and Joy asked in unison.

"All magical!" Van Bergen said, already halfway through the playground. Everyone stared after the headmaster as he strolled toward the building, stopping only to terrify the younger kids.

"That man is so hot, I swear…" Joy sighed.

"Do you think he's actively trying to be scary because he's worried we would lust after him otherwise?" Zak asked, a finger on his lip.

Eric made a whining sound, as he always did when Zak spoke positively about another guy. Mathias was about to come to his rescue, but Elodie spoke first.

"Being terrifying doesn't stop me from lusting after him," she said, causing general hilarity. "And his outfits… I wish every guy started wearing waistcoats again."

"That one waistcoat sure is tight…" Melissa sighed, and the other girls hummed in unison.

Elodie made a prayer sign. "Please, God, let me see him without his shirt one day, please!"

Thoroughly uncomfortable now, Mathias didn't bother to conceal his grimace. Xavier saw it and guffawed.

"Matt is jealous that Elodie loves Van Bergen!"

Everyone erupted in laughter, and Elodie's smile waned a little. "What can I say? I do like a good-looking man…" she said with a side glance at Mathias. He immediately looked away, only to meet Eric's bulging eyes.

After parting with the others, Mathias made his way back to class with Xavier, Zak, and Eric.

"Mathias."

With a discrete sigh, Mathias ignored his friend's call.

"Mathias. Mathias."

"…"

"Matt!"

"Please acknowledge him," Zak said, his eyebrows raised reproachfully.

Mathias turned to Eric. "*What?*"

"Elodie likes you."

"She does," Zak said, his eyes full of stars. "She really does!"

Mathias shrugged. "So?"

Zak scrunched up his nose. "So, so… am I really the only one who thinks you two would have incredibly gorgeous children?"

"Yes!" Xavier nodded fervently. "And Elodie's like, the best girl in the world! *And* she has taste. She's never agreed to sleep with me, you know?"

Zak slipped Xavier a perplexed look. "Do you even know the meaning of the words you're using?"

Eric suddenly released Zak's hand to stand in front of Mathias. "I saw you two at the party last Friday! Do you—"

"Eric, no," Mathias said impatiently. "I already told her: I'm not interested."

Eric then let out an uncharacteristically frustrated sound, going as far as stomping his foot before spinning on his heel and charging into the building. Zak watched him, his eyes wide, before rushing after him. Xavier followed them, muttering, "What did I say this time?"

Mathias, too, felt he had done something wrong again, and, eager to avoid a debate—or more questions—he decided not to spend the free hour they had before leaving for the game with his friends, but to hide in the infirmary instead.

In his exhaustion, he had forgotten one thing: today was a Tuesday.

21

GABRIEL

Everybody talked about the game. Zak mentioned it at length in the early morning in English Lit, and Camille lamented she couldn't make it because it was her mother's birthday. Zak promised to film the entire thing, and through Camille's hesitation, Alberto learned Zak was better suited for standing in front of a camera — not behind it.

Vexed by her distrust in his abilities, Zak had then redirected the conversation toward Mathias's hand. Eric wasn't so sure it wouldn't hinder his movements, even worrying about his grip. But after waking in Mathias's arms following his pathetic bender — with the wounded hand clasped firmly over his shoulder — Alberto could confidently vouch for Mathias's grip. The Colette team would win the game. As for Alberto… he was hoping for a different victory.

If only he could speak to him again, he could tell him what happened last weekend was all a big misunderstanding. Alberto had already decided never to use his own body as a cocktail mixer again, so he wouldn't text nonsensical stuff to Mathias in the middle of the night and force him to come to his rescue.

Alberto couldn't remember many of the events at the club, even less of what happened later at Mathias's place, except for one thing: he had made Mathias angry enough that the latter told him never to text him again or he would "kill" him. That request would have been really frightening, if not for two things: One, Alberto woke up in Mathias's arms, and, feeling so warm, it almost made him forget the pain stabbing through his head. Two, Mathias couldn't possibly be serious. Alberto was convinced of his goodness just as he was convinced that Mathias secretly still longed for him.

He had woken in his arms!

Alberto wouldn't give up just yet; he had enough willpower left to spare for one more attempt. What he would do instead is apologise for causing trouble, then dig around for answers, and if nothing worked, he'd just stick his hand down Mathias's trousers again, where he was sure to get an explicit reaction. And if Mathias got mad, Alberto would put the blame on him. *You shouldn't have held me that night. No, earlier than that: you shouldn't have said I was amazing. Wait, perhaps even earlier than that: you shouldn't have said you wanted to put it in when you invited me over that one time. In fact, let's go back to the beginning. You shouldn't have kissed me. You kissed me, you started it. You started it!*

Alberto had no cuticles left by the time classes were over. He stalked Zak, knowing his loud boyfriend wouldn't be far — and Mathias by association. He wanted to catch Mathias alone before he could leave for his football game. Alberto kept his eyes on the happy, carefree, *Friendship is Magic* group led by Eric as he waited for the break to end, which happened just as Van Bergen showed up to terrorise them. Things would have been easier if Kayvin hadn't bumped into Alberto on his way into the building. The sight of him brought unpleasant memories, and Alberto had to briefly turn away to collect himself. When he looked up again, the entire group had vanished into thin air.

Alberto searched for Mathias everywhere. In the lavatories, the cafeteria, the detention room, even the library. Worse, he couldn't even find Zak and the others. Desperate after almost an hour, he retraced his steps to the library and found Zak and Eric *inspecting the carpet* in the tech section, but still no sign of Mathias. With only a few minutes left before the five-p.m. bell, Alberto forced himself to stay calm and think. Mathias couldn't possibly have hidden in the infirmary, could he? If he had, then for sure, it meant there was still a chance between them.

Alberto bolted along one deserted corridor after another, his heart beating fast in his chest. Not bothering to take out his key, he slammed his hand on the handle and felt it open immediately. He came face-to-face with Mathias, who was swivelling in Sana's chair, the old thing squeaking under the strain. Alberto's heart lurched in triumph. Mathias, however, didn't seem happy to see him; he jumped to his feet, causing the chair to roll back and knock into the file cabinet behind him.

"Why are you here?" he asked, his face white.

"Same reason as you, I suppose," Alberto said without thinking.

"Me? I have a… I have a game to get to." Mathias checked his phone. "Right now, actually."

Picking up his duffel bag, he walked around Alberto and stormed out. Alberto ran after him, then retraced his steps to lock Sana's office before racing back. The bell rang just as Mathias was stepping out into the playground. Alberto went after him.

"Could you stop for a second?" he asked, panting. For now, they were alone out here, but it wouldn't last. "I wanted to talk about last weekend."

Mathias shook his head and tore toward the front gate. "Nothing to talk about."

"Wait!" Alberto gripped his sleeve. "I just… I wanted to thank you for helping me, that's all."

That wasn't all, but that had the merit of making Mathias slow his pace, even meeting Alberto's eyes — briefly. "You don't need to thank me for that."

"I do. I really appreciated your help, you know."

And the hug. I really appreciated the hug. How about you hug me right now? Urgency made Alberto feel feverish. He halted and watched as Mathias struggled to open the front gate.

"I really have to go," Mathias said, yanking the handle without method. "I… really… can't… What's with this fucking gate…? I can't lose this game!"

Alberto walked up to the gate and unlocked it for him. "I know, I know."

"What do you know?" Mathias grumbled, pushing past him.

Mathias was too fast, and Alberto was too slow. With the way it was now, he'd never be able to catch up to him. Alberto's shoulders sank. "I used to play football too, you know," he said in a small voice.

At the sound of his words, not only did Mathias stop, but he turned around, his eyes wide. "What?"

"I know." Alberto quietly closed the gate and leaned against it. "Unbelievable."

Mathias gawked at him. "I don't believe you."

No surprise there. Mathias never believed him.

"It's true."

"Which position?"

Alberto hesitated.

"Which position, Alberto?"

"Goalkeeper."

Mathias's eyes grew even rounder. "No way."

"*Way, way,*" Alberto said softly.

Mathias's lip twitched. He approached Alberto as though he wasn't sure it was really him. "You—Were you any good?"

Alberto gave a dry laugh. "I was terrible. I spent most of the time on the bench. I was afraid of the ball, you see. So, not so good for a goalkeeper."

"Then why did you play football?"

"My dad was really into it. He even tried to train me personally."

"Really?" Mathias sounded excited now. "Wait! Was your dad a football player? I mean, a pro, like Eric?"

"Not at all. He's just one of those people who really loves football. The sort that never misses a game involving their favourite team."

"I see…" Mathias's expression turned thoughtful. "That's too bad you didn't like it, then."

"Oh, yes. And he tried so hard, too! He used to—" Alberto's voice suddenly cracked. He held up a finger as he cleared his throat. "He used to blow his whistle and shoot penalties at me. I just froze every time. Got hit by so many balls, you'd think I'd have gotten better. But no, I was so hopeless. And he was…" Alberto cleared his throat again, "… he was disappointed."

"When was that?" Mathias checked his surroundings before he took another step toward him. "How old were you?"

"I was nine."

"So, what happened, then? Did you quit?"

"One day, Papà finally said I could stay home with Mamma from then on. It was a relief."

In fact, he said Alberto would get to stay home with his whore of a mother and he wouldn't embarrass him anymore. But Alberto didn't want to repeat that because, despite all the respect he had for whores, he didn't feel like upsetting his mother.

Mathias was observing him with a strange expression. Perhaps it was because Alberto had confessed to something so ridiculous out of nowhere, or because of the names he used. None of this mattered. Alberto didn't want to give him time to think or to speak, not before he'd say his piece.

"Anyway, I'm so sorry about last weekend…"

Mathias dug his hands into his pockets. "I told you it was fine."

"But you were so angry—"

"Oh, come on—"

"See? You're still angry."

"Not you—Shit!"

Something behind Alberto had caused Mathias's complexion to turn ashen. Alberto spun around and saw a black, elongated van-type vehicle coming to a stop before them. The windows were tinted, but when the one on the passenger slid open, he recognised Eric, and his mouth fell open.

"What are you doing, Matt?" Eric stuck his head out of the window. "We were looking for you everywhere. We have to go, now!"

Mathias looked completely frozen with his bag in his hand. "You… weren't we supposed to go by train?"

"Problem on the line. But look, I found us a ride!"

The driver's door also opened, revealing the headmaster. He

stepped out of the car and impatiently rapped his knuckles on the roof. "Go on then! Get in."

He was clearly addressing the two of them. After giving Alberto a panicked look, Mathias finally seized the handle and opened the door to the seat behind Eric. Alberto caught a glimpse of Zak waving at him from the inside.

"You too," Van Bergen said to Alberto. "Get in. Quick!"

Alberto shook his head. "I'm not getting into your…" He gave the massive trunk a wary look. "… whatever this is."

Van Bergen gasped in outrage. "Don't listen to him, girl," he said, caressing the roof of his beastly car. He shot Alberto a glare. "Suit yourself, then! But you won't make it to the game."

"I don't even want to go to the g——"

"Just get him in here!" Eric yelled from inside.

Zak heard him and pounced out of the car. Before Alberto could even protest, he was dragged inside. Alberto ended up sand-wiched between a chirpy Zak and a Mathias who looked like he was being taken to his place of execution.

"Sorry for yelling," Eric said, turning around. "I just can't be late for a game. It's a game. It's important."

"It's very important," Van Bergen agreed, clicking his seatbelt into place and checking everyone in the back was doing the same. "Don't think I go driving children around all the time. You need to win. And you'll be on time, don't worry."

"Are you sure?"

"Of course, I'm driving."

Mathias ostensibly cleared his throat. "Just… remember who our parents are."

Van Bergen gave Mathias a cold look in the mirror. "Is my mother here? Because I sense some hostility in the back."

Mathias returned his glare tenfold. "Drive carefully, okay?" To Alberto's surprise, the headmaster started the car without another word.

Thus began the longest car ride of Alberto's life. The worst parts of Eric seemed awakened by the mere action of being on the road. He was chatty, jumpy, and so loud. Soon enough, Alberto wanted to jump out of the car, despite being on the *periph**. Zak first attempted to soothe his boyfriend, probably worried the headmaster would kill him. But to Alberto's great misery, Van Bergen actually seemed entertained by him until Eric asked, "Are you married, headmaster?" while rummaging through his glove compartment.

Alberto felt everyone else tense in the car. No doubt, no one had ever dared ask Mr Van Bergen such an intimate question. The headmaster also thought it was odd, because he asked, "Why?" in a dubious tone.

Eric shrugged innocently. "You do wear a ring…"

Van Bergen glanced down at his hand and smiled. "I am happily, happily married."

Eric turned around to flash Zak a wink, who hissed at him to behave. "So, how's Mrs Van Bergen?" he asked slyly.

Van Bergen snorted. "What's your point, kid?"

Zak tried to stop Eric by waving his hands so fast, they became blurry, but his boyfriend ignored him, saying, "You see, I was thinking you might be gay a bit. But gay marriage isn't allowed in France." Eric turned to Zak again. "I *know* that."

Zak hid his face behind his hands, while on Alberto's right, Mathias let out a pained sigh. Alberto kept his eyes on Mr Van Bergen, who frowned as he abruptly changed lanes.

"What gave me away? My dazzling beauty, my excellent wardrobe, or did I leave my private invitations to a certain nightclub lying around in my office again?"

"So, you *are* gay?"

The headmaster gave a slight nod.

"I knew it!" Eric whipped a CD out of the glove compartment. "No straight man would have Najoua Belyzel's album, you know it!"

The headmaster erupted in laughter. "'Gabriel' is a classic, come on!"

"Alberto!" Eric said, suddenly excited. "Alberto, buddy! Isn't your middle name Gabriel?"

---

* France's busiest road, circling the city of Paris.

Alberto squinted in distaste at being called *buddy* and haughtily clicked his tongue. "I will forever regret the fact that you found my old ID. Forever." He felt Mathias flinch at his side and gave him a curious look, but Mathias was determined to keep his eyes on the side of the road.

Just as they were exiting the *periph*, Eric started singing his lungs out, screaming "Gabriel, Ga-bri-el!" for no reason. He was so horrible, Alberto feared the windows would burst in protest. The headmaster seemed to agree. His face splitting into a grimace, he rolled open his window.

"Give it here, I'll show you how it's done," he said, slapping Eric's hand away and putting the album into the player himself, selecting the right track by memory. "This is such an awful song, I love it."

A truly god-awful song started playing, causing Alberto much distress. Eric whooped in delight, and Zak was giggling maniacally, making Alberto feel completely out of place. As for Van Bergen, he was beaming. "Let's do this," he said. "Follow my lead."

Eric joined in the song with the headmaster. Both their French were impeccable, but in terms of singing skills, the headmaster was a lot better than the student. Meanwhile, Zak was bobbing his head up and down in rhythm, a smile on his face. Alberto discreetly checked out for Mathias's reaction. He looked miserable, which reassured Alberto a bit. He might never fit in with this merry-go-happy crowd, but at least he wasn't alone.

Van Bergen stopped Eric after the first chorus. "Sorry, I had to. Do the world a favour and stick to football, okay?"

Eric twisted his neck to give Zak a wounded look, and his boyfriend blew him a kiss from the backseat, which returned the fire to his eyes. "I'm gonna wipe the floor with them tonight. I can feel it. I feel really good. I'm gonna show you, Zak."

"Be gentle!" Van Bergen said. "The kids at the American High School are amateurs."

Eric bounced on his seat. "I. Don't. Like. To. Be. Gentle!"

"Don't I know it," Zak muttered.

Alberto actually snorted, surprising Zak — and himself — and Van Bergen slammed his hand on the klaxon. "Hey-oh!"

"Not even true!" Eric protested. "He's bullying me, headmaster. He does that all the time. I'm perfectly gentle — with *him*."

Zak stuck out his tongue, and that animal actually made a grab at it, but his trained boyfriend swiftly shut his mouth and withdrew to a safe distance from his fingers. Alberto skewered Eric with a glare, but the other shrugged it off with a laugh.

"Okay, let's try again," Van Bergen said. "Everyone, sing. You too, Rodin."

At the sound of Mathias's surname, a wave of desire rippled through Alberto. The song started again, and this time, Zak was singing, too. Alberto took advantage of the chaos of this new reiteration and covered Mathias's hand with his own, hoping to feel him squeeze back. Instead, Mathias jerked away as though Alberto had pricked him with a needle.

"Please let me out!" he said, shaking the handle.

Everyone inside turned their attention to him.

"Stop." Van Bergen snapped his fingers. "You, stop him."

Eric didn't even turn around. "Stop it, best buddy. We're on the freeway. You'll die if you jump out of the car."

"I choose death," Mathias said, his face red.

Alberto's brows knitted, and he returned his hands to his lap.

"Hang on." Van Bergen pressed the child-lock button. "Don't do anything stupid. Then, who will be the goalkeeper? Alberto?" He started laughing, joined by Eric and — to Alberto's dismay — even by Zak. "No, but seriously. Let go of that handle, or you'll end up in the cage."

Mathias immediately stopped fidgeting, and he rested his head on the window instead. After a few seconds, he closed his eyes and let out a sigh. Alberto didn't know what to think, but he started having a bad feeling about the whole situation. It was the impromptu karaoke that was causing Mathias to overreact, wasn't it? Alberto wondered, his right hand itching to give it another go.

Next to him, Zak shivered and tugged at his sleeve. "Look, there really is a cage…"

Alberto glanced over his shoulder. There was indeed a cage in the back, and he was almost certain it could fit someone like Zak.

Alberto blinked at it, then inspected the cabin of the vehicle before he turned around and leaned into Zak's space.

"It's a hearse."

"Huh?"

"The car, Zak. It's a hearse."

Zak gave him a look of disbelief. "How do you know?"

"I'm sitting where the coffin normally goes. See this? This seat was added later."

Alberto found himself in the place of the dead again. How entertaining! He let out a chuckle. Mathias gave him a quick glance before turning his gaze back to the road. Now shocked, Zak seemed about to ask the headmaster why he was driving a hearse, but Van Bergen increased the volume of the music and said, "Let's go again. Five, six, seven, eight—"

Zak forgot about his question and joined in the singing again. Alberto noticed Mathias's knuckles had turned white around the handle of the door. His expression carried a discomfort, a pain so intense that it shot right through Alberto's own heart.

How could he have been so selfish? Mathias was practically shaking next to him. It wasn't the song, it was him! *He* was making him physically ill.

Mathias didn't want Alberto in his life at all. Of course, he went and saved him the other day; he was that good a guy. But all this time he had tried to tell Alberto he no longer wanted to be near him, and Alberto did everything but actually listen to him.

Surrounded by Mathias's friends, whose happiness now felt like an insurmountable mountain, Alberto had an epiphany.

22

VICTORS

V.B. DIDN'T LIE. He dropped them off at the training field with plenty of time to spare and extracted himself from his vehicle under the mocking gaze of the American High School of Paris's bite-size headmaster. Mathias didn't care for politics and hurried after Eric toward the changing rooms, Zak and Alberto trailing behind them.

"Only players allowed beyond this point, I'm afraid," a bitter voice said as they were about to go in.

Mathias saw a man standing against the wall in the corner. Dressed in an expensive-looking but ill-fitted suit, he looked so cross and stuck up, he reminded him immediately of Kayvin. Eric heard him and scoffed, but he nonetheless turned to Zak and told him to find himself a good seat outside.

"It's not good for you to be in the changing rooms anyway," he said, flashing Mathias a wink.

Inside, Kayvin was as nervous as could be imagined. The last time Colette played against this "rival" school, Eric was too upset over his impossible crush on Zak, and they had lost 2 to 1. Kayvin had never gotten over it. This time, Eric was so confident, Mathias was almost hoping Zak would break his heart again. There was only so much happy he could take at the moment.

The car ride had been hell. Singing stupid songs while driving was one of Mathias's mother's favorite things, so the act in itself felt a bit like someone was jabbing at his heart with a knife. But having Alberto so close to him, and flirting—he touched his fucking hand!—was even worse. Already, his anxious apology had been too much to bear. Mathias didn't want Alberto to run after him, and he definitely didn't want him to feel sorry. He needed him to be a cold monster right now. He needed him to return to his other lovers, smash whatever was left between them to pieces, and disappear from his life altogether.

Mathias couldn't wait to get onto the pitch. His blood had turned to lava in his veins. The American High School of Paris's team was toast.

The sky had turned dark as they were getting ready, but the training field was brightly lit from all sides. The same man was on the pitch when Mathias and the rest of the team trotted out in their white and blue colors. Though he was accompanied by the headmaster of the AHSOP—and its many coaches—he stood out because of the disdainful way he was eyeing the Colette team. Even Kayvin was uncomfortable; blushing up to his ears, he ran straight for the center of the field, followed by his friends. The man then separated from the group and walked up to Eric.

"Been sold to Lyon, haven't you?"

Eric was busy waving at Zak sitting in the bleachers and gave the man a wary look. "Yes?"

Mathias was about to drag Eric away, but V.B. stomped toward them just as the man turned his attention to him, saying, "And here's the Rodin kid." Mathias's eyebrows jumped up to his hairline. The man squinted at him, disgust plain on his face. "He has his mother's eyes."

V.B. let out a booming laugh. "Blaise, I see you're dying to get your arse kicked again."

"You wish," the other retorted. "I donated enough to hire a new coach specifically to destroy your loser team this year."

"Did you?" V.B.'s eyes lit up. "But again, you always loved wasting money."

"Let's go…" Mathias said, pulling Eric away.

"Who's that guy?" his friend asked, a slight frown on his face. "How does he know your mother?"

"No idea. I don't know every goddamn asshole in town, Eric."

Kayvin blew into his whistle, cutting their conversation short. "You two, come here, I need a few words. We can't afford to lose this game."

He barked at his teammates for a couple of minutes while glaring at the opposite team. Mathias wasn't afraid of the AHSOP. They looked like regular seniors who already knew they were about to lose the game. One look at Eric would be enough to convince anyone; he practically had lightning bolts shooting out of his ass.

"How does my butt look today?" he asked when he caught Mathias looking at it.

"What? Ah, sorry. Looks fine, Eric."

"Thanks, buddy." Eric lowered his voice, "Zak's watching, I gotta give him a good show."

Mathias shuddered to think Alberto was sitting up there too, probably not staring at his ass but worse: at the side of his face. The nightmare continued. And speaking of, Mathias thought of something and, turning to Eric, he asked in an innocent tone, "How come you had that guy's ID?"

"Who?"

"Alberto."

Don't think I didn't hear your little conversation in the car. Alberto's outdated ID had not left Mathias's backpack since he'd found it on the floor of his bedroom during the Christmas holidays and decided it would be safer in his possession than back in Alberto's hands. And who could blame him? The picture above Alberto's Neapolitan address showed him at pure *girafon* stage, too cute to behold—definitely too adorable to be seen by anyone else.

"Oh, that," Eric said, shrugging. "I found it on the floor in class. No big deal."

"Which class?"

"You know, I can't remember." Eric pointed at the sky. "What do you think? Does it look like rain?"

Mathias reluctantly turned his gaze toward the clouds. "It's not freezing, at least. It might drizzle, but it should be fine… as long as it doesn't get worse."

But as Alberto said once, things could always get worse. Xavier detached himself from Kayvin and went to stick himself to him and Eric again. "So… Elodie likes you, right?" he asked, jumping up and down to warm up.

"Yes…" Mathias said coldly. "Apparently so."

"And you said no."

Mathias took a deep breath. "Yep."

"You don't like her?"

"It's not that. I just don't feel like dating her."

"But everybody wants to date Elodie." Xavier scratched the side of his face. "Did you know Kayvin really likes her, but she doesn't like him?"

"I didn't know, but I can't say I'm surprised."

"So, what is it about her that you don't like exactly?"

Mathias's hands balled into fists. "What the fuck do you want from me?"

"Nothing, I just…" Xavier stood before him looking like an idiot who'd just found out the Earth wasn't flat after all. "Mathias, do you like girls?"

"Hey!" Eric suddenly jumped right between them. "Rude, Xavier, rude!"

Xavier shrunk back. "I'm sorry for being rude," he said, causing Eric's mouth to fall open in shock. "But it's true. I've never seen you look at a girl, no matter how pretty she is. I thought at first it was a secret method to get them obsessed with you. Because it works! Elodie likes you, and she's not the only one. Melissa, even *Camille*, everyone calls you hot and mysterious. And Joy said you were the best-looking guy at school—after Alberto, of course."

"Really?" Eric pouted. "She said that?"

"So what?" Mathias asked, defiant. "What's your point?"

Xavier's mouth twisted. "If you don't like girls… does it mean that—"

"Shut up right this instant."

Being asked about his sexuality by a clueless *bisaster* was getting a bit much for Mathias today, but he was resolved to keep his hands to himself, unless it was to use them to stop the ball. No more punching people, no matter how annoying they were. And no more digging his fingers into Alberto's flesh—or any other part— anymore. He was done, done, done!

"Correct me if I'm wrong," he said through gritted teeth, "but my love life's none of your business."

"Love?" Xavier guffawed. "I'm talking about sex."

"There's no difference, asshole!"

Mathias whirled around and saw Alberto staring down at him. *Oh no. Don't look. Don't look. Don't think.* Between facing Alberto or Xavier… he'd take Xavier any day. Mathias looked at his watch: the game would start in another minute or two, so at least it would free him from this conversation.

"Mathias, seriously…" Xavier's face split into an awkward grin. "I wasn't trying to piss you off. In fact, I'm really impressed!"

"Why?" Mathias asked, suspicious.

"Because! Mother always says boys our age only think with our…" Xavier lowered his voice. "… penises."

Mathias shook his head. "Nope. Uh-uh, that's it!"

"I mean, look at Eric."

"Hey!" Eric clutched his chest.

"But you… you'd prove her wrong."

Eric stomped his foot. "Hey!"

"That's…" Mathias scoffed. "That's… bullshit."

He turned his back to the both of them. In truth, he was thinking about his penis right now. He was thinking of how beautiful Alberto was when he barged into the infirmary all disheveled earlier, and he was thinking of his adorable face when he realized he was sitting in a hearse. And although Mathias wasn't hard right now, he was already thinking of how it would feel to make out with Alberto once they'd won the game, and how aroused he'd be then. Every time he thought too much of Alberto, his penis took over.

So, really, Xavier was wrong, and Mathias wasn't so special after all. It's true his penis had never poked its head much before. It was a pretty tame penis, compared to other guys, he could admit it. It took some convincing to get to work, as Daphnée had complained about. But as Alberto said, Mathias's mother was really sick and then really dead, therefore, there wasn't much time to think about waving his penis around.

Mathias had truly never worried about his penis before; he had not even questioned the mechanics of his penis at all. He'd had plenty of sex after his mom's death, plenty of blurry encounters in the dark. And his penis had worked just fine then. Not great, just fine. Adequate performance for what it was: a mindless booze-fueled intercourse. It's only when Alberto showed up that his penis got a little too enthusiastic, dragging Mathias into this hell he was struggling to get out of.

Mathias suddenly realized he'd been saying penis a lot—enough for a lifetime. He got angrier at Xavier and simply walked off toward his goal, his face hot.

"Boys, girls, have you made your choice?" Alberto had asked once, taunting him. It finally occurred to Mathias that he had never cared about either.

If he really was as he feared, only attracted to long-legged Italians with demonic lips, he'd better give up on dating altogether for the rest of his life. He tried to think about that; he tried to scare himself with such thoughts, but a life without dating didn't seem scary at all to him. The only things that ever frightened Mathias were cancerous cells. The ones that stole his mom from him and the ones that had grown over his heart and his stomach, the ones he sometimes called Alberto.

Kayvin called everyone to gather around him one last time, saving him from his thoughts. "I can't stress this enough," he said, his expression murderous. "We have to win."

"Okay!" Eric said, squeezing Mathias against him for no reason.

Kayvin gave the two of them a quick look. "If you don't want to do it for me, then do it for yourselves."

Eric cocked an eyebrow. "Uh, okay?"

"Eric." Kayvin jerked his chin toward the rude man in the ill-fitted suit from earlier. "You see that guy? He's on the board of the AHSOP."

"Oh?"

"He said your boyfriend was ugly."

Mathias thought Eric would blow a fuse, but after a moment of confusion, he exploded in laughter instead. "No need to motivate me, Kayvin!" he said, his face glowing. "First, this is clearly a lie! I never pay attention to lies, and neither should you. Second, Zak is in the stands, and Mathias is in the goal. There's no way we can lose this."

"Good," Kayvin said, turning to Mathias, "because he also said Matt's mother was the worst person he'd ever met."

Silence fell over the team. Charles-Henry became as white as his socks, and Eric's arm turned rigid around Mathias's shoulder.

"Wow…" Mathias murmured, feeling the eyes of his team-mates on him. "That guy really did know my mother." He let out a laugh. "She *was* the fucking worst."

Chances were they went to school together, and she beat his ass at some point. Stupid guys didn't like being beaten by short girls in short skirts. Or at least, that's what Mathias's mother had told him.

A loud sigh of relief escaped Xavier's lips. Kayvin looked at a complete loss, but at least he didn't add another word and released them to their positions.

"Don't look up," Eric said as Mathias set off toward his goalpost.

"What do you mean?"

"I'm just saying don't look up." Eric smiled. "Whenever I see Zak's face up there, I get distracted."

Mathias frowned. "And why would I be looking at Zak's face, exactly?"

"Never mind, never mind," Eric said, rubbing the back of his head. He pointed at the goal. "Don't let anything in!"

"I never do," Mathias grumbled, and he punched his own palm.

Mathias recalled what Alberto told him earlier, how his father had tried to turn him into a good goalkeeper. It was a shame it didn't work for him, because Mathias was also trained by his parents, and it had worked out well for him. His mother used to ask his father to play the role of a goalkeeper. She would shoot penalties at him, and he would let them through most of the time, causing her to roar in laughter and tell Mathias, "Do the opposite of what your father does, and you'll do just fine." Mathias's father might have looked like a powerless victim at first, but when Mathias asked him if he was okay with all that, he replied, "Have you seen her smile? Of course I'm okay with that! Whenever the one you love asks you for something, you better do your best to give them what they need." Mathias decided his father wasn't a bad goal-keeper after all, and after learning from both of his parents, he had become somewhat skilled himself.

Three times, the ball came his way. Not once did it get in.

Xavier might have been an idiot and a *damn slut*, but he was a great defender. Charles-Henry was a solid midfielder, and Kayvin, for the first time, was being a real team player. As for Eric, he was a dumbass in love, but he was, after all, one of the brightest hopes of his division at the ***.

He scored eight times that day.

Even Mathias was giddy when the referee's whistle blew to announce the end of the game. Final score: 11–0. Eric was used to accolades and dodged V.B.'s attentions to tear down the pitch toward the changing rooms, bragging Zak would probably reward him for *each* goal. Mathias didn't expect the same treatment from anyone, so he took his time after the game. He genially shook every AHSOP player's hand, comforted their downtrodden goalkeeper, and grinned arrogantly at the man who had known his mother. When Kayvin also walked over, his own hand extended, Mathias shook it, albeit a bit roughly.

"Glad you were a team player today, Rodin," Kayvin said haughtily.

"I could say the same about you." Mathias noticed the furious expression of the man in the suit and shook his head. "I don't know who that guy is, but he really isn't happy about our score."

"He's my father," Kayvin said, and he walked off at a fast pace, leaving Mathias momentarily speechless in the middle of the pitch.

When he finally made it back to the changing rooms, Mathias was the last one in. It was V.B.'s fault. That boring old man was too proud to show off Mathias's skills, and Kayvin's father looked like he would have loved to punch him—if only that maniac wasn't so freakishly big. Eric got out just as Mathias was coming in.

"Oh, come on, Matt! Hurry! Zak and I want to celebrate."

"Then go! Why are you waiting for me? I can get home on my own."

"I guess…" Eric said. "Will you drive back with Mr Van Bergen?"

"I don't know…" Mathias hesitated.

"Alberto left already," Eric said briskly. "Zak said he didn't even wait for the end of the game."

A part of Mathias was relieved to hear that, but a small part only. Mathias's best save had happened only minutes before the end, and Alberto had missed it. Not that it would have changed anything, but… too bad.

When Mathias got out of the showers, the changing rooms were already empty. He'd only gotten around to putting on his underwear when he heard a door squeak open on the side. He jumped to his feet with his sneaker in his hand, ready to blast the first motherfucker daring to pull a prank on him.

But it wasn't that hack of a headmaster. Instead, it was a scary demon. Alberto slipped out of the storage cupboard he had been hiding in and smacked his lips at Mathias's appearance, his dry laughter reverberating across the walls.

"You win!" he said, his eyes flashing with arrogance.

There he was, the unfeeling monster Mathias needed to see. He had been hiding here this entire time, waiting for the right moment to hurt him. And he did. The sight of him felt like a punch in the gut. Mathias rushed to him, his fingers curling around his arms. In an instant, Alberto was once again pressed up against a wall, with Mathias glaring at him.

Like old times. *Almost*.

"Can't you leave me alone?" Mathias heard the note of despair in his voice and prayed Alberto didn't interpret it as such. "Please, will you leave me the fuck alone?!" Wanting to scare Alberto away once and for all, he tightened his grip around his arms.

Alberto tilted his head and blinked at him. His eyes were so big, he reminded Mathias of the boy in the pictures, the ones left to gather dust in the basement.

His resolve already falling apart, Mathias gave him a desperate shake. "Aren't you scared? Aren't you tired already?"

Alberto slowly shook his head. "I know you won't hurt me. Not really."

Mathias gave up. His fingers relaxed around Alberto's arms, and his head fell upon his shoulder. He spoke in a whisper, "Why can't you leave me alone?"

For a moment, it seemed like Alberto was smelling the top of his head, before he said, "Listen." His voice was soft, too soft for Mathias. "I have a proposition."

Mathias took his time before he hesitantly stepped away from him. "What is it?"

"Sleep with me one last time," Alberto said, holding his gaze. "I want one last round with my best fuck." His shoulder lifted in a half-shrug. "And I promise, you'll never hear from me again."

Mathias's heart had started beating furiously in his chest. "I don't think it's a good idea."

"You owe me, right?" Alberto said, his eyes flickering. "For that time you pushed me into the trash. You owe me."

"Didn't…" Mathias coughed in his fist. Guilt had formed a lump in his throat, choking him. "Didn't I help you the other night?"

"I didn't ask for your help that night." Alberto folded his arms over his chest. "You said you owed me, and I want to collect. Do you accept or not?"

Mathias hung his head. There was truth in Alberto's words. He owed him for throwing him into the trash, and more: for letting Kayvin humiliate him, for letting his stepfather put his ugly hands on him, for being such a loser, his mother would be ashamed of him if she could see him right now.

"When?" he asked, defeated.

23

GOODBYE

ALBERTO KNOCKED on the door three times. While he waited, he ran both hands through his hair, then he pushed them into the pockets of the thick black hoodie he was wearing, the one Mathias lent him at the museum so many weeks ago.

Mathias opened the door, dressed in the same outfit as always, and Alberto almost smiled. The sight of him had always been a relief.

"Do you want anything to drink?" Mathias offered as Alberto was kicking off his shoes. "Or to eat?"

He shook his head. "No, thank you."

There was a brief silence.

"Let's go to my room, then," Mathias said, leading the way.

Mathias's bedroom was messy. Only the tall lamp was switched on, revealing several culinary manuals scattered over the desk, dirty clothes littering the floor, and piles of clean ones that needed to be put away. The bed alone was neatly made.

"Are you planning a dinner party?" Alberto asked, pointing at the desk.

"Oh, that?" Mathias grimaced and started tidying up. "No. My culinary school entrance exam is next week."

Alberto was relieved. No dinner dates with Elodie or whoever else, then. Just because they were about to part ways didn't mean

Alberto would ever welcome the sight of Mathias holding someone else's hand. With any luck, he'd remain single until the summer. Then, he'd go to his new school to learn fifty ways to cook a chicken, and they'd never even lay eyes on each other again. With any luck.

Tonight was the beginning of the winter holidays*. Alberto believed the two-week break would be enough to wean himself from Mathias. That's why he had picked today to say goodbye.

"Sit down, if you want." Mathias said, gesturing toward the bed.

Alberto shed the black hoodie and did as he was told. Since when were they so formal with one another? Alberto silently prayed Mathias was still the same animal in bed or even their last chapter would turn into another disappointment.

"Are you going to join me?" he asked, his face growing hot.

"Sure."

Mathias approached in slow steps. Within seconds, they were both sitting at the edge of the bed, facing the wardrobe, their hands so close they almost touched, but their gazes were turned in opposite directions.

It didn't feel like their last time at all, but the opposite. They were awkward around each other, like first timers hoping sex would be half as good as people say and not half as painful.

"Here we are," Mathias said.

He looked wretched, sitting there with his head down. Alberto wondered if, between the culinary test, the mock exams, and the football game, Mathias had been stretching himself a little too thin. There was a time Alberto would have known what to do to relax the knot between his brows, but today, he was the one adding to his stress. It was plain on Mathias's face: he was anxious around him, and he was no doubt eager to be done with it.

Silver lining: at least he would have one less worry after tonight. As much as Alberto loathed parting from him, being a source of

---

* In France, the winter holidays usually take place in February (and can end in March, depending on the region). They are not to be confused with the Christmas holidays, which occur from the end of December to the beginning of January.

torment in his life was simply unacceptable. Since that car ride three days ago, when Alberto had realised he was the one making Mathias's life difficult, he had promised himself to break the leash, to open the cage. After all the good he did for him, Mathias deserved to be free.

"Here we are…" Alberto gave a brief nod. "I'm a little relieved, to be honest."

Mathias fidgeted on the bed. "You are?"

"Yeah. A little."

Not much, to be fair. The relief came from the fact he wouldn't have to keep hoping like a fool. The rest was all pain, but he could deal with pain better than hope.

"Yeah…" Mathias's expression twisted, then softened. "Me too."

Another silence stretched between them. Alberto wished they'd start fucking already. What else were they going to do? They were already bad with words, and Alberto was at his worst lately. It would be wise to keep his mouth occupied before he lost control of it.

"Why do you look so down?" Mathias's fingers twitched near Alberto's. "Don't tell me Alberto Gazza is going to miss me."

Alberto bit back the urge to curse him and stuck out his chin. "Even if I did… with my memory, you'll be forgotten in two weeks."

Mathias chuckled. "I believe you."

Alberto mentally cursed him anyway. *Now you believe me? You bastard!*

When, his elbows on his thighs, Mathias leaned forward and let out a long sigh, Alberto did a quick scan around the room. He wanted to remember how it looked, for posterity. His eyes fell on the picture on the nightstand. Arms wound tightly around her boy, Mathias's mother was laughing in his face. Alberto shivered and looked away.

"So… should we start, or?" Mathias asked, straightening up.

Alberto snorted. "How about foreplay?"

"Foreplay?"

"Yes, so it doesn't look too…" *Final.* "… Transactional."

"You mean, setting the mood?"

"Something like that."

"I don't have anything to fight about."

Alberto's fingers curled around his knees. "Did we really fight so much?" It had never felt that way to him…

Mathias didn't reply.

Fine, Alberto thought. He'd lead the way. Mathias might not want him in his life any longer, but Alberto wouldn't let him ruin their last time together by being awkward about it.

"Come on…" He edged closer until they were shoulder to shoulder. "Humour me a little."

"Okay," Mathias said to the wall. "Sure."

His little finger twitched again and accidentally brushed against Alberto's, who felt it *everywhere.* His scalp was still tingling when he leaned to Mathias's ear and whispered, "Tell me something you've never told anybody."

Mathias glanced at him. "That's your idea of foreplay?"

Alberto shrugged. *No, I just want to know your secret, before we say goodbye. Tell me why you picked me, for instance. Why me if you disliked me so much, if you despise me still? Or please, tell me you are gay, or tell me you are bi, and I'll tell you something even better.*

"Weirdo…" Mathias said in a quiet tone. "Why would I do that?"

"Because I'm asking you to."

Mathias's lips tightened. Alberto thought he'd tell him off again, but Mathias scooted back and lay down on the bed instead. "I started having that dream again," he said, the left side of his face plunged in shadows.

Alberto didn't dare move. He remained seated, his back straight as an arrow as he waited for Mathias to speak again, but in his chest, his heart was drumming with anticipation.

"What dream?" he asked faintly.

"Dream of that corridor at the hospital… Dream of the last door on the right." Mathias drew a long breath. "That's where my mother was. I was so angry at her one time, I… I said some things, some things I shouldn't have..." He paused. "I'll never forget the look on her face... I knew then, I knew I had let her down.

"I went out after my outburst to calm down, and when I returned, she didn't hear me come in. She looked so small, sitting on her bed, hairless. She looked even smaller because of what I'd said."

Alberto finally threw a look over his shoulder. Mathias met his eyes and loudly cleared his throat. "I can't stop seeing her face in my dream. The pain I had caused... and for nothing... You see, I don't want to live through that again. That... that guilt. I don't want to..."

He stopped talking, perhaps expecting Alberto to say something. But the latter was frozen, torn between wonder and terror at the thought he was listening to Mathias for what was probably the last time. Suddenly, each of his words, however hurtful they were in essence, were coming out of his mouth sounding like a symphony.

Mathias waited, waited, then spoke again. "I can't spend the rest of my life beating myself up... I'll lose it, I'll turn bad." He covered his eyes with his hand. "I deserve better, I think... and so do you." He exhaled a long breath. "So do you."

"I know," Alberto said. "I understand." He slipped his hand over Mathias's ankle. Mathias's guilt, he could understand it better than anyone. Alberto felt guilty all the time. Not for the same reasons as Mathias, of course. Alberto felt no guilt at being queer, nor would he ever feel guilty for not wanting to waste time on someone who didn't deserve it. His guilt ran deeper. Looking like this, for example. Looking like this and not being more grateful for it. And of course, being here. Being here and not being better at it, as people expected him to be. And the two were linked, constantly feeding into each other, making him feel even guiltier. So, yeah, he got it. He squeezed Mathias's ankle. He got it.

Mathias's leg jerked; he abruptly sat up. "Do you... Do you need help?"

Alberto blinked. "Help?"

"Do you need any help? At home?"

Help at home? Mathias wanted to ditch him, fine, but Alberto didn't need his pity. He huffed in distaste. "Why would I need your help?" Mathias shot him a look of confusion that threw him off guard. "No, thank you. I don't need your help at all."

That felt a lie too, but whatever. Mathias only believed what he wanted to believe anyway. In one sense, he was like the others. But that was another lie. Mathias was never like the others. He was the first to bother asking the real questions. Alberto did not know back then that those words had sealed his fate, just like that.

To answer his question, months later, the day of their parting… would it be right or wrong? Could Mathias be trusted in the end? If he could, wouldn't that make the parting worse?

Why bother? They were done. Alberto could both throw him a bone and satisfy that urge that had gnawed at him for weeks. *Look at me, Mathias, there's something I want to tell you. Something happened to me a long time ago. I saw the Plutonian shores. And though I made it back from the other side, a part of me still lingers over there, waiting. Waiting for me to return.*

"I dream of my mother, too," Alberto said, his voice barely more than a whisper. He lay down on the bed beside Mathias, who leaned on his elbow and stared into his face, his eyes both inquisitive and soft.

"You do?"

Alberto nodded. "I dream about this so often, it feels not like a dream, but a distant memory." His gaze turned unfocused as he recalled his dream. "I'm lying in a casket, at my own funeral. There's a crowd of people gathered around me, whispering, but I can't make out what they're saying. And then, my mother comes in. She leans over the casket, weeping. Her tears are so heavy, they roll like boulders down her cheeks. She starts howling and cursing the gods and everyone else for the loss of her *beautiful boy*, her nails gripping the edge of the casket, scraping the varnish. She keeps calling to me, calling me 'her beautiful boy', 'beautiful even in death.'" Alberto paused while his dream occurred in real time in his mind's eye, as clear as Mathias's ceiling above him. "All this time, she hasn't noticed my eyes are open, but they are. She doesn't hear me, and yet, I'm speaking. I tell her, *Look, I'm not dead, look at me! I'm not dead, I'm right here…* But she can't hear me. No one can hear me. Mamma is eventually dragged away from the casket, weeping for her *beautiful boy*." Alberto turned to Mathias with a sigh. "Dreams… They're weird, aren't they?"

Mathias was gaping at him, looking as stiff as a log. Alberto studied his expression and couldn't understand it. Not that it mattered anyway. Alberto didn't need to worry about how messed up he looked; he would never see him again after this. He forced his lips to curl into the semblance of a smile.

Mathias suddenly reached over and hooked his hand around his neck, pulling him forward until their lips met. Alberto briefly froze before relaxing in his grip, and when their tongues met, his heart leapt faintly in his chest.

So, that was it, then. Their final tryst had officially started. Talk about bizarre foreplay. But again, they were always weirdos, the two of them. Fighting and fucking, making out in infirmaries, in cemeteries… Always falling, but never landing. Until today.

Their kiss quickly deepened, turning frantic as usual, mouths devouring each other in retaliation for the words neither could say. When Mathias leaned back and bit into the flesh of his neck, tears seeped out the corners of Alberto's eyes, like rats fleeing a sinking ship. Holding back a sob, he hugged Mathias closer so he wouldn't notice. But Mathias had other things on his mind; his hands had already slithered under Alberto's jumper, who instinctively lifted his arms to assist him. Mathias blew over the bite mark he'd just left before he kissed it once, then again.

Within seconds, they were undressed, and within minutes, they were one again. Perhaps the fact that they knew this was the last time made it all the more special. Alberto felt lost during most of it. His head spinning, he relied on his touch more than his sight. Mathias led the way in the dark — *Mathias always leading in the dark…* Alberto shut his eyes. He was back on the carousel again, chained down to it for another ride. "Where am I?" he asked, his emotions in turmoil.

"You're with me," a voice replied — *Mathias's voice*. A kiss followed. "You're with me," it said again.

Alberto came. Of course he came. He was held in *his* arms again. Mathias followed shortly after. He was panting, his breath hot on his neck, and for a brief moment, Alberto wished he were crying. Tears streaked his own cheeks, and they had nothing to do with their intense bout of lovemaking, this time. It was distress, it was grief that struck him. Why? Why did they have to say goodbye? Alberto desperately clung to the sheets, terrified of the moment Mathias would slip out of him, and out of his life, forever.

"It hurts…" he choked out, overwhelmed by sadness. He bit into his lip to silence himself, late tears spilling out, burning a path down his temples.

Above him, Mathias's breath caught. He didn't kiss Alberto's neck, as was his habit when he pulled out. Instead, he hurriedly rolled off him and went to sit on the far end of the bed. In a moment of madness, Alberto reached out a hand toward him, but thankfully, Mathias was holding his head in his hands and didn't notice.

Sill stunned at his own words and actions, Alberto started cleaning himself up in silence. Mathias did the same with his eyes down. "Sorry," he said after a moment.

Alberto stared at his back in anguish. "Don't be sorry," he said. He added in a whisper, "I know you liked me… I liked you, too."

With a shake of the head, Mathias began putting on his clothes. "It's best if you leave now. My father will be here soon."

Alberto watched him, his ears buzzing. He felt as though Mathias's bed had become quicksand and was about to swallow him. He clumsily slid down to the floor and quickly gathered his clothes.

It took no time for Alberto to get dressed; he made sure his eyes were dry when he faced Mathias again.

"I guess this is goodbye, then."

Mathias grunted in response and stood up, his hands buried in his pockets.

Alberto thought of Mamma. Dignified, always. *Always*. He raised his chin. "Thank you for the bruises, Mathias. I'll cherish the last one." His hand was on the doorknob when he recalled something and chuckled.

"What?" Mathias said, somewhat meekly.

Alberto squarely met his eyes. "Anastasia."

Before new unwanted tears could smash his resolve, he walked out of the room, and of Mathias's flat, for good.

Outside, night had fallen, and it was raining again. *Good,* Alberto thought harshly. *Under the rain, no one can see you cry.* Shivering slightly, he took out his smokes and tried to light up, but it was windy outside Mathias's building, and he couldn't get his lighter to work. And why was it so cold? Perhaps he shouldn't have left Mathias's hoodie behind after all. To hell with it; it was over, over, over.

His arms wrapped around himself, Alberto set out toward *Rue de Sèvres,* but he didn't even make it halfway through Mathias's street when he heard him call his name. Whirling around, he lost balance and clung to a nearby gate. Mathias was running toward him, the black hoodie in his hands.

"Fuck you!" Alberto blurted out, the words spilling out before he even thought them.

Mathias skidded to a halt before him. "Okay." He looked miserable, at least. Good. GOOD. "It's just that you forgot this."

"It's yours, arsehole."

Mathias's handsome eyes flashed. "I know that, but it's fucking cold, and you're fucking standing there with no fucking clothes on again." He pressed the hoodie to Alberto's chest. "So take it."

"You take it!" Alberto pushed it back into his hands.

Something fell from the pocket and clattered to the sidewalk. It was Alberto's phone.

"Oh, shit," Mathias crouched and picked it up. "I didn't know it was in there."

Alberto retrieved his phone without a word. The screen was now cracked in three places. He glared at Mathias, who took a step back.

"Sorry, I didn't know."

"There's a lot you don't know, Mathias. Why don't you add that to the list?"

Mathias sighed and pushed the hoodie toward him again. "Please, just take it."

"I don't want it!" Alberto threw it back in his face.

"You stupid ass!" Mathias seized his wrist and tried to force his arm into the hoodie. Alberto struggled, and soon they were both entangled in it, pushing and shoving and hurling insults at each other, the rain pouring over them.

"Jesus…" Mathias panted, his face glistening. He had managed to force one arm into the sleeve of the garment, but it was the wrong one. "When did you become so fucking strong?"

"When did you become so fucking weak?"

"Oh, fuck you!"

Alberto let out a maniacal laugh. Mathias twisted both his wrists behind his back. "I'll show you," he grumbled, then he went, "Shit, shit, shit! It's my dad!"

Both boys instantly froze in the middle of the street. Mathias spun them around so they'd face the wall, and Alberto shrunk himself and hung his head, hoping that in the dark and the rain, Cyril wouldn't recognise them. The streetlights bathed the car in a warm glow as it drove down *Rue Rousselet*. Alberto threw a hesitant look over his shoulder. Indeed, Cyril paid them no attention at all; he was too busy chatting with the woman in the passenger seat.

Alberto's heart dropped to the bottom of his stomach. "It… it can't be…"

"That's her!" Mathias exclaimed by his ear. "That's your mo—"

"Mamma…"

The car drove past them and turned around the corner, leaving Alberto and Mathias standing like two fools in the middle of the street. Mathias released Alberto, and noticing he had no strength left in him at all, forced his arms into the hoodie. Alberto stared at him, slack-jawed. "You… you…"

"You saw them, right?" Mathias first appeared excited, but when he saw Alberto's face, his expression sagged. "Are you okay?" He leaned in and lightly touched his cheek.

"You were telling the truth? This whole time?"

Mathias's eyebrows shot up. "What? Of course I was! Did you think I was making this shit up all this time?"

Alberto clung to him. "Yes! Of course I did!" He spun around, the rain whipping his face. "It was all… it was all a ploy… It was a lie…"

"It's fine, calm down." Mathias gently shook him. "Calm down."

"No! This whole time… it was you… You sought me out…"

"Alberto?"

"You sought me out…"

At last, a great rip occurred inside of him. Overwhelmed by excruciating pain, Alberto took to his heels and fled.

Keepers

24

ANASTASIA

THE FIRST TIME Alberto watched a revenge flick, he was so mesmerised; he discovered something about himself: if the retaliation in the second half of the movie was satisfactory enough, there was no amount of abuse he couldn't stomach in the first half. *Catharsis*, he found out it was called.

Alberto was fond of that word. *Catharsis*.

He was robbed — he would say — several times, of his cathartic moment. When he woke from his coma, for example, he was told he could never go home. A few days later, he was on a train, and it was too late to seek answers, never mind revenge. No peace to be found there. Alberto had forever lost a part of himself, left behind in Mamma's room in the villa on the coast of Napoli, between her vanity table and the gilded mirror. More than blood and tears, he had forfeited his voice.

"I love you, Mamma," he whispered to the mirror. Alberto sat on a chair shaped like a throne in front of his mother's dressing table by the window. A different chair, a different table, and a different view. What about him? Was he still the same boy?

"Do you remember our dance, Tesoro?" Mamma had asked that day, the curtains swaying in rhythm with her long black locks.

He'd stared at her, transfixed. "Of course," he'd answered.

Mamma's wide smile had split the skies. "Yes? Let's put our costumes on."

It was almost a decade ago. Now sitting alone at her makeup station, Alberto opened every drawer and inspected their every corner, his head throbbing. Mamma wouldn't like to see him sneaking into her bedroom and going through her stuff. But so what? She wasn't here right now. Where was she again? Like that time at the beach… she was running away from him, and he was too small to catch up.

Alberto gritted his teeth. At the bottom of a drawer, he found her old sewing box. It used to contain thread and thimbles and colourful ribbons. Now it held a few treasures gathered throughout the years. Why didn't she tell him about Cyril Rodin? Why did she lie to him? Did she want to run away with him and leave him behind? There was no greater betrayal than the one inflicted by a mother. Her lie was pressing on him from all sides, filling his lungs with air he felt only invited more suffering inside.

Alberto flipped the treasure box open. Did Mamma also put him in storage with her other precious artefacts, beloved but safely tucked away? Ignoring the childish voice inside of him urging him not to do it, he searched through its contents, perhaps hoping to find a note explaining everything, perhaps hoping for another answer.

There was no note. No explanation. Beside a lock of his hair and a few faded photographs of relatives he'd never met, all he found were Mamma's old silver scissors. He held them up before him, and in their reflection, he saw his own hollow-eyed face. *My God,* they used to say. *What a beautiful boy. So much like his mother.*

The first slap he'd ever gotten was because he looked too much like his mother. And now the mirror reflected the same image, the same exhaustion at keeping up appearances. Alberto wanted release, he wanted surrender. Perhaps only then the worn-down carousel would stop spinning, its rusty gears would stop grinding and driving him to insanity. Would it ever stop on its own, or should he take a hammer to it?

Alberto laid his burning cheek on the glossy surface of the

table. When did it become like this? Maybe if he knew how it began, he would also obtain the tools to make it end. Slowly, he turned the scissors over in his hand. Focus — he had to focus.

Third time's the charm.

No, that wasn't it. He knocked his forehead against the table, hard enough for black dots to fill his vision. The whispered voice in his ear vanished; he let out a sigh of relief.

To him, life had begun like everyone else's — a painful extraction from the safe haven of his mother's womb and out into a brutal world. Except the pain never ended. To most children, the source of their joy or their torment was decided at birth. It was the primary concern of every therapist out there: Who are your parents? Who are you to them? And how do you survive a parent who doesn't love you at all?

Alberto unfortunately knew the answer to all of these questions. He knew that even when a child escapes them, their parents' shadow won't leave them be. With every decision they make, they'll hear the sound of their steps hot on their heels, feel their breath on their neck, hear their words like thousands of needles prickling their thoughts, day after day, night after night.

"Shut up." "You're useless." "You're so weak." "Why are you always crying?" "There's no way you could be mine." "You look so much like your whore of a mother." "Look at you, boy. You're rotten to the core."

Napoli lost the Coppa Italia against Ternana on the 11th of September, 2002.

2-nil.

Mathias was telling the truth: he really wanted to catch his parents in the act. It was never about Alberto at all. Somehow, Alberto had convinced himself Mathias had liked him from the start. He could bury that truth under a lot of lies, but, yes, the arrogant part of him believed this whole time, Mathias had lied to get close to him. Alberto just had to hook him — and hook him again and again and again. Right until he had met him, he thought he knew all there was to know about mankind.

People want good-looking partners because it makes a statement about themselves. It's all about themselves. Look whose hand I'm holding, whose lips I'm kissing, whose arse I'm fucking. Who's the best now? Nothing had ever been about Alberto. His entire life, it seemed, people had used him to work out their personal issues. He had never mattered to anyone but Mamma. And then everyone recoiled and clutched their chests when he dared ask, *What is it? What is there to smile about?*

Nothing. It had never been about him. And now the same thing happened again. Mathias used him to work out his own bullshit and then pushed him away when he became an inconvenience. Alberto gave everything up to be with him based on the stupid assumption that Mathias had sought him out, that a part of him was desperate for him, and Alberto only had to show him "Hey, look, I'm desperate for you too! I'll do anything for you. I'll change my hair, my clothes, my personality, I'll do anything, and I'll be... I'll be worthy of your love."

Mati.

Watching that car drive away into the rain with his fingers curled around Mathias's jacket, Alberto finally understood the only hooked one was him. Now Mathias had released the line, and Alberto was back underwater. *Don't believe for a second I'm like the others*, Mathias had once told him. But he was. He was just like the others.

God, there was no way out of this. Alberto was long out of Diazepam, and he didn't find any in his mother's treasure box. Ever since the day he took clippers to his hair, she had been hiding her pills away. Instead, Alberto turned and turned the scissors in his hands. There was so much pain around. It was everywhere. Dark clouds hanging over people's heads, poisonous gas corrupting their lungs. It was in everyone. In Joy, in Xavier, in Gwen and Kayvin, in Zak... maybe even in Eric... In Mathias, for sure, grief was like a nest of vipers slithering in his veins. In Mamma, pain was a vice-like hand around her throat. In himself... a constant feeling of drowning.

Even if things got better, he'd still carry around his scars. Probably be fucked up for the rest of his life. He was fucked up already. *A fading slut, letting the worst kind of people ride him.*

He was a hindrance, a burden, really. Mathias wanted to be rid of him, and now his mother was hiding things from him. Who knew the amount of people he'd hurt if he kept trudging along… and for what? For Mamma? How tiresome it was to stay alive only for the sake of another. Everything for Mamma. Everything to see her smile again. Except she never smiled.

Smiling gives you wrinkles.

Alberto turned and turned the scissors in his hands, his thoughts in disarray. He wondered what good he could ever accomplish in this world and came to the conclusion there wasn't. He glanced toward the window for a sign, and that's when he saw her.

Trotting up the lawn, Stasia was coming up to the main house in her workout clothes. From the vicious smile disfiguring her plain face, she was hoping to find him alone. Who knew how many people *she*'d hurt in her lifetime… More than he ever could. Stasia, who was never worried, who knew she could fit him in her schedule any time she wanted. Doing Pilates at six, torturing Albertino at seven, then heading out to Le Baron for a night of fun. *Cakewalk.*

Alberto turned and turned the scissors in his hand — one, two, three times. Then he got up.

"Close the window, Albertino." She said half a minute later, strolling into Mamma's bedroom. "I know you're so freaking high all the time you don't even feel cold, but I do!"

Alberto didn't reply at first. He stretched his neck out of the window. Fresh air bathed his face and gave it momentarily relief. "Just once, I wish you'd shut up."

"Can't hear you." When he turned around, Stasia's eyes widened. "Dear, dear! Look at those bloodshot eyes! What happened? Did you find out you were adopted or something?" She laughed. "Though you wish you were. You could tell people, 'Yes, he's a psychopath, but he's not really my dad!'"

Alberto huffed. More pain. *Thank you.* He shut the window and hurriedly walked out of the room, narrowly avoiding Stasia's attempt to grab him. Relentless, she followed after him.

"Why were you in your mommy's room? Do you love her that much? You're even worse than I thought."

Alberto raced back to his room, but before he could lock the door, she was already pushing with all her weight from the other side, laughing as she did. Even in his current state, she was stronger than him. After a brief struggle the door flew open, and he was flung back into his shelf, sending its contents toppling to the floor. Suddenly, Mathias was standing in front of him, a tennis ball in his hand. *Where did you get this? I despise you for what you've done.* Alberto's heart jolted in his chest. When he stepped back, the crunching sound of broken glass reached his ears. The blue elephant had smashed into pieces at his feet, revealing the key he had hidden inside.

"Ha!" Stasia cried, triumphant. "There it is. Give it to me." With a shake of his head, Alberto took another step back. Her washed-out blue eyes fixed on his face, she slowly advanced on him. "What do you think you're doing, exactly?"

Eventually, Alberto's back met with the window, and his hands scrambled around stupidly, looking for a way out.

"You done?" She sounded bored already. In her mind, she was just doing her job. She had to do it; he had to endure it. Those were the rules of the game she had designed for them long ago.

Alberto slid a glance toward his computer. It was all lonesome in the middle of the desk. If he stayed put against the wall, she couldn't miss and accidentally break it, so he held up his hands in front of his face and waited. She tugged at them half-heartedly at first, then rained blows over him with increasing strength, as though his lack of reaction only stirred up her rage. She beat him until she got tired, until he was crumpled on the floor, his arms draped over his head. When he finally lowered them, Stasia was sitting on his desk chair, smoking, her cheeks flushed from her efforts. After a minute or two, she put her joint between her lips and played with his bedroom key, tossing it from one hand to the other.

"What's up with you?" she drawled. "I didn't even hit your nose."

Alberto could barely make out her words. Her face, like the

walls of his bedroom, were undulating in a sickening rhythm. When he looked down at his hands, he saw red and mumbled, "What?"

"Your nose is bleeding." Stasia snickered. "Look at you, you can't even feel a fucking thing. Hey! Do you think if I hit your head really hard, your brain will come out of your nose?"

He groaned. In fact, his head was throbbing from the pain, but he was worried she'd kick him if he moved. He blinked helplessly at her until she clicked her tongue.

"I was about to offer you some Advil, but it's not painkillers you need at this point… It's an exorcism."

"Help me up," he said.

"You can still talk? I should have hit you harder." She sounded so calm; Alberto could hear the disappointment in her voice. With great focus, he studied her face. A veil of sadness shrouded her eyes. Like the time Alberto was shocked at his own lack of emotion when Zak dumped him, Stasia probably wondered what she would have to do to him to feel something at last.

"Help me up," he said again.

She jammed her foot in his side. "I can't do that."

Anastasia.

How similar the two of them were in some aspects. They both hated their life and blamed it on the interlopers who had moved into their space. She loathed him so much, she could never call him by his real name. As for him, he used her name as a safe word, because he knew he'd rather suffer endless torments than to say it out loud. He did it as a dare, at first convinced Mathias would one day stop the games and really hurt him. And he did, in the end, just not with his hands. How long had Alberto lived on the edge like this? Longing for both love and punishment?

"You're a monster," he whispered.

She briefly glanced at him. "Are you talking to yourself?"

"You'll never know what love is."

"And you will?"

Alberto didn't answer. His back sore and his ears ringing, he rose with difficulty, using the corner of his desk for support.

"Oh, no!" Stasia shrieked with laughter. "Are you talking about *him?* Still going on about that guy, huh? Don't you remember? He ditched you." She stubbed out her joint on Alberto's keyboard. "You want to know why he did that, Albertino?"

Alberto bit his tongue. Mathias was off-limits. He wouldn't let her worm her way in using him as a weapon.

"You know it already," she said. "You're unlovable."

When he shook his head, she abruptly rose from her chair, and Alberto fell back on his arse against the wall. She approached, filling the space above him until all he could see was her distorted face.

"But you are," she said, her eyes brimming with fake empathy. "My sweet, if you weren't unlovable, your daddy wouldn't have hit you so hard, you'll wonder for the rest of your life if you were born that stupid or if he's the reason you're so slow." Her eyes gradually filled with tears. "Albertino… Don't you sometimes wish he'd finished the job? That you hadn't woken up to make your mommy's life miserable? Moving from country to country, from stepfather to stepfather, never able to settle down…" Her eyes grew darker as she bent her neck and brought her face so close to his that the stench of her breath reached his nostrils, turning his stomach. She was in a trance, her expression betraying the glee of someone who was about to finally get to enjoy a meal they had taken a long time to prepare. "Have you forgotten? The one time your mother did something good for you and gave you the chance to become someone… you… what? Shaved your fucking head and threw a tantrum and passed on a million-dollar deal? Surely you couldn't have been that stupid by design. Or maybe… maybe you always were, and your daddy saw it, and he couldn't cope with it."

There was no light left in the room. All there was was Stasia, her round face, her laughter, her glistening eyes. All there was in his world was pain, and the prospect of more to come.

"Why?" he ventured, awed by her cruelty. "Why are you like this?" He caught in her eye a brief glimpse of confusion.

"Why don't you ask yourself?"

Alberto's head was throbbing too much for her words to make sense. He attempted to grip the side of his desk and missed. "Tell me…"

"Tell you what?"

"Tell me what I have to do, to make you st—"

She drew back, and suddenly, light surged into the room. Alberto could finally draw in a breath. His lungs filled with air, and he became lightheaded.

"Disappear," Stasia said, her eyes narrowing. "That's all I ever wanted. This house may be large, but there isn't enough room for all of us. I never wanted this, I will *never* want this. It's *my* house, and it's *my* dad."

She bore down on him again, and he flinched. Papà had similar eyes, black with hatred. In their reflection, Alberto saw himself. Tall and yet small; frail little bird with no voice. He wondered if his mother saw a similar sight the night he almost lost his life.

"And if I leave?" he asked, his hand fumbling around for the side of his desk again. This time, he found it. Alberto slowly pushed himself up to his feet. Something warm trickled down his nostril, and he wiped it with his sleeve. "If I disappear? You wouldn't have to share your house with me anymore."

Stasia drew herself to her tallest. "Depending how you leave here…" She cast him an ominous smile. "I'll get your mother next."

There was a slight pause, a deafening silence. Golden dust particles floated between them, lightweight yet clear. Then a thundering crack split the air when his hand, like a whip, met its target. The dust particles scattered.

The force of the blow was such that Stasia fell against the door to the closet with a cry of surprise. She glared, she smirked, she puffed out a laugh. But Alberto's pain was gone, and his voice, *his voice* was found again. His hands felt strong as they curled around her shoulders.

When he saw she was still gleeful, her hand clutching her cheek, his rage burst out of him. He shook her. He hurled insults at her as he did. And he shook her, again and again. And again and again, she crashed and bounced against the doors like a rag doll. He shook her until she stopped laughing, until her curses turned to shrieks, then to sobs, until two powerful hands yanked him away from her and hurled him across the room. Alberto landed on the edge of his bed and sunk to the floor, his heart pounding and his throat dry.

When his vision came into focus again and he met his mother's eyes, he was submerged with horror at what he had done.

25

WHERE THIS DEMON LIVES

For a few minutes, Alberto felt eerily calm. Nothing mattered anymore. He was vaguely aware of something hot and wet trickling down his face, yet it was no concern to him. Feeling the weight of his mother's arms around him as she helped him take a seat on the bed, he watched Dimitri comfort his daughter. Her gushing tears were a thing of beauty. So were the sobs shaking her athletic frame, casting the illusion of frailty. A distant and familiar voice in the back of Alberto's mind suggested to tell her she was born with great acting skills, *commedia dell'arte.*

"You're right," he mumbled when he recognised the voice. Mathias had turned up for him, if only in his head.

Mamma wouldn't let go of him. He found her embrace both reassuring and suffocating.

Standing in front of them, Dimitri was beside himself. "What if we hadn't shown up at the right time? Did you intend to kill her?"

Alberto didn't reply; he had nothing to say in his defence. In fact, he perfectly understood Dimitri's anger. He would have reacted the same if he had found some arsehole playing life-size maracas with his precious daughter. Alberto was done for, really… and it was fine. He hadn't felt that amazing in a long time. One glance at Stasia told him that, despite the handprint on her cheek, she hadn't felt that amazing in a long time either. After all, she finally got him to snap.

Like father, like son.

Alberto inadvertently chuckled.

Dimitri turned to him, his arms full with his evil daughter. "And you think it's funny?"

A little bit. A little bit, really.

Dimitri's face swelled with anger. "You little psychopath. You're not gonna laugh so much when I press charges." He faced his wife, and his voice turned pleading when he said, "Olympia, please! You can see he's not normal. Look! Look at him!"

Alberto shut his eyes, afraid of glimpsing his mother's expression. When her arms tightened around him, he opened them again. Also nestled in her father's arms, Stasia was watching them carefully. She was biding her time, and soon enough, behind everyone's back, she would smirk at him. She would. She had to. Because she wasn't hurt, was she? He hoped she wasn't, even now. Even if he had lost to her, failed to prove her wrong.

"He's not normal…" Dimitri was saying, his mouth twisted in disgust. "He's not normal…"

"He came at me out of nowhere." Stasia spoke in a quivering voice. "His eyes… his eyes were all bloodshot. At first, I thought he was on drugs… *illegal* drugs."

Alberto's mother flinched, but she didn't release him.

"It's not the first time he's acted weird around me, but…" Stasia let out a string of sobs, hiding her face in her father's neck. When she drew back, tears were flowing down her cheeks again. "I've always known there was something off about him, but I never thought he'd hurt *me*!"

Dimitri pressed her closer to his chest. "That's all right, my darling."

Alberto shut his eyes again. Mamma's perfume filled his nostrils, and as always, the refreshing floral notes carried him back to the villa in Napoli. Funny how it was almost preordained. No matter how hard he had willed himself not to become his father, he still ended up throwing a girl against a wall.

"I don't want him around my daughter anymore," Dimitri said.

His tone was firm, his stance powerful. Still clutching Alberto, Mamma said nothing. "Now we know he's dangerous. Olympia, do you hear me?"

If she did, Mamma didn't show it, but her grip around him had grown so fierce, Alberto started struggling for breath.

"Olympia!" Dimitri pleaded. The look in his eyes suggested he was desperate for his wife to side with him. Alberto wondered if he had often dreamt of this, of being rid of him at last. "It's not just that," Dimitri said after a pause. "There's also… There's also…" He turned away from them, his shoulders slumping, then he started pacing around the room.

Alberto stared at him from the corner of his eye, as though watching a puzzling movie whose denouement left him absolutely indifferent. *He looks like a blood orange now,* Mathias's voice spoke in his ear. Slowly, Alberto nodded in agreement.

Dimitri abruptly stopped pacing and stood in front of Alberto's mother. "Weeks ago…" His voice was softer now. "Weeks ago, after our party, he returned home in the middle of the night." He waited, but when Mamma didn't react, his jaw clenched. "I didn't want to say anything, but I have to. I really have to. He was drunk when he came home. Stumbling up the stairs and shouting… He made such a racket, he got me out of bed. And when I came to check on him, he…" Dimitri balled his fists. "He kissed me!"

Ouch. Mamma's nails dug painfully into Alberto's flesh. As he lifted a hand to stop her, something finally clicked in his brain.

"What did you say?" he asked, at the same time as his mother.

Dimitri only had eyes for her. "It's true, I swear, it's true! He may have been too drunk to remember, but I wasn't—" He paused for a brief moment. "I went to his room to scold him for making too much noise, and—"

"He *kissed* you?" Mamma spoke quietly, but in a tone as cutting as a blade. Alberto's heart stopped momentarily in his chest. "Alberto *kissed* you."

"Yes! I was in shock, naturally, I—"

"My son. My *son* kissed you, and you never thought to tell me?"

"I didn't—"

"What did you do, then?"

Dimitri hesitated. Mamma slowly released Alberto.

"What did you do?" she asked again. "Did you kiss him, then?"

"No! I stopped him, I did! And then I… then I… I left him alone…" Dimitri stopped talking, his gaze falling on Alberto, who had started laughing, quietly at first, then gradually loud enough to cover his voice. Hiccups of laughter shook him until his sides started hurting.

"Did I…" He wiped tears with the back of his hand. "Did I really kiss you?"

"You *did*," Dimitri said, in a tone laced with scorn. "You threw yourself at me, and I pushed you away— Stop it! Stop laughing!"

But now that it hit Alberto, he feared he'd never be able to stop laughing. "We had an audience that night, did you know that?" To Alberto's delight, Dimitri's orange face turned grey from shock. "Truly, we did. My friend was here. He…" Alberto's laughter died in his throat. "He saw *everything*."

Stasia's tearful eyes narrowed. She only now realised her mistake. She may have simply believed "Alex" too insignificant to tell her father about that night, preferring to poke at Mamma instead. And Mamma had evidently never told her husband about Mathias's visit, because Dimitri lunged at her in a frenzy.

"Olympia—"

Suddenly, Mamma was gone from Alberto's side, and his laughter returned, unrestrained. So *that's* what Mathias had seen that night. It had nothing to do with him finding his pills in the bottom drawer under the bathroom sink. It wasn't because he thought Alberto was a pathetic sack of shit, unworthy of his time. Poor, foolish Mathias. What a shock it must have been! No wonder he disappeared after that. Did he think he and Dimitri were secret lovers? What a mess, what a disaster. And yet, Alberto could only laugh. And the more he thought about it, the more hysterical he sounded.

"Look! Look!" Dimitri pointed at him. "He's not sane! He's not normal!"

Mamma pretended — or not — not to hear him. All but buried in the walk-in closet, she was pulling clothes off the rack and throwing them into Alberto's favourite duffle bag. *Vegan leather*, that's what it was made of. Alberto didn't wear animal skin or their fur, not even wool. If anyone would ask him, he'd say since the day someone had plucked off his wings, he'd convinced himself he wouldn't hurt a fly. Now he realised there wasn't much truth to it. He had wanted to swat Stasia for years, and he just did.

She's not really a fly though, is she? Mathias's soothing voice said. Alberto could vaguely see him, sitting low in a chair with his arms folded over his chest, a glint of mockery in his eye. He adverted his gaze; it was all too tempting to agree with him.

"*Be still, my heart…*" Alberto whispered, earning himself a glare from Dimitri. "*Thou hast known worse than this.*"

When she was satisfied with the amount of outfits she had crammed into the bag, Mamma rushed to the bathroom next and dumped a pile of things on top of his clothes, so very like the way Alberto had packed months ago, febrile from the pleasure of having Mathias standing by his side in this very room. The more Mamma added to the mess in the bag, the more Dimitri panicked. He followed her every step, his face increasingly sweaty.

"Olympia, fine, I take it back. I won't press charges, just listen to me!"

Alberto's mother was hyper-focused. He could see that from how wide her eyes were and how rarely she blinked. She didn't spare her husband a glance, and she only stopped when the bag was full and she couldn't zip it closed no matter how hard she tried. When her nail snapped and he rushed to her aid, she seized the bag and stepped away from him.

"I'm taking him away from here."

"Where?"

She hesitated. "Somewhere… safe."

"Olympia, don't be ridiculous. I'm not going to hurt him."

Her face red, Mamma turned away from him. When Alberto met her eyes, she bit her lip. "Meudon. That's where I'll take him."

Where do demons live?

Alberto had his answer now.

Mamma spun on her heel and, gripping Alberto by the arm, she pulled him up and led him outside the room. The sudden movement filled Alberto's vision with black dots, and he almost tripped. In confusion, he even waved at Stasia, and he saw her lift her hand back.

"Olympia, why won't you look at me?" Dimitri rushed after them. "I didn't kiss him, he kissed *me*!"

Alberto personally believed Dimitri was telling the truth. That night, naive as he was, he had mixed his medication with wine when Mathias took him home and ended up staying in his room. Alberto was certainly messed up enough to mistake the two in the dark, but Mamma didn't know that, and perhaps finding out your husband kissed your son and didn't feel the need to mention it was terrifying enough to justify her reaction. If only Alberto had known… he would have told her weeks ago. Then they would have moved out of this house, and he wouldn't have hurt Stasia.

Not that any of this stuff mattered anymore.

Mamma's voice was shaking when she spoke again. "I know *you* were drunk too when you went to bed that night."

"What are you saying? I mean, sure, yes, I had a few drinks, but it's not like—"

"He'd just turned eighteen!" Mamma snapped, clattering down the staircase, Alberto in tow. He was so lightheaded, he felt like he was gliding down the stairs. He checked his nose, but he wasn't bleeding anymore. Maybe his brain really did come out of his nose, since he couldn't think or feel anything. He thought of telling Stasia, share a last laugh, but Mamma was tearing across the hall and pushing him outside.

They were met with a rainfall. Mamma rushed down the front steps, slamming her thumb on the key to the Jaguar while pulling Alberto by the hand, and she slipped. Dimitri caught her before she tumbled down the stairs.

"You're upset, Olympia," he said in an emotional voice. "At least have Oleg drive you there."

Mamma looked at Alberto, and after a moment of hesitation, she brushed his hair away from his face and said, "Yes, okay."

Dimitri rushed back inside, while Mamma stood on the front steps shivering. Then she let out a sound of surprise. "What's this?" she asked, stepping onto the terrace. "What are these doing here?"

The old pair of silver scissors — now broken — was lying,

abandoned, in the middle of the terrace. Mamma lifted her head toward her bedroom window and saw that it was closed. Then she turned to Alberto.

"Did you do this, *Tesoro?*"

Alberto did have a faint memory of throwing them the moment he pictured himself sticking them into Stasia's neck. He gave his mother a nod of admission. It reassured him, somewhat, that before he snapped, he had every intention of avoiding hurting her.

Whatever Mamma made of this, she didn't say a word. She walked back to his side, and when Dimitri reappeared accompanied by Oleg, she dragged Alberto toward the SUV and pushed him in. The door slammed shut, and everything turned quiet.

"You believe me, right?" Dimitri asked, his voice muffled. Through the window, Alberto could see the fear in his eyes. Mamma was talking back, her voice too faint to be heard.

Alberto checked himself and felt no fear. He was glad to leave, and even happier to be put away. He closed his eyelids. Where was Mathias right now? Probably congratulating himself on proving to Alberto he was right about their parents. Would Mamma marry Mr Rodin now? None of this mattered. Alberto was done now.

When he reopened his eyes, Mamma was already in the seat next to him, and the car was reversing, crunching gravel and casting a bright light on Stasia's face. She was smiling at him. A triumphant smile.

"I'll leave," he said softly. "I'll be a model, you'll see. I'm irresistible... gorgeous enough to bring the world to its feet."

When Stasia waved, Dimitri whirled around and snapped at her. Only then did she stop smiling, and then the car turned, and she was gone from his sight.

The night was black, and the now pouring rain was obscuring the sides of the road, but the headlights from the cars on the opposite lane sometimes cast a glaring light on Mamma's tear-streaked face. And at last, concern and resentment grew within Alberto. All those years enduring to ensure she wouldn't weep because of him, all for nothing.

"Why did you do this?" she asked, her voice weak. "How could you…"

"I'm sorry."

The rain pounded against the windows and the roof of the car. Sorry was the right word, indeed.

"How could you do this to that poor girl?"

Why? Alberto couldn't say, so he wept, too. Mamma was looking at him like she'd never seen him before.

"Are you off your meds?"

"Yes."

Shock brightened her eyes. "Why?!"

They were making me slow.

I had a man to catch.

And they were making me slow.

She stared at him, and she saw her first husband, probably. *Like father, like son.* The rest of the journey was spent in tears, and in the mirror, Alberto caught the worried face of Oleg. There was silent judgment in there, too. After all, it's a terrible thing to make your Mamma cry.

Don't tell your mother, Alberto. If you tell her, it will destroy her.

"Don't ever let me out," he told the receptionist. First, she asked his name, and since Mamma was rummaging through her bag, he was faced with answering. He said, "Hello-my-name-is-Alberto-and-I'm-a-dumb-white-gay."

She blinked at him in confusion before asking his mother, "Is *Alberto* off his medication?"

"Yes," Mamma said, her voice strangled. When anxiety brought her down, her jaw would clench so hard, she couldn't even have water. She would lose the feeling in her fingers, too. Alberto knew that. She was on antidepressants way before him, but even then, she needed extra help sometimes. He used to force the pills through the small gap of her teeth, and half an hour later, when she could finally open her mouth, he was able to give her the water she needed. Once, it had to be through a straw, because of the punch Papà had given her hours before. She couldn't get up, and she was so afraid of leaving Alberto alone with his father, she had made herself sick from worry. Nothing bad happened that night. Sometimes, even Papà felt guilty.

"I don't know how long it's been," Mamma said at last, "since he's stopped taking them. He's in a state, like last time."

"Oh, so he has been with us before?" She looked him up on their records.

"Yes, in 2007."

Shit year, it was.

Yes, yes it was.

The receptionist asked, "Is it true, Alberto? Have you stopped taking your medication?"

Alberto would rather speak to Mathias, who was there, next to him, speaking to him. *So, you decked that poor girl, huh?*

"Not everyone has your legendary self-control."

Mathias laughed, like in all of Alberto's fantasies. *You're so weird,* he said, and the corners of his eyes crinkled when he smiled.

Alberto said, "I needed to be fast, to catch myself a werewolf."

"He's not making any sense." Mamma looked sad. So sad.

She asked about Doctor Roland. There was a lot of talk, about the clinic's rules, his treatment, his dietary restrictions, and how things were different now because Alberto was no longer a kid. They spoke of a room just for him, with a view of the grounds. They gave him a pen, asked him to sign some papers. Got the date wrong. Signed more papers. Then Mamma gave her credit card, and just like that, thousands from her savings were gone.

Like father, like son.

"Don't ever let me out," he told the woman who led him into his room. Mamma apologised for him and sat him on the bed.

At this hour, the heavy curtains were pulled shut. Nice view, nice view. His favourite.

He couldn't rest, his blood wouldn't let him. His messed-up brain was recovering from the brunt of Stasia's blows, and now he was left pacing the room like a caged animal, afraid of losing control of his limbs. Afraid. Terrified. *What will happen to me?* Didn't matter. Didn't it? What would happen to him? His mother watched him from the armchair, weeping silently. Once or twice, she begged him to sit on the bed, no, better, to lie down.

Do you always do what your mother tells you? Mathias laughed in his ear.

Alberto laughed, too. "You're still here," he said, overcome with joy.

Where else would I be? Mathias asked, and they were interrupted by Doctor Roland, who took one look at him and went *tsk tsk tsk*.

"I can't talk to him when he's like this," he said in the same old condescending tone.

Mamma had always been afraid of him. He probably looked like her father. She nodded anxiously, and a nurse stuck a needle in Alberto's arse after he said, "Go ahead, do it." A few seconds later, his lungs expanded, and he could finally breathe.

"That's better now, isn't it?" The doctor looked at his file. "So what happened, Alberto? Are we in the middle of a little crisis?"

Punch that asshole, while you're at it, Mathias said while inspecting the contents of the nightstand. Alberto didn't reply.

"Change into your pyjamas," Mamma said, and her fingers brushed his shoulders. She let out a sound of surprise when he slapped her hand away.

"Please don't touch me."

Perhaps it was indeed fear in her eyes. But if he undressed in front of her, he would have more explaining to do. And now, he was dead tired.

He saw while he was changing in the bathroom Doctor Roland and Mamma talking in hushed voices, then she was hugging him, her face wet, and reassuring him she would come back tomorrow.

Suddenly, Alberto was in bed, in his favourite pyjamas. Mamma was pulling the comforter over him. A comforter to comfort him. Thank fuck for all his blessings!

"You'll be just fine," Mamma said, and she kissed him.

"Don't ever let me out," he replied.

Then it was dark, and he was alone in the room.

To his doctor, to Dimitri, to Stasia, to the *world*, he was just a big fuck up.

I'm a fuck up too, Mathias said.

Yes, Alberto knew that. But Mathias didn't need to worry. Alberto saw him for *everything* that he was. He looked at him and how his beautiful body covered his own. How his eyes were burning into him. Burning for answers. The timid first, then the growing, threatening opportunity. To Alberto, Mathias was *that* guy.

Lights out, Mathias said, somewhere in the back.

"Wait, wait!"

Alberto thought if he saw him again, he would tell him all that. He would stop playing aloof because he was afraid. He'd tell him *I know we're over, but you should know that you made my heart beat hard and fast, and it wasn't out of fear.* He wanted to say *thank you, thank you for that opportunity, for allowing me to feel something different.* And then the medicine really took effect. Words first, then thoughts slipped away from him, vanished into the ether, and soon, he had forgotten all of what he wanted to tell Mathias about.

26

THE OTHER GUY

It was well after 9 p.m. when Eric banged on Mathias's front door. Still dressed in his gym clothes, Mathias opened the door with a frown.

"I told you I was busy tonight."

Eric pursed his lips, his gaze lingering on Mathias's bare arms. "You said you were going boxing, and now you're back. Come on, let's get Zak and go to the movies."

"Pass."

"Why?" Eric's nostrils flared. "Don't tell me you're going to bed this early on a Friday night." When Mathias didn't react, Eric pushed him aside and stepped into his home. "That's it, Matt. I'm tired of you spending the holidays cooped up in here alone."

"I'm not alo— Hey!"

Eric was already dashing toward his bedroom, with Mathias on his tail. "There better be someone hiding in here, or I swear—" He shoved the door open and stopped. "Oh… It's empty."

"What the hell, Eric?" Mathias tried to slam the door shut, but Eric kicked it open.

"Were you replacing your bed?" He let himself in and laughed at the chaos reigning in Mathias's room.

"Fixing it, actually."

Tired of the squeaking and creaking that only got worse after he and Alberto last saw each other, Mathias had ordered a new set of slats for the frame. When he removed the mattress earlier, he found underneath a small black lock. *LOCK AWAY*, the engraving said on the back. It obviously belonged to Alberto, who hid it under there for some reason, as he had done before. Mathias once searched for his hi-fi remote for days, thinking it lost, before he found it hidden under the same mattress. Why? Mathias knew better than to assume there was no explanation for Alberto's bizarre behavior. Now here he was with a lock and no key. He was still obsessing over the absence of the key when Eric had started banging on his door.

"How does that happen?" Eric was asking, his tone sly. "How d'you break it?"

Mathias exhaled a sigh. "As you can see, I'm busy. So, unless you wanna help…"

"I always want to help. So, tell me: Did you fail your entrance exam this week?"

Mathias hesitated. "No, it went well, I think."

He showed up on time, did what he was told without questions and in order. Neither awful nor extraordinary, in his opinion, he had passed the test, but he couldn't be certain until the school wrote back to him to let him know.

"You would have told me if something went wrong, right?" Eric asked.

"Sure."

"I don't believe you." A muscle twitched in Eric's jaw. "I want to know why you've been ignoring me for a week. I'm not leaving until you tell me."

"Then suit yourself, but you'll find the place a bit lonely. My dad's away for the weekend, and my sister's at a sleepover." Mathias pointed at the door. "But *I* have shit to do, so you can let yourself out—*after* you fix my bed."

"Don't!" His arms outstretched, Eric stood in the doorway. "Don't shut me out."

"You're the one blocking my way out."

"Wait!"

The earnestness in Eric's eyes was unbearable. That same look probably wore Zak down until he capitulated and accepted him as a clingy boyfriend. He probably used the same trick on everyone. *Look at me, I'm so cute! Matt, Matt! I love you!*

That bastard.

Yet, Mathias averted his eyes, his face hot. He pushed his hands into the pockets of his sweatpants and closed his fist around the small lock until the pain numbed his palm. "If I asked you to go somewhere with me," he said in a gruff voice, "would you? Just you and me, without Zak. Would you?"

Eric's eyes briefly narrowed, betraying his surprise. "Of course, where do you want to go?"

"Home," he said, before shaking his head. "I mean, my former hometown."

The smug expression Eric then adopted irritated him, but in the end, he said nothing.

An hour later, after an unmemorable train ride, the two of them stood outside an apartment building in Massy. Because he wasn't ringing the intercom, Eric leaned into Mathias's space until the other snarled at him.

"So, what's happening?" Eric asked once he'd stopped laughing. "Why did you absolutely need me to come?"

"I never said I absolutely needed you to come."

"That's what I heard anyway."

Mathias lit up a cigarette and patted his shoulder. Eric returned the gesture with a warm smile.

"This is Sylvain's place," Mathias said. "We used to go to the same school and we hung out together with the same guys, before I punched one of them when he… said something he shouldn't have. This week, Sylvain texted me to invite me to this party."

"A party? That's it?" Eric wrinkled his nose. "Sometimes, I really don't understand why you insist on keeping the most banal things so hush hush. I canceled on Zak to be here, and now he's having a pajama party without me!"

Mathias glared at him. "For *once* I invite you somewhere… You see Zak every day. You probably see him every night too!"

"Not in his special pajamas, no I don't! They're called special for a reason!" Eric jerked his head. "You know what? I'm going back." He made to turn away, but Mathias clasped a hand on his shoulder.

"Wait! It's not just a party, I swear. There's someone here I need to talk to, and I'd prefer if the others don't notice me slip away."

Eric turned around and glanced up at the rows of windows above with a perplexed expression. "Okay, I'll stay."

"I need you to create a diversion," Mathias said, serious. "Keep them busy so that I can be alone with that person." He added after a beat, "They've never met an American. Play along, they'll think you're Jack Bauer or something."

"Sure." Eric gave a nod. "Who's Jack Bauer?"

"For fuck's sake! Do you only watch Disney movies or what?"

Sylvain's mouth fell open in shock when he opened the door a few minutes later, the quiet hallway suddenly alive with French rap music. "I didn't expect you to come," he said. "But I'm glad, honestly!"

Mathias took sight of the old crowd gathered in the living room and asked hurriedly, "Does Clément still live here?"

Pushing his long hair away from his face, Sylvain laughed and frowned at the same time. "Yeah. He should be back from work soon, but he's not going to hang out with us much. He's gonna pilfer a bottle of vodka and drink it alone in his room. What do you need him for anyway? He's all out of weed, he said. Hey, man!" Sylvain finally noticed Eric, who introduced himself in French. He shook his offered hand. "Do you guys want some beer?"

"Wait, wait." Mathias craned his neck toward the others. "What about Mathieu, is he here?"

After a pause, Sylvain gave him a knowing smile. "Nope, he's working tonight, and it's better this way. He hasn't forgotten that punch. He probably never will." He suddenly became serious. "I get it, though. *I'm* dating Daphnée now, and I wouldn't let anyone talk that way about her." Noticing the alarm in Mathias's eyes, he added, "Don't worry, she's not here either. No chicks tonight. Cocks only."

That last line had Eric giggling like an overexcited dolphin. As they followed Sylvain into the living room, he nudged Mathias with his elbow and whispered, "Straight guys, amirite?"

"What?" Mathias pulled him to his side. "Stop talking, get over here."

"Yes, sir."

With the relief that he wouldn't have to face another one of his demons tonight, Mathias introduced Eric to his former school friends, purposefully letting him know he was American. That was enough for them to get interested. Once each of them had shaken Mathias's hand and listened to his monosyllabic answers, Eric was deemed the funnier of the two, and that was before he even told them he was a proper football player. Mathias let him take over while he leaned against the wall by the kitchen and drank liquid courage in the form of whisky and coke, his free hand absently clutching the lock in his pocket.

It took some time, but eventually, Mathias felt someone's eyes on him, and he turned around. With his pale skin, his round baby-blue eyes, and his blondish hair combed back in a good boy hair-cut, Sylvain's stepbrother looked the same as he ever did. Hopelessly vulnerable and kind, *too* kind. Mathias's lips instinctively stretched at the sight of him, and the pressure in his chest eased when he received a smile back.

"*Mathias Rodin,*" Clément said, stepping out of the shadows. "Here's one person I never thought I'd see again." The genuine sweetness in his expression was much more than what Mathias expected… or deserved, in his opinion. He felt exposed, and he dipped his head like a told-off child.

Clément and Sylvain had been thrown together at the age of eleven, when their parents got married and moved together into Sylvain's apartment. At school, Sylvain was the stocky, sporty one, competitive and popular. Clément was the opposite. Awkward and soft-spoken, he would have preferred not to be noticed at all. For a long time, Sylvain pretended he didn't know him, but eventually, people found out they lived together. Sylvain resented that, and he never lifted a finger to defend his stepbrother when the boys at school ultimately decided Clément was bullying material. To this day, Mathias couldn't help wondering how he could have wasted so much time hanging out with those guys, and therein lay the root of the problem: wasn't he, after all, one of them?

His fist closing around the lock in his pocket, Mathias signaled Eric with a quick nod, who immediately launched himself into a tirade in English, and in an unwarranted southern accent. Mathias left him to do his thing and walked over to Clément, noticing, up close, that he hadn't grown much since he last saw him and was significantly shorter than him. Yet, when he addressed him, it was with his eyes on his shoes.

"Can we talk? Alone?"

Clément took a moment to reply. "Sure… Come to my room, we'll have a joint together, like old times." He pointed at Mathias's empty drink. "I'll get you a refill as well."

Mathias wordlessly followed him down the corridor. Back in the living room, Eric's bad impression of a cowboy caused general laughter. At least Mathias could count on his friend to keep the others busy.

Clément invited him to step into his tidy bedroom. When Mathias caught him locking the door behind them, he gave a sheepish smile. "Wouldn't want to be caught alone with the school *fag*," he said, a hint of bitterness in his tone.

Mathias's eyebrows drew together. "Do they still call you that?"

With an exaggerated shrug, Clément shuffled to his desk and leaned against it. "I am, in fact, gay, so… they were never wrong." From his shirt pocket, he removed a joint and waved it in front of Mathias, who tilted his head toward the door.

"But… won't it look suspicious if I'm locked in a room with you?"

"God, you're right!" Clément pounced forward. "I didn't think about that, I'm sorry. I—"

"That's fine." Mathias caught his wrist before he reached the door. "I don't care what they think."

His gaze lingering on Mathias's hand, Clément's expression grew dumbfounded. "Let's have something to drink, shall we?" He pointed at the improvised mini bar on top of his shelf. "I can even make us some Old Fashioneds."

"That's actually my favorite drink," Mathias said.

Clément turned his face away. "I know."

As he applied himself to make their drinks with slightly clumsy fingers, Mathias stood silently in the middle of the room. There were no posters on Clément's walls. No clutter lying around either. It was familiar to Alberto's room, except it was a fraction of the size, and the walls here were painted in much darker shades of purples and grays, with matching bedding. Mathias felt at ease in this room, even with the memory of Alberto gnawing at his stomach like a bad indigestion.

Clément gave Mathias his drink and perched himself on top of his desk. Now his eyes were at the same level as his, which made talking easier, somehow. He took a generous swig of his drink before he spoke.

"I always wondered, Mathias. Did you punch that guy because you thought he was wrong, or right?"

Mathias blinked at him. Clément laughed, revealing faint dimples and slightly crooked teeth. "I guess I've always wanted to ask, and now that you're inexplicably here… I'm afraid I'll never get another chance."

"I also came here," Mathias said, "to talk about that." As he spoke, he rolled the lock between his fingers in his pocket.

Clément watched him, his gaze soft. "I'm really happy to see you, you know?"

"You are?"

"That seems to surprise you. But listen to me, I'm being so rude! Tell me, how's life? How have you been since, you know…"

The last punch.

Mathias emptied half the contents of his drink in one gulp. "I'm okay." It felt odd to say the words, but more so to be able to talk to someone from his past. And especially Clément, whose warm welcome was unexpected, to say the least. That must have been why his voice came out sounding so muted. "My new school is mostly rich kids. I thought I'd hate them all at first—some are really the worst clichés you can think of. But I've made some good friends. I mean, I've made *one* good friend—"

"Do you have a boyfriend?"

The question stunned Mathias, and he must have looked

dumb, because Clément laughed behind his fist. "Don't look so shocked. I used to wonder whether you were… you know, and now you show up after all this time, you don't flinch when I tell you I'm gay, and you're okay being locked in my bedroom with me—"

"You used to wonder about me? Why?"

Clément stopped laughing, a flush creeping up his cheeks. "I don't know. You never called me names, for one. For years now, everyone's been calling me the same stuff, but not you, not once. You went as far as punching a guy for making fun of me, so…"

Mathias knocked back the rest of his drink and, drawing closer, flung it to the side. The glass spun endlessly on the surface of the desk in an irritating clatter until Clément laid his hand flat on top of it and there was silence again.

Unnerving silence.

"I just don't like bullies," Mathias said.

"Is that why you punched him, Mathias?" There was a glint in Clément's eyes. "You punched a guy twice your size because you don't like bullies? Or…"

"Or what?" Mathias held his gaze. "You know why I punched him." He added resentfully, "And he wasn't *twice* my size, he was—"

"Big. And you knocked him down on his ass because he called me a fag."

"… Yes."

"It's not the first time you heard them talk like that about me, I'm sure. You never punched him before, so what was different that time? It was because you knew, right? You knew it was true, and—"

"Because I felt bad."

"Why?" Clément leaned forward. "Why did you feel bad?"

Mathias tried to remember how it was back then. The memories were blurry, shifting shadows he couldn't grasp, except for a face, clear in his mind.

"My mom, she was sick. I was angry with the world. And I was dating Daphnée…"

"Oh yes, Daphnée." A hint of distaste laced Clément's voice. "That's it? Nothing else?" Mathias's hesitation inspired him to hand over his drink to him. Mathias thanked him and took a careful sip.

"The gymnasium. I felt bad about the gymnasium. It was an accumulation, really. When he started talking, I just… I felt I owed you that, at least."

"So, it did happen, then. The gymnasium. It wasn't in my head." Clément let out a quiet laugh. "This should make me so happy, but, instead, it just makes me sad."

Mathias took a step closer. "I just remembered recently. I've been—"

"Good, because *I* never had the chance to forget—"

"—thinking about you."

Clément was shaking his head, then he processed Mathias's words, his eyes lighting up. "You've been thinking about me?" When Mathias nodded, he groaned and shifted in his seat. "There's no point hiding it now; we're not kids anymore. I've had a crush on you since the first year of collège*."

Mathias had been suspecting that for a while now.

"That's a long time," he said softly.

"I'm sure you understand why."

Now, that's the part he never understood. He blinked cluelessly until Clément puffed out a laugh.

"You weren't like the others. You were good at everything, kind to everyone. Your best friend was a girl, and it wasn't a secret either. You were proud of Daphnée, even when people were making fun of you two."

"I wasn't—" Mathias shook his head. "I wasn't good at everything. And I wasn't popular at all."

"I didn't care about that! You don't remember? You would pick me when no one would in sports team. And you would steer assholes away from me, time and time again. You did, I *saw* you. And you, you would smile at me when nobody else would…"

"I was just trying to be nice."

Clément unexpectedly seized his hands, and Mathias almost

---

* In France, collège precedes high school, and welcomes pupils aged from 11 to 15 years old.

dropped his glass. "You *are* nice, Mathias. You're nice. So nice that I started thinking… maybe you liked me, too." He seemed to realize what he had done and released him just as abruptly. "Until that day in *quatrième**, at the gymnasium. Do you…" He bit his lip. "What do you remember?"

There was laughter somewhere in the apartment. Mathias thought of Eric playing the idiot to buy him time. He couldn't afford to pussyfoot around. He had to get going.

"We were left to clean up after handball," he said. "It was pouring when we came out. We took refuge under the covered courtyard."

"And?"

"I thought you wanted to kiss me. It was written all over you."

"And…"

Mathias's shoulder lifted in a half-shrug. "I thought you were cute that day. You wanted to kiss me. I felt I could kiss you too."

There was a silence. Clément was watching Mathias through squinted eyes, his mouth twisting in a displeased—but sort of cute—pout. "So, why didn't you? Because I'd been waiting for so long…"

Mathias lowered his eyes. "I didn't want to deal with the consequences."

"Of… being gay? Even with your—"

"No." He looked up. "Of having to disappoint you."

"Why?" Clément's eyebrows drew together in confusion. "What does it mean?"

"I wanted to kiss you, that's true. I was curious about it. But I wasn't into you the way you were into me. I thought if I kissed you, then I'd have to be with you, and I didn't want to do that."

Mathias's admission had Clément looking stumped for a moment before his shoulders sagged. "Thank you for telling me," he said, barely audible.

When he was a kid, Mathias never worried about saying the wrong thing. He didn't have to. One day, everything changed. One day, he wasn't a kid anymore, and it seemed everything that came

____

* 8th Grade (US) Year 9 (UK)

out of his mouth was not what people wanted to hear. But now, he couldn't hide anymore, he had to own it. Even if his words were painful to Clément, he owed him—and himself—the truth.

"I'm sorry," Mathias said. "I really am. Because I really did like you. *You're* nice. So, I'm sorry I couldn't be what you wanted me to be."

Clément let out a sigh. "No, you're actually everything I want you to be, that's the problem."

"It's not only that. I came here because… I wanted to tell you I'm sorry for frightening you."

"Frightening me?"

"You never spoke to me again after that punch."

The snort of laughter that followed wasn't what Mathias expected. While he stared at him with round eyes, Clément snatched his drink back and finished it before discarding it to the side.

"Mathias, you adorable idiot. That wasn't because I was afraid of you. That was self-preservation! Yes, you went overboard when you punched that guy in the face because he insulted me. But from my point of view, you were a hero. After that incident, I was even more in love with you than before." With another laugh, Clément seized Mathias's hands again. "I avoided you to protect my own heart, or I would have been at risk to follow you around like a love-struck puppy, and then people would have started making assumptions about you too. About being… a *fag*."

Mathias squeezed his hands. Briefly. "I'm not a fag."

"Apparently not."

"Neither are you."

There was a pause, then Clément slowly smiled. "You did like me, even if only a little. You felt like kissing me that day."

Mathias gave a small nod. "I felt like kissing you that day."

Even now, Clément was cute. He had a lovely smile. And he had a pretty neck, long and slender, and a flat chest. Mathias definitely had a thing for those. Sure, he was blond. But Alberto's beautiful dark locks came with even darker secrets, so no, thank you.

Clément wouldn't call Mathias an asshole. Clément loved him since they were kids. Clément was *such* a good idea.

So when he playfully hooked his foot behind Mathias's knee and brought him closer, between his legs, Mathias said nothing and stared into the hopeful face in front of him.

27

FIGHT OR FLIGHT

Clément stuck the joint between Mathias's lips, chuckling as he did. "Let me light you up," he said, forcing a smile out of him. After he did, Mathias took a long drag to steady his heart.

"So you weren't afraid of me this whole time?"

"Afraid? If you're asking if I ever feared you'd hit me, the answer is no. The only times you ever put your hands on me was when you peeled me off the floor every time I fell during P.E. Trust me, I know. I counted those times."

Relief flooded Mathias to the point where he almost felt euphoric. He clutched Clément's hands, who turned scarlet. "You were counting?"

"The only person I've ever seen you touch was Daphnée, so it made me feel special. Even when your mother got sick and you were… distracted… you always had a kind gesture for me." Clément took his joint back, his other hand still clutching Mathias's. After a hefty puff, he carefully blew the smoke to the side. "When you punched that idiot because he insulted me, the only thing I was afraid of was you getting kicked out. But, hang on! Didn't you punch the *same* guy last year?"

"No!" Mathias chortled, and Clément's gaze fell on his lips. "No, it was Mathieu, Sylvain's friend."

"Oh, that guy is so very punchable. What was it, then? What did he say?"

"Something not worth repeating."

"Oh, come on."

Clément returned the joint to Mathias.

"Okay," he said after a couple of drags. "So when I punched the guy who insulted you, his nose bled, so his girlfriend stuck a tampon up his nose."

"Not bad."

"Thanks. Because of that, people started calling me—"

"Period Master!" Clément bounced on his seat. "So that's why!"

"Right. Then last year, Mathieu started spreading the rumor that that stupid name was actually because of Daphnée. Because I made her bleed or some shit, you know, because I was her first."

At that, Clément erupted in laughter. "Besides how vulgar that guy is, he's stupid, too. Does he even know what periods are?" Still laughing, he laid his forehead on Mathias's shoulder.

"I didn't think to ask," Mathias said. Clément's hair was tickling the side of his face. "Damn, I think I'd been wanting to punch him for a while, and he gave me the perfect reason. I really don't like people going on about Daphnée."

"What about me?" Clément drew back and took Mathias's hand again. After a hesitation, he interlocked their fingers.

"You what?"

"I'd love to ask you about her. Can I?" His palm felt hot against Mathias's.

"Why?"

"Because it's been torturing me for years. I've been asking myself, 'Why, why on earth would he date her?'"

Mathias let him swing their joined hands while he thought about it. He was relieved that Clément had never feared him. More than relieved: set free. And maybe that feeling, coupled with the joint and the amount of whisky he'd drank, turned him mellow enough to overshare.

"Daphnée was my best friend. For a very long time."

"So?"

"So I loved her."

Clément cocked his head. "I love my best friend too, but I'm not interested in fucking her." After a careful look at Mathias, understanding dawned on his face. "Neither were you, evidently."

"I loved her." Mathias rolled the joint between his fingers. "I sort of noticed a change of behavior, but I thought it was because she was getting older, you know, turning into a woman or something. I thought it was logical that she would go through stuff I'd never get. So I just kept doing what I always did, going with the flow. She was *Daphnée*. I knew she trusted me enough to tell me if something was wrong. And she did, one day." Mathias drew on the joint until his throat burned and he gave a light cough. "She showed up at my place and said she was in love with me. 'I can't be around you if we're not dating,' she said. 'You understand.' I understood jack shit. Anyway, you know what happened. If I'd said no, she'd have left me." Mathias found saying the words aloud for the first time was as painful as it was liberating. "You know, when my mom noticed something different about Daphnée and me, she asked me about it, but I was too awkward, too stubborn. I didn't want to tell my fucking mom about this stuff. 'Don't do anything I wouldn't do,' she said. But I knew her: she would have done anything for a friend."

"But that must have been awful!" Clément said, the corners of his eyes reddening. "For you I mean."

"For *me*? What about Daphnée?" Mathias let out a dry laugh. "I let her live this lie. Anyway, she's gone now, and good for her; she's free, and she's dating Sylvain."

"But as I recall, you were dating a long time."

"Because a few weeks after we started this charade, my mother was diagnosed. I had a good excuse to be a shitty boyfriend, and it worked most of the time. And Daphnée couldn't break up with me while my mother was sick—or worse, after she died. She would have felt bad."

"It would have looked bad, mostly." Clément's grip tightened around Mathias's fingers. "I think she shouldn't have given you this ultimatum in the first place."

Mathias shook his head. "I shouldn't have said yes. If I'd

understood what it really meant… I had no clue what I was getting into, and I really shouldn't have done that, I know that. But what the hell did I know? I was fourteen, and she was my best friend. And most of the time, it was fine between us; it really was. We were just hanging out, doing the same things we'd always done. It's just from time to time I had to, you know, do real boyfriend stuff."

Clément shuddered. "That's what I said: it must have been awful."

Mathias let him cling onto his fingers with a thin smile. "It wasn't that awful."

"But she's a girl! And you—"

"I don't know. I couldn't tell the difference at that point."

"Whatever you say." Clément's free hand came to rest above Mathias's heart. "You've always defended her, even when she left you. Even when she started dating your best friend."

"*She* was my best friend. Not fucking Sylvain."

"And now, what is she?"

"I don't know." Mathias pulled on the joint one last time and returned it to Clément's lips, who maintained eye contact as he smoked. He thought of Alberto doing the same thing with Xavier. "Another bad memory."

With a sigh, Clément drew him closer until their foreheads were an inch apart. "You always did so much for other people, and for what? You know Daphnée still speaks of you like you betrayed her because you weren't a good boyfriend? No wonder why your sister couldn't stand the sight of her."

"That's why?" Mathias's eyebrows rose. "I always thought Ella didn't like Daphnée because she hated Naruto." He laughed. "*Mi niña preciosa.**"

The thing was, Daphnée was right: he *was* a bad boyfriend. Took forever to return her calls and took even longer to… Anyway. She was right. He was about to tell Clément, but the latter reached up to stroke his scalp, and Mathias grew still under his touch.

"And your hair?" Clément asked. "When the time came, you

---

* My precious girl. (Spanish)

shaved your head alongside your mother. She's been gone for years now. Don't you want to—"

Mathias jerked his head to the side. "I can choose to shave my head. It's none of your business." He gritted his teeth, cursing his bad temper. "Sorry."

"That's okay." Clément's voice fell to a whisper. "All I'm saying is… you don't seem very happy, that's all."

Mathias hung his head. "I don't know how to be happy." He didn't deserve to be happy in the first place.

His words hung in the air long enough to make him feel embarrassed. He could feel the temperature in the back of his neck rise up, and he was about to find an excuse to piss off when Clément blurted out, "What if I could help you?"

Mathias gave no answer besides a confused look. Clément cupped his face between his hands. "I could kiss you now. I've been wanting to kiss you since I was twelve."

Mathias grimaced. "I had glasses at the time."

"So? I liked you."

"Okay."

"I still like you."

"Okay." Mathias looked away.

"Mathias, you're so sexy, even in that crappy hoodie. I'd really like to—"

Sexy, huh? Mathias gave a faint burst of laughter. That was so nice of him. Alberto also used to call him sexy. *Hot.* He was often acting completely manic when they were fucking, like he was a different person, able to let go entirely. It was amazing. Alberto could burn with desire for a few precious minutes, then turn as cold as the dead as soon as he was done.

His freak. His demon. His… Thinking that word tore at his chest, and he gave a pained grunt.

"What?" Clément brushed his fingertips against his cheek. "What is it?"

"Nothing."

"No, you can tell me. You can tell me anything."

With a certain sadness, Mathias realized he didn't want to. That despite this sweet reunion, Clément was actually more of a stranger to him than Alberto ever was. But they were alone in this room, and he was so sweet, and he wanted him so much that Mathias had the feeling he could make him come just by zipping his pants open. *Give him what he wants*, he thought. *Such* a good idea, *the best.*

What about what *he* wanted? Right. If that ever mattered, he wouldn't have come here in the first place. He would be... *No.* Mathias swallowed the words, wrapped his arms around Clément's waist, and kissed him.

It felt different, of course. Unfamiliar. Not unpleasant, not mind-blowing; just as it was before, with the others. But ultimately, uninteresting. Mathias broke the kiss.

"What's wrong?" Clément panted.

Mathias cast his eyes down. "There's..." *Go on, then, say it.* "There's a guy."

"Oh, no..." Clément released him. "You *do* have a boyfriend."

"No. It's not like that."

Hope returned to his eyes. "Are you or are you not with this guy?"

"I'm not," Mathias said, and his jaw clenched alongside his stomach.

"So don't feel bad! I can be your rebound guy, or whatever you need." Clément scooted to the edge of the desk. "That's all right, really. I won't ask for much. One night, that's fine." He took Mathias's hands again. "What do you say? I *really* want to be used by you."

Not a bad offer; not a bad offer at all. All Mathias had to do was let go. But then he recalled the time Alberto said *You can have my body, everybody else does,* in his bored, languid voice. A wave a self-loathing overpowered him, and he shut his eyes, his fingers closing around Clément's.

The gesture might have looked like he was taking the offer, because Clément leaned in and joined their lips together again, and Mathias responded aggressively, desperate for that kiss to blow away his unwanted thoughts. Surprisingly, Clément was nowhere near as shy as his frail appearance suggested. Within a few seconds, his hands were already trying to sneak into Mathias's pants.

Breath against breath, jeans buttons popping, and the memory of a smile he never got to see… In the end, all of this felt too familiar: a played-out song he couldn't bear to listen to anymore. Mathias stopped him before it went too far.

"I can't, I'm sorry."

Clément's fingers froze down below, and he took a breath before leaning away. "Do you love him?"

Mathias said nothing. There was nothing to say.

"Oh, Mathias…" Clément sighed, shaking his head.

"What? Why does it matter anyway?"

"It matters, Mathias! What the hell are you doing here if you love this guy? You should tell him, because there's no way he wouldn't—" He stopped himself, his teeth digging into his lip again. "You should tell him."

Mathias had no intention of getting into this with Clément. Stepping away from him, he stuck his hands in his pockets and felt the comforting weight of the lock between his fingers. "Don't you think I'm a bad person?"

Clément slid off the desk with a snort. "What are you talking about? What have you ever done that was so bad?"

"I don't know."

But he knew.

You let Alberto believe… His conscience nagged him in the back of his head. *You encouraged him to believe he was nothing to you. Because the thing you were most afraid of was looming over you, and you only know fight or flight.*

You couldn't fight him… So you fled.

Coward.

Mathias closed his fist around the lock. "The last time we were together"—he gave Clément a pointed look—"something happened." *It hurts,* he said. Mathias had hurt him. "He was in such a state… Anyway. I tried checking on him since, but he seems to have blocked my number."

Clément leaned back against his desk with a frown. "What did you do to him?"

"I…" Where would he even start? "What if he's afraid of me?"

"Because you're a bad person?"

"Yes."

"Hm." Clément gave a slow nod. "I should tell you he probably blocked you and you should move on. I really should." He swiped his tongue over his lip with a grim expression. "Go talk to him. Chances are, he's as afraid of you as I am." He gestured toward the door. "Now let me lick my wounds, please."

Mathias shuffled toward the door, but he turned around instead. "Clément," he said, his chest heavy. "You deserve better than to be a rebound guy."

Though his eyes were now red and glistening, Clément still had it in him to smile. "Since you kissed me after years of pining, I forgive you." He paused, his forehead creasing. "I hope I was helpful at least."

He was turning away; Mathias stopped him, and, slowly and carefully, he kissed his parted lips. Clément returned his kiss tentatively at first, but then his arms moved on their own. He pressed Mathias against him for two heated seconds before pushing him away.

"All right, all right, no need to overdo it. I'm that close to kidnapping you already."

Mathias brushed his cheek with the pad of his thumb. "Goodbye, then."

"Goodbye."

Mathias was already halfway through the door when Clément spoke in a mournful tone, "I envy him. Truly. He must be something."

He's a demon, Mathias thought, though his heart wasn't in it.

"I used to envy him too," he said, not looking back. "Then I got to know him."

Mathias returned to the living room, where Eric was signing autographs and distributing them to the others, the tips of his ears all flushed. "What are you doing?"

Eric winked. "Your friends said that if I ever became a famous footballer, they could sell them on eBay." While Mathias gave the group a reproachful look, he went as far as drawing a tiny heart next to his signature. "I like to be of service!"

"I can see that. Come on, let's go home."

Sylvain overheard him and let out a sound of protest. "Already? But I haven't even talked to you—" Mathias ignored him, pulling Eric toward the exit. "See you around, then?" Sylvain called after them.

"I don't think so," Mathias grumbled, slamming the door behind him. He pressed the button to call the elevator and exhaled a breath of relief. As they waited, Eric stuck a stick of gum into his mouth—*Tutti-Frutti*—and pulled out his phone.

"I have to try to get into those pajamas," he said as he typed, switching back to English. "Unless you still need me for something."

"Sure, sure," Mathias replied absently.

Eric looked up from his phone. "Everything all right? You seem…"

"Everything's fine."

"How come your jeans are open?"

"…"

Shit! His cheeks burning, Mathias buttoned himself up, but it was too late: Eric laughed all the way down, and he was still smirking when he pushed a confused Mathias into a taxi a few minutes later.

"Hang on," Mathias said. "Aren't we taking the train back?"

Eric gave him a pointed look. "You were in there a long time doing God-knows-what with your pants open, and there are no more trains back to Paris."

"There's a night bus."

"Aww, buddy!" Eric's laughter returned. "A *night bus*."

"Sometimes I forget you're rich," Mathias said, scowling.

"You're *very* forgetful, that's for sure."

The driver reversed onto the road, and the two friends were silent for a while. Mathias was grateful for the quiet, but of course, Eric couldn't endure it for more than five minutes.

"Are we going to talk about what happened in there or—"

"Nope."

"Okay. But also, who's Clément?"

"N-o-p-e."

Eric pouted. "I'll ignore you then and talk to Zak instead."

"Fine by me."

Leaning as far from Mathias as possible for good measure, Eric resumed his text conversation with Zak. At this time of night, the roads were deserted. It would take no time to return home. Mathias felt strange, like he was floating; perhaps that's what it felt like to be numb. In his pocket, the lock had turned hot from his touch.

Minutes later, Eric put his phone away with a cry of triumph. *"A moi les pyjamas!** God, that was almost too easy. I thought he'd give me trouble, but me thinks he can't get enough of *this*."

Mathias rolled his eyes, but Eric's laughter had him stretching his lips despite himself. "You're so cocky."

Eric popped his gum. "You like cocky. It makes you laugh."

"Bull…" Mathias shook his head, still smiling. "Fine."

Outside, there was only darkness, briefly interrupted by flashes of light. It was like Eric and he were on a train to nowhere. *A train to nowhere.* Someone would have liked that.

Alberto. His dad chose his name.

"My mother wanted to call me something else. Something French."

Gabriel.

Mathias turned away from the window. "Are you in love?" he asked. "With… the *pajamas*?"

An eyebrow quirked, Eric popped another bubble. "Huh? I thought it was obvious." He met Mathias's eyes. "Yeah, I am."

"How does it feel, then? To be in love?" Mathias tried his best to ignore the frantic beating of his heart. "You're just… happy all the time? Is that it?"

"Hmm…" Eric's nose wrinkled as he turned thoughtful. "It's a bit like a roller coaster at first. I've always been sort of happy-happy, but now I also feel… stronger? Like I'm not alone, you know? Zak really believes in me, and that's just enough for me to want to be… everything."

Mathias dropped his gaze down to his lap. "No one can be everything."

---

* The pyjamas are mine! (French)

"You can be everything to someone." Eric smiled at the thought. "That's it, really."

Mathias didn't think he could, actually. Be everything to someone. When he didn't think he amounted to… anything.

"You in love with Clément?" Eric asked, not losing any opportunity to torture him.

"No." Mathias felt his eyes on him and hurriedly changed the subject. "So the others, all these girls, you didn't love them?"

Eric answered with a bright laugh.

Mathias insisted. "You dated them even though you didn't love them?"

"It's not like that! I liked each and every one of them. I just had no clue what real love was, that's all."

"But that's what I'm asking!" Mathias said, frustrated. "How do you know the difference? How do you know if you love someone or if you just like them, then? How does it feel?"

Eric shrugged. "You don't know what love is until it starts hurting. *Really* hurting."

Mathias froze, dumbstruck. "Hurting to be around them?"

"No." Eric looked like he was about to laugh, but he shook his head instead. "Hurting *not* to be around them. When Zak was with Alberto and I was watching from the side, knowing I'd lost him. That pain, that's how I knew he wasn't just a crush, that I really loved him. But in the end… it was all worth it."

People kept saying that. Worth it, worth all the pain. Mathias's father would say the same to anyone who'd listen. Knowing he would lose her, he would still do it all over again. What nonsense. Why would he inflict such torment on himself?

Mathias knew too much about pain. The force of it tore him in half when his mother died. He hadn't been able to take a real breath ever since. He was standing in the dark, ready to snap. *Losing someone you love. That's pain.* The day of the funeral was the day he promised himself he would never feel that agony again, because he would never allow himself to feel such love again.

Nothing was ever worse than this. Nothing. Never. Never again.

"Are you ready to talk, or what?" Eric's voice startled him.

Mathias looked around him; they were standing on the front steps of his building, and the taxi was gone.

"… The hell?"

Eric didn't notice his confusion. His eyes were full of concern. "Why won't you let me help you, Mathias?"

Eager for the comfort of his bed, Mathias shivered in his jacket. "I don't know. Maybe I think I don't deserve you."

Eric cackled. "Maybe you're right. After all, I'm really awesome." He waited for his friend to join in the laughter, but Mathias just looked embarrassed, his cheeks prickling, not from the cold.

"I…"

"What?"

Mathias gritted his teeth. "I love you too, you know."

Eric's eyebrows rose just as his jaw dropped. "Oh, that's—that's not what I—that's…" He blinked several times. "Thank you? I mean… that's nice to hear."

Mathias scowled. "Like you didn't already know."

Eric opened his mouth, then changed his mind and pulled him into a hug instead. Mathias let himself be squeezed for half a dozen seconds before he felt he had to protest.

"No wonder why Kayvin hates you so much, if you were doing the same to him all the time."

Eric laughed without releasing him. "I never felt like hugging him, unlike you; you smell nice. Stop rolling your eyes."

"You can't even see my face."

"I can feel you rolling them anyway." Eric released him, only to hug him again. "Hang on, little bit more."

Mathias exhaled a sigh. He returned Eric's hug, but only for five seconds.

"It's not so bad, is it?" Eric asked, before they parted ways.

Mathias returned upstairs to a dark and empty apartment. He fixed his bed and then stood a while before his fridge. Starved, and yet without appetite. A familiar feeling of dread weighing on his stomach.

Never again, he reminded himself as he climbed into bed.

But what was it, then, that was keeping him awake in the night, the sheets crumpled in his fists, but a familiar old enemy? The specter of loneliness gripping him in the depth of night, its dark and smooth voice whispering to him tales of failure, of anguish, of loss. Laboriously kept at bay during those nights he'd held the one in his arms, it had finally crawled its way back with a new line…

This young man, you have lost him too.

28

IN YOUR CARE

It was thirty-five minutes in, and Alberto hadn't said more than good morning.

Doctor Roland took his silence as arrogance; it was obvious from the way he was looking at him. Alberto thought him a patronising old fart, so at the very least, the dislike was mutual. He was perfectly fine allowing the both of them to sit here in silence. In any case, Doctor Roland was being paid handsomely for his time, and Alberto believed his mother's money was best spent in silence.

"I hear you've had some… difficulties," Doctor Roland said, lightly shifting in his large chair. His face, framed by a grey beard, carried a strict countenance. "Your mother said you stopped taking your medication. Do you want to tell me why you did that?"

Though the drugs were clouding his judgment, Alberto chose not to answer. The fact that Mamma had talked to him annoyed him. He shrunk back in his chair.

Doctor Roland glanced at his watch. "The first time you came here, you didn't want to speak either. I can't help you if you don't want to help yourself." His eyes were cold when they met Alberto's. "Is it help you want, or a place to hide?"

A place to hide sounded about right. When he first met Doctor Roland years ago, Alberto already knew this man couldn't help him. He couldn't take the risk of having his secrets repeated to his mother. Alberto had always worried about his mother. The thought lingered in his mind, turning almost bitter.

"I shouldn't be here," he said, and a silence ensued.

"And why do you think you're here, Alberto?" Doctor Roland asked.

Alberto gave a shrug.

Roland pointed his pen at his face. "You're here because you lost control, and you hurt someone." He glanced down at his notes. "Your stepsister."

Through the large windows overlooking the park, Alberto could glimpse the early strollers, seeking comfort from an elusive sun. Spring was only two weeks away, but the past few days had been so warm, the trees in the park were already showing signs of budding. He knew in another fifteen minutes he'd be out there on his favourite bench, listening to the sparrows' song, his thoughts lost to a medicated fog.

"You don't get it," he said. "That's not what I meant."

"What did you mean, then?"

Even through the closed windows, Alberto could make out the song of the sparrows already. Fourteen minutes now. He could do this. He leaned back and settled in his chair. "Napoli lost to Ternana on September 11th, 2002. Two-nil." Alberto gave a thin smile. "When Papà came home that night, he was in a terrible mood. I'll never forget it. It was the ninth month of the year; I was nine years old; I was in a coma for nine days."

The law of three. His lip twitched, and the smile turned into a grimace before vanishing altogether. "Believe it or not, I was a different child after that."

Buried in his massive chair, Doctor Roland wasn't moving. Outside, the sparrows were singing.

"The meek, frightened sort, you know the type. A doormat, a fool, a perpetual loser. The sort who makes his mother cry…" Alberto arched an eyebrow. "Did you know I was homeschooled for years? Papà kept us locked away, and I never questioned why. When I woke up and Mamma bought our freedom, we rode the train out of Italy, and she said, 'We'll get to see the world now,' and I didn't want to. I didn't want to see the world at all. What was there to see, honestly? Do you think people are better in France than in Italy? What about London? San Francisco? I was nine years old, and I wanted to hide in her arms forever." Alberto's jaw clenched. He was eager for a cigarette.

Doctor Roland's eyes darted between him and his notebook, his pen scratching over the smooth surface of paper in an even, mechanical rhythm.

"Mamma is always worried. Worried about me getting hurt, worried about me turning weird. Once we moved to London, she really tried her best to make me open up. She got me the best tutors in London… Not that I could remember much of what they were trying to teach me. Through one of them, she met Martin. They were married within three months." Alberto paused, attempting to recall the image of his handsome stepfather. "He was okay, really. Young. Younger than Mamma anyway. He exercised a lot, and he let me borrow his horror movies. He said it'd be our secret, but Mamma found out anyway. She gave him an earful, but he laughed it off, and even though I knew she worried about me watching this stuff, I kept doing it in secret."

Catharsis.

"Eventually, I was deemed ready, and I was sent to school. The first time I saw the other kids, I had a fit. All those people over-crowding me. Just like before… *Such a beautiful boy, so much like his mother.*"

Tick, tock, tick, tock.

"Do you know what it's like, believing your resemblance to your mother is the reason your father can't stand the sight of you? Do you know how hard it is not to start resenting it? It made it tough to look in the mirror, you know—for years. But little by little, I got better at handling it, I really did. Perhaps I was too reserved, for a kid, and not particularly great at school, but I was doing fine. Better to have a few headaches than to cause them."

Alberto slowly twisted his neck to check the clock hanging over the door behind him. "Unfortunately, with such looks…" Not long now. A few more minutes. "It would have been a waste not to try."

Soon there would be the park. The bench. The swallows.

"Mamma wanted me to go on a shoot. She was certain

modelling would save me. But no matter how I looked, nobody really cared. I was fourteen years old; there were lots of kids more beautiful than me. I looked a little bit too much like a girl, in my opinion. But Mamma wouldn't give up; she asked everyone she knew. She told me she called in a favour from an old friend, but I heard a different tale. I heard she begged." Alberto let out a sigh. "Whatever she did worked, because he said he'd see me. Mamma was over the moon. He was world famous. A genius, really."

He's my life, she told him, while Alberto stood behind her, his gaze on his feet. *I leave him in your care.*

The soft chime of the clock announcing eleven o'clock didn't startle him. Alberto looked up, stared into the good doctor's face — with full-on dead eyes — and he waited.

"Your time's up," Roland said, a sharp hint of judgment in his tone. "Another fifty minutes spent in silence. Suit yourself, Alberto, you're an adult." He added under his breath, "And I'm being paid the same."

Not my fault you're not a mind reader. Alberto resisted the urge to smirk, picked up his coat, and, with a muffled goodbye, he shuffled out the door. *You're like everyone else: you want me to say it out loud, but I don't owe it to you.*

Located at the edge of the woods of Meudon, The Clinique du Parc Fleuri was a beautiful place, a manor rehabilitated into a private mental health centre a century ago by some bored heiress with a heart. Visitors were allowed three days a week, but not on Wednesdays, so Alberto had the rest of the day to himself, without having to stare at his mother's tear-streaked face. He dragged himself to the entrance, and after an accidental encounter with a potted plant, he gave the woman at reception an awkward smile that she returned with kindness. Outside, his favourite bench was free, so he stretched out right in the middle and, at last, released a breath.

Alone; that's what he liked. He ignored the knot in his stomach and fished in his pocket for his pack of cigarettes. Perhaps the smallest part of him wished his long monologue had actually passed his lips. Perhaps it would have been more freeing than letting the same old thoughts bounce against the walls of his mind. Stupid, stupid carousel.

He really was beyond help. What he wanted now was, indeed, a place to hide.

Berko arrived then. He stood behind Alberto's bench with his own pack of smokes, and watching him struggle to find his, he leaned forward and offered him one. His skin was so dark, the cigarette looked white as snow in his hand, and Alberto's fingers when he plucked it, looked cadaveric in contrast. Berko didn't seem to mind; he was smiling.

"So," he said, lighting Alberto's cigarette, "I have a question for you." He edged close enough that Alberto could smell mint on his breath. "I've been thinking about it all morning."

"Okay," Alberto said. "I think I know what you want to ask."

Berko flashed him a dangerous grin. "When you're in session, do you use the divan or the chair?"

This time, Alberto was slightly surprised. Since they'd met shortly after his arrival, Berko had done nothing but hit on him in a brazen, almost ridiculous way.

"Goodness," he said, blinking. "A real question."

Berko's grin widened. "I aim to surprise you until you fall for me."

"Obviously." Alberto was more amused than annoyed. "What do you think?"

"I'm thinking divan. So you can look like a Renaissance painting, and I can think about you looking like a Renaissance painting when I fall asleep tonight—no, before I fall asleep."

Alberto scoffed at the implication. "You have no shame, and you're wrong. I always pick the chair."

Berko clutched his chest as though Alberto had stabbed him in the heart. "No! I was so sure of myself. I always use the divan. How come you don't?"

Alberto studied the burning end of his cigarette with a wan smile. "I try to avoid lying down on old men's divans. As a rule," he added with forced enthusiasm.

The carousel's gears hiccuped and whined. *What's wrong with me?* The question fluttered in his mind until his forehead creased.

Berko peered at him through clever eyes. "Not a bad tip, if you're not into older men, but I am. It's not bad, you should try it sometime."

Alberto replied with a grimace, but again, he wasn't annoyed.

Berko and Alberto were cut from the same cloth. Like Alberto, Berko was a model. The supermodel kind, top of the top. He was also fucked up, or he wouldn't be here, looking gorgeous and hitting on Alberto despite his lack of reaction. He had a minor quirk—as he called it—which along with his addiction to a particular kind of narcotics, consisted in being extremely promiscuous. He was shagging everything that moved, as long as it had a dick. He had favourites, he had types, he had dares. And Alberto, being a model, Italian, and fucked up, was what he called his trifecta: his favourite patient here, his type, and a good dare. Though he was an adult and voluntarily signed himself up every year, Berko did not take therapy seriously; he really was cut from the same cloth as Alberto. And Alberto therefore couldn't help feeling a kinship toward him, so they'd spent a lot of time together since his arrival. In any case, Berko's relentless attempts at convincing him to have sex were a better distraction than day time TV in the break room.

"Roland isn't so bad," Berko said. "But he is a homophobe."

"Someone should tell him he chose the wrong profession."

"You'd be surprised."

Would I, would I.

Berko got tired of leaning over the bench and slipped in the space beside Alberto. He put his hand over his. "Did you know the first time I saw you, I thought to myself, 'Who is this gorgeous Wolfman?'"

"Wolfman?"

"Because of your badass ring and your bloodshot eyes, you looked like a wild animal. Then I thought no way, he's too sweet to be a predator. And now, look at you: a ruthless tease."

Alberto glanced down at the ring with a dry laugh. "That ugly old thing…"

"You don't like it?" Berko asked.

"Not really, no. I don't know."

"If you don't like it, give it to me." Berko stretched his hand toward the ring. "It's a Denizon. I can sell it for two thousand, at least. Then we can leave this place for a night; I'll treat you like a king."

Alberto quickly hid his hand in his pocket. "No."

Berko laughed at him. "Why are you wearing it if you think it's ugly?"

Alberto didn't reply. It was a reminder; he knew it now. A reminder not to remember. And it was no longer working. Next to him, Berko was becoming restless.

"Alberto, throw me a bone, will you? I couldn't even focus when I was doing that guy last night."

"I can see therapy's going well for you."

"I know, right? Just wait, I'll get you one day, I know it." Berko patted his hand a few times, then released it. "And you're going to love it. You'll ask me to marry you, and I'll say no, because you made me wait for weeks."

Again, Alberto didn't reply. His attention was drawn to a sparrow feeding its young in the tree right across the path. There was only one of them, its beak open in a grotesque manner.

"What are you thinking about?" Berko asked, unnerved by his silence.

"My mother."

"Therapy doesn't agree with you. Don't let Roland fix you too fast. He's only got three cars; he needs us to finance the next one."

"I'm glad to know our misery makes for a lucrative business."

"Hey, didn't I tell you not to overthink things? It's a waste of time and energy." Berko flicked the butt of his cigarette and leaned closer to him. "Think about that instead: you, me, the most attractive fuck ups in this place, both single at the same time and brought together by fate. To not take advantage of it, that would be truly devastating… and… and… you spaced out again, *amore*." He clicked his fingers under Alberto's nose. "One day, I'm going to take advantage and kiss you."

Alberto gently pushed his hand away. "You wouldn't dare."

"No, I wouldn't. But let me ask you a question."

"Go ahead."

"You'd like me on top, wouldn't you?"

Alberto snorted smoke through his nose and went into a fit of coughing. "That was your question?"

"I just wanted to see you blush."

"Did I?"

"No. Seriously, what do they have you on?"

Alberto searched his pockets for his prescription. Berko read it and returned it with a frown. "Has anyone ever told you you're overmedicated?"

"Yeah, I thought so. I mean, it's starting to make sense."

"Why don't you ask them to change it?"

"Every time I saw Roland, he just increased the dosage. Eventually, I stopped feeling anything, so I figured it was working."

Berko turned morose. Alberto didn't like it. He nudged his new friend with his little finger until his enthusiasm returned.

"I know your secret now: you're overmedicated! Somehow, that's a relief. For a minute, I thought you were bored."

"Both can be possible, you know."

"Ouch!"

Alberto apologised by offering him one of his own cigarettes. They were crumpled, of course, since he had forgotten they were in his back pocket, and he had sat on them all morning. Berko took this poor offering with a delighted smile.

"With that shit in your system, can you even get it up?"

Alberto taunted him with a quirked eyebrow.

"You're not for real. How is that even possible?"

"I don't know. Maybe that's why I like it rough. I can really feel it, you know. Deep inside."

Berko gave him a smouldering look. "You like it rough."

"I really do."

He couldn't help it. There were times when down on his face on Mathias's bed, taking it from behind, the red sheets clutched in his fists, a savage pleasure lit up his spine and shot through him just at the thought of how debauched he was, what everyone would think if they could see him now. Would they still find him gorgeous with bitten lips, his skin sleek with sweat, tears seeping from the corners of his eyes? Would they still act like they knew everything about him? In those precious moments, his body was his—his to do as he pleased. And so, he wanted to hurt it, bend it, break it, turn it inside out until there was nothing to think—or worse—to forget about.

It was almost similar to the wild ideas which popped through his mind when he was staring down at train tracks. One of these days, one of these days… See who'd dare call him irresistible after that.

Letting a silence settle over them, Alberto lit another cigarette. Berko scooted closer and asked softly, *"Amore?…"*

"Sì?"

"You're a sad, sad boy."

"Would I be here if I weren't?"

Berko clicked his tongue. "You and I are so different. How did you end up here?"

Alberto shook his head in resignation.

"Come on, you can tell me! It's always the same thing, really. Trust me." Berko spoke with confidence. "Your daddy didn't like you, or your mother's a bitch, or both. Or maybe you had a drunk uncle—"

Alberto held up his hand to silence him. "My daddy didn't like me."

"That's it?" Berko pursed his lips. "And I thought you were different."

"God, no."

"And Mom? Is she a bitch?"

"No." Alberto's heart lurched, his stomach twisting. "I…" His voice failed him for a second. "I love my mother." Something occurred to him, something he couldn't grasp fully yet. "I'm tired, Berko, really tired. I think I should lie down, forget about it."

Berko patted his hand a few more times then got to his feet. "Can I see you tonight?"

"Of course."

"Can I see you, see you?" He gave him a pointed look.

Alberto blinked at him, unsure.

Berko let out a theatrical sigh. *"Amore mio!* How can you be so insensitive? I worship you." He plastered a hand over his chest.

"And still, you reject me. Tell me, your majesty, what does a guy have to do to sleep with you?"

A heavy, impossible sadness suddenly fell on Alberto's shoulders, the weight of it nailing him to the bench. He looked up. "You really want to know?"

"Yes." Berko eagerly resumed his seat.

Alberto put his cigarette to his lips, and when he exhaled, the words came out in a cloud of smoke. "Give me a glass of wine, tell me I'm irresistible. A beautiful boy." He blew the smoke away; his breath caught in his throat. "Move fast. And don't forget to hold me down, before I realise what's going on."

In a blurry flash, Alberto remembered the way he felt afterwards, standing in front of his mirror at home, depleted. And then, catching sight of it, right there, red, unmissable, on the back of his thigh. It was all he could see, then. Truth, in the shape of a handprint. Then, he remembered thinking he must have liked it, or he wouldn't have let it happen, so fast and so quietly. Alberto had turned his back to the mirror from that day onward. And not just to the mirror; he had disguised his shame in a deep part of his mind, wrapped a little bow on it, labelled it with a slur. All so that he wouldn't remember something quite not right had happened under the neon-lights in that cold white office. He felt all of sudden the weight of Berko's arms around him.

"What are you do—"

"I'm holding you until you stop crying."

"I'm not crying."

Berko swiped his thumb under Alberto's eye and showed him the glistening pearl coating it.

"Have you ever told anyone?"

"No."

"Why not?"

"Because…" Alberto whispered, before quiet sobs took over. "I love my mother."

If he had told her, it would have destroyed her.

29

SAY THE WORD

THE NIGHTS WERE TOO LONG, the bed too empty. Clinging to Alberto's pillow, Mathias had conversations with the dead. *Yeah, really.* He had reached the point of having imaginary talks with his mother. One sided tirades, questions unanswered. *Mom, I met a guy. Mom, only you could have understood, because I remember the intensity of your love. You loved me and Ella more than anything in the world, you told me so many times. And when you needed me the most, I betrayed your love.* Throwing the covers over his head, curling into a ball, he would turn Alberto's little lock between his fingers. *I did it again, Mom. I betrayed him; I betrayed myself, too.* He would fidget under the sheets, stuff them into his mouth to swallow back tears. *Mom, I wish I could cook for you again. You always said, 'This is the best, you are so good, I love you, Mati'. You always said the right things, always.* He would kick back the covers, hit his own chest with his fist when air failed to fill his lungs.

When he was calm again, pulled by exhaustion toward a fretful sleep, he would press the lock to his lips, to his heart. *Mom, I met a guy. You would have loved him, too. And I'm sure he would have loved you. Five minutes around you, and he would have laughed with you and told you all his secrets. And then you would have told me... told me how to take good care of him, not ruin it as I did. You always knew everything. Tell me, is it too late?*

That one night, she spoke back for the first time. It was going to be okay, she said. He was ready to talk now, ready to admit it. *Ready to beg?* There was no need for that. "Remember, he's alive," Mom whispered as his damp eyelids quivered shut. "He needs you. He's not me."

He slept that night, but in the morning, he felt like shit again. He hated ghosts, he hated secrets. He hated everything and almost everyone; most of all, he hated himself. He took refuge in his kitchen, tried to make something beautiful. It was Elodie's birthday. Eric asked him to make a cake, so he would make a fucking cake. He'd do anything for Eric, who loved him. How long until Mathias fucked that up, too? Did it even matter? Eric would be off to Lyon in a couple of months, and he would shine there. He'd make a million new friends; he'll be too busy to keep in touch. Life would go on for him. Only Mathias would cling to the memory of him, the best friend he'd had since Daphnée. There might have been more than eggs, flour, and sugar in the base of Elodie's cake; he couldn't say.

Mathias tossed the cake in the oven and watched it rise, his heart in his throat. Was it too late? Was there a chance? Did Alberto even care? His heart racing, he pulled out his phone and called his number. He thought about what he should say. *Hey, pick up, I need to tell you I'm sorry. Like, really sorry. I know I'm an asshole, but is there any way we….?*

The call went straight to voicemail, as it always did. Mathias was blocked, and that's what he deserved. What the hell was he thinking? Alberto deserved better than an apology over the phone anyway.

When the cake was ready to be packed, Mathias gave it a long inspection. It looked decent, great, even. He really was good at this when he could be bothered to try. Mathias recalled how he'd started learning how to make maki after the holidays, when a certain someone confessed he loved them. He was caught by his sister and fed her a lie about opening his horizons. She was right to smirk. She knew how old-fashioned he was. Just like she knew the mini marshmallows in the cupboard were only for Alberto's special cappuccinos, but she kept his secret. She'd stopped complaining about Alberto a long time ago. She liked him. She liked him, indeed.

Without thinking, his palms sweaty, Mathias called Alberto's number again, thinking of maybe leaving a message. *Can we meet? I need to tell you something. That night after the club, I should have told you I'm jealous as hell, and I hate your other lovers, and I'll come pick you up every time you're drunk even if you don't like me, because I want you to be safe, always.* When it got to voicemail, and he heard the beep, he chickened out. He thought he'd hit the gym tonight, whatever Alberto might say.

His mother had said it last night: he was ready now. Today was the day.

They had set a green picnic blanket in a corner of the playground, to overlook the fact they weren't sitting on grass but on a slab of cement. Everyone was there, pretending the day was warmer than it was. Eric and Zak, Xavier, Charles-Henry, and the twittering Melissa and Joy, all of them surrounding Elodie as she blew the birthday candles on her cake. When Mathias brought it out, Elodie, visibly moved, asked why.

"I wanted to say sorry."

"To me? What for?"

He shrugged, she smiled. What for? Because apologizing to her was easier. She wasn't Alberto; he hadn't hurt her the same way at all. It would never go down so easily with him. And baking him a cake wouldn't do. Baking a cake was enough to tell the girl who had a crush on you, "Sorry I didn't notice, and sorry I rejected you. Please, let's be friends." It was his own way of making up for his lost friendship with Clément. How on earth was he going to tell Alberto what he needed to tell him? *Hey bro, remember the holidays? It was the best time I had in years. I really regret the way I treated you. I was frightened, because, in truth, and maybe you know it already, but just to be sure, you need to know—*

"Cake?" Eric was pushing a paper plate under his nose.

"Thanks." Mathias took it and absently passed it to Joy. He couldn't focus on the impromptu birthday party. He was too busy twisting his neck in every direction, looking for Alberto, to no avail. It had been three weeks already since they parted outside his home, and he hadn't seen him since. Mathias had tried to keep an eye out between classes, but Alberto always succeeded in eluding him. It wasn't a surprise; Mathias knew how good he was at hide and seek.

What would happen it Alberto refused his apology? Because he could apologize for being a grouchy ass, but what about those times he failed to protect him? And the time he actually hurt him? How do you get forgiven for that? Did he even deserve forgiveness, after everything that happened? No, Mathias decided. It didn't matter. Whatever the consequences, he would apologize. Alberto deserved it, and he deserved the truth. Mathias would respect whatever he decided after hearing it. He could be there for him from a distance. Was that creepy? It sounded creepy, come to think of it. The best outcome would be Alberto agreeing to resume their affair—the secret, sweaty one. Then right after the act, Mathias could lay it on him. A combination of three words that only worked when told in the right order, in the right tone.

Mathias jerked his head impatiently. He was ready—as ready as one can be. Where on earth was Alberto?

Joy tore him out of his thoughts when she leaned into his space. "I hope you'll make one for me, too."

"One what?"

"Cake! Maybe I could go to your place, and you could teach me. We're neighbors after all—"

He turned away from her with a grunt. He thought he'd caught a glimpse of Alberto and froze, but it was V.B., who, from having grey hair to being about six times bulkier than him, couldn't look less like Alberto even if he tried.

Hovering at his side, Joy gave a sigh. "I don't know what happened to me," she said in a dejected tone. "I keep backing the wrong horse. It's maddening."

Mathias ignored V.B.'s attempt at a wave, his gaze falling back on Joy. "Are you talking about me? Am I 'the horse'?"

"It's an expression. I know you're not really a horse! I'm just saying, this year, it feels like I can never get the things I want."

Mathias huffed. "Perhaps if you stopped thinking of people as things or horses, you'd have better luck. I don't know, have you thought about that, or are we just here to make you feel special?"

"You—" Joy stepped back. "You sound like Alberto." Her lip was trembling. "Congratulations on being an asshole, too!"

"Thanks. It's rewarding, you should try it." Mathias smirked. "Oh, wait."

Eric slipped between the two of them. "Someone woke up on the wrong side of the bed." He pulled Mathias away from the others. "Let's take a break, shall we?"

Watching Joy's eyes brimming with tears, guilt welled in Mathias's chest. He broke free from Eric's grip and took a steadying breath. She was right; he was an asshole. But today, he felt nothing but resentment toward Joy and the likes. All those things people said about Alberto, he had listened to them all. Desperate as he was not to see the good sides of him, he had been quick to believe every little nasty rumor said about him, without any care for the truth. But then it became clear Alberto wasn't the asshole people portrayed him to be. Bitter, yes, and weird, so weird. But that arrogance, that selfishness people loved to talk about, it didn't make so much sense anymore, especially after the Christmas holidays. Not after seeing the soft side of him, or how funny he was in his dark, morbid sort of way. As for his sweetness, hiding inside like the most delicate filling... He was a vegetarian, he "didn't want to be a bother," he only remembered the bad memories. All alone at the museum, so small on the bench, and later in the shower, his body black and blue.

"You're so cool."

Mathias closed his eyes. He could still see them, the cheap angel wings fluttering with each of Alberto's moves, spinning around in the bedroom, mischievous as a cherub. In fact, whenever he closed his eyes, Mathias saw him standing amidst a snowfall of feathers, dreamlike. Mathias's chest constricted painfully from his longing, his heartache. That day...

That day, he already knew he loved him.

He loved him, and he couldn't stop time. He thought he didn't know what love was, and it's true he had nothing to compare it with. But it was love, it was. And he knew it still later on, during Eric's party; his love threatening to burst out of his chest, he had wanted to tell him one way or another, but he didn't know the words. He should have gone on his knees and shown him, shown him the way he had failed to at the museum but succeeded later at home, to tell him it never mattered that he was a guy, but it really bothered him that he was Alberto. The most frightening human being Mathias had ever met, the only person in the word capable of crushing him under his indifferent gaze, mocking him, laughing at what—and who—was precious to him. Mathias always thought he was special and maybe a part of him felt a little superior, because his cock, like his heart, weren't easily stirred, unlike everyone else around him. The one time he felt something, it had to be for Mr Model, the handsome face everyone dreamed of. In truth, he could never forgive Alberto for the crime of being so magnetic that he had to resort to extreme measures just to spend a minute alone with him. He would have done *anything*, that was the truth, he would have done anything if that meant obtaining his heart, including hiding the worst parts of him. But he could never hide, in games or in matters of the heart. His mother always found him.

Mathias's chest was so heavy now. He lifted a hand to his throat and found the new chain around his neck. His fingers traced it down until they felt the lock under his shirt. He squeezed it to give himself some fortitude. "Anything," he whispered to the wind. *I would have done anything for you. You only had to say the word, and I would have done it. If you'd told me you cared for me, I would have fought, robbed, killed. I would have ripped your stepdad to shreds, I would have kidnapped you and hidden you somewhere safe, in my home, in my bed, in my chest; I would have taken care of you. I would have stopped being so empty inside. I would have lived; I would have lived again.*

He feared if he didn't tell him soon, he would simply be pulverized, crushed under the weight of the words. One more chance, just give him one more chance. Where the hell was Alberto?

"Matt, you okay?" Eric asked. His expression was too serious. When he was like that, he looked five years older.

"Yeah..." Mathias appraised him with a frown. "Are you okay? Did I accidentally step on your toe or something?"

"No." Eric gave Zak a long look, then he turned back to Mathias. "It's just..." he spoke in a strange, strained voice.

"What?"

"Nothing. It's just..." His lips stretched into an awkward grimace. "My butt. It hurts, this morning."

Mathias lips immediately tightened shut.

"Yeah, that's it!" Waving his arms in the air, Eric bounced on the balls of his feet. "My butt hurts. I'm very happy being of service and all, though honestly, I prefer the other way around, you know, with me on top, but Zak was determined to have his way with me, and it sounded fun at the time! But now, my butt hurts a bit." He slapped his hands on his ass with a bashful smile.

Mathias stared at Eric in silence. All the romantic thoughts and feelings that were filling him to the brim a second earlier had vanished, replaced by the image of his friend holding his own butt.

"You are joking," he said, scowling.

Eric gave him a strange look of frustration. "What, what? You can't relate?"

"... No."

"Really?"

"*Really.*"

Eric crossed his arms over his chest with a sneer. "Oh, so you're saying it didn't hurt Alberto the first time you stuck your dick in his ass?"

Just like that, and with a metaphorical crack, the ground split open between Mathias's feet, and he had to cling to Eric for balance. "W-what?"

All traces of a smile had vanished from Eric's face when he slammed his hand on his shoulder. "Drop it, Mathias. I've known all along." He paused, his lips pursing. "I mean, depending on when it started, I've known all along."

"Wha—"

"Enough with the what! You a parrot?"

Mathias swallowed the brick that seemed to have been jammed in his throat. Then it occurred to him he didn't care. None of this stuff mattered. He simply didn't give a shit anymore. Shaking his head, he gripped Eric by his shoulders. "Do you know where he is?"

30

DOWNPOUR

Eric's eyes widened in surprise. "No, why? Isn't he at school?"

Mathias ignored his question and started shaking him. "Does Zak know where he is?"

"Fuck, no! Why would Zak—" When Mathias released him, Eric abruptly fell silent. "What's going on? Is everything okay?"

"You have no idea…" Mathias's arms dropped to his sides. "I haven't seen him all week, and before that… he…"

"Let's go ask Zak, then." Eric gave him a reassuring pat on the back. "Come on."

Mathias was dragged back toward the others. The cake was gone, reduced to crumbs in the middle of the group. When Joy saw them approach, she turned her head to the side with an angry huff.

Eric tugged on Mathias's arm as he sat between Xavier and Elodie. Mathias followed suit, his stomach in knots.

"Did you like the cake, Zak?" Eric asked. That wasn't what Mathias wanted him to ask, but Eric seemed to feel the tension emanating from him and gave a light shake of the head. Mathias kept his mouth shut.

Zak was licking his fingers off one by one. "I loved it. Maybe you should learn to cook like Mathias, and make dishes just for me."

The smugness in his tone… Mathias realized Eric might have been telling the truth about what they did last night.

"Maybe! We'll talk about this later, at *home*." When his tone turned serious, Zak's cheeks grew two shades darker. But before he could retort, Eric abruptly asked, "What's up with Alberto? Has he got kicked out at last?"

Mathias unconsciously balled his fists and shoved them in his pockets.

"No," Zak said, eyeing his empty plate with regret. "Why do you say that?"

"Haven't seen his long face all week."

Zak stopped licking his fingers, turning thoughtful. "That's true. He must be sick again. I heard him tell Mrs Paquin he's often sick. I honestly believe he doesn't get enough B12 in his diet, you know? He doesn't eat meat."

Recalling Christmas's Eve, Mathias's eyelid twitched. Zak knew everything about Alberto, whereas Mathias knew fuck all. How hard would it have been to make the effort to get to know him, really? Why had it seemed so insurmountable at the time, when today, all he wanted was to corner him and beg him to speak to him again?

"Oh, but has he texted you, then?" Eric's voice rang false, but no one else seemed to notice. "For homework or… something?"

"No…" Zak furrowed his brow. "What are you insinuating?"

"Nothing. Just that, you're friends and all, so…"

Zak immediately started shaking his head hard enough to unscrew it from his neck. "We're not friends! We're not close at all! He… He didn't even invite me for his so-called cemetery birthday party—" Zak looked to the others for support. "He didn't! Even though I invited him to my party."

Mathias's heart skipped a beat. Cemetery party…? Did he mean—

"No, I did." Eric gave a nervous laugh. "I did… that." His eyes darted toward Mathias, who opened his mouth to ask something, but once again and to his dismay, Xavier beat him to it.

"Alberto had a birthday party in a cemetery? When?"

Zak gave the lot of them a bewildered look. "I don't know!

Months ago! His birthday's the 4th of January, so around that time, I guess."

The light in Xavier's vacant eyes flickered. "He didn't invite me either."

Across from him, Melissa's mouth fell open. "Yeah, like you're so close," she said, scathing.

Next to her, Joy's face was a mask of resentment, but she kept her lips pressed tightly together.

Though Xavier pretended not to hear Melissa, Mathias noticed his face was flushed. "Has anybody seen Alberto at all this week?" he asked, now completely alert. "Anybody?"

His question was met with a puzzled silence.

Mathias tried to recall the 4th of January. Right after the Christmas holidays, after the museum disaster. School resumed on the third and the next day they… they went to visit Mom's grave. Did this mean that the whole time, it was Alberto's birthday, and he didn't say a word? But why? Either he didn't care enough to tell him, or… or he didn't think Mathias would care. Probably the latter, Mathias realized, his stomach churning.

"What about during the holidays?" Xavier asked, pulling his phone out of his pocket. He glanced at his text messages, then opened up Instagram and a handful of other apps, before addressing Zak again. "When's the last time you heard from him?"

"I don't know…" Zak's voice weakened. "Before the holidays? What's going on?"

Seething in his silence, Mathias agreed: what the hell was going on? He felt Eric nudge him lightly with his elbow and forced himself to stay calm.

"Do you have regular conversations with Alberto?" Eric asked Xavier.

"Sometimes, but he hasn't replied any of my texts during the holidays, so I…" Xavier's face was turning ashen before their eyes. "I thought he might have gone abroad." Dialing a number, he abruptly got up and stomped off, surprising everyone.

Mathias, his face hot, also scrambled to his feet. Eric followed, but not before reassuring the others with a calming gesture. "Everything's fine."

Xavier stood in the middle of the playground, his phone stuck to his ear. Mathias crudely invaded his space, causing him to turn to the side. "Any answer?" He could hear the tremor in his own voice and was aware he'd be found out soon if he didn't keep his cool; but how could he stay calm, when dread was building up inside of him like dark clouds gathering before a storm?

"Straight to voicemail."

It seemed Xavier, too, was blocked. But why was he acting so concerned? His worry was obviously, and painfully, genuine. It disoriented Mathias, who didn't know if he should shake the truth out of him or comfort him as he himself wished to be.

Xavier looked lost, his phone in his hand. "I texted him, of course…" he muttered, as if to himself. "But he never replies to my texts, so I didn't think anything was wrong. But if nobody has heard from him for three weeks… Nobody at all…" He gripped his phone. "You think… you think the school would have told us if something had happened, right?"

Mathias's blood rushed to his head. Sweat prickling his armpits, he reached out toward Xavier's shoulder. "What the fuck are you talking about, if something had happened?"

Instead of answering, Xavier turned away from him.

"What do you mean?" Mathias insisted, his voice cracking. "What could have happened?"

Eric gently called Xavier's name. "Buddy. Do you think something could have happened to him?"

Xavier turned back around. His gaze was frosty when it fell on Mathias. "Yes, something could have happened to him. He's… He's not well."

Mathias's hands almost flew to grip Xavier's jacket. He buried them, shaking now, in his pockets. "What are you saying?"

"All this time spent together, and you've never noticed?" Xavier cocked his head with a wry smile. "It's you, isn't it? The one he likes? The one he suddenly rushes to my parties for?" He rolled his eyes at Mathias's stunned silence. "Fine, whatever. I don't care." He faced Eric. "He's on antidepressants."

Surprise stole across Eric's face, replaced by a doubtful expression. "What? How do you know that?"

"I saw them," Xavier said, serious. "This summer, in Aurons. When that drama teacher forced us to share the same room, Kayvin asked me to look through Alberto's luggage, to find out stuff about him, or stuff to, you know…"

Steal? Mathias's mouth twisted in distaste.

"I found his prescription meds in his suitcase. I recognized them because my uncle used to take exactly the same antidepressants. Then it made sense to me, why he's acting like a zombie, like he's not really here. The stuff he takes is so strong, no wonder why he falls asleep everywhere." Xavier tossed Mathias a resentful look. "You've never noticed?"

Hovering by Mathias, Eric looked slumped, like his worldview had been shattered. His eyes darted between the two of them, his jaw slack. Upon hearing Xavier's confession, Mathias didn't look any better.

"I don't…" Mathias shook his head. "I don't…"

Misinterpreting his bafflement for a denial, Xavier gave an exaggerated shrug. "You don't *what?* Alberto never wants to hang out with me, but the moment you two met at my party, suddenly he's everywhere. And suddenly you disappear at the same time, and he's smiling more, and you're smiling more. I know he's not coming to my parties for my sake. And after what Gwen and Kayvin did to him at my Christmas brunch, he would come back? You think I'm dumb, fine, but I'm not blind! I keep an eye on him all the time! You know who he keeps his eyes on?"

Mathias stomach lurched.

"Your ass, that's right." Xavier's tone grew bitter. "Oh, and dude, I saw what you did at my party. The moment Kayvin moved, you were on him. To say nothing that Alberto actually came to watch a football game. That's when I knew, even though you refused to admit you don't like girls. Alberto *hates* football, for some reason. My cousin Gwen told me." Xavier cast them a dim smile. "Eric's not the only one who knows but pretends he doesn't."

"What about Kayvin?" Eric asked. "Does he know?"

"Kayvin has suspicions… not about Mathias, but about us. Me and Alberto. But we're not lovers! We're not! He has it all wrong."

At last, Mathias broke out of his stupor. "Stop bullshitting, I saw you kiss!"

"So?"

"You did what?!" Eric started blinking super fast, like a malfunctioning cyborg. "You did wha—"

"It was nothing. Just a kiss between friends."

Ignoring Eric's gasp of horror, Mathias puffed out a laugh. "Sure! Do you kiss all your friends like that?"

"At least, I take care of my friends. Alberto feels safe with me."

These words stabbed Mathias right into the gut. He fell into an aggrieved silence.

"Okay, but…" Eric intervened in a tinny voice. "That's all a bit gay and all…"

Xavier turned to him. "It's best if you don't tell Kayvin about that, okay? Or anyone on the football team. Or anyone at all. I didn't see the problem at first until… you know. Until my party last time. Kayvin was furious, he accused me of doing stuff with Alberto behind his back and all. It took me ages to calm him down. So, I didn't invite Alberto on purpose, but he still showed up!"

"I remember," Eric said. "You told me you didn't invite Alberto to avoid trouble, but when I spoke to him I… I thought he had already been invited. It's my fault he showed up at your party."

"When Kayvin saw Alberto dance with Melissa, he really lost it. He thinks everyone he knows is turning gay out of nowhere, and he's already mad about it, but he really hates it when girls like Joy and Melissa give all their attention to 'the gays'. He can't stand it."

"So, you're just friends?" Eric asked, unsure. "You and Alberto."

Xavier nodded. "Yes, friends. I care about him, that's all. After I found his pills and I noticed how fragile he is"—Mathias scoffed—"I felt like I had a responsibility, you know… to watch over him."

"Why don't you watch over your own uncle, then?" Mathias snapped. He poked a finger in Xavier's chest, his face burning. "And leave Alberto to me!"

Xavier pushed his hand away in an impatient gesture. "My uncle's dead. He shot himself years ago."

Mathias stood back, horrified. "Shit… I'm sorry."

"I know. Everyone's always sorry, after the fact." A hint of defiance shone in Xavier's eyes. "You all think depression's a joke. Or maybe you don't think about it at all until the consequences hit you in the face. You say I should leave Alberto to you, but you don't even know where he is. You don't even know how he felt, what he was going through. You don't know anything, so don't you start going all Kayvin on me."

Mathias's world tilted. Is that how everyone saw him? Charles-Henry, Eric, even Xavier. He was just a Kayvin in the making, a worthless bully, another asshole drawn to a career that would allow him to shout at people without consequences. "I'm sorry," he repeated.

"I was watching over him when you were just fucking around." Xavier's expression twisted. "So don't you dare look at me like that. Don't you fucking dare."

"I said I'm sorry, okay?" Mathias spoke in a hollow voice. "Because I am! I'm sorry—I'm sorry—I'm—" He stopped himself. He was worse than a parrot now. "I didn't know."

A warm weight fell on his shoulder. Eric had swung his arm over it. Mathias said nothing, grateful for this gesture of support.

"You're right, Xavier," Eric said. "If anything had happened, the headmaster would know about it. We should go and ask him."

Just then, they were approached by Elodie and Joy. Sweat pooling at his armpits, Mathias forced himself to stand straight. What did they want, this time? He really couldn't deal with them right now.

"Have you found Alberto?" Elodie asked.

Mathias didn't answer. His jaw was wired shut with dread. Eric was uncharacteristically quiet, his eyes shrouded by concern. Xavier took upon him to answer with a shake of the head.

"There's something you should know, maybe… I don't know."

"What?" Mathias finally asked in a raspy voice.

Elodie gently nudged Joy to speak.

"It could be nothing, but I'd hate…" Joy's voice was quivering. "I'd hate it if something had happened to Alberto. I know we're not friends, but I… I don't think he's a"—she gazed at Mathias—"a horse, or a thing…"

Mathias's shoulders relaxed a little. He even managed to offer her a faint smile.

"What is it?" Xavier asked impatiently. "What do you know?"

"I saw something at your party, a month ago. Kayvin had cornered Alberto outside your house. He had him against the wall, and I…" Joy hesitated and turned to Elodie, who nodded in encouragement. "I overheard him threaten Alberto if he ever got near you again, Xavier."

"Really? What did he say?"

"I really don't want to say." Joy sounded terrified. "Please don't ask me. But it sounded bad, and now he's missing or something? I don't know. Maybe you should ask Kayvin if—" She gasped in surprise.

Mathias was already gone. His head swimming, he tore across the playground toward the lockers, where Kayvin held court. He was on him before the bastard could understand what was happening.

Adrenaline gave Mathias such strength that he lifted him off the ground. Kayvin found himself pressed against the lockers with a dumbfounded expression.

"What did you do to him?" Mathias was beside himself, the rage rushing through his veins blurring his vision. "What did you do to him?"

Kayvin's eyes were twice their size, all white, the usual conceited pride all gone. "I-I-I don't know who you're talking about!"

Mathias's fist smashed into his locker. When Kayvin saw how the metal had bent from the impact, he let out a yelp. "W-what's your fucking problem?" His voice was as shaky as Joy's a minute ago.

Mathias gripped him even harder. "Where's Alberto, Kayvin?" When Kayvin failed to answer, he slammed his fist into his locker again. The metal screamed, but Mathias felt no pain. "Speak! What did you do to him? What happened after Xavier's party?" So what if he sounded unhinged? Nothing mattered more than finding Alberto.

"Nothing, man, I…" At last, understanding dawned on

Kayvin. His lips flapped stupidly until he found his words. "I swear I did nothing to him. I threatened him a little. He was… he and Xavier—"

"What did you do to him?"

"Nothing! God! Nothing!"

Mathias didn't believe him, and his fist found Kayvin's locker again. "Tell me, you fucking piece of shit!"

Coming from behind, someone wrapped their arms around him to separate them, without success. Mathias could only see one thing, his reflection in Kayvin's bulging, frightened eyes. He saw his future in the stupid look on his face: a frustrated, angry loser, without anyone by his side. "I hate you!" he yelled, pounding the locker until his hand grew numb. "I fucking hate you—"

The sound of the airhorn announced the imminent arrival of the headmaster. Mathias instinctively let go of Kayvin, who let out a sob of relief. Mathias watched him slump against his destroyed locker with a cold indifference.

"You're a fucking psychopath!" Kayvin shouted, his eyes red. "You're all fucking crazy here!"

"I don't want to be like you." Mathias stood numbly, eyeing V.B. as he crossed the playground toward him with a stony face. "You don't get it… I need him back."

Next to him Eric was standing, his lips parted in silent astonishment. Mathias realized everyone on the playground was watching him. His friends, their expressions alternating between shock and horror, and other faceless students pointing their fingers at him. They all looked like cardboard cutouts, all except Van Bergen, who shoved Eric and Xavier aside to slam his beefy hand on his shoulder.

"Just give him back to me," Mathias mumbled.

V.B.'s hand felt light on him. Everything else was a blur. Mathias glanced up toward the building, and a faint feeling of hope rose in his chest. *Let's go, let's go.*

"Please, Headmaster," Eric said, his face full of anguish.

"Don't even bother." V.B. didn't even look at him and pulled his charge toward his office.

"You've got to expel him, or I'll call my father!" Kayvin shouted, somewhere in the back. He sounded really far away.

Let's go.

Mathias floated more than he walked toward the main building. Where was Alberto? What happened to him? Did it occur to him to let go, to leave this world then? Was he gone, like Mom? Did Mathias lose him, too?

Death. The prospect kicked the stuffing out of him. His knees buckled, and he would have fallen flat on his face, if not for the headmaster, who yanked him right up. "You're really busting my balls," V.B. muttered through clenched teeth.

Back inside, V.B. pushed Mathias in his office without ceremony. "What the hell is your problem?" he boomed, slamming the door shut behind him. "Do you want to get kicked out so bad?" He stood against the far wall of his office with his arms crossed, his muscles stretching the gray fabric of his shirt.

Mathias eyed him warily for a moment. His wits were slowly returning to him. He was exactly where he needed to be, in the headmaster's office. Where no one could hear.

"Where's Alberto?" The cold anger in his voice made V.B.'s brow wrinkle with incredulity.

"Who?"

That only angered Mathias further. "*Alberto.* Gazza. Première Littéraire A*."

The headmaster looked around the room. "What the hell—"

Wrong answer. Mathias reached out behind him and swiped a pile of files off his desk. "Where's Alberto?"

"Okay…" V.B.'s incredulity turned to mild amusement before Mathias's eyes. "Before we do this, just know that trashing my office won't achieve anything except pissing me off for disrespecting the cleaning staff."

"Oh, really?" Mathias sneered. With a movement of his arm, another pile of documents was pushed off the desk. They burst open on impact, littering the floor with sheets of papers. Van

---

* 1. The specific class he belongs to.

Bergen glanced at the mess with a click of his tongue, but he didn't move a muscle.

"Just tell me where he is." Mathias's voice was shaking.

"Who, Alberto?"

"Yes, asshole!"

At last, V.B. reacted. "Hold on…" Raising a hand, he thoughtfully raked his fingers through his hair. "Are you dating that kid?" His eyebrows shot up. "Under my nose?"

With a sound of frustration, Mathias grabbed his name plate and hurled it in his general direction.

"Hey, watch the face!"

Mathias met his glare head-on. "Don't you get it, yet? I will destroy your office bit by bit if you don't tell me where Alberto is."

"Have at it, then!" V.B. shrugged. "I can't give you that information. It's private. Do you know what *private* means?"

"Do I? Do I?"

So, he knew where he was, but he wouldn't fucking tell him? With an angry curse, Mathias flung his pen holder across the room, and when the headmaster snorted, he did the same with his desk lamp, his diary, then the greyhound statuettes near his picture frames.

"Hey! Not the dogs, come on." V.B. leaned down to pick them up one by one.

"Where is he?!" Mathias shouted, and his tone froze V.B. on the spot. He held up his hands, his entire face frowning.

"I don't know what's the matter with you, but you're acting crazy. You need to get your shit together."

Mathias couldn't care less. He raised his arm, his hand hovering over the largest picture frame in the middle of the desk.

Van Bergen's eyes grew cold. "You wouldn't dare."

Mathias seized it and held it up between them. "I would, I really would."

"Mati—"

"Don't *Mati* me, you bastard! I will break it, so help me god, I will hurl it out the window if you don't tell me where he is."

"Just stay calm now." V.B. kept his hands up. "Your mother's on that picture. Surely you wouldn't want to do that to her?"

"My mother?" Mathias burst out a laugh. "My mother?! She would tell me to burn this place to the ground, and you, and your statuettes and your pictures with it, if you refuse to tell me where my… where my… where my…" Mathias choked on the words. Tears began streaming down his face, as hot as lava. "Tell me!"

"I can't!" V.B. pleaded. "I can't! Even for you. I can't do that. It's confidential. I can't…"

"Oh, God…" Mathias's knees weakened again, and he had to lean on the desk to support himself. "I pushed him away, just like Mom. Oh, God… He's dead, isn't he?"

"What?"

"He's dead, he's dead—"

Suddenly V.B. was right in front of him, his arms reached out as if to hug him. With a cry of despair, Mathias landed a blow on his shoulder, then another, then another, until he was reduced to a mushy pile of tears and snot, sobbing at the headmaster's feet.

"Alex!" he cried, burning with fear and grief. V.B. had trapped him in an embrace tight enough to crack his ribs. "Alex…"

"It's okay… I know…"

"I want my mom…"

"I know, my boy. I'm here."

"I did it," Mathias gritted out between sobs, twisting Alex's shirt in his fists. "I killed her. That time… I was so angry at her, I told her… these things… and then she gave up. She gave up because of me."

"Is that what you think?" Alex cursed under his breath, his hand rising to cup the back of Mathias's head. "Your mom loved you! And she knew how much you loved her. She didn't take it like that. And she didn't give up either. That wasn't her style. Don't you remember your fucking mom? You really think a snotty brat like you could have made her flinch?"

Right then, the door burst open, and Mathias looked up to see his dad and his sister rushing inside. The sight of his boy crumpled on the floor with tears streaming down his face brought fear to his father's eyes. "You texted code red?"

Without releasing Mathias, V.B. glanced at him. "I don't know what to do this time."

Dad and Elisa each picked a side, and Mathias found himself choked in a group hug. He should have hated it, but in truth, he was so exhausted that he reveled in their warmth. He even reached around his sister to hold her closer.

"Your office's a real mess, Alex," Dad said. "Way to set an example to the kids."

"That's right!" Ella squeaked, almost buried under her godfather's arm. "You should clean up a little."

"Ha, ha." V.B. extirpated himself from this sorry pile of humans with a wounded look at his tear-soaked shirt. "Cyril, did you know about Mathias and that Alberto kid? This one thrashed my office to get me to tell him where he is."

Mathias froze. He made eye contact with his sister. Elisa shook her head, his lips pinched.

"Is he alive?" Mathias asked anyway.

"Of course, he's alive!" Alex clicked his tongue impatiently. "Cyril, did you know they were a thing?"

"Maybe." Their father shook his head helplessly. "What can I say?"

"You're my best friend," Alex muttered. "I've known you two decades. You could have told me."

"And yet, it's really not my place to say."

"He's as good as my nephew, and now I find out he might be gay, like that? What if he needed me as a role model—"

"Who the hell would want you as a role model?" Mathias said darkly. "Unhinged fucker."

"Ah…" Dad let out a sigh of relief. "He's better now."

As if they all knew he had reached his limit, Dad and Elisa released him to stand on their feet. Alex stood by, a smile tugging at his lips. Disoriented, Mathias remained sat on the floor, his eyes fixed on his father.

"Are you sleeping with Alberto's mother?" he managed to spit out.

"What? No!" Dad said, and relief washed over Mathias. "It's not like that!"

Part of Mathias wanted to ask what the deal was, but at the same time, he couldn't make himself care. His mind was still full of

Alberto. What was he supposed to do now? Wiping his face with the back of his hands, he slowly got to his feet.

Elisa picked up a box of tissues off the floor and handed it over to him. "Alex," she said, turning up her nose, "you're not going to expel Mathias, right? Kayvin's the biggest bully. You always tell me to punch bullies in the face, how can you expel Mathias now?"

"I don't know." Alex shuffled toward his desk with a troubled expression. "Let me deal with this stuff. Cyril, you need to take him home."

"I can take myself home," Mathias said.

"Can you?" Alex sunk in his desk chair with a sigh. "Mathias. You've been acting up all year, and I let you get away with it every time. You broke out of the detention room, for Christ's sake! And I still let you get away with it." He swiveled in his chair to face Mathias. "This time, you really did it. Kayvin's father is the last person I want to deal with. So, be good and wait at home while we fix your mess."

"Fine." Mathias met his eyes. "*After* you tell me where I can find Alberto."

Alex scoffed at his insolence. "Your boyfriend's mother called me, and naturally, asked me to secrecy. I'm not going to betray her confidence, even for you. If I do, I could lose my job, and much more."

Mathias hadn't originally thought about that. Now that his mind was clear, he could see why that would be a problem. "I'm sorry, I hadn't thought about it."

"No, you hadn't." For the first time in years, Alex looked genuinely tired. "So, anything you want to know, you're gonna have to ask Miss Gazza." He motioned toward the door. "Now please, get the fuck out my office and go home. Ella, here's a note. Get back to class immediately. Your dad and I need to talk."

Mathias trudged toward the door in silence. From the moment Alex mentioned Mrs Gazza, a glimmer of hope had rekindled the fire in his heart. Alberto's mother knew everything, and he knew where she lived.

Spring

"I pictured myself rising above the wreckage
with one hand raised to shield my eyes,
and the other holding on to you."

Onlookers

31

MOUNT OLYMPUS

MATHIAS STUMBLED OUTSIDE, his ears buzzing. The playground was empty. Everyone was back in class, except for him. He forced a deep breath into his lungs, trying to clear his muddled thoughts, until he felt a hand on his shoulder. Eric was standing behind him, his expression full of concern.

"You should be in class."

"So should you." There wasn't a trace of laughter on Eric's face. "So, where is he?"

For a moment, Mathias said nothing. He appraised Eric like he'd never seen him before.

"How long have you known, exactly?"

His friend's ears turned pink before his eyes. "Does it matter?"

"How long?"

"A while."

Mathias replayed their interactions in his head, couldn't think of anything special except Alberto's ID. "What gave me away?"

Eric's shoulders dropped, betraying his reluctance. "I mean… it wasn't just one thing, you know. First, there was that time I saw you two alone in Xavier's pantry. I thought, 'Oh? What do we have here? Who would want to be alone in a room with that guy?' No need for death stares, Mister. It was suspicious, if you ask me, but to be fair, I quickly dropped it. But then there was that time when I rode to your apartment the morning after Joy's party, and there he was, outside your place, in his fancy clothes. That was strange. But since strange stuff happens all the time around me, I thought I'd let it go. It's not the only instance I thought there was something fishy going on, but there was always another explanation. Like that time I found Alberto's ID under your chair in class. That was a big hang on a minute! But after all, I couldn't be sure. It was under your chair, doesn't mean it necessarily fell off your bag! Of course, all of these were just tinfoil hat conspiracies, so I couldn't share my concerns with anyone, but at this point, I was almost convinced you were hiding something from me. Something big. Or should I say tall. With a face." Eric gave Mathias a smug look. "All I could do was investigate, and prove to myself that maybe that girl who was driving your little stick-in-the-mud self nuts was no girl, but Alberto, because he'd drive anyone crazy, he's so—"

Mathias silenced him with a glare. "So, that's what did me in, huh? That damn ID. I knew I shouldn't have taken it; it was wrong of me in the first place."

"Oh no!" Eric eagerly shook his head. "That's not what gave you away, buddy. No, the thing that really did it for me was when I saw you two fucking in my mom's office!"

For the second time today, Mathias felt like the ground split open beneath his feet. Eric, oblivious to his shock, went on with a smile. "Yeah, that was definitely the moment I went like, 'Wow. Probably not just roommates, then.'" Eric turned thoughtful. "I really tried to make you admit it since then, but you're a tough nut to crack."

It took a moment for Mathias to recover, but he eventually stammered, "For your information, we were not… we weren't…"

"What do you call what you were doing then?" Eric looked bewildered. "Buddy, do you know what *fucking* means? Knowing you, nothing's certain. You know I've tried all year to work out your deal, and I still have no clue. And please, don't make that face, I'm the one who should make that face. I'm pretty sure I *invented* that face when I came upstairs to get more tonic from my mom's mini fridge and I saw you two—"

"But we weren't doing it, I swear!"

Eric ignored him. "My man, always acting all stuck up, but in reality…"

Mathias harrumphed, and he was about to hurl him into a bush when he realized someone was standing right behind them, and they both cursed in fright.

"Hi." Elisa lifted her hand.

"Little girl!" Eric shouted. "Don't ever do that again!"

She slipped him a condescending look that would have made Alberto proud.

"What are you doing here?" Mathias asked, aghast. "Did you hear what we just said?"

"Every word." She drew closer. "I caught them at it, too, you know. Wayyy before you did."

Mathias bared his teeth. "We thought we were alone! Why is there always some weirdo watching?"

"Anyway"—Elisa cut him off with a wave of her hand—"what's the plan?" When Eric and Mathias exchanged a wary look, she sighed. "I know you're going to check on Alberto. Why are you still here?"

Mathias hesitated. "I don't know what to do. I don't trust his mother… Or his stepfather… I don't trust anyone. Who knows... What if they're keeping him prisoner in that shitty house?"

"What?" Eric's eyebrows shot up. "Why would they do that?"

Mathias briefly considered telling him, then he shook his head. "I can't tell you more, but trust me on that. I may have to sneak in, and I—"

"I'll help you!" Eric started jumping in place. "I'll create a diversion, like last time."

"… Thank you." Mathias appreciated that he didn't even have to ask. "Really."

"I'm coming, too," Ella said. "He's my friend. I want to help." She averted her eyes when he blinked at her in disbelief.

Mathias hated to admit it, but Ella was smarter than him and of course, less aggressive. Also, she was so small and cute. It would be good to have someone like her around to defuse the situation in case things turned sour. The three of them left school before Alex could put two and two together and hopped on the metro toward Alberto's home.

"So, what happens when you see him?" Eric asked once they stepped onto Robert Schuman Avenue. "What are you going to tell him?"

"I want to make sure he's okay, first. It seems he blocked my number, and possibly Xavier's."

"How do you know?" Elisa chimed in. "Does it ring, or does it go straight to voicemail?" She added slyly, "Trust me, I've blocked a lot of people."

"Straight to voicemail."

"Sounds like his phone is turned off."

Her words only accentuated Mathias's concerns. "Let's just find out if he's okay, then I'll improvise, I guess."

They reached the imposing black gate. Mathias turned to Eric and Ella, his jaw set. "His stepfather will probably be at work, but his mother will be here. If she lets us in, great. But if she doesn't, we'll need a diversion so that I can get up to his room and speak to him face to face."

"Alright." Eric said. "What's it going to be?"

Mathias thought about it while trying to ignore how fast his heart was pounding in his chest. "Someone's gonna have to seduce her." He glanced at Eric, who blushed profusely.

"Oh no. No, no. I'm really not a fan of this plan."

"What happened to 'I'd do anything for you, best buddy'?"

"When did I ever say that?"

Mathias gave him a pointed look.

"Fine! That does sound like me. But when I said it, it didn't occur to me that you'd ask me to seduce Alberto's mom!"

"Yeah, well... you said it, so now..."

"Oooh..." Eric furiously rubbed the back of his neck. "I don't know..."

Mathias felt he won the upper hand. Eric was just too sweet, too good for this world. "Go on. Try to make yourself sound more mature. Deep voice. And act sexy."

"Hang on, why me?" Eric suddenly rebelled. "You're sexier than me, everyone keeps going on about it."

"What?"

"Seriously, you're super hot! So, you do it."

Standing between the two of them, Elisa was watching in silence, her mouth agape.

Mathias clicked his tongue impatiently. "Seducing Alberto's mom? While you're going up to his room? Sounds logical to you? Even if I could seduce the mother of the guy I love—"

Eric gasped. "Did you just—"

"Shut it! Even if I could do that, which is wrong on so many levels, how do you think Alberto will react when he sees you, of all people, sneaking into his bedroom?"

"Okay, but…" Eric wrung his hands. "I-I don't want to seduce her. I'm… I'm married in my heart."

Mathias slapped his forehead. "No one's asking you to go through with it!"

"Buddy…" Eric's smugness returned. "When I take the shot, I score."

"Oh, for fuck's sa—"

"Excuse me?" Elisa interrupted, her hand raised. "Can I just say something real quick?"

The sight of her tiny hand, raised politely, immediately softened Mathias. "Of course, what is it?"

"Just a simple question: What the hell is wrong with you?" She ignored their bewildered expressions. "What in the world makes you think Alberto's mom would be seduced by a seventeen-year-old boy?"

Mathias didn't have an answer for that. He and Eric exchanged a sheepish look in the middle of the pavement.

"*Cristo*…" Elisa shook her head. "Eric, you don't need to seduce anybody. Just talk to her, make her smile, you'll still be free to marry Zak later. If he still wants you," she added through gritted teeth.

Eric nodded, obviously relieved. After a steeling breath, Mathias raised his hand to press the doorbell, only to be stopped by Eric.

"Hang on, Matt."

"What?"

"I want you to know something." Eric spoke in a reluctant tone. "You know, all I really wanted was for you to be happy. So, if you... if this whole time, you hid Alberto away because of me, I sincerely apologize."

Mathias gave his shoulder a pat. "Don't beat yourself up. You were just a convenient excuse. It's true I would have preferred if you liked him, but in the end, it wouldn't have changed anything. I would have found other reasons to push him away. I did, actually."

Just then, the gate abruptly opened, revealing Mrs Gazza and a middle-aged man who appeared—by the look of his equipment— to be a pool technician. "I'll see you back tomorrow with the missing piece," he said, accidentally bumping into Eric. With a quizzical look, the man skirted around them to return to his van parked across the street, and Mathias found himself facing Alberto's mother. Even dressed casually in slacks and flats, she was extremely tall, her cold beauty simultaneously intimidating and riveting. But his time with Alberto had taught Mathias better than to trust the unapproachable facade.

"What is it?" Mrs Gazza asked in a faint voice.

Mathias noticed how glassy her eyes were, how frail she looked once the shock of her formidable appearance had waned. He forced himself not to turn back and was relieved when Eric took charge.

"We're friends of Alberto. Can we see him?"

Alberto's mother gave Eric a bleary look, then Mathias, then Elisa. "Alberto's sick. He can't have visitors."

"He's been sick a long time," Eric said. "We haven't heard from him in weeks."

"He has an infection." She sounded hesitant. "He won't be back for a while."

Just as Mathias had feared. He slipped Eric a quick glance, but Elisa spoke first. "That's okay, we just came to bring his homework. Can we come in?"

"He's resting. I don't want to wake him."

"No problem!" Eric flashed her a bright smile. "We'll just give it to you then." Despite his friendly tone, he was already letting himself in as he was speaking. To Mathias's surprise, she let them do so without reaction. After Xavier's confession, it was easier for him to put two and two together. Recalling his own father acting similarly after his mother's passing, Mathias concluded she must be on some antidepressant, just like her son. She led them to the pool lounging area and despite the cold, resumed her seat on one of the chairs.

"I remember you," she told Eric. "You play football… You're Alberto's good friend."

"Oh yes! That's me!" Eric hid his discomfort behind a boisterous laugh. "We're best friends. I love the guy. *Love* him." Like a kid in urgent need of a bathroom, he started dancing on his feet at the edge of the pool.

Unlike Mathias, Alberto's mother didn't register his nervosity. "Come closer, I don't want you to fall," she told Eric. "The heating system broke; the water's really cold." Her shoulders visibly sank. "Alberto falls in there all the time."

"Can I use your bathroom?" Elisa bellowed out of the blue. "I'm very small and have a tiny bladder."

Mathias skewered her with a glare, but Mrs Gazza nodded and waved toward the house. "Of course. There's one right as you come inside, second door on the right."

"Thank you." Elisa grabbed Mathias by his sleeve. "You, come with me."

Noticing Mrs Gazza's brow furrowing, Mathias spoke fast. "I'm her big brother; I have to watch over her."

Before she could react, Eric plopped on the nearest chair and leaned toward her. "Would you like to know about the first time I met Alberto? So, he was sleeping—"

Mathias and Elisa left them, making their way toward the house as casually as possible. Once inside, Mathias started running, Elisa at his heels.

"We must hurry," he said, flying up the stairs. "Eric won't be able to say nice things about Alberto for more than a minute or two."

Yet he stopped before Alberto's door, to give his heart a second to recollect. Then he knocked gently. *Please be in there*, he prayed to whomever would listen. *Please, be in there.*

Alberto wasn't in there. Mathias realized before the door was even fully open. The curtains were open and the bed was made. Across the room, the desk was neat and the computer screen black. The place looked pristine, like no one currently occupied it.

"Look alive!" Ella joked, pushing him inside.

"She lied, he's not here. Why would she lie? What is she hiding?"

"Who knows, maybe to protect him."

Mathias spun around like a top, not knowing what to do. Ella put her hand on his arm. "Think. Where could we find a clue?" Mathias's gaze fell on the computer. They could maybe check his emails. Elisa read his mind and pushed him toward the chair. "Good idea!"

He sat down, and she stood behind him, gripping the back of his chair with both hands. Mathias shook the mouse to wake the screen and glanced over his shoulder.

"It's password protected."

"As expected."

"But what's the password?"

"Why are you asking me?"

"I don't know!" Mathias stared at the black screen in a panic. "How about his date of birth?"

"Do it."

With a wordless thanks to Zak for this precious information, Mathias typed different combinations, but it kept being rejected. "Now what?"

"I don't know… What does he like?"

"I… I don't know that."

"Are you serious?" Ella shook the back of his chair. "How is that possible?"

"I..." A wave of guilt swept over Mathias. "I never asked."

"How could you not ask? Give it to me." She leaned over him to grab the keyboard. He held her at arm's length.

"Stop it, what's wrong with you?"

"You suck!" She gripped the keyboard with both hands. "What would Mom say? *¡Tú tas loco, pollito!**"

"*¡Cállate la boca!*[†]" Mathias pulled the keyboard back to him. "*Diabla infernal!*[‡]"

Just as he wrenched the keyboard away, someone lightly cleared their throat, getting their attention. Mathias shot up and pulled his sister close. It was the woman he'd met in the kitchen that time he played hide and seek with Alberto.

"I know you..." The intensity of her gaze unsettled him. "Are you Dina?"

The woman nodded, then she checked the corridor was empty before stepping into Alberto's room. "Are you Alberto's boyfriend?"

"Yes," he said without hesitation. "Do you know where he is?"

She shook her head. "His mother took him away when he hurt that awful girl."

"What awful girl?" Elisa asked.

"I cleaned this room myself after he left." Dina approached and put a small USB key in his hand. "He'd left this plugged in his computer, so I took it back, for safety. There's nothing I can do with this. I can't afford to lose my job. But you... you could do that for him."

Mathias frowned at the thing in his hand. "What is it?"

"Something his mother should have seen a long time ago. Something her father should know." Dina's expression twisted with worry. "If you see my little one, tell him I miss him and I pray for his happiness." She made to leave, turned around. Walking past the two of them, she removed a Post-it Note from the back of Alberto's iMac. "Password, right?"

"Yes," Mathias said, his heart racing.

"Alberto has a bad memory, so he keeps hints around. Something she wouldn't understand."

When she was gone, Elisa stretched on her toes to read the Post-it with a perplexed expression. "What does it say?"

---

* You're insane, little chicken! (Spanish)
[†] Shut your mouth! (Spanish)
[‡] Infernal demon! (Spanish)

"*Favorite band.*" A feeling of helplessness fell over Mathias. "I don't know what it is. I never wanted to know anything about him. I... I couldn't—"

"Mathias..." Elisa clung to him affectionately. "*Tú tas loco.*" She pushed his ass back into the chair. "Who's the awful girl he hurt?"

Mathias had a good idea of who it could be, but he wasn't sure whether Elisa should know yet.

"Let's deal with this first." He brought the keyboard close and typed a few names half-heartedly. World-famous bands. No luck. What songs did they ever listen to but the ones left to Mathias by his mother? Alberto never spoke about music. The only band he ever mentioned with affection was...

With a stab of hope, Mathias typed in Bloodhound Gang. In two words, then in one. To his dismay, it was rejected. "I'm all out of options," he said grimly.

Elisa's small hands fell on his shoulders, their grip surprisingly strong. "What's your favorite band?"

"It's not gonna be my favorite band, El."

"Just type it anyway."

"Why?"

"Because, honestly, the only thing I ever saw him care about was you."

Mathias puffed out a dubious laugh, but his fingers moved on the keyboard all the same. "All right." He typed in Garbage, slammed the Return key, and his heart thundered in his chest when the screen brightened, revealing a mess of open folders. Ella let out a sound of triumph.

"That's so weird," Mathias muttered, dumbstruck.

"How did you two end up this way?" Ella asked, her tone full of the judgment.

Mathias shrugged himself free from her grip, ashamed. It ended up this way because he was a moron, nothing else. But now he knew for sure Alberto loved him once. And with that knowledge, the violent hope that maybe, *maybe* he could get him back, they could be together—*really* together—resurfaced. They could have it all. The mornings, soft; breakfasts, lunches, and dinners, face to face; holding hands in the streets and in the dark, under the covers, where they would be one again.

Hope is a bitch, Mathias recalled abruptly. His mind was already racing to make up improbable scenarios instead of focusing on the task at hand. Hope wasn't real, it wasn't tangible. Finding out where he had been taken was.

The open folder right in front of them showed a string of videos recorded with the iMac's webcam. Mathias's gaze instinctively shot up toward the top of the computer where he noticed a small piece of black tape covering the spot where the recording red dot would be.

"I'm not sure I want to see this," Mathias said, remembering that time he stayed the night. "And I'm not sure you should, Ella."

"Shut up. I'm press, remember?" Elisa slapped his hand away from the mouse and clicked open the latest video.

The recording was several hours long. They went through it as fast as possible, spotting Dina cleaning the room, Mrs Gazza standing awkwardly by the bed, then sitting on it and hugging the pillows. Elisa rushed to open another file, and after a bit of fast-forwarding, they found some harrowing footage: Alberto's stepsister Anastasia openly mocking him as he was painfully obviously attempting to get away from her, and how she proceeded to beat the shit out of him. Though they couldn't see the beating itself, they could definitely hear it. And they could hear Anastasia's subsequent words, which filled Mathias with dread. "His dad really gave him that scar..." he whispered, stunned.

"What scar?" Elisa asked. "Oh, shit!"

The resounding slap Alberto gave Anastasia was caught by the camera, as well as the way he gripped her and shook her like a rag doll afterwards. Mathias watched her ordeal without empathy. He only stopped the video when her father intervened. "I don't know what to do with this," he said, his blood pounding in his ears.

Elisa pushed him out of the way and plugged the USB key. It was filled with snippets of assaults taken from the security cameras located throughout the house. Some showed mild stuff such as Anastasia running up the corridor with Alberto's clothes bundled in her arms, to some more alarming scenes like the one where she was laughing her head off while chasing him with a knife. A look at the dates informed them this had been happening for years.

"He was preparing something," Elisa said. "Did his mother know?"

Mathias shook his head. "If she did, would she have let this happen?"

"I don't think so." Elisa grabbed her set of keys. Hanging from a ring was her own USB device. "I'm gonna copy this real quick, in case this one gets lost somehow. Then we're showing his mother."

She transferred some of the snippets to her own phone. Mathias quickly checked Alberto's emails in case it contained clues about his location, but his inbox wasn't at all as Mathias expected, filled with flirting men waving their dicks in grainy pictures. No, it was mostly spam, like, an insane amount of spam, so much that Mathias promised himself to have a talk about it with him later, if the occasion presented itself. Afterward, they hurried downstairs, only to stop dead in their tracks once they emerged outside. Anastasia had returned home, and, clad in a fur coat, she was walking toward the pool, where Mrs Gazza and Eric were still sitting.

"Hello there," she saluted in a singsong voice. Her gaze fell on Eric, who got up from his chair. "Who are you?"

Eric's mouth had fallen open, but no words were coming out, so Mrs Gazza answered for him. "That's Eric. He stayed over once."

"I don't think so, no. Someone's lying to you, Olympia." Anastasia's tone suddenly dripped with contempt. "What's going on, here?"

From her position, she could see Mathias and Ella approaching. She pointed a finger at them. "That's him! He's the one who stayed over. Aaaand"—she squinted at Elisa—"I don't know the toddler next to him. Why are you lying? What do you want?"

Mrs Gazza threw a quick, anxious look at the both of them. "I feel like you were gone a long time."

Elisa approached her. "Do you like movies?"

"Not—"

"Great, watch this one." Ella pushed the phone between her hands and pressed play.

"What's that?" Anastasia's eyes fell on Elisa's phone, and her smile turned into a cruel grimace. In that moment, Mathias imagined she was surprised at her own lack of judgment. After all, she had allowed her bullying to be recorded time and time again on video. Perhaps she had so little respect for Alberto, it never occurred to her he might use that footage against her. And now, here she was, exposed.

Alberto's mother was quiet as she watched video after video of her stepdaughter's assaults on her son, but Mathias noticed her knuckles turning white around Elisa's phone.

"We were just playing," Anastasia said. Her unconvincing tone caught Mathias's attention.

"Playing?" Mrs Gazza stood up. She towered over Anastasia, her blue eyes stark against the red tinge from her unshed tears. "What sort of game do you call this?" She shoved the phone under her nose. "Why would you do this to him? He's just a boy!"

Anastasia dropped all pretense and gave Mrs Gazza a look full of disdain. "A boy? A boy?" She let out a laugh. "Is that how you see him? That explains so much. He's not a boy anymore, *Olympe*." She grinned maliciously. "He's a waste of space!"

Eric gasped in shock, his fingers gripping Mathias's shoulder. Elisa gritted her teeth. "Hey! Watch your tits, Satan!"

"Clam it, microbe." Anastasia spoke without even sparing her a glance.

Alberto's mother looked like her world had been turned upside down. "Why, why?" She kept repeating, her voice shaking. "He's so sweet. He's suffered so much already."

"Oh, cry me a fucking river."

"No, you're wrong… You're angry, Stasia. You're—"

"Of course I'm angry!" Anastasia squinted at Mrs Gazza as if she were mere dirt under her shoe. "My life was perfect before you sunk your claws into my daddy."

"Then… Then…" Mrs Gazza sounded wretched. "Then why didn't you come after me? Why Alberto? You know what he's been through!"

Despite her countenance, Anastasia, too, was upset. Mathias could see it from the way her body faintly trembled from rage. "But

I did," she said with a forced smile. "I did. I went after what you loved the most."

Anastasia was telling the truth; it was plain in her eyes. Overwhelmed by shock, Mrs Gazza stumbled back and almost fell on the lounge chair, but Elisa rushed forward to hold her hand.

"This is so absurd," Alberto's mother whispered. "We could have been a family. I wanted... I wanted to give him a family."

"Guess what!" Anastasia snickered. "I don't want to be part of your family." She approached Mrs Gazza with murder in her eyes. "I'm glad I did what I did. I don't get what the fuck happened between Daddy and that retard, and honestly, I don't even care to know. But I'm glad your marriage is dead. Glad!" Her eyes had turned black with hatred. "Your son's a little bitch, and so are y—AAH!"

What she intended to do to Mrs Gazza, no one could tell. Before she could put her hands on her, Elisa went, "That's it!" and delivered a precise kick in the center of her chest. Anastasia was thrown into the pool, where she landed with a resounding splash. Shock, anger, and the cold water made her screech like a hellish creature from a b-movie.

That's what a real demon sounds like, Mathias thought absently. Unconsciously, he squeezed the lock around his neck.

As Anastasia, bogged down by her expensive coat, kicked and shrieked in the water, Eric turned to Elisa. "You... you kicked her!" His eyes were as round as the tennis balls he so affectioned." You kicked her in the fucking chest!"

"Did you expect me to kick her in the face?" Elisa shrugged. "I'm not an animal."

Eric made a helpless, and rather squeaky sound. "How..."

Mathias put his hand on his shoulder. "Don't believe her size."

"But..." Eric was shaking his head. "But how—"

"Ten years of taekwondo."

"*Diez años!**" Elisa raised her hand and waited.

"*Diez años.*" Mathias high-fived her, then recalled he was her

---

* Ten years. (Spanish)

brother after all. "Bad, Ella, bad! You're supposed to be the chill one!"

Smart, small, and cute, my ass! Another demon sent to ruin him!

"What?!" She crossed her arms with a disgruntled expression. "I warned her to watch her tits."

Alberto's mother, despite her state of shock, had had enough presence of mind to draw Elisa to her chest to protect her from getting splashed when Anastasia fell into the water. Now, she held her tighter as Mathias half-heartedly scolded her. Back in the pool, her stepdaughter was still struggling to get out of the pool and making hellish sounds. Alerted by the racket, a mean-looking bodyguard rushed out of the house and stopped in front of Mrs Gazza with an inquiring look.

"Don't help her out, Oleg," Alberto's mother said, her tone colder than steel. "She'll be just fine on her own."

"*Sì, Signora.*" The man stood back obediently.

At last, Mrs Gazza turned to Mathias. "Who are you? Are you Alex?"

Mathias felt small under her gaze, sharp for the first time. "Sometimes. My name is Mathias. *Rodin.*"

Her lip twitched, and her brow furrowed briefly. She swallowed her discomfort and straightened up. "Well… Why have you come? What do you want?"

"Alberto." Mathias didn't avert his eyes. He stared into her face, his jaw set. "I want to see him, make sure he's okay."

"Why?"

Despite his lack of answers, his eyes held no deception.

"You?" She murmured, her eyes widening. After a while, she gave in with a resigned sigh. "He's in Meudon."

Overcome with relief, Mathias took one step back, his hand finding the back of a lounge chair and gripping it for support. Mrs Gazza saw it, and after another sigh, she used Ella's phone to type something in the browser. "This is the address." She returned the phone to Mathias's sister with a smile. "There. You're a fiery little thing."

"I'm sorry." Elisa glanced up at her like a wrongfully accused puppy. "And thank you. I don't know." She dragged her feet toward Eric, who gave her a long, perplexed look.

"Tell me," he said, arching his eyebrow. "How long does it take to learn that kind of kick? Does it really take ten years, or can I get away with it like, today?"

While Ella patiently replied, Alberto's mother took Mathias to the side. Behind her, Anastasia had finally made her way out of the pool and was crawling on her hands and knees, half-sobbing, half-cursing to kill them all, toward her dependency.

"You think you care for him now, but it's not so easy," Mrs Gazza said, her eyes mournful. "You can't be fooled by the beautiful wrapping; Alberto has been through enough, as you may know."

"I think I'm beginning to understand… to understand many things."

"Mathias." Her voice was soft when she addressed him. "To be with him is to accept that. It's not going to be easy, not when he's like today, in a bad place. You can't even think about it without considering the amount of patience, of work, of care…"

"I get that," Mathias said almost defensively.

"Do you, really?" She absently straightened his jacket for him, before gently running her finger along his cheek. "If you do, then you need to keep your distance for now. Because he's in a place of rest, and he needs that space right now. If you really care for him, you'll agree with me."

"I get it," Mathias repeated, his gaze drifting toward the phone in Elisa's hand. "I'll keep my distance." Raising his chin, he cast Mrs Gazza a smile. The truth was, he didn't even feel remotely guilty for his lie.

32

OF LOVE AND VIOLENCE

ALBERTO WAS a beast of leisure now. He thought so as he lounged on a low chair in the substantial break room, his legs stretched out and resting on the opposite chair, where Berko sat. Originally, Berko had given up on trying to sleep with him since last time; he had turned sweet and was even tiringly caring at times, until Alberto lashed out and told him he preferred the previous version. This morning, Berko changed his tune and offered to take him outside and suck him off behind the dumpsters, but instead, he dragged Alberto to a storage room. Alberto thought for a second he might do it in there, but Berko only wanted to show him where they stashed the stuff patients had lost or no longer used, and they dug up an old game that was just a knockoff of Tetris. Alberto sucked at it, and that was amusing enough for the both of them. The tip of his tongue sticking out in concentration, he was in the midst of his third attempt at clearing a low level when he heard a soft voice calling his name. He looked up blearily.

"What?"

"You have a visitor," Aïcha said. She was Alberto's second-favourite receptionist. Half-hoping, half-dreading, he tossed a glance at whoever was standing in the doorway, and it was dread which settled on his chest. There, stood Mathias, his eyes riveted on the feet Alberto had propped between Berko's legs.

"Who's that?" Berko asked in a whisper. He subconsciously pushed Alberto's feet off the chair. Yes, Mathias had this effect on people. He made them believe Alberto belonged to him. Alberto believed it once, too. He knew better now; as far as he was concerned, whatever they had was over, so what could Mathias want from him now? Alberto considered telling Aïcha he didn't want to see him, but in the end, he said nothing and gave a small nod. Aïcha turned on her heel and headed back toward Mathias, her white shoes squeaking on the waxed hardwood floors.

"Hey." Berko leaned into his space. "Who's that?"

"Nobody."

"Nobody's really hot. Does he like men?"

Alberto lacked the energy to even sarcastically laugh. "No." Even though they were over, he still didn't want Mathias to get with another guy. Ever.

"Liar."

After getting the green light from Aïcha, Mathias was now traipsing toward them, his hands buried in his pockets. Alberto straightened on his chair. "Forget about him, he's got issues."

"Don't we all?" Berko said with a grin. "I'd love to work out some of my issues with him."

Alberto slid him a cold look. "Don't you have somewhere to be?"

Berko laughed in his face. "Nobody, my ass." He rose and snatched the Tetris knockoff from Alberto's hands with a click of his tongue. "And look, you lost again!"

"To everyone's surprise."

Alberto shooed him away. Unbothered, Berko blew him a kiss as he took his leave. He and Mathias passed each other in a charged silence. Berko whirled around to give him a not-so-subtle once over, then trotted away when Mathias threw a look over his shoulder and caught him ogling.

"Hey."

Alberto didn't answer. Mathias took a seat opposite him, avoiding Berko's chair, and pulled it closer. His familiar scent, somehow reminiscent of the forest, was nothing but a reminder of weeks spent lying to himself about who led whom by the nose.

Mathias's smell was a dangerous memory. Alberto wished he had a blocked nose.

"It's nicer than I thought in here," Mathias said, rubbing his hands up and down on his lap. His eyes, green and gold in the afternoon light, scanned around the room, momentarily stopping on the high ceiling, before falling on Alberto's face. There was something different about him. What was it?

"You think my mother would send me to a horror asylum?"

Mathias seemed stumped by his tone. "No, I don't know." He fidgeted for a moment, his knuckles popping one after the other. Alberto wondered what his hands were doing out of their pockets. "It's just… it's nice." Mathias was silent for a bit, and when he saw Alberto wasn't volunteering anything, he asked, "How are you?"

"Me?" Alberto pointed at his own chest, deliberately aloof. "Peachy."

"Is it nice, here? I mean, do you… do things?"

"Mm. We have activities and such. They coddle me, really." Okay, maybe he should rein it in, or he wouldn't sound believable. "We have movie nights. Yesterday it was…" He trailed off. He couldn't actually remember what he was shown. "Someone was in a cape, I'm sure."

Mathias studied him with a half-frown that made Alberto wish Berko had left him the video game. At least he'd have something else to look at other than those eyes.

"Did you make any friends?"

"One."

"That tall guy I just saw?"

"The very one." Alberto nodded with feigned enthusiasm. "Berko's great. Earlier, he offered to suck me off behind the dumpsters."

"That's…" Mathias's expression hardened then sagged, all in a blink's time. "That's nice of him."

"You don't do dumpsters, I remember. Just like throwing people in them." Alberto's attempt at a smile must have looked frightening, from the anguished look he received in return.

"Did you?" Mathias asked after a pause, his voice quiet.

"Did I?"

"Let him suck you off behind the dumpster."

Alberto thought about what to say. A part of him still wanted to take jabs at Mathias, but he didn't understand why. After a month spent in here, the memories of his times with him, good or bad, had become little more than a blur. Gone, the edges. Faded, the colours. Muffled, the cries they breathed into the night. And now here he was, assailed by Mathias's smell, the intensity of his gaze, and now the sound of his voice… Alberto abruptly recalled the way Mathias used to call him a good boy in his ear.

My good boy.

"I did not," he whispered.

Mathias shifted on the chair, eyes cast down on his red sneakers. He didn't want to be here, not really. Why was he here, anyway?

"I heard you met my mother," Alberto ventured.

"Yes."

"I'm curious. What were you doing at my place?"

Mathias looked up. "She didn't say?"

"No." Alberto shook his head. "I mean, she said you came to give me homework, and caused quite the ruckus. She also told me she told you to stay away." He arched an eyebrow. "So…"

"I know…" Mathias hesitated. "But mine told me to come anyway."

Alberto opened his mouth to retort, then thought better of it. Unsettled, he bit into his lip until pain blossomed around his teeth.

"I know, I know what you're thinking," Mathias said, his hands balling into fists on his lap. "Or maybe I don't. I don't know what you're thinking, and that's the problem."

There was a silence, punctuated only by the tick tock of the gigantic clock over the equally massive fireplace, and the discrete clattering of the chess pieces two other patients were using a few feet away. For the first time since Mathias sat down, Alberto felt a twinge of fear.

"What's gonna happen to you now?" Mathias asked. "Are you getting out of here soon?"

"Why would I want to get out of here?"

Mathias gave him a look of surprise. "You don't want to stay in here forever, do you?"

"Of course not. In any case, since your visit, my mother's been planning another escape. I think it's not long before she moves us again."

"Where?"

"Europe, hopefully. Somewhere old, with decrepit buildings, old graveyards, some good wine…" Alberto jerked his legs impatiently. "Why are you here, Mathias?"

That question seemed to give him pause. At last, he shoved both hands in the front pocket of his hoodie. The sight of it only increased Alberto's discomfort.

"I wanted to say I'm sorry. For the way it all went."

Now Alberto wanted to roll his eyes. So, that fool went all the way to his house and caused all that trouble to what? Say I'm sorry? Was he serious right now?

"What?" he said harshly. "Why?"

"I think I treated you horribly, and if I… if I…"

"If you'd known I was already fucked up, you wouldn't have done it?" Alberto scoffed. "I thought you didn't like pity, so why are you throwing yours at my face right now?"

Mathias froze on his seat, as though the notion hadn't occurred to him before. Alberto was about to sneer in bitter victory, only to fall silent when Mathias's eyes started glinting suspiciously.

"I need to tell you, about that time, that night I spent at yours…"

"The night you spent at mine…" Alberto recalled with a jolt. He scooted forward, surprising Mathias. "You saw it. You saw me kiss my stepdad, right?"

"Yeah." Mathias's voice was croaky. Alberto burst into a laugh, enjoying how wide his eyes were.

"Did you think I was sleeping with him?"

Mathias didn't reply. Alberto tut-tutted. "Oh, Mathias, Mathias… Always assuming the worst about me. Or, wait. Did you think he was, what? Molesting me?"

The shock on Mathias's face quickly made way to annoyance. "Any… anyone would have at least wondered…"

"Is that why you refused to spend time with me afterwards?"

It took Mathias a moment to reply. "I was ashamed."

That was unexpected. Alberto blinked as the cogs in his brain worked out the reason why, but in the end, he still asked, "Why?"

"I didn't defend you. Just like at Xavier's. I let someone… someone…" The words, uttered in a thick voice, died in his throat.

A wave of longing submerged Alberto then, and he clung to the armrests for fear of being swept away. Instead, he gave a nonchalant shrug.

"Meanwhile, I thought you'd found my sad, sad boy pills and decided I wasn't good enough for you anymore. Oh, don't look at me like that. You were in my bathroom. Didn't you open every drawer, just out of curiosity?"

"What? No!"

"Ah…" Alberto let out a sigh. "Ah, Mathias…"

Ah, Mathias indeed… He really couldn't do anything like other people.

"Alberto." Mathias abruptly leaned forward. Alberto blinked fast as he clutched the armrests. "Did you want to be with me, at some point? Did you—"

"No!" Alberto tossed his head back. "No, not at all." He plastered a fake smile on his face. "In any case, thanks for the apology, but as you can see, I didn't need it. My stepdad's an idiot, and perhaps he was as drunk as I was when he stumbled into my room. But he's not that kind of guy. Honestly? I think I may have kissed him, you know, thinking he was you. After all, he doesn't look orange in the dark."

Alberto chuckled at his own joke, then he fell silent when an unexpected wave of sadness fell over him.

For a long time, Mathias just sat there, his gaze on his feet, not speaking, not moving an inch, and the twang of fear Alberto experienced before returned, coupled with the longing, and suddenly it seems the walls of the leisure room were slowly closing in on him. Alberto wanted safety, and peace. He didn't want to keep making the same mistakes over and over again. So why did he feel like reaching out, taking Mathias's hand and pressing it to his own cheek? Why did he feel like burying his nose in his neck to inhale his scent one last time? Why did he feel the need to reassure him when he should just reject him as he was rejected, and send him on his way?

"Is it true Elisa kicked Stasia in the tits?" he heard himself ask, his resolve shrinking.

"Yes," Mathias confirmed, somewhat subdued. "She really did that. She was with me when I… when I found your computer… and your password…" His shoulders sagged. "I thought…"

"Oh, right." Alberto's eyes narrowed. The subconscious worked in mysterious ways. Or, so it seemed. Who would have thought that he would leave Mathias the key to his dark secret? If only he could laugh…

"Then your maid… Dina. She's the one who gave me the USB thing."

"Mm-hm." Alberto knew Mathias had seen the little horror movies left on his computer, and at last, was able to put two and two together. Truthfully, he really didn't want to talk about it. But Mathias had found his password and had done what he could to help, saving Alberto from having to tell his mother himself. So, he sighed, softer, this time. "Dina's really kind. She makes friends with everyone—including the guy in charge of my stepdad's security. She got the footage from him."

"Is it true what Stasia said? About your dad?"

Alberto hesitantly met his eyes. Perhaps the difference in Mathias was that he looked older. Or maybe he always looked like this and Alberto hadn't noticed because he was always either high on his meds or losing it from abrupt withdrawal. Or did he look sad? Maybe not sad, more like guilty. Guilty, that was it. It was guilt he felt at having messed around with the mentally fragile Alberto. Now Alberto was surprised he didn't bring a gift. Flowers or something. A get well soon card. Bitterness rose in his throat, and he shrunk back in his chair.

"Yes, I told you already, about my jaw. Why it clicks."

"I thought you were joking at the time."

Alberto's attempt at a dry laugh resulted in an ugly sound. "I wasn't. It's not that he hit me often, mind you. He didn't, not with my mother watching over me. She made sure he couldn't find me when he was in one of his moods, by hiding me in that musty antique wardrobe. But that one time, there was nowhere to hide. He overdid it, and I fell against the marble mantelpiece. Cracked my head open like a watermelon." He looked up thoughtfully. "I was in a coma for nine days, and then I woke up, and I was fine."

"Fine?" Mathias said in disbelief. "You were fine?"

"Yes. Well, except for a few things, like my memory, and the headaches; I've had bad headaches ever since."

Mathias seemed absorbed by the floor, but his fist raised to his mouth as though he wanted to hide behind it. When he lifted his head, his eyes were a different shade. "Why did he do that?"

Stupid questions warrant stupid answers, Alberto thought faintly. "Well, Mathias, it seems he didn't like me."

"But how could... how could your *dad* not like you?"

"Why do you care?" Alberto gave a limp shrug. "You don't even like me."

"Is that... is that what you think?"

"Doesn't matter what I think."

"Doesn't it?"

"What do you want me to say?" Alberto asked impatiently. "You thought I was a bad person, you even told me."

"Right." Mathias gave a slow nod. "At my place, that night, after Joy's party. I said horrible things to you."

"Well... I probably deserved it."

"That's not true!" Mathias leaned forward. "This stuff, about you and Stasia... That's why you hated her so much, why you said those things. I get it now." He raised his chin, met Alberto's eyes. "You shouldn't be in here."

"I'm perfectly fine here," Alberto said. "Normal guys don't hit girls. It's better for me to be here, where I can't hurt anyone else."

Mathias frowned. "But she was hitting you all the time, the stuff I've seen—"

"So? I still hit a girl. I deserve to be here."

"No, you don't!" He looked cross now. "She had it coming, didn't she?"

"So, it's fine because she had it coming?"

"No, it's not fine, but for fuck's sake, it was self-defense!"

Alberto's lips parted, but he was all out of words.

"It was self-defense," Mathias repeated, a glint in his eye. "And if you'd done it earlier, things would have been different, things wouldn't have turned out so bad—"

"You don't know that. You just don't know that."

"You think you're going to turn into your father because you slammed a bitch against a closet?" Mathias said, incredulous. "Trust me, it's going to take more than that."

Right then, it occurred to Alberto with a vague amusement that Mathias would never be against a bit of violence as long as it was justified. Not just him in fact, but both Rodin siblings. And that being a girl didn't stand in the way of their straightforward justice. If he weren't so high, Alberto would be turned on by him again, and that, that was an inconvenience. Alberto folded his arms over his chest.

"Is Elisa going to be in trouble for that kick? Stasia has a very powerful father."

"I don't think so." Mathias finally cracked a smile. "Elisa also has powerful friends. But..." he hesitated. "Your mom told my dad, and he was kind of furious. Well, mostly disappointed. I got him to admit he and your mom know each other, but he said nothing happened. The truth is, I didn't dare ask too many questions. Between skipping school and going all *This is Sparta* on Anastasia, Elisa and I have done enough to turn his hair grey, so we've been avoiding conversations with him."

Alberto shut his eyes, invoking the delectable image of Elisa kicking Stasia in the pool and taking his time to savor it. "Who would have thought your sister was such a little beast?"

A sudden flush darkened Mathias's face. "Now you know violence runs in our family."

"Pff." Alberto waved his hand dismissively. "What do you know of violence..."

Mathias didn't answer, his hands fidgeting inside his pocket.

"But you," Alberto said, "you see me."

"What do you mean?"

"Now you know everything about me."

He knew about Papà, he knew about Stasia, he knew about the

pills Alberto took just to get through the day, he knew everything about the sad, pathetic life he'd lived, and he knew enough about the future he'd have.

"I doubt it," Mathias said.

"Still. You know enough."

"Alberto." He paused, looking terribly reluctant. "You have no idea how sorry I am. For everything."

Shut up, Mathias, I'm not mad at you! Alberto wanted to shout, but he pressed his lips tightly together instead.

Mathias had come in here to take a good look at him and apologize for his misgivings, and Alberto stupidly let him get away with it. Now, Mathias could move on with his life and forget all about him. It wouldn't matter, because he said all the right things, and no one could blame him for being an asshole to poor, sad Albertino. Bitterness took its hold in his chest. If he spoke now, it would only be venom. Better that way: he hated goodbyes anyway.

"Right." Faced with his silence, Mathias thought for a moment, then fished something out of his pocket. "I wanted to give you something." He laid the thing on the table between them.

"A book." Alberto said in a dubious tone.

"Yes." Mathias pushed a battered paperback toward him. "Just in case you wanted to… you know."

"Read?"

"Travel… to some other place."

"Thanks."

Alberto's voice was laced with venom after all. And why the hell not? Mathias brought him… a book. That's what you get for three months of fucking, crying, and holding on to each other at night. A stuttered apology and a shitty book. And not even a single offer to get him off behind a dumpster.

Possibly searching for his reaction, Mathias looked into his face a long time. Long enough that Alberto felt his countenance waver, even with powerful meds to back him up. When he first met Mathias, he was the same, took the same meds and still…

Alberto was once a doll, a rare and exquisite item whose body was stitched so delicately, and yet, everyone was desperate to touch him, until little by little, the fragile seams burst, the fillings spilling out, and he was left alone to make his own repairs. But the damage was done. He had long admitted defeat. And then came Mathias with a ball of thread and a giant needle.

Remembering these things were bad. Alberto shook the memories away with a shrug, his gaze slipping down to the little book between them. "I never finish them."

"Books?"

"I can only get through the beginning. After that, I keep getting stuck on the same page. Not remembering what happened before… what's supposed to happen next…" He steadied himself. "And they give me headaches."

"You could just read the beginning, then," Mathias said. "The beginning's fine."

What's your deal? Mathias had asked, that day in November, standing in the damp parking lot. *Why are you so weird?* No one ever cared to ask the way Mathias had asked. Like it was vital for them to know. Alberto could have told him the truth straight away, but then he would have had to watch him run as far from him as his legs could take him.

"I'm gonna go," Mathias said, confirming Alberto's fears.

He got up, then he carefully put his chair back to its original spot before turning away. Alberto stared at him, ready. A few more steps, and it would be over between them. For good, this time. No hoodie to return, no apologies, no get well soon in the form of a second-hand paperback. The break room was immense; Mathias's steps were slow and heavy. Alberto could have stopped him anytime, but he just watched, and watched, and watched. He was ready.

And yet, when Mathias reached the exit, Alberto's shoulders tensed and his heart lurched in his chest. He blurted out, "Mathias?"

"Yes?" he said, stopping in the doorway. He was so handsome, one foot out of the door, one foot in. The most beautiful man in the world. Alberto was drowning in his bitterness, and he spoke before reason could convince him not to.

"You're gay."

Alberto leaned back, triumphant. He'd spoken loudly. A few

heads turned, and Mathias stood very still with his foot out the door. After a brief silence, he gave a single nod, his lip stretching in a half-smile.

"I know."

And just like that, he was gone, leaving Alberto struck dumb, unable to blink. Frozen, he sat amongst the midcentury furniture, the oversized bouquets of flowers, the Satie-like background music, and the faint laughter of the others patients. The other patients, whoever they were, with their own problems to fix. Mathias would never end up here, because he had already fixed his problem, while Alberto would grow cold and bitter and rot in here alone. People talk about the birth of their kids, but he'll never have any. They talk of their wedding day, but he'll never get married. They talk of their childhood, which he spent in a dungeon, of space and time-defying friendships, which he'd never experienced. They talk about this or that great romance, while he'll most likely be anybody's fuck boy and nothing more. His best memory was a tale of escape, a boy's arms wound around his mother's on a train, a frozen image jittering back and forth like on an old VHS.

He'd thought he was doing so well, and now once again, the weight of the world was pressing down on him like the sides of a coffin. Clutching his chest, he forced himself to swallow the bitterness inside of him and almost retched between his feet.

Alberto knew his exercises. He breathed in and out, slow and steady, until he calmed down. One, two… seven times. It wasn't so bad. It never was. He could teach himself to be happy for others. He'd have plenty of time here. So what, if Mathias had a great future? Alberto had Berko, and his offer to suck his dick behind the dumpster.

He made his way upstairs, eyes wet and throat dry. Berko was waiting for him in his bedroom, standing by the window. He pointed outside with a smile.

"Nobody's leaving."

"He sure is," Alberto said, tossing the book on his bed. He joined Berko by the window. Indeed, the figure of Mathias, his head down and his hands in his pockets, was visible in the distance.

"He's really hot. Imagine how he'd look if he were dressed in proper clothes."

Instead of answering him, Alberto looked away, annoyed.

"What's that? He gave you a book?"

"Yes, but I don't read."

Berko leaned against the windowsill. "I've seen you read."

"What do you want, Berko?" Alberto asked in a cold tone.

"You, Alberto, what else?"

Alberto didn't return his smile, and Berko's expression grew serious. "What's wrong, *amore*?"

Alberto watched the figure of Mathias finally disappearing beyond the gates. His eyes started burning. He screwed his eyes shut and bit into his lip again, the pain helping him regaining control of himself. But when he reopened his eyes, they were still burning. "Don't you wish you'd fought back, sometimes?"

"Fought back? Fought who?"

"I don't know. Just fought back."

Fought back when people pushed him down. When they made assumptions about him. When they pushed him in the pool or wrapped their hands around his throat… When exactly a month after his fourteen's birthday, he returned home bewildered and with another man's fingers etched around his thigh.

"Fuck," he said, gritting his teeth.

"Do you wish you'd fought back?" Berko asked. His tone was light, but he was eyeing Alberto carefully.

"Every. Damned. Day."

Berko drew close. Alberto squinted at the spot where Mathias had vanished until his vision turned blurry. And the more he stared, the more impatience grew within him.

"Can I hug you?" Berko asked.

"No. You can leave me alone."

"I can't do that."

"Then go stand in a corner. I'll call you if I'm bored."

Berko started complaining about him loudly and in French, but he stayed all the same. Flinging himself on the bed, he lifted the book Mathias had brought over his head.

"Can I read this?"

"Whatever." Mathias was gone. Alberto would probably never see him again. He threw a look over his shoulder at the sublime Berko, beautifully stretched across his bed. He wondered about him. Why he would keep coming back here if therapy wasn't working. Whether he was just like him. "What's the book about?" he asked, his brow furrowed.

"It's by Stephen King. It's called *Different Seasons*, and there's a bookmark to a story called *Rita Hayworth and the Shawshank Redemption*, which is, I don't know if you're aware—"

"I know the movie."

"It's an escape sto—" Berko abruptly fell silent. Alberto turned away from the window, intrigued.

"What?"

Berko had sat up, his brow raised in astonishment.

"What is it?" Alberto asked again, restless.

With an exaggerated sigh, Berko got up. He closed the distance between them and pressed the book into his hands. "You should stay here," he said. "If you stayed, I would worship you."

Alberto shook his head. "You only like me because I'm fucked up," he said, mildly amused.

"Still." Berko leaned forward and kissed his cheek. "I'll see you soon."

"Wha—"

"You'll be back." Without another word but with a gleaming smile, Berko walked out of his room.

Nonplussed, Alberto wrenched open the book to the bookmark, and a series of papers gently fell to the floor. Alberto picked up the scribbled note first, his pulse racing.

Alberto,

I saw you sitting out there, but you're not alone, and I guess my courage left me. I don't know, with you, I never know anything at all. So, I wrote this note real quick at the reception to tell you that I'll be waiting at the Saint-Lazare

Waiting to get picked up from the floor was a train ticket to Deauville. His hand shaking, Alberto glanced back at the note. Mathias had given this book, with its hidden note, after their painful conversation. After Alberto had told him the truth, about his dad, about Stasia, about himself. Mathias had chosen him anyway. Mathias wanted him, despite all this shit, despite everything. Alberto couldn't tear his eyes away from the note. Two words were standing out, sending his heart beating madly around his chest, trapped little bird about to make his great break out.

"You're alive."

33

THE CABIN

STANDING on the platform with his hands in his pockets, Mathias was berating himself for his half-baked, absurd plan. The same inability for logistics. There he was, waiting, sweat gathering on his palms, gaze flickering back and forth from the platform to the departures board. In fifteen minutes, the train he'd booked would be leaving for Deauville, with or without them. He'd watched a few of them arrive and depart already, indiscriminately spilling out scowling and smiling faces, business suits and rowdy children, while he stood there, uncertain. He thought he'd arrive at Meudon and sweep Alberto off his feet in a great-escape-type gesture. But after their earlier conversation, he felt stupid waiting here. He *was* stupid, and Alberto was not coming. Furious at himself, Mathias removed the chain with Alberto's lock from around his neck and shoved it in his pocket. One of the suits knocked into him, and he staggered back, but before he could bark at him, his phone vibrated in his hand, and his heart stopped.

ALBERTO

I got my phone back.

Suddenly, all of Mathias's anger was gone, and he was jumping in the air. "Yes!" Ignoring the spooked gasp of a passerby, he landed on his feet, his free hand clenched into a fist. In his chest, his heart was now drumming erratically. "Fuck, yes."

The next person who knocked into him apologized and received a smile, almost followed by a hug. "That's alright," he said. "No harm done." Everything was fine. Alberto was texting. With shaking fingertips, Mathias went to reply, but his phone vibrated again, announcing another text.

ALBERTO

I saw that.

Mathias froze, his head snapping up. Passengers were descending on the platform in droves, obscuring his view. Mathias tore his neck trying to find Alberto, but once again, he seemed to elude him. And then, at last, a fair distance ahead of him, he caught sight of an angelic face, eyelids heavy with sleep, his phone lifted over his head. Mathias glanced down at his own phone, a laugh of relief breaking from his chest.

ALBERTO

So, I'm on the wrong platform.

I can see that, Mathias thought, his eyes prickling. He made a gesture with his hands toward the shops. Alberto clumsily made his way in that direction, and Mathias did the same, his burning gaze fixed on him. He barreled through rows and rows of stunned tourists and hissing Frenchmen without a care, until Alberto was right in front of him, within reach. Unsmiling, as always. Only then did Mathias stop, his pulse thrumming, his mouth dry.

Uncertainty paralyzed him, something he couldn't understand. What to say? No. What to do. Mathias recalled that one time he did something right. Grabbed him in the parking lot under his building where they kissed for the first time. When everything fell into place.

Fingertips itching, he reached for him, hooked his hand around his neck, and pulled his face to his own. Their foreheads met. Alberto said nothing. Mathias felt his fingers slowly but resolutely gripping the fabric of his hoodie and pulling him closer. Hating himself for setting up a reunion in one of the busiest locations in Paris, Mathias maneuvered them both toward the side of a kiosk. Now that they were skin to skin, close enough to see through each other's lies, Mathias gradually calmed down. There was no need for struggle now. They had found each other again.

He didn't realize how tight he was holding him until Alberto poked him with the tip of his nose.

"You're—"

Mathias jumped back, embarrassed. "I'm sorry."

Alberto spoke again, but his words were lost to the bustle of the crowd agglutinated around them.

"What? What did you say?"

From now on, Mathias didn't want to miss anything he would say. Not one word. Never again.

"I don't mind," Alberto said.

"Don't mind what?"

"Being held by you."

Mathias stared into his face. He wouldn't say it now in the middle of the station like an idiot. He almost took the *girafon*'s hand to lead him but ultimately refrained from doing so. If someone saw them like this... if someone dared protest, or worse, sneer at Alberto or attempted to touch him, Mathias would end up throwing them off the platform. He couldn't take the risk of anything breaking them apart.

"Come," he said, numb from relief. "We should board the train."

He still took Alberto by his arm, right above his elbow, and led him down to their coach. He took his duffel bag, too. It felt too light, like a bag packed in a panic by a runaway.

"How did you get out?" Mathias asked.

"Checked myself out."

"That easy?"

Alberto nodded as he climbed onto the train. "They only keep me around as long as I'm paying. I no longer want to stay or pay. So, they let me go."

"Ah." After a quick glance at his ticket, Mathias led the way toward their seats. "So, you were just... hanging out?" *At the mental health center… with that long-legged blowjob-distributing bastard whose name I don't care to remember.*

"I was resting."

"And I disturbed your rest."

"You tend to do that." Before Mathias could apologize, Alberto added, "That's okay."

They stopped in the middle of the aisle while a group of four ahead of them fought for the window seats. Alberto watched them argue through glassy eyes.

"Your mother…" Mathias said, regaining his attention. "You should tell her you're with me. So she doesn't freak out and have me murdered or something."

"I already texted her. She knows I'm going to Deauville with you." Then his brow creased in an adorable frown. "It's Friday. Don't you have school?"

"Hum…" Mathias was tempted to lie. "I called in sick. I thought this was more important."

The guarded look he received in response filled him with doubt. Alberto came, so that meant he wanted to be here with him, right? So, why did it seem like there was a giant wall standing between them?

The group of four finally settled, and Mathias and Alberto reached their seats. Mathias put their bags in the compartment overhead and slipped into the window seat. Alberto slid into the other one and was immediately pulled into a yawn.

"I like trains," he said, his voice raspy.

He was a stray cat, a creature that barged out of nowhere into Mathias's life, then became a necessity. Mathias tentatively reached out to stroke his hand.

"You do?"

"Mm-hm." Alberto didn't react to the touch, so Mathias retrieved his hand in silence.

It was the middle of the afternoon, and the sky was cloudy, as usual. It should clear by the time they'd reach Normandie, which is what Mathias was hoping for. Next to him, Alberto was quiet, his eyelids heavy. Mathias wanted to touch him again but didn't know how to ask. He tried, "Do you want the window?"

"No, thanks. I'd fall asleep straight away."

"You can fall asleep, it's fine."

Alberto cast his eyes down. "I don't want the window."

A few seconds later, the conductor announced their departure. As the train slowly and smoothly left the station, the last-minute passengers claimed their seats and made themselves comfortable for their two-hour journey. To everyone, Mathias and Alberto were just two friends on a train. To Mathias at least, the truth was different. They had so much to talk about, but he knew this wasn't the right place for a heart to heart. For ten long minutes, he steeled himself, before a look at Alberto's sleepy face convinced him to act.

"Come here," he said, beckoning him closer. "Here."

"Are you sure?"

"I'm sure."

Alberto accepted his offer, leaned into his embrace, and fell asleep with his face half buried in his clothes, Mathias's arm wound around his shoulder.

At last, Mathias exhaled a long breath. Gray suburban buildings flew by as he held Alberto close against him. He received a few odd looks from passengers on their way back from the bathroom, but nothing like the old lady facing them a handful of seats farther across the aisle. Her narrowed eyes lingered on the two of them, her mouth twisted in displeasure. Mathias calmly held her gaze. After a huff of distaste, she forcefully opened her crosswords magazine. He never blinked. Eventually, she looked away.

Mathias briefly buried his lips in Alberto's hair before returning his gaze to the window. His hair smelled the same. Lavender, with faint notes of mint. Mathias, despite his calm countenance, was overwhelmed with joy. It's true there was a chance, as small as may be, that their train might crash, or someone might come in and attack them, or they might just drop dead from a heart attack, and it would be the end of the world. But if it weren't, if nothing happened, and they made it to The Cabin, then Mathias would tell him… everything.

"What is this place?" Alberto asked, his brow wrinkled.

About three hours later, they had finally reached their destination. Before them stood a stylish apartment complex built in the Norman style, with its half-timbered facade and checkerboard brickwork. Mathias pointed at the sunlit corner unit situated on the ground floor.

"It's The Cabin." In truth, it looked everything like a luxurious little apartment and nothing like a cabin, but because it was on the beach front, its owner, Van Bergen, called it The Cabin. "You like it?" Mathias asked, unsure. "It's nice. There's a pool."

Alberto slid him a pointed look.

"We don't have to use the pool," Mathias said quickly.

"Thanks."

Mathias led them inside after a brief struggle to open the door with a key set on a cumbersome keychain—an inflatable life saver in the Dutch flag colors. Alberto dropped his bag on the polished hardwood floor with an incredulous expression.

"Did you rent this?"

"No." Mathias dumped his own backpack by the door. "It belongs to a friend of my parents. He lets us borrow it whenever we want."

"Oh." Alberto looked thoughtful. "Would that be the same friend who buys the equivalent of an entire flower shop every week to adorn your mother's grave?"

"Yes."

"I see."

Mathias jerked his thumb toward the door. "Why don't you settle down, take a shower, whatever you want. I'm gonna stop by the grocery store and get us something to eat. You must be starving."

"Not really." Alberto shuffled across the living room toward the terrace. His eyes brightened at the sight of the ocean only a short distance away. "Although, a salad would be nice."

"A salad. Got it."

When Mathias returned from the store, Alberto was wrapped in a giant towel and sleeping face down in the master bedroom, his mouth open, as if he'd tumbled out of the shower and landed right in the middle of the bed. Mathias left him there and returned to the kitchen to prepare the salad, his thoughts wondering as he broke a fresh lettuce into parts. Alberto wasn't aloof on purpose, nor was he uninterested in people as he seemed. He was just high on whatever he was given. Like Dad after Mathias's mother had passed. Six months in the dark where Mathias took care of everything, the meals, the chores, the grateful Elisa, while his father lay in bed, tear-soaking the sheets, ignoring his best friends' calls and eventually turning to the drink. Now, Mathias felt he understood. If he had almost no energy, he wouldn't care for company either. For stupid, pointless conversations. He wouldn't waste his time taking chances on needy or narrow-minded people. He would probably be sleeping all the time.

Mathias stopped slicing tomatoes and glanced down at the knife in his hand. If he were that tired, he wouldn't have the energy to go to clubs, get drunk, and sleep around. Did Alberto change during the course of their fucked-up relationship? Wasn't there a time where he seemed different?

Mathias wondered if Alberto would sleep all evening after sleeping so much on the train. He wondered if he'd have the chance to speak to him tonight. He wondered how to even bring the topic up. Alberto never said what he wanted him to say, infuriating him, but he wasn't any better. In fact, he was worse, because this entire time, he was never mad at Alberto, but at himself. He was the one, he was the one who should stop fucking around and tell him how he always felt about him. Then perhaps Alberto would let his guard down, finally revealing if his feelings were mutual.

To his surprise, Alberto joined him twenty minutes later with quilt marks on his cheek. He mumbled an apology Mathias nervously waved away.

"Come sit." Mathias hurried to pull out a chair for him. "Here's the salad, vegetarian of course. There's also bread and cheese." He took a step back, his stomach in knots again. "I don't know what you like."

Alberto took his seat with a blank expression. "Domestic."

"What?"

"Nothing."

Mathias was hoping they could open up while eating, but Alberto thanked him for the food and ate his salad in silence, and while the cogs in Mathias's brain were working so fast for a way to unload without sounding like an ass, he found himself unable to say anything at all.

"It's really nice," Alberto said, his plate far from empty.

"It's okay if you don't like it. You don't have to force yourself."

"Oh." He pushed the plate away with relief. "It's just that I don't have much of an appetite these days."

"That's fine." Mathias got up. "Don't worry, I'll clean this up. Sit down, make yourself comfortable."

After a brief hesitation, Alberto immediately returned to the terrace, opening the double doors and wrapping himself up in a blanket before claiming a seat outside. He watched with a dazed expression as the sun bled into the sea.

When he was done with cleaning, Mathias put his jacket on and joined him outside. He sat on the chair closest to him, his pulse pounding in his ears. An unnerving silence settled between them. Mathias didn't know how he'd be able to go ahead without help from the gods, but Alberto broke the silence first, his voice so gentle, it was almost stolen by the waves breaking on the shore.

"Our house in Napoli also had a view on the ocean. I could hear the other kids laughing through the windows of my mother's bedroom. Sometimes, I would watch them play."

"Did you…" Mathias hesitated, afraid to spook him. "Did you go there yourself?"

"Rarely. My father didn't like us going outside. Not without him anyway. We just stayed in the house and waited for him to return." A slight frown marred his face. "It was a big house. It wasn't so bad."

Mathias disagreed with that, and brought his chair closer to him. "I have so many questions."

"Oh, no." Alberto shook his head, his eyes falling on him. "You can ask me one. One question."

"Only one?"

"That's the rule."

"No take-backs, I assume."

Alberto gave another shake of the head.

Mathias bit the inside of his cheek. One question. What was the one question he really wanted to ask, now that they were here at the edge of the world? Emotion rose within him when at last, he found the words.

"What happened?" he asked. "Between us. What happened?"

"It got boring."

Alberto's answer was followed by a pause, then a sudden puff of laughter from them both, followed by real, belly-deep laughter coming from Mathias, who feared he wouldn't be able to stop, fat tears welling in his eyes. When he regained control of himself, he stole a glance at Alberto. He was staring at the horizon, the ghost of laughter still on his lips.

"I'll tell you what," Mathias said, sniffing. "It was a mistake, saying goodbye. I don't want to say goodbye."

It was a moment before Alberto spoke again. "You said we were done."

"I should have never said that." Mathias leaned toward him. "I was wrong. I'll never say it again."

In lieu of an answer, Alberto gave him a cautious look, as if trying to get a read on him. "The sun is setting," he finally said. "Darkness is coming."

"That's okay." Goose bumps flared on his forearms as Mathias held out his hand. "There's beauty in darkness, too."

INSIDE

ONCE THE SUN had dipped below the horizon, the mid-March winds would rise, cuttingly cold. Mathias waited for Alberto to slip his hand into his, then he took him back inside, locking the doors after them and closing the curtains.

"Do you want anything to drink?" He made his way around the room, switching on two side lamps and refraining from turning on another.

Still wrapped in his blanket, Alberto settled on the sofa, the lamps casting a gentle light on his features. "No, thanks. We know too well what I turn into when I mix my meds with wine."

Mathias cocked his head. "I didn't offer you booze."

"I thought you would. There's no way this place doesn't have a bar."

Mathias's eyes darted toward the mini bar concealed by the TV. "I'll get you some water." He backtracked toward the kitchen. "Stay put. Don't move."

"Can I get some coffee instead?"

"Okay."

"The way you made it this winter, at your place?"

"Sure." Mathias made an offhand gesture. "No problem."

He walked away with a sigh of relief, congratulating himself for thinking of buying mini-marshmallows earlier, and when he returned with their drinks a few minutes later, Alberto shed the blanket and wrapped his hands around his "special cappuccino." The soft glint in his eyes made Mathias want to overturn the coffee table and shout *Fuck it, be mine!* or some other sickening shit. Instead, he sat gingerly on the edge of the sofa, berating his heart for pounding so fast he feared Alberto would hear it.

Alberto took a sip of coffee, the corner of his lip twitching slightly. Mathias regretted not buying a magnifying glass earlier to verify whether what he just saw was the hint of a smile, but it was too late now, the shops were closed, and he was acting crazy—even by V.B. standards.

"You called me a lot," Alberto said, his eyes carefully kept on the steaming mug in his hands.

"Did I?" Mathias played innocent. "Maybe once or twice…"

"I had my phone turned off while at the clinic. When I turned it on, I saw you had called me a lot." He added with a frown, "So did Xavier."

"All this time, I thought you'd blocked me."

"Why would I do that?" Alberto's frown deepened. "You're the one who's always snappy with me. Why would you assume I'm angry at you?"

"Maybe…" Mathias lowered his eyes. "Maybe I want you to be angry at me."

"Why?"

"For the way I treated you."

Alberto's eyebrows shot up. "This again? I don't care you didn't punch my stepdad when you saw… *whatever*, that night. In fact, I'm actually glad you didn't. His guys would have broken both your legs. To say nothing of what Oleg would have done if he'd thought you were a danger to my mother."

"I'm not just talking about that."

"Then what?"

Fine. Since Alberto's memory was unreliable, Mathias would have to do the heavy lifting.

"The last time we were together, in bed… Afterward, you said I hurt you."

Alberto first shook his head, as if he had no idea what Mathias was talking about, before suddenly pinching his lips. "Oh, right. That day, I was having a… a headache. It had nothing to do with you."

Mathias studied his face, unconvinced. "Really?"

"Yes."

"But I said plenty of mean things to you, all the time we were together. Things—"

"Not all the time, and so did I." Alberto shrugged. "It was our way of doing foreplay, wasn't it?"

Mathias blinked. "I don't…"

Alberto gave a dramatic sigh. "You're like that," he said, putting his coffee down. "A sheep in wolf's clothing."

He scooted closer. Mathias's muscles turned rigid when their knees brushed against each other's.

"Do you remember the first time we met?" Alberto asked, his voice low.

Mathias shook his head, his pulse quickening. "Did I scare you?" he asked in kind.

"You… intrigued me, I think. I remember I felt… something. But fear? No."

"I pushed you against the wall."

"I guess you really wanted to put your hands on me." Alberto puffed out a laugh, then he retreated to the back of the sofa and picked up his coffee. "Anyway, even then, I wasn't afraid of you." He drank from his cup. "I know you see yourself as a piece of shit. You told me that time, outside the museum. You see yourself one way, I see you another."

"How…" Mathias voice was croaky. He closed his fists on his lap. "How do you see me?"

Perhaps he could lead the conversation toward the only thing that mattered to him. Could they get back together or not? Would he feel the warmth of his lips against his own, or was Alberto done with it all? Because so far, all Mathias had felt growing between them was an incomprehensible distance.

"Honestly?" Alberto said, his gaze falling on Mathias's hands. "You never did anything to me I didn't ask for. In fact, you always did what I wanted, in bed. You were the one negotiating at first, arguing we should take it easy. Maybe I didn't like when you told me I was a bad person, but in your actions at least, you were quite sweet. Think about it. We always did what *I* wanted."

"That's not how I remember things—"

"The only things I never asked you to do were the stupid, sappy ones. Like kissing my neck, my face, holding my hand when we did it… Spooning at night. You didn't even realize you were doing it. You can deny all you want, and I can see you want to call me names right now, but I'm not afraid of you. I was never afraid of you." He turned pensive, his lips hovering over his mug. "How could we have done what we did if I didn't trust you? I gave you my body. Willingly. God knows I don't care for that kind of stuff."

Mathias was still scowling from hearing his gestures of affections were *stupid sappy things*. His expression only softened when Alberto covered his hand with his own.

"Mathias, I know violent people. I've known violence, and I've known cruelty in many forms. You're neither violent nor cruel. It was never your temper that scared me, if I was ever scared. It was…"

"It was…?"

Instead of answering him, Alberto grew silent. Pain flashed in his eyes, and for a moment, Mathias felt he was within his reach again. "Let me ask you something," he said. "If you could do anything, *anything* to me right now, what would you do?"

Caught off guard, Mathias hesitated. "I don't know."

"Yes, you do." Alberto nudged him with one of his feet. "You do."

"Then I…" Mathias gripped the hand covering his own. "Then I would pet your hair. Maybe hug you against my chest a bit. Kiss your… face. This sort of thing." He grew bolder. "Hold you, but gently, and doing things, but slowly."

"Scary stuff indeed." Alberto retrieved his hand in a brisk gesture. "What a big bad wolf you turned out to be." He almost sounded disappointed.

"Alberto…" Mathias already missed the warmth of his hand beneath his own. He grew desperate. "Alberto… Did you ever like me?"

Alberto made a sound of frustration. "Why do you keep asking me that?"

"At the clinic, you said no. But then, you came to the station."

"It's your fault! Writing notes like this… I guess I got emotional." He shrugged, as if the matter was inconsequential.

Mathias scoffed, wounded by his indifference. "Yes, because you're usually so emotional."

Alberto shot him a rare dark look. Mathias realized that perhaps angering him wasn't the right way of confessing his feelings, although it weirdly felt the most natural. So, he recalibrated, and spoke more kindly. "But your password, why was it my favorite band?"

Alberto answered with another shrug.

That was too much for Mathias to bear. Slapping his own forehead in frustration, he rose and retreated to the back of the room. "Tell me the truth, please. Did you ever want us to be together?"

Alberto also stood, slowly and carefully. If he weren't afraid of Mathias, why was he acting so guardedly, like he wanted to tell him off but was worried about the consequences?

"Maybe, yes. At one time."

At one time. A tendril of panic seized Mathias's chest. He turned away from Alberto to conceal his turmoil. "Really?"

"Yes…"

"But not anymore."

"I don't—"

"What changed?"

"I don't know. Everything?" Alberto gave a sigh. "I… I was certain you'd sought me out. That you'd lied about our parents so you could get close to me. I convinced myself of that, and when we saw our parents together, I sort of lost my mind, so…"

"Why? Why did you care so much about our parents' stuff?"

"Power, I guess."

"Power?" Mathias repeated, his forehead creasing. "What does that even mean?"

"I'd been clinging to that amount of power I had over you. Knowing you always came back, needing me in your bed. Without it, I was afraid of losing myself, and I was afraid I would start asking for things I could neither receive nor return. When we saw my mother with your dad, it made me realize you never sought me out. I never had power over you. It was all bullshit, as you say. So, yes, everything changed after that. For me, at least."

For a moment, Mathias was stunned into silence. Tonight was the first time he heard Alberto speak for more than one or two sentences, and in clear terms. If only what he was saying were more agreeable… When at last, the meaning of his words reached Mathias's brain, he whirled around to face him.

"But! But it wasn't, though!"

"What?" Alberto asked in a dubious tone.

"False!" Mathias's voice came out high pitched, betraying his distress. "I did it, all of it!" When he heard this, Alberto's eyes widened, and confusion marred his features. "I really did use whatever our parents were doing to lure you to spend some time with me. You think I'm not capable of asking my dad a straight question? He's the nicest guy on the fucking planet. Anyone can steamroll him, you have no idea. All I had to do was ask. But instead, I thought… now I have a good excuse to… to push you against a wall, I guess!" Mathias let out a dark laugh. "God… I'm such an idiot!"

If only he hadn't been so fucking traumatized, and if only he'd known then what that kind of love felt like, he could have just been honest with him. None of this shit would have happened. Maybe they'd be together. It was all his own damn fault.

Across the room, Alberto was as still as a marble statue. His eyes red, his lip trembling, he was gazing at Mathias with a strange expression. "You kept acting like a beast when I suggested you were gay."

Mathias turned away from him. Now that Alberto had destroyed his hopes of a relationship with a few words, he felt drained. With a dismissive wave of the hand, he shuffled toward the sofa. "I don't fucking care about that."

"You—" Alberto's mouth fell open. "What did you just say?"

"What?" Mathias blinked at him. "I don't care about that stuff."

"You don't—" Alberto huffed. "You gave me shit every time I suggested it, asshole!"

"Being gay wasn't the problem, *asshole!*" Mathias glowered. "It was you!"

"What the— You know what?" Alberto returned his glare tenfold. "Fuck you. I mean it. Fuck you, fuck you, fuck you!"

"Fuck me, fine!" Mathias sank into the sofa. "Christ! You really never say the right things." He started rubbing his face with both hands. "Why can't you ever say the right things? Not once..." He glanced up at him. "You're killing me over here!"

"Oh." Alberto's expression gradually relaxed. "Sorry." After a while, he cautiously edged back toward the sofa. "What was it?" he asked, resuming his seat with a straight back. "What did you want me to say?"

What's the point? Mathias thought. He wondered what he'd do now, stuck in The Cabin with a guy who didn't want him. He wanted to run away, to disappear. Become someone else. Someone Alberto would fall in love with.

"*Fuck me,*" he said. "You were actually right the first time."

"But what else did you want me to say?" Alberto asked softly.

Mathias had nothing to lose. He carefully cast his gaze on the black screen of the TV to avoid the upcoming sight of Alberto smirking at him and accidentally locked eyes with his own downtrodden expression.

"That you like me," he said, resigned. "That's all I ever wanted from you. Even if I didn't know it then. If you'd said you liked me, I..." With difficulty, he swallowed back the flood of emotions rising up in his throat. "But you always acted so inapproachable. I knew you'd crush me if I confessed altogether. You're so scary that way..." Mathias ignored Alberto's gasp of disbelief. "But we grew closer, didn't we? During the holidays... I could feel it, just as I feel that distance between us right now. Like you're miles away even though you're so close. But the one night I wanted to ask you out, that stuff with your stepdad happened, and I panicked. If that stuff hadn't happened, I..."

"You wanted to ask me out, the night of Eric's party?"

"Oh yeah." Mathias gave a small nod. "Yep. That was the plan."

"Fuck." Alberto's shoulders sank before Mathias's eyes. "It all went so wrong."

"I'd say."

"Like it wasn't meant to be."

There it is. We were not meant to be. Mathias's heart plummeted. In how many more terms would Alberto annihilate him tonight?

"It would be stupid to keep making the same mistakes…" Alberto continued. "Wouldn't it?"

Mathias glanced at him. "We don't have to—" He paused. Alberto had lifted his hand to his forehead, his features twisted in obvious pain. "Are you okay?"

"Yes." He screwed his eyes shut. "Just a headache."

"Do you need some aspirin?"

Alberto nodded, so Mathias went to the medicine cabinet to retrieve some, and brought him a glass of water. Alberto swallowed the pills, all the while avoiding meeting Mathias's eyes.

"I'm fine, really. I've just done too much thinking today."

The sight of Alberto like this reminded Mathias of how he looked at the museum, and how stupid Mathias was not to notice he really was just human, like him. Sometimes, impossible to deal with. Other times so… vulnerable.

"Do you have them often? These headaches." Mathias kept his tone as quiet as he could, while resisting the urge to comfort him, push Alberto's hair away from his face… kiss his temple… tell him everything would be okay from now on.

He had missed his shot.

Alberto shook his head, then nodded, then shook his head again. "I don't know. Usually, when I read small print for an extended period of time, stuff like that. Mostly, I'm just, you know…" He shrugged again. "Add that to the happy pills, I'm pretty much useless, as everyone knows."

"Come on, now." Mathias forced a smile. "You're not useless."

"You used to say I was useless."

"Yes. I used to say a lot of crap." Mathias laughed at his own stupidity. "You know that was BS, right? Why would I keep coming back if I found you useless?"

"Well…" Alberto smirked. "I do have one talent."

There was a pause. Was that an attempt at humor? Or was it really what Alberto thought of himself? What was really going on in that head of his? Mathias recalled Xavier's fierce expression when he accused him of not knowing anything about Alberto. His chest tightened with guilt.

"Why do you take antidepressants?" he asked, his hand moving on its own to touch Alberto's forehead. He received no complaint, so he pushed his luck, plunged his hand into his hair and pulled it away from his face. "Because of your father?"

"I don't know." Alberto suddenly became flustered, jerking away from him. "Things. Life. Stasia. I don't know."

Mathias regretfully withdrew his hand, his fingers still singing from the touch.

"My father, yes!" Alberto then blurted out, and he looked strangely relieved. "My father."

He glanced at him, hesitant. Mathias's burning fingers ached to grip him and pull him closer.

"During the holidays, you told me you missed him," he said, working hard to retain his self-control. "Was that true?"

"Yes, sometimes. The notion of having a father, I guess. Someone to watch over me, and teach me things, and…" Alberto's throat bobbed as he swallowed. "It doesn't matter, does it? What's done is done."

"But…" Mathias's voice fell to a whisper. "Do you know what happened to him? After he…"

"After my mother took me from the hospital, and we escaped? Yes, I do. He has a new family now. Hopefully, it worked out better for them than for us. Maybe he's a proper dad to his new children. Maybe they can play football and don't look like their mother. I don't know."

It surprised Mathias that Alberto didn't look upset while talking about this. He looked like he had made peace with the fact that his dad almost killed him, whereas since finding out about it, Mathias had had nightmares about meeting the bastard in a dark alley and dealing with him in ways better left unsaid.

"You're not even angry at him?"

"Oh yes, I am." Alberto gave a curt laugh, and a faint glow brightened his eyes. "I really am. Sometimes, I think about him, his big shadow towering over my mother's crumpled form in her bedroom, and how small she looked then, and how she'd done nothing wrong but dress us in costumes and dance to her favorite song, but he hated it so much somehow that he felt he had to break her into tiny pieces. It's like he couldn't stand looking at her face, or mine for that matter, and I never knew what I did to him, and I never learned to stand up for myself. *Fight back.* And that's it. That's *why* I'm angry at him. Not just because he hit my mother and broke my jaw and shoved me into that stupid mantelpiece. I hate him for forcing my mother to give away every last cent of her modelling money in exchange for a divorce, leaving her with nothing but her charms to secure our future. But taking away my voice…" Alberto gritted his teeth, his lip trembling. "This, this is the worst thing he ever did to me. Robbing me of my ability to say… 'Stop.'" His gaze grew distant. "'Don't do this to me.'"

He seemed to be shuddering. Mathias instinctively took hold of his hand. "You'll never see her again."

"What?" Alberto looked straight through Mathias for a second before his gaze focused again. "Yes, you're right."

He abruptly tossed his head back and flashed Mathias a smirk, but his eyes were brimming with tears, canceling the effect. Shaking from the ferocity of his feelings, Mathias bit viciously into his own lip. When a single tear fell from Alberto's eye, and he slapped his hand over his face with an embarrassed sound, Mathias's heart lurched violently in his chest.

"I can be your voice…" he said, forgetting himself.

The words were out, carrying with themselves the brunt of his feelings. But once again, they were met with laughter.

"Okay."

"No." Mathias spoke quietly. "I mean it."

Alberto threw him a look of disbelief, but Mathias's expression gave him pause. His gaze hardened, his lips parted in surprise. "Why?"

"What do you mean, why?"

"After all this… all this… Why on earth would you say something like that?"

"I don't—"

"Why would you say something like that? It's—"

"What the fuck do you think?" Mathias sprung up from the sofa. "Because I love you, that's why!" He covered his face with his hands. "Fuck's sake! You're impossible to talk to! You're—" He stopped talking, his blood draining out of his face.

Fuck.

Of all the ways to tell someone… after all this time… He couldn't even manage a confession! Mathias stood frozen in the middle of the room, too horrified to look over his shoulder. When he finally dared steal a glance, Alberto was still sitting on the sofa, his mouth agape.

"I…" Mathias began, his face burning.

"Look at you…" Although Alberto's eyes were wide with shock, he still managed to taunt him. "Great, great orator skills."

"I know."

"Assolympic Gold Medal."

"I know."

"Undefeated champion of pricks."

"Okay. I get it." Mathias shoved his hands in his pockets. "I deserve this."

"Hang on, I have a couple more…"

"Please." Mathias approached him. "I'm sorry, Alberto. Clearly, I…" He let out a weary sigh. "I'm the one who never says the right things. It's always been me who… fucked everything up."

His eyes never leaving him, Alberto attempted a laugh, but only a strangled sound came out. He started fidgeting on the sofa, a deep flush creeping up his face. Mathias didn't dare make a move. He waited, his heart pounding in his ears.

"You bastard." Alberto said at last, his gaze turned fierce. "You little French bastard."

Mathias had no idea how to retort. His mouth opened, but no

sound came out. Alberto watched him, his jaw set, before pointing at the seat next to him.

"Come. Sit."

Burning with apprehension, Mathias did as he was told in silence and folded his hands on his lap again, waiting.

"You love me," Alberto said, his brow furrowed.

"I think so, yes," Mathias replied quietly. "Yes."

"You don't want to just hook up again. You actually love me."

"Yes."

"*Me?*"

"You, yes."

Their eyes met.

"You *love* me." Alberto sounded almost aggrieved, his mouth twisted, his eyes glinting.

"Yes."

Alberto fell silent, his teeth digging into his lip. In his eyes, darting in all the corners of the room, Mathias could see his fear, his shock, and maybe even a flash of hope. He wanted to confess to him again, normally this time, thinking it might convince him, but Alberto spoke first.

"Prove it."

All of a sudden, he was on Mathias's lap, his hands gripping his hoodie, trying to force it open. His fingers fiddling with his zipper, he smashed their mouths together until Mathias's wits returned and he kissed back hungrily. At last, Alberto conquered Mathias's hoodie, and with a needy sound, he slipped his hands under Mathias's shirt and started grinding against him.

"Let's do it like we used to," he said against his lips. "I need it. I need you."

In answer, Mathias held his hand in a tight grip. And just like they used to, Mathias did as he was told. Here they were again, thrashing around the apartment until they found the bed and toppled heavily on it. This time, the baseboard held strong. Alberto was manic again. Mathias's clothes were practically torn off. Alberto intertwined their legs while groping every inch of him, and they rolled off the bed, almost falling. "I've got you," Mathias started, but Alberto stopped him with his lips, while frantically kicking off his pants.

"Stop talking." Alberto kissed him again. "Use your fingers. I want you inside me."

This wasn't the way Mathias had planned it, but it was enough just to be with him again. Yes, he pushed him down, and he did him from behind, hard, following his directions and savoring his rewards in the form of lustful moans. If that was what Alberto needed, Mathias would prove his love by performing as instructed. But also, he took advantage of the chaos to kiss his shoulder blades, his neck, his hair, and to lock their fingers together. To murmur stupid, sappy things in his ear, until he started begging.

Once again, they were two bodies becoming one in the dark, their sweat and their voices merging, their grievances forgotten.

35

THE GILDED MIRROR

ALBERTO'S MEDS kept him in a state of constant drowsiness. Only the purest form of anxiety could keep him awake. And tonight, he lay on his side of the bed, eyes wide open, waiting for a slumber which refused to come. Through the bedroom window, he watched the ocean lapping at the shore, relentless, while flush against him, Mathias slept soundly, an arm loosely thrown around him.

This should have been the best day of Alberto's life. Mathias told him the impossible. He was in love with him. And yet, here he was… staring at the waves instead of enjoying his warmth against his skin.

Alberto gently removed the arm wound around his waist. There, he could breathe a little better. He brought his knees up to his chin and basked in the silence so characteristic to long nights.

Maybe the horrible truth was that he didn't love Mathias after all. Not after everything that happened. He loved him once, but Mathias had broken his heart, and now, Alberto no longer wanted him. Did that even make sense? Just thinking of Mathias's confession was enough to send a delightful chill through his spine. There were feelings still, and not a few. He could have him. He could, and that would be it. He wouldn't be alone anymore.

…

…

And then what?

Alberto wasn't fit to date anyone. Only a month ago, he had committed himself to the fancy loony bin, and until a few hours ago, he was determined never to get out. Mathias may have lured him out with his unexpected note and his subsequent confession, but that didn't mean Alberto was going to fall into his arms. Stasia was right about him: he wasn't lovable. His father hated him. No one liked being around him. He didn't even like being around himself.

Alberto should know better than to be wooed by a few words. He fell for that stuff once, ignored his instinct urging him to leave, and he was left with the consequences. If he chose to be with Mathias now, wouldn't that be the definition of madness? Doing the same crap and expecting different results? Remembering Mathias's confession earlier, his vulnerability as he professed his love, a heavy weight settled on Alberto's heart. Even when offered the world, he thought only of a way out.

Alberto exhaled a sigh. There was no point counting sheep; he knew sleep wouldn't come. His gaze fell on Mathias, his naked body handsome in the moonlight, his expression peaceful at last. His secret was out, and now he could rest.

It occurred to Alberto he already knew the answer. He got up and dressed, and with a final look at Mathias, he climbed out of the window and set off toward the beach.

Whether horrible or soothing, the truth was love wasn't enough.

Love wouldn't make him sane. Love wouldn't make him healthy. Love wouldn't smother the nightmares visiting him at night. It was for love he had taught himself to shut the doors of his mind, and it was love who tightened his lips when he burned to shout himself hoarse.

And at this exact moment, standing on the empty stretch of sand facing the Atlantic, it was love again that threatened to drown him.

Alberto wondered…

If, tonight, he stepped into the ocean, it would be like walking straight into the abyss. No one would find him again. Or the waves would return him such that nobody would recognise him. Maybe these were the Plutonian shores he often dreamt about.

It was right there, staring him in the face. Why couldn't he make sense of it?

Mathias said *I love you.*

Shouted it, actually.

And he proved it, too.

His gaze lost to the black-and-blue sea, his heart full of unrest, Alberto mentally wrote his own note to Mathias.

Dearest Mati,

The ocean at night is a great, frightening thing. All sorts of creatures fighting for their life under the rolling waves. And above them, men in ships braving the storms. Hulls breaking against rocks, bodies flung overboard. Lungs, devoid of oxygen. Last breaths stolen, along with final words.

And then, you.

For the first time ever, I pictured myself rising above the wreckage with one hand raised to shield my eyes, and the other holding on to you.

The waves carried with them the briny scent of Alberto's childhood, rare innocent times spent in his mother's arms, smiling at their reflections in the gilded mirror. The memory of it almost drew a smile from him. The sand, the sea, the wind in his hair… The only thing missing was the scent of Mamma's locks.

With a quiet sound of resignation, Alberto took out his phone and sent a text, before throwing his phone aside and falling to his knees on the sands. Above him, the moon hovered in the sky like a spotlight. Alberto thought of Mathias in the bedroom back there, his sculpted body stirring, his forehead creasing as he took in his absence by his side.

He thought about him long enough to lose track of time, until a loud, sudden racket disturbed his reverie. A car was swerving near the entrance to the beach, tires shrieking as they mounted the pavement. Alberto threw a look over his shoulder and sprung to his feet in time to see a familiar SUV abruptly flattening a bollard and rolling straight onto the beach, tires flinging sand behind them until they screeched to a stop.

The driver door flew open, and out came Alberto's mother

dressed in jeans and sneakers, her loose hair and her Burberry trench coat flapping in the wind.

"*Tesoro!*" She didn't bother closing the door and ran straight to him. "*Mon petit poulain*," she said, pulling him into a hug. Only worry could make her use her favourite French nickname for him, a term he believed too cringe to even translate.

"Mamma?" He gave her a look of pure shock. "How long was I out here?"

"Ten minutes?" She blinked at him. "I wasn't far. Oleg drove me to Deauville when I received your text this afternoon."

Alberto couldn't believe his eyes. His mother was here, in Deauville, right in front of him, her SUV parked — *very* illegally — in the middle of the beach. And to make matters even worse, Cher was singing "Believe" on the radio, her vocals drifting through the open door of the car.

"What the fuck?" he said weakly.

Perhaps Mathias had done a number on him, and he came so hard, he actually died, and he was now trapped in some sort of Limbo.

"*Tesoro*, don't swear," Mamma said in a reproachful tone. "It's not elegant."

"Elegance, Mamma?" Alberto resentfully pointed at the car. "Look at how you parked!"

"Is it bad?" She gave her surroundings a quick glance. "There's no one here to fine me."

Alberto was too shocked to disagree with her logic. "How did you even find me?"

"Your phone! I can always find out where you are, as long as it's turned on."

"Oh… Right."

Although Alberto had agreed to have a tracking app installed on his phone, as well as his mother's, for safety a few years ago, Alberto had quite forgotten about it. Now, he considered the implications. His thoughts fluttered toward all those nights spent at the Rodins', and heat rose to his cheeks. "What do you mean, always…"

His mother seemed to have read his thoughts. "Don't worry,"

she said. "I'm not tracking your movements. I only use the app when I'm really worried about you. Like when you sent me that text just now." She tightened his coat around him. "I saw you were alone on this beach, and I didn't want you to get silly ideas, like swimming at midnight when the water is so cold."

From the shaky notes in her voice, Alberto understood what she was implying. "I'm happy to see you," he said, softened by her fussing. He pulled her into a hug, which she returned eagerly before kissing his cheek, her eyes glinting.

"Do you want to sit inside?" She took his hand and led him toward the car.

"I would prefer a cigarette." He plopped himself on the hood of her car. His mother watched him take out his pack of cigarettes and light up with a disapproving look. "I know. It's bad for me." Before she could protest, he asked, "Where's Oleg?"

After a moment of hesitation, Mamma took a seat by his side. "Back at the hotel."

"Isn't he Dimitri's employee? He's still following you around like a puppy?"

"Ah, well…" She tilted her head with an innocent look. "Don't you have puppies of your own?"

"Mm…" Alberto hummed vaguely. He suddenly recalled the number of calls he received from Xavier and bit his lip. "I can't believe you're here," he said, changing the subject.

His mother reached out to touch his hair, her fingers grazing along his ear. "I wanted to be near, in case you needed me." Alberto leaned into her touch with a sigh.

"What's wrong, *Tesoro*?" Mamma swung her legs back and forth in a rare anxious gesture. Her sneakers were Converse, like his, but classic blue. "Why are you out here alone at midnight?"

"I was watching the ocean through the window, and it reminded me of the house in Napoli."

"That was a lifetime ago." Mamma's hand slipped into his own. "You shouldn't think about it too much. Return to bed and get some sleep."

"I can't. I'm too full of thoughts."

"Thoughts?" Mamma repeated. "What sort of thoughts?"

"Like…" Alberto's shoulders tensed. "Tell me the truth, Mamma. What's going to happen to us?"

She gave him a look of confusion.

"Now that it's over between you and Dimitri."

"Oh." She looked thoughtful as the wind whistled past, messing their hair. "We'll get a divorce. Maybe a bit of money, but not much." Mamma pushed hair away from her face. "I don't want to hurt him. He was always good to me."

"So, he agreed to a divorce, then?" Alberto asked, surprised.

"Yes. We both know it's impossible to fix things now. Anastasia hates us, and he loves her. He must stand by her. And…" She made a sound of resignation. "… Truthfully, it was over before I found out about her. We were done the moment I found out about that…" A small shiver rocked her. "That night. And now, I'm left to wonder—"

Alberto stopped her, anxious to alleviate her concerns. "He was never weird around me, you know. Not that way anyway. I think it was just a big misunderstanding."

"You'd think that," Mamma said with a sigh. "But you don't know men as I do."

Alberto lowered his head. "Where are we going to go?"

"How about Eastern Europe?" Mamma offered, leaning into his side. "We could live really well there once I sell my clothes, my handbags, some presents… At least until we can figure something out. What do you think?"

She waited for his answer, and when he gave none, she softly called his name. "Alberto?"

"I don't…" he said, his head low. "I don't want to go."

It was his mother's turn to fall silent. "Why not?" she asked at last in a small voice.

"Because…" Alberto pictured himself stepping into the Atlantic and diving under the waves. "I'm tired of moving, Mamma. I'm tired of… everything." He tried to fill his lungs with air, and felt them strain with the effort. "All this time Stasia gave me hell, I was bearing it because I didn't want you to have to leave Dimitri when he was making you so happy."

"*Tesoro…*"

"I knew you'd get me out of there in a heartbeat, just like before. Just like London. And I didn't want to go."

"You shouldn't think of those things." Mamma reached out to hold his hand. "It's my job to worry about you, *Tesoro*. Not the other way around!"

"It wasn't just that, Mamma. It's more… complicated than that." Alberto watched their joined hands with a tight chest. "Maybe part of me needed her to treat me like garbage because I…" his lip curled into a grimace. "I often think I'm garbage."

"No." Mamma gripped his hand tighter, all the while shaking her head. "You're not garbage. How could you even think that?"

Alberto stared at her face, beautiful even when racked with worry. "I'm a whole person, you know. Independent of you. I've lived my own life, my own experiences, my own… secrets. So much stuff you don't know about."

Mamma forced a smile, but her eyes were gradually filling with tears. "I wish you'd told me about her, and about your fears! You always keep everything to yourself. You insist on carrying these burdens, and then you explode… Twice already. And I'm left to wonder what happened to you." She bit into her lip; her expression a mirror image of his own. "You never told me why you shaved your head, that time," she added quickly, "I know, you told me you didn't like modelling. But why shave your head when you could have just told me you didn't want to go back?"

"I don't… I don't know…"

Once again, Alberto saw himself standing in front of the mirror, the red handprint stark against his pale skin. His fingers tracing over it. His mouth falling open in awe.

"Perhaps I did," Alberto said, and a strange feeling grew in his chest. Something small yet resilient, like a seedling breaking through the soil of a barren wasteland.

"What?" his mother searched his eyes, confused.

"Mamma?" he abruptly asked. He dried an unwanted tear with the back of his hand before gripping hers. "Mamma…"

"Yes, baby…"

"Why did Papà hate me?"

There was a sudden flash of pain in his mother's eyes. After a hesitation, she pulled him close, close enough that he wouldn't miss a word.

"Your father didn't hate you, *Tesoro*. He hated himself." With the pad of her thumb, she wiped another tear from his cheek. "Some people, they take their anger on themselves, some take it on other people. You've never done anything to deserve that. You were a perfect child. But he had his demons, and he chose to follow them, over me, over us." Mamma fell silent, no doubt haunted by memories of her own. Her own carousel of heartache.

"What does that mean?" Alberto sniffed. "What demons?"

"Your father is a proud man." Mamma affectionally cupped his cheek. "What he wanted, he got. And he wasn't one to share. So, the more you started resembling me, the more he believed you weren't his at all."

Alberto thought of the ridiculous painting Dimitri had commissioned on the bedroom ceiling. Even Mathias had thought, initially, that his mother's likeness had been his own.

Alberto hesitated. "And am I? His?"

"Of course you are." Mamma leaned away from him with a stern look. "I loved your father. I've never cheated on him, or anybody. Contrary to some…"

"Who would…" Alberto's eyes widened. "Martin?"

Mamma nodded.

"No way!"

"Oh, yes."

"I can't believe it…" Alberto was genuinely stumped. "That bastard… And I liked him, too! He was kind to me." He was also devilishly handsome, and the first man to ever give Alberto unusual dreams at night, but there was no point telling his mother that. "And he was fun, acting a bit like a kid at times."

"And a bit of a rabbit as well." Mamma's lips stretched into a thin smile. "He was sleeping with everything that moved." She shrugged at his outraged expression. "I'm a whole person, too, you know! I have secrets of my own." She held him closer. "*Tesoro*, you're well aware by now, you can look like this and still have garbage thrown at you. It's all fake. To find somebody who loves you, truly loves you, that's the difficult part. That's what I told that boy when he came looking for you. I wanted him to know what he was dealing with. You can't be separated from what happened to you. It's a part of you like it's a part of me. And this one… he's got his own baggage to deal with."

"But his mother's dead…"

"*You* almost died, *Tesoro*. My soul shattered when I saw you bleeding out on that floor. And when you returned to me, you weren't the same. You wouldn't play, or smile… But you're stronger than you think. You only gave me the strength to go on."

"Mamma…"

Alberto leaned into her embrace. For most of his life, he thought he was a horrible person, a horrible child, and that's why those things had happened to him. But now, he had proof that even if he had been a model child, it still wouldn't have been enough. His father's hatred had nothing to do with him. And if Alberto had been wrong about this, perhaps he had been wrong about other things. Perhaps he wasn't as bad as he always believed himself to be. Not rotten, not a whore… and *not* irresistible.

He closed his eyes, and the image of his younger self standing in front of the mirror gazed back at him. The red handprint. In front of him the entire time.

In his chest, the small seedling grew. Relief came to Alberto in the form of quiet sobs, smothered by his mother's loving arms.

"What's going on, *Tesoro*? Please, talk to me."

"It's the worst…"

"What is the worst?"

"I think I'm in love…"

All but surrendered, Alberto allowed his tears to fall freely. An astonished look on her face, his mother gave him a tissue, unaware her own eyes were streaming.

"He's not the first one who asks, you'd say, but he kind of is, really. The only one who really asked about me. 'What's your deal' he said, and that was it. I was doomed. I should hate him for it, and I do, I really do! He's so… stubborn! And when I'm near him, I feel like I'm going to explode from how much I want him." Alberto wiped his eyes with a groan of frustration. "And the worst part is… he says he loves me."

"Cyril's boy?" Mamma asked, sounding wretched. "Really?"

"*Cyril's boy?*" Alberto gave her a cold look. "No, not to me. He's not Cyril's boy. He's *mine.*" The seedling which had taken root in his heart was now expanding to his lungs, giving him voice. "He's mine."

"Fine," Mamma said, reluctance plain on her face. "Mathias, then. I should murder him for getting you out of therapy."

"No, you should thank him."

"Oh, really?"

"Yes, he saved me. I hate Meudon."

Mamma recoiled in surprise. "What?"

"I hate it!" Alberto too was surprised, at the accent of resilience in his tone. There was no stopping him now. "Roland's a mean asshole. My only friend there wants to sleep with me. And I hate my meds. I hate being asleep all the time watching my life pass me by. If I stay there, I'll fade. I'll give up, I'll take the meds, and I'll take Berko, and I don't even want to!" Alberto paused to catch his breath. His mother was observing him with rapt attention. "What I want, what I really want, is to change. For him… For you. For *myself.*"

He waited, but his mother only offered silence, her gaze falling on the sea. "You're right," she said at last. "It sounds like giving up. Like what I did all these years. I felt so guilty about what had happened to you with your father… watching you turn away from the joy of being a child… Watching you…" she closed her eyes momentarily. "When they gave me a way out, I couldn't resist, and I did what I'd always done. Take it. I didn't want to keep dreaming of that night, and the pills kept the nightmares away. But look at us now. If I'd been a better mother, you wouldn't feel the need to hide things from me to protect me. You wouldn't have had to hit Stasia."

"So…" Alberto slipped her a sheepish look. "So, you're not mad that I hit her?

"No, baby. I'm mad at myself that I didn't. And mad, so mad at myself for not noticing how she treated you. You say you don't want to watch your life pass you by… Well, I don't remember the last time I was awake enough to take proper care of you."

She pulled him into her arms and pressed a kiss to his forehead.

He let her hold on to him, his chest warm, until she pulled away, her cheeks glistening. "It's because I want to be there for you that I have to tell you… I don't think Mathias is right for you."

Alberto had not expected the conversation to take this turn. He stared at his mother wordlessly.

"His father told me of his anger issues," Mamma went on. "Expelled for hitting two boys. You expect me to trust him with you? How long until he hits *you*?"

Alberto took a moment to consider her words. Was there a part of him, as small as may be, who thought Mathias was capable of it? He kept searching for signs and he saw none. When he pushed him to the limit, all he got was the kind of sex Mathias knew was his thing. He wondered what Mathias would be like, once assured of Alberto's affections. Defanged, probably. Pawing and nuzzling at him like a *lupetto**.

"It's not all black and white, you know…" he said, his heart leaping in his chest. "He punched someone to defend his friend from a bully. I know it's not ideal. I know. But sometimes, I think if the first time Stasia hit me, I'd put a stop to it, it wouldn't have gone that way." Alberto paused, thoughtful. "But that's the thing with bullies. People like her, and people like Papà, they're counting on it, on our silence, on our inability to fight back. They thrive on it while we get smaller and smaller. Until we fade away."

Alberto lifted his gaze toward the inky sky. The moon still hung like a spotlight over them, bathing them in cold light. "You couldn't hit Papà back, and that's not your fault. But if Mathias wants to use force to protect me, I'm not going to cry about it."

"Alberto…"

"You don't get it! I've never felt safer than when I was with him. Just being near him gave me more confidence. I trusted him in ways I've never been able to trust anyone, and he's never hurt me." Alberto suddenly recalled the times they spent together at Christmas. Mathias was always scowling at him from a distance, but one dark joke from Alberto was enough to soften his features, to earn himself a kiss. "Of course, I'm afraid of him sometimes. I'm afraid

------

* Wolf cub. (Italian)

he'll leave… He did, once, and that's when I stopped taking my meds. I wanted to be normal, just for him. But I had it backwards. I should focus on myself first. That's what it means to fight back."

Mamma still held his hand, a faint smile dancing on her lips. "You're in love, *Tesoro*," she whispered, her eyes welling once more. "It hurts, and it's beautiful."

"Beautiful…?" Alberto tossed a glare at the sky, as though it were responsible for his troubles. "If feels like I'm at the edge of a precipice, and I'm afraid. I'm so afraid to jump…"

Mamma squeezed his hand between her own. "If you stumble, I'll catch you. It's my job. I promise I'll do better from now on. For you, for us… and for myself."

Alberto looked at her face, so similar to his own. Despite their perfect features, their eyes carried the exhaustion of older people. And then it hit him. It was always going to end this way. He and Mamma against the world. The two of them tonight, facing the ocean.

"The truth is…" He was calm as he spoke. "I can't be with him if you don't want me to, Mamma. If you don't like him, or don't trust him… It's always going to feel wrong to me. It was always us, always, from the beginning. I'm not going to let a man stand between us ever again."

"Nor will I!" Mamma shook her head with such force, tears flew in every direction. "Never again. But if he loves you, and if you love him…" Alberto shuddered. "If you love him, I love him, too."

There was a silence, punctuated only by the waves, indifferent to the delight swelling in Alberto's chest. "He said he loves me… You should have been there… It was so romantic…"

Well… to him, at least.

His mother smiled fondly at his bashful expression. "Go on then, be in love, you deserve it."

"Mamma…"

They fell in each other's arms again. Alberto's tears were no longer caused by worry, but by overwhelming relief. "My tissue's completely soaked," he complained when they parted.

His mother gave him another one. "There, I have more."

"Are you sure you're okay with this?"

"Yes. In any case, if Mathias hurts you, I'll take it up with his father."

Her words, uttered with complete confidence, broke the spell between them. Alberto leaned away from her, all traces of joy vanished from his face.

"Now that we're here…"

His mother seemed to read his mind. Blinking fast, she slid off the hood of the car. He held her hand in a tight grip. "What the hell is going on between you two?"

"Don't swear, *Te*—"

"Mamma!"

"What!" her defiant tone gave Alberto pause. "Can't I have my own thing?"

"No, you can't!" Alberto stood up as well. "Mathias and I have been hooking up for months. Do you know how it feels to find out you two have *your own thing*? That's gross!"

His mother's mouth fell open in outrage. "*Alberto!*"

"No! I don't want you to get married to his dad! Gross, gross, gross!"

"But I don't want to marry Cyril!" Mamma snapped, looking genuinely offended. "He's my friend!"

"Don't lie to me." Alberto scoffed. "You don't have friends, Mamma. You have mean girls and guys who want to get in your pants. I know what I'm talking about," he added, speaking from experience.

"I have this one, and I want to keep him!" Mamma folded her arms over her chest. "I'm not letting him go."

"But—"

"No buts. It's such a relief being around someone who's *not* interested in getting into my pants." She tilted her head. "Cyril's a very faithful man. He's never given me a single thought of that kind!"

"But what *is* the deal between you two? Mathias claims he saw you together several times."

After a hesitation, Mamma gave in with an unladylike sort of groan that had Alberto arch an eyebrow. "All right," she said, her entire face flushing. "It's a bit embarrassing, and obviously, I never told Dimitri, because he wouldn't like me having a friend who's a straight man."

"Go on…" Alberto said, worried.

"Back in September, when school resumed, I attempted to come to the first teachers-parents meeting. I was concerned about you, so I wanted to see your teachers, your class. Become more involved. But I arrived late because I drove myself, and the traffic at that time was madness."

Olympia explained that she hurried on her new pumps, a gift from Dimitri she couldn't walk with, twisted her ankle as she was entering the building, and basically face-planted into Cyril Rodin's arms, who was so shocked, he let go of her as if she had the plague. Her emotions got the best of her, and she burst into tears. Overcome by remorse, a horrified Cyril took her for a coffee in the break room, where Mamma's defenses broke down when faced with his genuine kindness. She ended up oversharing, telling him of her worries concerning her son.

"Cyril's very nice. Instead of embarrassing him, my behavior encouraged him, and he ended up telling me about his wife, and how his own son, like mine, hadn't laughed in years. We exchanged numbers, and sometimes, when life is hard, we meet, and we talk."

Alberto gave her a dubious look. "And you promise you've never, ever slept with him?"

Mamma scoffed. "Alberto, no! Cyril is like a pen pal, except we don't write. We sob miserably over a cup of coffee, and we blame ourselves for being useless parents." Mamma laughed. An occurrence as rare and as delightful as a shooting star briefly lighting up the sky. "I told you; Cyril is still in love with his wife. I don't think he's even noticed I'm a woman. To him, I'm just a friend. It's an amazing feeling, really," she added with a smile. "I told him of my recent troubles, and he said he'd introduce me to his gay friends so that I wouldn't have to be alone."

"O-kay." Alberto's brow wrinkled. "You don't seem to be all that saddened by your divorce."

"I've never been on my own," Mamma said, shrugging. "But now you're old enough to make your own decisions and choose your own path. You choose Mathias, and I choose to swear off men for a while. Maybe I should focus on myself getting better instead. How does that sound?"

"It sounds… good." Alberto gave a small nod. "I'm just happy to see you smile, for once."

"And I want *you* to smile, *Tesoro*. Do you know how you look when you smile? There's nothing more beautiful in the entire world."

"But Mamma… You keep saying smiling gives wrinkles."

His mother's eyes widened. "*Tesoro*, my love, I only started saying that when you stopped smiling so you wouldn't feel bad! People noticed and were constantly going on about it, and I could see it was making you miserable. I didn't want you to force yourself; I wanted you to be okay. So, I came up with this line so you wouldn't have to pretend to smile."

Alberto stared at his mother. "You… You made that up for me?"

All this time, he had misunderstood her intentions. He who claimed he was the best at reading people. Maybe what he was the best at was misreading intent, or seeing everything in a negative light. Poorly analyzed through the lens of his childhood trauma.

"You can smile, baby," Mamma said, her own lips curled into a gentle smile. "You can do whatever you want. On your own terms."

All this time, the radio had been spitting out old tunes, relics from the past intended to warm the heart. Just as they stood, now shivering in the cold, Mamma's favorite Italian song began. They both stilled, challenged by their memories of a certain night.

"If only we could change the past…" Alberto whispered, the thought of Mathias lying alone in bed becoming more and more unbearable.

"We can change the way it affects us," Mamma said wisely. "Like this song."

"It was your favorite before that night."

Mamma nodded, but she was still smiling. "Do you remember the moves?"

Alberto puffed out a laugh. "I don't know. It was a lifetime ago."

"Should we find out?"

"Mamma…"

"Come on, you and me, for one final round. No one to bother us this time."

The eagerness, the childish mirth in her eyes would have convinced even the gods. Alberto got up.

They did dance, that night. Two shadows in the middle of the beach, taunting the dark waves hugging the shores. Not silent, but laughing, as loud as they could in tandem with the wind.

And she was right: no one bothered them this time.

Alberto removed his shoes and his socks before he climbed into the darkness of the house. On the bed, his face lit by a bedside lamp, Mathias was sitting with his head in his hands. He started when he heard Alberto. His face pale, his eyes wide, he looked like a little kid.

"I thought you were gone," he said, his voice hoarse. "I thought you…" He didn't finish his sentence.

Alberto removed his coat and draped it over a chair. "I was, and now I'm back."

Confusion blurred Mathias's features. Perhaps, like Alberto, he was worried about saying the wrong things. Alberto stood in front of him and waited. Mathias looked fearful when he finally met his gaze.

"What happened?"

Alberto chose his words carefully. "There was something I needed to do."

"What—"

"Shh…" Alberto slowly slipped on top of him, straddling his thighs. "It's all done now." Mathias's hands hesitated before settling on his waist.

"What you want…" Alberto said in a whisper. "I want it, too."

Mathias studied his face, his chest rising and falling rapidly. "You do?" he asked in the same tone.

Alberto nodded. "Let's do it your way."

He caught his lips in a soft kiss, a tentative gesture which

Mathias received with a broken sound, before he cupped Alberto's head between his hands, deepening their kiss with the same gentleness.

"Mati…" Alberto called, his voice hoarse with desire.

"That's my name," Mathias replied, before joining their lips again.

They stood slowly, at the same time. The room twisted and turned. Alberto gave all his attention to the kiss, the mutinous intimacy of it, and barely registered being laid down on the bed, until inspiration struck, and he rolled them both over until he was on top.

Something shone in Mathias's eyes. Striking enough for Alberto's heart to briefly stop in his chest. Alberto pushed away the impulse to run.

How do you tell someone you like them? *Actions, not words.* Alberto slowly undressed, removing his shirt by lifting it over his head, and he did the same for Mathias, goose bumps flaring across his skin with every breath. Hands took their time to explore shoulders, neck, waist, and chest, and then lips took over. Eventually, they were fully undressed, and Alberto was still on top, and on top he remained for some time. Their love was gentle and awkward as a colt's first steps, its newborn eyes meeting a wondrous world filled with light. And then, the silence. Silence which filled the room and blanketed their satiety and never threatened it.

There were no tears. Only morning.

36

MATHIAS

MATHIAS WOKE FIRST. He experienced a mild confusion, typical of rousing in an unusual place; next to someone else. Then it occurred to him the someone else was Alberto, and his breath caught just as his fingers itched. Through the window, the sky was clear, the sun bright. It was probably late, and Mathias didn't care.

Morning-Alberto, trapped within his arms at last. A sleepy, cuddly creature to be woken with kisses. *Mathias's way.*

Mathias pressed their bodies together under the blanket. Alberto's skin was warm; almost impudent in its softness. Mathias breathed in its scent, his lips finding the other's nape. Then he heard it: the same sound that nearly undid him all these months ago. Almost a moan, but not quite so. A gift, a testimony of his consciousness returning to him. Inspired by its invitation, Mathias's hands wandered with ease, from the shoulder to the thigh. With tender fingertips, he counted Alberto's ribs, explored his narrow waist, caressed the outline of his back until he reached the place he longed to bury himself in. He kissed, he licked, he willed and hummed his lover awake.

And then he stopped, waiting.

"Don't…" the creature at his side said, his voice thick with sleep.

"Don't… what?"

"Stop." And sounding almost scornful, "Don't stop." Reaching back, Alberto caught Mathias's hand and placed it on his stomach. "Like this, but lower," he breathed.

Mathias stretched his neck to see his face. He was already panting under his touch, shivering almost, his hips jerking as he seemingly attempted to merge their bodies together. And then his eyes snapped open, and he wriggled out of Mathias's grip.

"Hang on, I need to…" He gasped when Mathias's fingers closed around his already significant erection. "Pee," he finished, in the most uncertain of tones.

No, no, no. Mathias released his cock to hold him against his chest, cutting short his plans of escape. "Unless you *really* need to go, you should stay right here." And he swallowed his garbled words of complaint with a kiss.

It worked. Alberto became soft and docile between his hands. Mathias rolled him over. With painstaking care, he made his way down from the column of his throat, his tongue sliding over his collarbone and a puckered nipple, which he regretfully abandoned to kiss his way to the greatest reward yet: his navel, in which Mathias buried his tongue. Finally, he ducked his head between Alberto's legs with a familiarity that surprised even himself.

"Breakfast?" he joked, glancing up.

The darkness he found in Alberto's eyes resonated with his own desire. *Take me, but fast,* they dared him. *Lest I escape you again.* Mathias took this challenge head-on and swiped his tongue along the length of Alberto's erection until he heard an Italian slur, one he'd looked up long ago. With a puff of laughter, Mathias swallowed his entire cock, his lips stretching when Alberto gripped the headboard with a drawn-out moan. For a moment, the room was filled with sounds Mathias had almost lost hope he would ever hear again. Until Alberto grew quiet again.

"Is it always like this?" he asked, looking down. The vulnerable look on his face tugged at Mathias's heartstrings.

"It can be," Mathias said, his own eyes soft.

They held each other's gaze for a long time.

"Go on then," Alberto said at last. He parted his legs a little wider, and his eyes shone a little wilder, and Mathias remembered to be a wolf again.

He took his cock first, then he took him entirely. Spread his legs open and buried himself between them, slow and steady, until Alberto's eyes rolled back in their sockets, and he came all over his own stomach, Mathias's name on his lips.

And *then*, Mathias made him breakfast.

Alberto watched him dress with a curious look, especially when Mathias recovered his chain from his pocket and put it around his own neck.

"Is that… my lock?"

Mathias shrugged. "You left it at my place. It's mine now."

"I didn't know you liked that brand," Alberto said, sounding surprised. "If you had told me, I would have gotten you something better."

Mathias was so stumped, his arms fell to his side, but Alberto missed it, already on his way to the shower. They reunited a few minutes later in the kitchen, where Mathias was setting the table.

"I know you like grapes," he said, his brow arched uncertainly.

Alberto plopped on a chair and, with a quick thanks, he immediately plunged his hand in the bowl of grapes. Mathias turned to the coffee machine with a sigh of relief.

"Can I ask you a question?" Alberto asked with his chin in his hand, watching him work.

"You can ask me anything. Anything." He whirled around to face him.

"You might live to regret that," Alberto said, reaching out for a glass of water. He ingested a small white pill with an indifferent expression. Mathias realized he had never seen Alberto take his medication before.

"I don't think so," he said absently. "What was your question?"

"What did you mean by, 'It's not being gay that's the problem, it's you'?"

Maybe it was Alberto's gaze fixed on him with obvious affection, or the simple fact that he was asking him such an intimate question, but Mathias's face started burning, and he would have taken to his legs if not for the flash of desire in Alberto's eye suggesting he was into it.

"I-I don't—" he stammered. "Sorry. What are you talking about?"

Alberto rolled his eyes, but his own face was flushed. "When I touched you, you were fine, but you didn't want to touch me… and when you finally did, you kicked me out of your place…"

"Yes, I did," Mathias admitted, his wits finally returning to him. "Because… Because you laughed in my face!"

"Did I?" Alberto's innocent blink wasn't as convincing as it was charming. He seemed to be aware of this, because he shoved several grapes into his mouth and went into a small fit of coughing.

"The thing is…" Mathias said, wondering if his heart could take any more of this, "I'm not… comfortable with touching people. I don't even realize I'm doing it. It's just… I only touch the people I'm really close to. I've always been like that. I wasn't about to get on my knees the first time we hooked up. Part of me didn't want to hook up with you at all. You acted like the sort of guy who'd shit all over my feelings." Mathias's brow furrowed. "I'll never forget the way you laughed at me…"

His mouth still full, Alberto grimaced, suddenly absorbed by the ugly modern art painting hung across the room. Thankfully, a series of beeps announced the coffee was done.

"You're the one who assumed I was afraid of dicks," Mathias went on, pouring coffee into a cup. "But it's *your* dick I was afraid of. I've spent my entire life not being into anybody. Then I met you. It's not like I understood anything that was going on." Mathias set the steaming cup in front of Alberto. "If you say I'm gay, fine. I'm gay. I must be, since I'm so into you."

Alberto finally swallowed. "That's okay," he said in a small voice. "You don't need to say more."

"No, I want to." Mathias smiled. "To me, admitting that I like men is admitting that I like you. I can't separate the two. I just didn't want to tell you, 'Fine, I'm gay, I'm into you,' before making sure you wouldn't laugh in my face again."

Alberto's lips pursed into a pout. "Meanwhile, all this time, I was hoping you'd admit it. All. This. Time."

Mathias leaned across the table until they were face-to-face. "I think I admitted it pretty loud and clear since then."

"Do you mean last night?" he teased.

"And this morning."

For some inexplicable reason, Alberto leaned back in his chair, his expression turning mournful.

"Would that every morning be as the one we just shared," he said in a dejected tone, the expression of melancholy.

Let me in, and it would be.

Mathias couldn't bear to look at him. He knew he would sound too sappy if he said he loved him again, so he busied himself around the kitchen instead, his pulse racing. "Talk some more," he said. "Please."

"What do you want me to say?"

"Whatever you want."

"Hmm…" Alberto assumed a thoughtful pose. "I want to say all the wrong things so that you get mad again, push me down on the bed, and—"

"Okay, settle down." Mathias pointed a spoon at him. "Let's try to have a conversation that doesn't end with you on all fours."

Alberto's subsequent burst of laughter caught Mathias by surprise. He dropped the spoon, which bounced and clattered on the tiles until he stepped on it.

"O-kay." Alberto cocked his head. "Let's be real for a second. I find it hard to believe that you've never been into anyone."

"Why is it so hard to believe? How many people have *you* been into?"

"… Good point."

"Funny…" Mathias gazed at him thoughtfully. "I used to think I was traumatized. It turns out I'm just different."

His words made Alberto sputter with another laugh. "You're right, it's funny." He shook his head with an amused expression. "You thought you were traumatized, but you're just different. I thought I was different; turns out, I'm just traumatized."

Mathias's body momentarily froze. He wasn't sure how to react. But Alberto only laughed some more.

"Look at us." He held out a grape and waited until Mathias got close to feed it to him. "So domestic."

Reassured by his good humor, Mathias took his offering and made sure his tongue lingered on Alberto's fingers while staring into his eyes.

"Since we're asking questions…" he said, his voice low, "can I ask who your other lovers are?"

Alberto suggestively pushed the fingers Mathias had just licked into his own mouth. "My other lovers…?"

"Three more, you said. Three more. Remember?"

To his shock, Alberto reacted by slapping both his hands over his face. "Oh, Mathias…" His fingers parted, revealing a gray eye glinting with mirth.

"What?"

"My other lovers… They were my toys!"

"Your… what?"

"Toys! Sex toys!" Alberto gave Mathias an appraising look. "What? you don't have any?"

"No." Mathias gave him a scornful look. "Why would I need that stuff? I have you."

Alberto chortled. "And how did you manage before me?"

"With my hand, like everyone else."

"Good for you. I have my hand, and I also have toys… which I tend to name after my fictional crushes." Alberto smirked at Mathias's helpless expression. "You were boiling with jealousy that day, it was so hot. I wanted to push you even more."

"Oh."

"Mathias, don't look so sad. My toys may have preceded you, but you were the first brave knight to breach that sacred land."

"I was your first?" Mathias grinned, delighted at the prospect.

Alberto didn't answer, instead turning away from him to get more grapes. "So, what should we do today?"

"Hang on." Mathias just had a realization. He caught Alberto's wrist, who gave him a startled look.

"What?"

"If I was your first… Didn't it hurt?" Mathias recalled Eric's stupid face as he was holding his butt with both hands. "It must have hurt."

"Yes, maybe…" Alberto's cheeks took on a rosy hue. "I guess it did a little bit, but I loved it, so don't worry."

Mathias stepped back, horrified. *"Don't worry?* Of course I worry. Why didn't you say anything?"

Alberto shrugged. "I was afraid you'd stop!"

"You—" Mathias gave a groan of despair. "Alberto, *pollito*, you don't get it! I don't want to hurt you. I really, really don't want to."

"Oh, yes you do!" Alberto's expression turned scandalized. "You want to bend me over that table right now and teach me a lesson."

He flung himself into Mathias's arms and pressed their mouths together, before sinking his teeth into his lips. With a grunt of pain, Mathias leaned back, unimpressed.

"You are so unbelievably slutty."

"Deal with it!" Alberto turned away from him with a flourish. "I'll stop being slutty when you stop looking like this."

"Fair enough." Mathias caught him and held him from behind. "Look outside, Alberto. The weather's nice. My dad's friend's car is parked outside. Do you wanna go for a ride?"

Alberto glanced at him over his shoulder. "You can drive?"

"Of course I can drive. You can't?"

"Do you know anyone who'd let me drive in my state?"

"Oh, right." Mathias dropped his head. "Sorry."

"Now you have to make it up to me."

Mathias obliged, with a little bit too much fervor. The table rattled for a minute or two while they shared a… *passionate* kiss. Mathias feared it would actually end as Alberto had said, with him bent over the table and taught a lesson about the consequences of teasing, but thankfully, Alberto broke the kiss first.

"Mathias?"

"Yes, *pollito*?"

"Why do you love me?" He gave Mathias a look that dared him to mention his face. "Why me?"

Mathias thought he could lose himself in those eyes. Just *drown* in them. His chest tightened from the thought. "Because…" He dared the truth, for once. He brought his lips to the side of Alberto's face and breathed the words like a secret in his ear. "You're so weird…"

The greatest reward was the softening of Alberto's features. His lip curled, his eyes narrowing in an endearing way. "You like that, huh?"

"Uh-uh," Mathias replied, *drowning*. "I love that."

Mathias had to concede, being in love was the strangest thing. Suddenly, he wanted it all, not for himself but for the one at his side. His own comfort felt like an afterthought. Mathias cupped Alberto's face and gave him a kiss he hoped conveyed enough of the burning love he felt for him.

In response, Alberto shuddered, before taking his hand to lead him back to the bedroom. Mathias followed him, his gaze fixed on his nape, wondering where their actions would actually take them.

Gratitude, affection, perhaps love. Mathias wondered what Alberto could give him. He didn't dare hope much. He was content to have him in his arms once again. He felt like he had fully woken from a bad dream, his fears finally put to rest. Inevitably, the two of them fell into bed again, and Alberto's mouth, crafty and cherishing, brought him to the edge, their fingers interlocked. Mathias, breathless, felt Alberto's pulse against his own. "You're the most beautiful man in the world," Alberto said when Mathias reached his climax.

"Don't be silly," Mathias panted, his vision swimming. "You should know… you should know better."

"And I do," Alberto said against his lips. His kiss was as soft as a petal, leaving Mathias wanting. With a contented sigh, Alberto curled up on his chest, and Mathias closed his eyes. His thoughts drifted, peacefully, toward an old, buried truth.

The first time Mathias saw Alberto was on the first day of school.

He was hard to miss, tall as he was. A tower clad in black, expensive clothes, perfectly tailored to his long and thin body. Perceived, at the time, as an unmistakable sign he had parents, alive and well, who took good care of him. Made sure he looked his best and felt it, too. Rendering him, intentionally or not, unforgettable.

And Mathias thought, with bitterness at first, *Wow. Imagine being this guy.*

Until their eyes met. Accidentally of course. Alberto stared right through him and yet… Mathias's heart thumped in his chest. In the hollowness of his gaze, Mathias saw himself, a crumpled boy robbed of the light of his life. Never once had he met someone with eyes to match his own, their emptiness suggesting a kinship that was yet to come bare. Mathias stared and grew angry at himself. He scoffed, he shrugged, he forced his gaze away. And he hoped never to learn his name.

But he never forgot.

Without his knowledge, Mathias had never expected Alberto to join in this stupid quest to find out their parents' secret. It was the dumbest plan, born from the dumbest guy. But he was hoping for it. He never expected Alberto to really be as weird as people said, but he was hoping for it, too. He never expected Alberto to let him when he kissed him the first time, or to jump headfirst down that rabbit hole the first time they touched each other almost for a dare.

Alberto was never what he was expecting to find.

He was even *better*.

Mathias, on the other end, was the predictable one.

Since the first time he caught sight of Alberto as he stood, surrounded but alone at the school gates, cool gray eyes raised to the matching sky. Since the first time he stopped to look and failed to smother the strangest thought as it occurred to him.

Wow.

Imagine being with *this guy.*

37

ALBERTO

Alberto was a beautiful boy.

From the moment of his birth, it was settled. His appearance was a constant cause of wonder, one he was well aware of. In fact, he had known since he was old enough to understand words.

From dawn to dusk, friends, co-workers and relatives of his parents would come forward, one after the other, to pay homage to his mother and father. Old men grinning, ladies swooning, wave after wave of faceless strangers marvelled at his features, all of them with the same words on their lips.

"My God. What a beautiful boy."

So much like…

After their lovemaking, sleep took him almost by surprise. When at last he woke, still curled up on Mathias's chest, the open window offered him the tinkle of laughter of children playing on the beach, and Mathias… Mathias was holding on to him as if he were afraid he would leave again through that very same window.

So, no, Alberto did not quite know yet how to broach the subject. What would happen afterwards? Would the light dim in Mathias's beautiful eyes?

Would he wait for him?

Would Alberto wait if he were in his place?

"Wake up, Mathias," Alberto whispered, pressing a kiss to his cheekbone. Mathias did so, slowly, with a languid smile. Alberto felt his stomach lilt.

"I want to go to the beach."

Mathias stretched out his hand to cup his face. "Let's go to the beach, then."

What did Alberto say again? *Defanged.*

They left through the front door this time. It was clear they had overslept. The afternoon was late already and surprisingly warm. As they strolled alongside the shore, Alberto, who had taken only half his medication that morning, allowed himself to be distracted by the sights. A group of teenage girls reading magazines. Toddlers shrieking in laughter as they pushed around a beach ball, their parents' eyes lovingly fixed on them. A few feet away, an old man was watching the horizon with his dog in his arms.

Alberto and Mathias walked on, their hands lightly brushing against each other's with each step. When the wind carried to them the laughter of a young couple splashing about in the waves, Alberto slowed his pace to watch them. The guy was hot, but not nearly as hot as Mathias. The girl seemed to agree, her gaze briefly sweeping over Alberto's face to linger on Mathias's golden arms.

The fool who held Alberto's heart at ransom didn't notice, too busy kicking seaweed clumps out of his way, his expression clear of worry. Alberto leaned in and kissed his cheek, and in return was granted an open smile.

In the afternoon sun, Mathias's hazel eyes were almost pure gold. In the darker hour, they would turn amber—and pleading, most likely. Alberto had the feeling neither of them were actually human, but other. Incompatible with this amount of love. His heart ached at the thought.

Nearby, a friendly-faced vendor was selling French fries, the smell turning Alberto's stomach. Sadness rolled in waves within him. He felt he was drowning again.

"What will happen to the pictures in the basement?" Mathias then asked, catching him by surprise.

"What? Why?"

"You're going to move, right?"

"Yes."

"You know where yet?"

"Only that we're staying in Paris."

Alberto caught the flash of relief in Mathias's eyes, his stomach twisting painfully.

"So, what will happen to the pictures in the basement?" Mathias stopped walking, bringing their promenade to an end. "Will you hang them in your new place?"

Alberto studied his face. He was so loath to hurt him. There was only one other person he would be willing to upend the world for.

"It's my mother who wanted to keep them. If it were up to me, I would have already tossed them away. So, I'm probably going to toss them away."

"Don't." Mathias took his hand. "Don't make your mother sad. It's the worst feeling in the world."

Alberto retrieved his hand and immediately regretted it. Mathias looked so lonely whenever his thoughts drifted back to his mother. Alberto spoke kindly, his hands moving on their own to rest on Mathias's chest. "What you told your mother that day… at the hospital. The thing that's haunting you. I'm sure it wasn't as horrible as you think."

"No, it was." Mathias's expression soured but his tone remained gentle. "I have to live with it now, for the rest of my life."

"Would you tell me what you said? Is that okay?"

Mathias nodded. "I don't mind telling you. I want you to know who I am."

"Mati…"

This time, the sound of his nickname brought pain to Mathias's eyes. His shoulders sagging, he turned his face away. "I told her she was abandoning me, and Dad, and Elisa, so I couldn't understand why she felt it was okay to make jokes about it. It's a shit thing to say to a dying person. She needed me. I don't deserve forgiveness."

Alberto flinched at the harshness of his words. It pained him to imagine what they had in common was an acute self-loathing. "I think you do," he said, sounding shy again.

Mathias gave him a clipped smile. "You're way kinder than you let on, you know. It's even scary at times. I don't think *you* ever made your mother cry."

"I did worse. I made her faint, once."

The sight of Mathias's dumbfounded expression was amusing enough for Alberto not to regret his confession. But he was experiencing a profound need to speak up, to reciprocate Mathias's candour. Open the door, just an inch, and experience the warmth of mutual sympathy.

"You're not joking?" Mathias asked, his brow furrowed.

"Nope. Cross my heart and hope to die."

"Don't speak like that." Mathias's frown deepened. "You're not allowed to die, ever."

Alberto did as he always wanted to and pressed his finger right in the centre of Mathias's forehead until the latter's scowl turned into a smile. His hand was snatched and kissed before it was released.

Alberto was loved.

"When I was younger, Mamma took me to a former colleague of hers for my first attempt at modelling. But I was bad, so bad… You should have seen the look on her face. Like she couldn't fathom that anyone could be so bad at this."

Perhaps he had misread her reaction that time as well. Perhaps she was simply sad for him, for his inability to smile, even then. Perhaps if he had not been missing the voice he had since reclaimed, they would have left the studio that time. And never returned.

"The third session we did together, Mamma thought I couldn't relax with her hovering around nervously, as she tends to do. She changed her approach and left us *between men*, as she said. The photographer was famous, but he didn't act like it. He was kind to me. I confessed I was nervous, and he was really sweet about it. He said…" Alberto trailed off, doubt rising in his mind. *Where was he going with this?*

"What did he say, *pollito*?" Mathias asked softly, and unhelpfully. His fingers reached toward Alberto's wrist and made but the briefest contact. That simple touch was enough to bring Alberto back to his senses.

"He said 'Third time's the charm.' I didn't know this one. It made me laugh at the time."

"And did it work?"

Alberto gave Mathias a long look. He didn't feel like answering. He searched for his next words with a frown. "One of us got what they wanted."

Mathias's smile froze at the edges. "What does that mean?"

"Well…" Alberto gave a practised little shrug. "Don't you love the pictures?"

"Oh!" Mathias's expression relaxed. "It was *those* pictures! He took them after his pep talk."

Alberto acquiesced with a nod.

"I still think about them, sometimes… Your little face in the basement."

"Pervert."

"Don't joke about that stuff!" Mathias made a grimace of disgust. "It's not like that… It's like… It's like he captured your innocence perfectly."

With a dry laugh, Alberto briefly pressed himself into Mathias's side. His *lupetto* was so good. Nothing to be afraid of. "Yes… he was artful that way. But guess what? I wasn't impressed. Since he warned me my mother wouldn't get it, and since I didn't want to make her cry, that's how I got the brilliant idea of shaving my head. Right before the next shoot." He did a little bow. "Hence the nickname…"

"Britney," Mathias breathed, his eyes flickering.

"With the scar on the back of my skull, I looked like Frankenstein's pet, so when Mamma saw me, she didn't cry, but she fainted. And weirdly enough, she put all the blame on her husband Martin. I didn't get it until last night, but he was kind of an asshole, and she might have thought he gave me the clippers on purpose. And that's how I ended up moving back to France, to her new friend Dimitri's house." Alberto paused, wondering. "What the hell was up with that? It never occurred me to ask. It was around this time I just stopped caring about everything. *Just like that.*"

Alberto had nothing more to add. He waited for Mathias's reaction. Mathias appeared lost in dark thoughts of his own, his hands searching for his pockets despite having left his hoodie at The Cabin. Already missing his smile, Alberto eagerly changed the subject.

"Do you want to know something cool?"

"Huh?" Mathias returned to reality with a start. "Oh, yes. Always."

"I asked my mother last night. About her, and your dad. And they are truly friends."

It took a moment for the information to reach Mathias's brain, but the results were worth it: the coveted smile returned larger than before. "Truly, truly?"

"Truly, truly. They met at one of those useless parent-teacher meetings and realised they were both as miserable as their children. Isn't that neat?"

"Oh…"

"So, don't worry. You can keep fucking me like a wild beast day and night, it won't be awkward a bit."

"Christ, *pollito*." Mathias's cheeks darkened from embarrassment—or something else. He stepped away from Alberto. "That mouth of yours!"

"You love it, admit it."

Mathias seemed about to say something, but he pressed his lips together instead. Silence stretched between them, unnatural this time. Looking at him, Alberto's stomach twisted again, and the pain brought a grimace to his face.

"Are you okay, Alberto?" Mathias asked in a muted voice. "I feel like… I feel like something's not okay."

Alberto scanned their surroundings. They were far from being alone, but they were also isolated enough that they wouldn't be overheard. "Let's sit down. There's something I have to talk to you about."

Mathias immediately tensed. His gaze drifted toward the ocean before falling back on Alberto's face. "Okay." The hint of resignation in his voice gripped Alberto's chest with guilt, but he too was concerned, stretched taut by the weight of his expectations. What would happen once the words had left his mouth?

Would he wait for him?

Would Alberto wait if he were in his place?

"Thank you. For taking me here. I really like this place."

"I'm glad you like it," Mathias said. "You can stay as long as you want."

"I can't. I'm leaving tomorrow with my mother."

Mathias's expression fell, the corners of his mouth turning down.

"I have to go," Alberto said too quickly. "I can't just wish everything away, and we can't just keep using sex as some sort of messed up therapy, because it clearly wasn't working."

"Is that what we were doing?" Mathias sounded surprised.

"What did you think we were doing?"

"I have no idea… I just wanted to be close to you. Any way you'd let me."

"You got pretty close," Alberto teased.

Mathias wasn't amused. His brow was furrowed, his lips had turned pale. "But are you going back to Colette?"

"I don't think so, no."

"Is it because of Kayvin?" And there was a sudden flash of hope in Mathias's eyes. "Because if it's because of Kayvin, you don't need to. He's been expelled."

Alberto had every intention of saying his piece. But this particular bit of news made him lose the train of his thoughts. "Kayvin has been expelled? Seriously? Why?"

"Why?" Mathias leaned away with a stunned look. "I know he threatened you. Joy told me she overheard him."

"Oh."

"She won't say what Kayvin told you. But I've been wondering—"

"There's no point talking about that." Alberto didn't want to revisit that conversation, which he suspected had pried open the door he had so carefully kept locked in his mind. "But I never complained, and it happened outside of school, so…"

"Kayvin had a history of threatening others, he punched Eric last year, and there were already complaints against him. But somehow, whatever he said to you was bad enough that Van Bergen lost it when Joy finally told him. Kayvin was gone the same day." Mathias waited a moment before adding, "School's kinda okay without him. Eric's captain of the football team again. You should stay."

Alberto rolled his eyes. "Oh well, if Eric is captain…"

"Okay, okay." Mathias held up his hands with a half-smile. "You're really not going to tell me what Kayvin said to you?"

"No. And it has nothing to do with Kayvin. I'm just going away."

Mathias said nothing for a while, his gaze fixed on the ocean, no doubt battling thoughts about the best way to react to all this. A bitter taste rose in Alberto's throat, and he swallowed with a grimace.

"You really think that's what you were doing with me, then?" Mathias spoke at last. "Sex as therapy?"

"I'm not sure," Alberto said. "But despite what my good friend Berko says, sex is definitely not a viable form of therapy. For me, at least."

Mathias's gaze darkened, but he kept silent, his head dipped between his knees. "You want to go back to Meudon?"

"Not Meudon. Somewhere else."

"Where?"

"I don't know yet. Somewhere nice. Somewhere I can get better. I want to live without meds, or at least without that constant feeling I'm in the shadows. Mamma said I'd get a new therapist, a good one this time, and—"

"A new long-legged friend who distributes blowjobs behind dumpsters."

Alberto was forced to snicker. "Look at you. You're so possessive."

"I know. I know. It's just…" Mathias closed his eyes. "I just told you that I loved you."

"I know."

"And you're saying that you're leaving."

"I'm leaving to get better so I have a better chance at…" *Life.* "Everything."

Mathias shot him a quick glance.

"So *we* have a better chance."

"We?" Mathias hung his head. He didn't appear to believe him. The thought threatened to shatter Alberto's fragile confidence.

"And if you have a mind to you know, wait…" he offered anyway, a tinge of fear in his voice. "Then maybe, we can… when I come back…"

"Oh." Mathias lifted his head. "You want me to wait?"

Alberto hesitated. His face was burning, his stomach was in knots. One more word, and it would be done. He would know.

"Yes."

Alberto waited. His blood pounded in his ears, relentlessly. His vision was filled with the sand covering Mathias's sneakers. The grains seemed to pulse in rhythm with his heart.

Waiting. Waiting. Waiting.

"All right then," Mathias said. "That's settled."

"You—"

"I'll be waiting."

He knew.

The unbearable amount of tension Alberto had been carrying — since Mathias's confession, since the note, since the visit, perhaps even since that first fateful kiss — left Alberto so abruptly, he became lightheaded. "I should be sitting," he said, his arse already firmly settled on the sand. He gripped Mathias's bicep for support. "Really?" he dared, just to make sure.

Mathias was smiling. There was sorrow in his eyes, and a deep affection Alberto was still unfamiliar with. He patted his hand, then linked their fingers together. "Whatever you want, Alberto. Whatever you need."

A sudden arrival of tears threatened to turn this scene into another embarrassing memory. Alberto promptly wiped them with the back of his hand before Mathias could notice, and doing so, he caught sight of the French fries shack waiting for customers. The smell was no longer turning his stomach.

"You know what?" Alberto said, perplexed. "I'm feeling hungry."

The notion of feeding Alberto always seemed to make Mathias perk up for some reason. "Really? Do you want me to make you something? I could—"

Alberto motioned toward the shack.

"Junk food?" Mathias asked, shocked. "You want junk food?"

"I really do."

Mathias didn't say more. He sprung up to his feet in a cloud of sand. "Be right back."

He returned shortly after with a steaming portion of fries wrapped in greasy paper and doused in both ketchup and mayo. Alberto couldn't remember the last time he ate anything like this, if ever. He stared at his portion with an adoration that could have made Mathias jealous.

"Don't tell my mother how much I wanted this, okay?"

With an amused snort, Mathias crouched by his side and leaned in to kiss him.

Alberto froze when their lips met. He immediately looked over his shoulder. "Wait!"

"What?" Mathias was smiling. "No one knows us here."

Alberto flattened his hand against his chest and gently pushed him away. "You're not afraid?"

"Of what?"

"Getting beat up."

Mathias shook his head. "Let them come," he said, holding up his fist. "I'll introduce them to my gay agenda."

The nonchalant confidence with which he spoke gave Alberto pause. He realised his mouth had fallen open again. "I'm not gone yet."

"I know."

"We still have time."

"Okay…"

"Let's eat fast, and you can have your way with me again." Alberto arched his eyebrow suggestively. "Think you can take me?"

The light in Mathias's eyes brightened, the big bad wolf within rearing its sensual head again. Alberto shoved a handful of fries into his own mouth to avoid telling him the *stupid sappy thing* seeking release from his chest. The sudden burst of flavour hitting his tongue elicited from him a gasp of surprise. So deliciously inde-cent, he salivated.

"It's better than sex," Alberto said, mildly astonished.

"No, it's not," Mathias replied with an aggrieved expression. He turned away from Alberto. "Not sex with you, anyway."

His wounded tone made Alberto laugh. When Mathias glanced at him next, his smile had extended to his eyes, warm and soft.

Alas, the wildlife had other plans. Alberto had not enjoyed more than a handful of fries before a bastard French seagull swooped down from the sky and snatched the entire packet from his hands.

"That fucker!" Mathias burst out, rising to chase after him.

Staring at his empty hands, Alberto couldn't help laughing. "Leave it, Mathias. It's not worth the trouble."

"Oh, it's definitely worth it." Mathias's eyes were burning. "I'm not gonna let it get away with this!"

As Mathias wasted time and energy—better spent in bed—hopping after the expert seagull who was no doubt laughing at him, Alberto remained seated, watching.

He remembered the house in Napoli. The fluttering curtains, the floral scent of Mamma's locks. The gilded mirror reflecting her face, all black and blue. He remembered the fear, his heart pounding through his chest so hard he could see it, crouching at the bottom of the antique wardrobe, waiting for the violence to end, and for his mother's quiet sobs to begin. He remembered two dark eyes bearing down on him before his vision turned black. He remembered floating for a long, long time. He remembered a journey on a train, the dazzling swagger of Martin, horror films, Philip's smile, and the flash of his camera. The heat of his breath on his neck. The neon lights. The crack in the mirror. The hand-print, visible, and the moment he turned away. He remembered the clippers, the way Stasia laughed at his scar the first time they met on her manicured lawn. He remembered Eric's coldness, the scorn in his eye, the way he strolled away. He remembered Zak's sharp tone as he said, "I heard that," and the way Michael's hand reached out to him. *Are you okay?*

His eyelids fluttered closed. Unseen by all, Alberto's chest rose and fell evenly.

He saw it. *All.*

He saw himself sitting in a cosy room, flowers in bloom, telling a blonde woman about his secrets. He saw his departure, Mamma driving, the radio on, her radiant smile to come home to. He saw himself rushing forward in a straight line, falling again in Mathias's arms. And then the roller coaster. The sex, the fights, the meals shared face-to-face. Secrets whispered in the night. More sex, more fights, a horrible breakup that would leave them both scarred, amputated. He saw himself rise from the wreckage again, and again, Mathias's hand holding on to his. He saw the cake, the guests, the moment they glimpsed each other. Superior. *I do. I do.* He saw all that, and more.

A short distance away, out of breath, Mathias had given up but wore a triumphant look, his fist lifted over his head. Three fries clutched within it. He looked like a god, backlit by a setting sun.

Alberto saw him, and he smiled.

A real smile.

The End

Epilogue

Reunion

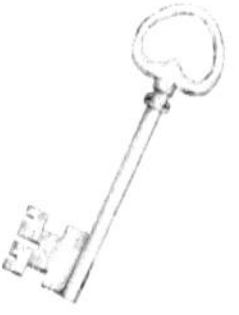

CLOSE TO THREE months had passed. Mathias had been accepted in his first choice of culinary school, where he would start at the beginning of September, and he was confident enough he'd score well at the Baccalaureate tests scheduled later this month.

Class before the exams was a weird business. First years like Elisa, who didn't have tests to deal with, had already left school to enjoy their three months off. *Premières* like Zak and Elodie only had three relatively simple tests to prepare for and were mostly watching movies in class. And senior year students like Mathias weren't really doing anything except pretending to revise, but mostly they were playing games with their amenable teachers. This Friday morning, Mathias and a few of his friends were just hanging in the corridor instead of attending class. Charles-Henry was playing with his PSP. Xavier, trying to get Eric to wrestle with him, was being repeatedly told by him to take a chill pill, while Mathias watched on without interest.

Mathias was near the end of his time at Colette International and should have been able to rejoice, but once again, he was surly, his hands shoved in the pockets of his sweatpants now that the late-spring weather had robbed him of his hoodies.

"Stop it!" Eric was wailing, caught in a headlock by a maniacal Xavier, who wanted to make the most of his final days at school.

"Come on, fight me!"

With a bored sigh, Mathias grabbed Xavier by the shoulder and hurled him into a locker. "Thanks," Eric panted, his cheeks flushed.

"No problem."

Just then, Van Bergen walked out of his office, carrying a glinting trophy cup. He walked by Xavier's form, which had slid down the locker like a wet piece of toast, before he stopped in front of Mathias.

"Here it is!"

The Colette football team had won this trophy for their victories over the other international schools of Ile-de-France. Van Bergen, all misty-eyed from secondhand pride, wanted to place it in the main hall's display case with other prizes won throughout the school's history. He did so with emotion, placing it on a shelf above the one Mathias's mother and her friends had won for some dance contest during their own stint at Colette's, right next to their greatest achievement: the record for Earliest Detention ever received—within seven minutes of the start of their first year at school, a story she never told him.

"Wow," Eric said, watching the headmaster set down the cup with a bright eye. "Such an honor."

Mathias gave his friend a fond look, his lip curling despite himself. Eric was used to much bigger trophies, but he would still politely pretend to be impressed by this one.

Van Bergen clapped Mathias around the back with a smug look. "Somehow, I never lose."

"Meh." Mathias shrugged. "Let's see how the team does when Eric's gone."

"Ho ho!" The headmaster locked the Plexiglas case with care. "Why are you so negative all the time?" Something occurred to him, and his tone softened. "Have you heard from him yet?"

"No. Not a word."

V.B. and Eric exchanged a look. Eric was now aware that Alex was a family friend and Elisa's godfather, but he had kept his promise not to tell anyone, including Zak. Mathias still clung to his secrets, for a reason he couldn't grasp. He felt safer when he was compartmented, like the partitions of a train. In this wagon, his mother, *his Mamma,* the sun of his life. In this one, at the very end, Alberto, light and shadow, moon of his life: Gone twelve interminable weeks now. And in the middle, Alexander Van Bergen and his *twelve lesbians.* Mathias vaguely wondered if he had introduced them to Alberto's mother yet.

"Come on now," Van Bergen bellowed, suddenly all authoritarian. "Fun's over! Get back to class!"

"I don't want to!" Xavier whined, kicking his—empty, by the sound of it—backpack across the floor.

"De Dampierre, don't mess with me." V.B. whipped out his riding crop. "You're dangerously close to doing a hundred push-ups as it is!"

"But *why?*"

"I don't know. You're too tall. Your hair's stupid. I'm the boss, why do I need a reason?"

"But…" Xavier's expression suddenly fell, his mouth falling open. "Shut the fuck up…"

There was a general gasp in the corridor. Charles-Henry looked up from his PSP, his face white as a sheet.

"What did you just say to me?" Van Bergen bore down on Xavier. "Do you *want* to die?"

"M-Mathias… L-look," Xavier stammered, his finger pointing at something behind them. "Look!"

Everyone, not just Mathias, spun around to see what he was pointing at. Save for Eric, who gave a small oh, no one made a sound, least of all Mathias, whose heart had stopped when he had recognized Alberto.

He was here… awkwardly standing in the hall, his thumb scratching his brow.

As tall as a baby giraffe…

His feet glued to the linoleum floors, Mathias swallowed a lump.

Alberto wore a black short-sleeved shirt and matching linen pants, with tan fabric sneakers. A pair of sunglasses hung from his shirt, revealing just enough skin to make you want to peel the thing open button by button, heartbeat by heartbeat. His hair was the same, pulled back, looking even softer than his shirt. And his eyes…

Strange how absence can make people look different. Twelve weeks and Alberto seemed taller, older, and… so devastatingly handsome, he looked almost poisonous.

Mathias stared and stared, transfixed. He was no longer certain he knew the person standing before him. He felt the muscles of his face twitching, his lashes working, his eyebrows drawing together.

Standing by his side, it seemed Eric felt the same. He was ogling Alberto, his mouth slack, his expression torn between alarm and admiration. "Alberto… You look… good."

When Alberto opened his mouth to reply, his voice was drowned by an obnoxious, "My man!" Xavier rushed to him with open arms. "You're back! Can I hug you?"

"No," Alberto said, deadpan.

The finality of his tone would have made anyone else vaporize into nothingness, but Xavier had a thick skin. His hand hovered uncertainly over Alberto's shoulder—Mathias's eyes narrowing at the sight. But surprisingly, Xavier seemed to understand no meant no, because he backtracked with a laugh, his forehead shiny with sweat.

Mathias instinctively turned to Alex, but his father's friend seemed baffled himself, and was peering at the lot of them as if he weren't sure whether to start cheering or punishing them.

"Class," he muttered at last. "All of you, get back to class…"

"I'm not going back to class," Mathias said.

All this time, Alberto's eyes had not left him; Mathias finally found the strength to take a step toward him.

"He's not going back to class," Alberto said, his voice as gentle as ever. The severely missed lilt of his Italian accent caused Mathias's blood to rush to his head. "It's almost lunch time."

V.B. checked his watch. "In ten minutes." His eyes darted between Alberto and Mathias for a moment before he waved his hand. "Fine, GTFO. But you—" he added, grabbing Mathias by the shoulder, "you better be back here on Monday. No more of that *I stole your keys and eloped without a word of warning* bullshit."

"I'll be back," Mathias said vaguely, his attention riveted to Alberto's face. "*Take a chill pill.*"

With a drawn-out sigh, Alex pointed his riding crop at Xavier and the others. "I don't like kids."

Charles-Henry peeped, "Can someone tell me what's going on?"

Van Bergen replied by whipping the air with his riding crop. "Oi! All of you! One hundred push-ups!" He started herding them like cattle. "Your boyfriends will thank me."

"Pfft!" Xavier gave him a wounded look. "I don't even have a boyfriend!"

"And you won't get one with this attitude. Two hundred push-ups!"

Eric was already on the floor. "You heard him, guys! Go, go, go!"

"Let's go," Mathias told Alberto, his hands feeling clammy in his pockets.

The two of them stood outside, a reasonable distance from each other. The sun was at its highest, and Alberto had hidden his gray eyes behind his sunglasses. Mathias had no idea what he was thinking.

And no idea what he himself was supposed to think.

Although Alberto had warned him he would cut off contact to focus on his therapy, Mathias had not expected not to hear a single word for three months. Lots can happen in three months. So much that he was hoping he wouldn't have to speak first, because he had no clue where to begin.

They went to that little restaurant near Place Monge the students frequented because the staff spoke English. It was Mathias who offered, panicked at the thought of finding himself completely alone with that version of Alberto—whose steely gaze was threatening to undo him.

Mathias hid behind the menu; Alberto didn't bother. He was staring at Mathias staring at the menu. When the waitress came, she did a double-take at the sight of him, and Mathias almost screamed, "Right? How am I supposed to talk to him when he looks like that?"

"What can I get you?"

"I'll have the salad, please," Alberto said in a polite but detached tone.

"Which one? We have three different salads."

"The vegetarian one."

"We don't have a vegetarian salad."

At last, Alberto tore his gaze away from Mathias to look at the young woman, who blinked fast, her face reddening. "I'll have whatever one's the cheapest. And you know that one step where you add the meat to the salad?"

"Yes."

"Just skip it. Thank you."

The girl turned to Mathias impatiently. "And you?"

"Same," Mathias muttered.

With a loud sigh, she turned on her heel and walked away.

"Didn't you miss Paris?" Mathias asked in a sarcastic tone. He was playing with his fork, unable to meet Alberto's eyes.

To his surprise, when Alberto spoke to him, it was in a much smaller voice. "I did, a bit."

His tone acted as an encouragement for Mathias, who remembered he was supposed to be a tough guy and looked up, only for Alberto to turn his face toward the window.

"Are you good now?" God, that sounded stupid. "You look… good."

"Thanks." Alberto pinched his lips. "I feel good."

"Yeah?"

"Mm-hm."

"No more meds then?"

"New meds." Alberto turned away from the window to meet his eyes. "New dosage, too."

"Oh." Mathias felt himself flinch under his gaze. "Are they… good?"

"They're better."

"And your therapist?"

"Also better."

"Good. Good. So—"

They were interrupted. The waitress set the plates in front of them and left without a word, but Mathias didn't know what he was about to say anyway.

The salads were nothing to write home about. Alberto didn't even touch his. Mathias played with his, but he wasn't even a vegetarian, and what the hell were they doing here anyway? Why were they acting like a divorced couple, and why did he feel like the forsaken one, burning yet dreading to ask, "Have you met someone new already? You look like you've met someone new."

"You're not eating," he said gruffly.

"I'm not hungry."

"Why did you order something, then?"

"I thought it was expected of me. Being in a *restaurant* and all."

Alberto spoke in a haughty tone, and Mathias immediately felt his stomach twitch from longing. He could be such a dick, sometimes. And Mathias loved it. He almost blurted out, "Okay, but do you still want to be with me?" *Straight to the fucking dessert.* Because Mathias, personally… he was game. He was so game.

This lunch was probably one of the worst things they ever did together, and that included that stint at the cinema a lifetime ago, or that night they said goodbye at his place, when Mathias should have grabbed his dick and told Alberto to stay. Twelve weeks was enough to screw everything up. Twelve weeks was too long a time. In fact, they hadn't even totaled twelve weeks of "relationship" before Alberto had left!

There! He had been gone longer than they had been together, or whatever else you want to call it. Alberto looked like someone else, and Mathias…. well… Mathias was a hundred percent the same.

The same old sulky, stupid guy…

Except for one thing.

This time, he wouldn't let him get away. Not if there was a chance. No, this time, Mathias chose to grab his dick before things got out of hands. He took a long breath, pushed away his plate, and asked point-blank, "Do you want to get a coffee at my place?"

The flash of alarm he caught in Alberto's eyes was unexpected.

"I'm just saying," he quickly said, nervous, "it'd be easier to talk things out in a… familiar place."

"Oh, right." Alberto sounded relieved. "Let's go, then."

They both tried to pay the check at the same time, flashed each other awkward smiles, split the bill, and fucked off with their heads low and their hands in their pockets.

At home, Mathias feared Elisa would be here, but she was in her gamer phase, so she basically lived at her other gamer friend's place. He told Alberto when he asked about her.

"Elisa's got a boyfriend?"

"No, I mean, I don't know." Mathias walked into the kitchen, Alberto right at his heel. "I think he likes her, but she hasn't noticed. He came here once, and he was looking at her funny."

"You should have scared him for good measure." Alberto leaned against the wall and crossed his arms over his chest. "Glared at him with those eyes of yours. As a dad would do."

"I did, actually," Mathias confessed, and they chortled at the same time.

Mathias became aware of how hot his face was, so he turned his back to him.

"Is Elisa straight?" Alberto asked.

"I don't know. I never thought to ask."

Alberto tut-tutted behind him. "It's a thing you do."

Did he sound judgmental? A little bit, maybe. Mathias whirled around to ask, but Alberto spoke first, his eyes wandering around the room. "You said something about coffee?"

"Oh. Yes!"

Mathias was glad to busy himself, although he found it hard to ignore Alberto's eyes burning holes through the back of his skull while he was wrestling with the coffee machine. His fingers seemed to have turned into knackwursts.

When coffee was ready, Mathias chose his best mug and poured Alberto a cup, but instead of drinking, Alberto gave his mug a skeptical look.

"Oh," Mathias said, realizing what the problem was. "Sorry about that. The mini-marshmallows went out of date a while back. I didn't know if—I mean when you'd come back, so I… so I didn't buy more."

Alberto just stood there, blinking at him. Mathias inwardly

hurled his fist into his own nose. Did he sound resentful just now? But maybe—and despite how wrong he knew it was to feel that way—he was, in fact, resentful. At least a little.

Alberto was gone for so long, and now he was back looking like a deadly viper. One bite in a form of a word, and Mathias was a goner.

He waited, but Alberto remained silent, puzzling him.

Mathias's mother never set foot in the kitchen, so he led the way back to his bedroom and stood near the nightstand where he could see her picture. Moral support, and all.

Alberto walked across the room and stood awkwardly on the other side of the bed with his cup in his hand. "This is weird."

"It is," Mathias conceded with relief. At least they were still on the same page, sort of.

Alberto stepped toward Mathias's desk, and, after a hesitation, set his cup on it. His lips pursed, he turned around to face Mathias.

"So, I've been gone for a little while, and—"

"A little while?" Mathias blinked. "Three months isn't 'a little while'."

"I guess." Alberto shot the door a quick glance. Apprehension rose within Mathias, settling on his chest like a stone. "But…"

"But what?" Mathias's heart gave a loud thump. He took an unconscious step toward the door.

"Now I'm back."

"Now you're back."

"So…"

"So…" Mathias held his breath, dreading the next words like a helpless wretch waiting for the judge's sentence.

"So…" Pink bloomed like watercolors on Alberto's cheeks. He gave the smallest of shrugs. "Do you want to kiss me?"

For a brief moment, Mathias only stared at him. Then he burst out, "Yes!" and lunged forward.

Alberto was opening his arms, but Mathias was too fast. They collided and crashed into the old dresser, the same dresser Alberto once tumbled into so many months ago… the day Mathias had unknowingly fallen in love with this unexpected angel.

Their kiss, after weeks, no, months of separation, of anxiety, was desperate and greedy, messy and raw. The force of it blew away every concern and doubt. Mathias tasted the sweet joy of relief in the enthusiastic way Alberto returned his fervor; he knew then for certain he was loved just as he loved, twelve weeks was nothing, twelve weeks was small game. They were *it* for each other, no one else would do, *Game Over, everyone else. Fuck off.* Reveling in ecstasy, Mathias laughed in Alberto's mouth, and received a laugh back. They parted, but only for an inch, forehead against forehead, their fingers curling around each other's clothes.

"This is…"

"This is—"

"—So much better."

"So much easier… Than talking…"

They laughed again into each other's necks.

"God…" Mathias's chest was so full. He screwed his eyes shut. "I've missed you so much."

"You did?"

"You've no idea. And you, did you miss me?"

"… I did. I… Ah… I thought about you every day."

"Every day?"

"Every day—ah! Now, that tickles."

There was more kissing. And hands… febrile hands snaking around, settling in interesting places.

"I wasn't sure…"

"What…"

"I wasn't sure you still…"

"Shut up, you're insane."

"Wait… ah… Fuck… Look who's talking—"

More kissing. Alberto's hands sneaking under his shirt, stealing a dangerous sound from Mathias.

"Mathias…"

"Hm?"

"I've waited so long…"

"Hm?"

"So long… to suck your cock…"

Mathias gulped, gripping his arms.

"I want to do it…"

"Hold on—"

"… Real bad," Alberto purred. He dragged his fingertips across Mathias's crotch. "Real bad…" Mathias cut him off with a kiss. "And I want to…"

"What, *pollito*?" Mathias was dizzy. "What do you want?"

"I want you to meet my mother." With his eyes, he searched into Mathias's face. With his hand, he searched and found his way inside Mathias's pants. "Properly, this time."

"Fuck, yes—I mean…" Mathias cleared his throat. "I want to —ah! Wait, wait." He clung to the front of Alberto's shirt. "I want to…"

His hand working inside, Alberto spoke by his ear. "What do you want?"

Not given much choice in the matter—and not complaining— Mathias tried to speak between kisses.

"I want to—"

"Mmm?"

"Take you—"

"Oh? How nice—"

"—to prom."

Alberto stopped moving, his eyes wide with shock.

"I mean," Mathias said, flustered. "Prom is stupid, and it's gonna suck, and people… I hate people… but—"

"Okay," Alberto said. He glued their bodies together, smiling. "Okay, let's go."

Mathias kissed him until he was liquid, then he sunk his teeth into his neck and felt the consequence as it burned through his clothes, long and hard. He leaned back to admire the desire in Alberto's now dark eyes, the way his chest rose and fell rapidly. With a swipe of his tongue over his lip, Mathias tentatively brushed his fingers along the opening of Alberto's shirt, pressed his palm against his heart, and felt the passion beating within.

"That shirt… That shirt's got to go."

"Agreed," Alberto said, his eyes glinting. Gripping the hem of Mathias's shirt, he abruptly lifted it over his head, only to gasp in shock.

"What?" Mathias recoiled, worried he might have grown pustules overnight. "What's wrong?"

"You still got that thing?" Alberto pulled on Mathias's chain. "And you're wearing it, too!"

He was talking about the little lock Mathias had once found hidden under the mattress. With a low chuckle, Mathias buried his nose in Alberto's neck and nuzzled it fondly. "Since you have a bad memory, I will tell you again, but only because you have a bad memory." Alberto nodded like an expectant child, and Mathias let out a soft sigh. "I don't know if you recall," he whispered against his ear, "but I'm in love with you."

In response, Alberto shuddered, his length growing even harder against him. "I choose you," he said.

"What?"

"Say you choose me. Say it first, then—"

"I choose you." Mathias smiled.

"And I choose you," Alberto said, finding his eyes. "We choose each other."

A tad confused, Mathias linked their fingers together. "Okay."

"And now…"

"And now?"

Alberto pursed his lips into a pout. "Where's that good pounding you once promised me?"

With a great burst of laughter, Mathias joined their lips together again. Then he enveloped Alberto into his arms and lifted him from the dresser to the bed as carefully as he could. Alberto didn't care for his caution and was trying to tear his pants off.

"Let me see you," he was saying. "Three bloody months. I need to feel your skin."

As always when it came to him, Mathias did as he was told. Awkwardly fending off Alberto's frantic tugs, he removed his pants, but Alberto wasn't happy until he stood bare in front of him.

"God, you are so hot!" Alberto threw himself back on the bed. "I'm ready to burst already."

"Shut up!" Mathias turned his face away, embarrassed. He laid on top of Alberto to hide his burning face in his neck. Alberto let out a feral sound, his lips clamping on his earlobe, and Mathias's eyes started prickling again. "I feel naked."

"You *are* naked."

"What about you?"

Up close and without the veil of his former meds clouding his eyes, Alberto was the most terrifying person on earth. Mathias felt ten years old again. Alberto spread out his arms, teasing. "All yours."

"You are so beautiful," Mathias said to his clear—and scorching—eyes. He came for his shirt, button by button, heartbeat by heartbeat. The thing slid off like silk. Heat curled through Mathias's veins at the sight of his bare skin. He was so hard by now, it had become almost painful. "*So* beautiful."

Alberto's gaze flew up toward the ceiling, self-consciousness painting his cheeks a deep red. Mathias feared it would be ridiculous to tell him he loved him again; he did it anyway. Alberto didn't say it back. His hands were trembling. Mathias took this opportunity to slither down, pressing kisses to his skin all the way. "I'll take care of you now."

He undressed him carefully, and he took him in his mouth for a short while, ecstatic to taste him again on his tongue, before Alberto's long fingers gripped his shoulders, and he begged him to stop.

"Don't you like it?"

"It's not enough," Alberto said. Mathias climbed up by his side.

"Not enough?"

Alberto arched an eyebrow seductively. "Do you remember how to do it?"

Mathias's lips stretched in a confident smile. Long arms wrapped around him, and fingers felt him from his nape to his tailbone and below. "I'll remember everything, from now on."

Mathias got to work.

The heat was stifling. In his groin, his gut, and his chest, and between Alberto's cheeks where it was tight like a vice. The fingers clutching his face were burning as well, and Mathias's defenses crumbled entirely. He said the words again between kisses, breathed them into his mouth. Again, Alberto didn't say them back. He looked away, his legs shaking. Mathias could read fear in his eyes. Not of him, not of his temper, but something else entirely. Perhaps it was the same kind of fear that had devoured Mathias the past few months, that had told him lies about Alberto not wanting him anymore, about having replaced him with someone else. The little lock had burned into his skin both lovingly and painfully when he was nurturing these thoughts.

Three long months… reduced to nothing by the feeling of each other's skin again.

Rocking his hips faster, he said the words again, to himself this time. He added, *Please let me keep him, and keep him safe, don't take him away from me.* And he hoped the look in Alberto's eyes meant he was wishing the same.

With a cry of pleasure that bordered on agony, Alberto came first, tears spilling out the corner of his eyes. Mathias pulled out at his request, and Alberto got on his knees and finished him with his mouth, both hands gripping his ass. He looked entranced as he swallowed everything, and lapped at Mathias's softening cock for a while before he fell on the bed with a sigh.

Mathias grabbed a freshly laundered towel before falling at his side. He wiped Alberto's stomach lovingly, before leaning down to press a kiss to it.

"Are we together now?" Alberto then asked, a quiet whisper in the comfortable silence following their entanglement. They were face-to-face, their legs entwined, Mathias's fingertips caressing the outline of Alberto's face; Alberto's hand, not as well-behaved, was tracing small, flaring circles over the skin of Mathias's ass.

"I hope so," Mathias replied in the same way.

He received a smile, before Alberto hid his face behind his other hand. "Are you my boyfriend, then?"

"Yes, I am." Mathias pried his hand away. "I'm your boyfriend."

"Look at me…" His eyes were glinting. "I got myself a man."

"You've got yourself this one, at least." Mathias kissed him again, and then the dumb part of him gave in the remnants of his fear, and he asked, "Did you…? Did you hook up with anyone else during…"

Alberto jerked his head back and skewered him with a glare.

"No!" Then something flickered in his eyes, and he swallowed noisily. "Why? Did you…?"

Mathias blinked at him. "You're kidding, right?"

"What?" Alberto tried to wriggle away. "I was afraid you'd move on. Who would wait for three months?"

"Me!" Mathias held fast and didn't let him slip away. "I said I'd wait, why would I go back on my word?" When Alberto stopped struggling, he relaxed his grip around him. "I was afraid you'd moved on, too."

"Really…?"

"Of course. I thought maybe… maybe once you'd get better, you'd might want someone better, too."

"Mati…" Alberto became all soft against him. His voice fell to a whisper again. "We chose each other. We can never move on."

Mathias and Alberto held each other and talked for a long time, until afternoon bled into evening and shadows started filling the room. When Alberto fell asleep, Mathias got up, cleaned himself, and answered a few—very demanding—messages from friends and relatives who spent *too much damn time* prying into other people's lives.

Although Eric's text: "I can't believe I'm gonna have to be friends with Alberto now," accompanied by a sobbing emoticon, did steal a quiet laugh from him.

When he heard a sleepy voice call from the bedroom, Mathias turned off his phone to join him. With a rare presence of mind, he leaped onto the bed to hug the *girafon* before he could get up—and get dressed.

"Is your father back?" Alberto asked in a groggy voice. "Or your sister? Should I go?"

"No!" Mathias grimaced at his ridiculous notion. "I texted them to stay away this weekend. We have the place to ourselves."

That cocky bastard Alex could feed them, for once. And his house had at least thirty bedrooms. Meanwhile, Mathias had only one bed, and it was forever reserved for Alberto.

Alberto's face split into a lazy smile that launched Mathias's heart into an impromptu drums solo. "For real?"

Mathias nodded. "Please, stay." He leaned down to kiss Alberto's lips. "Are you hungry?"

Despite the sleepiness in his eyes, Alberto's hand immediately reached between Mathias's legs. "Yes."

"Not that." Mathias shook his head with a smile. "*Real* food."

"Oh, right." Alberto rose to his elbow with a grunt. "You want to feed me again?"

"If we're to be together, you'll have to taste a lot of things."

"Okay, okay."

Mathias peeled him off the bed. Alberto found his underwear and threw one of Mathias's t-shirts over his head. They skulked to the kitchen holding hands.

"Tell me what you like," Mathias said, opening the fridge. "What you *really* like."

Alberto gave a little shrug. "I like annoying, complicated things. Things you don't know how to make."

"I'll learn them, then." Mathias pulled him into his arms. Cool air from the fridge had caused goose bumps to flare on his arms and thighs. Mathias buried his lips into his neck to elicit some more. Alberto dug his fingers into his biceps with a gasp. "I'll make you anything you like. I'll make you vegetarian salads with rainbows of colors." He kissed his way up his neck, swiped his tongue along his jawline, and felt Alberto grow hard against him again. "There's this Japanese sweet potato that's purple inside. It's gorgeous, you'll see."

"I know." Alberto's voice had grown thick. "I know, I love Japanese food. And I love your… ah… pasta."

"Oh?" Mathias briefly sucked on his earlobe. "Looks like we're getting somewhere."

Alberto pushed his face away. He was flushed, his hair sticking to his forehead, his eyelids half-closed from desire.

"Come back to bed with me."

"Now?"

"Help me build up my appetite."

Mathias took him back to bed, where Alberto received a gift, then showed off his own skills in a loving, thoughtful, yet brutally efficient way, before he fell asleep almost immediately. Mathias observed his face, satisfied by the peace he found there, then sleep took him as well. Stress left his muscles as he wrapped himself around Alberto and held him close.

In the middle of the night, Alberto stirred and turned to the other side to bury his face in Mathias's chest. That was the only brief interruption. They slept a long time, and in the morning, Alberto woke to the feeling of Mathias's lips in his hair, finding his scar, pressing upon it the softest kiss. He shivered, before asking for more. They enjoyed each other before breakfast, soft and slow.

It was during these effusions that a few crucial words left Alberto's lips and floated in the air but for the briefest moment before Mathias caught them and etched them deep into his heart. Afterward, when everything was still and quiet, Mathias kissed Alberto's parted lips, satisfied.

There, Mathias thought.

I finally stopped time.

Extra

Endings
AND BEGINNINGS

Alberto was panting.

There was no air in this room. Throwing his head back, he caught the green light of the emergency exit. Sweat began gathering on his forehead, threatening to mess with his hair. Pressed against him, Mathias was raining kisses down his neck, only stopping once to drag his tongue across the jut of his throat. Alberto, with a mental curse, curled his fingers around his arms and pushed him away.

"What?" Mathias leaned back, his tone full of protest.

Alberto readjusted his Armani jacket. "We'll be late."

"So?" Despite his tone, Mathias stepped away from him and switched on the light.

"So?" Alberto gave him a haughty look. "You said you'd take me to prom, and now you're changing your mind at the last minute?"

Mathias narrowed his eyes, either at the sudden light or Alberto's coyness. "I took you to prom."

"You took me to the gymnasium, then you dragged me into this office and tried to get into my very expensive suit. We never made it to the party itself."

It was the truth; they could even hear what sounded like an eighties revival playlist through the wall of the office. But Mathias still chose to lie, shrugging. "It hasn't started yet." After a pause, he added, "I just wanted to see it."

"See what?"

He licked his lip. "Your tummy."

"Tsk." Alberto shook his hair away from his face. "That old thing."

"Right." Mathias watched him reset his tie with a frown. "Show me your tummy, and then we can go."

"My shirt will get wrinkled."

"Ah… because *that's* important."

"What's so good about my tummy anyway?"

"You don't get it." Mathias trapped him between him and the desk for another heated kiss. Alberto felt his resolve melt with each swipe of his tongue.

"Not… f-fair."

His face suddenly serious, Mathias released Alberto. He glanced at the door with a sigh.

"What is it?" Alberto asked. "You're worried the others will think we're together?" He kept his tone light, but deep down, he was becoming anxious.

"No," Mathias said, and he sounded distant now.

Alberto's anxiety grew. "What is it, then?"

"I just wanted to make good memories for us in here."

In case something bad happened out there?

Alberto unknowingly took a step back. Mathias was right. Nobody out there but Eric and Elisa knew about their relationship, about the past two weeks of absolute bliss they had shared, especially that first weekend where they practically never left Mathias's bed. Going to prom was a fun idea in theory, but in the end, they'd have to pretend to be acquaintances at best. No kisses, no *touching* at all for the next few hours. Alberto understood why Mathias didn't want to leave the office. Now he felt the same.

With a sigh, he tugged on his shirt. "Here," he said, lifting it.

With a mouthed "bless you," Mathias knelt down with no regards for his own navy-blue suit and started kissing him, his lips fluttering all over his stomach until shivers rocked Alberto, and he tried to push him away. Mathias resisted, wrapped his arms around his waist, and whispered against his navel, "I'll come back for you later."

"Disgusting," Alberto said.

Tenderness overcame him; his grimace turned into a smile, then a flustered laugh. He kissed then ran his hand over Mathias's scalp. "It's too hot in here; I can barely breathe. Let's go."

Mathias sprung up to his feet and smacked their lips together. "Almost ready." Before Alberto could ask, he cupped his face with one hand, his thumb finding Alberto's cheek, then his lower lip, which he flickered lovingly. "Say it, to give me strength."

Alberto let out a dramatic sigh. *For show.* He pressed himself into Mathias's space, clung to the lapels of his jacket, and said the words against his lips. "I love you, Mati."

Then he hurried out of the room, worried one look at Mathias's face would end, once again, with him on all fours.

Outside the gymnasium, wearing a light-blue suit and hair gel, Eric was holding court. His tie was loose and his shirt half untucked, but the effect was irritatingly riveting. Standing too close to him in a bright mini dress, Joy was laughing at his jokes, unaware of the dark looks Zak was throwing her. As she wasn't a senior, she had to have come here as someone's date, and since Melissa didn't appear present, Alberto concluded she had come here with Xavier. Also present, Charles-Henry was standing next to an Elodie clad in the tightest black gown, and was blinking at her as though he couldn't believe she'd agreed to go with him.

Alberto felt himself tense, his fingers flexing, wishing he could hold his man's hand. Mathias seemed no better. The way he bumped into Alberto as they walked toward his friends felt purposeful, and the way he placed his hand on the small of his back as he apologised even more so.

"There you are!" Joy said to Mathias. She gasped when she recognised the one at his side. "Alberto?"

Zak's mouth had fallen open. "My God, it's really you… What are you doing here?"

Alberto shot Mathias a quick glance. He hadn't thought about that. Although he and his mother had had a long talk with Van Bergen, who encouraged him to take his exams at the end of the month instead of repeating a year, Alberto hadn't returned to school yet, preferring to study at home in Mamma's small rented flat. In fact, Zak, Elodie and Joy hadn't seen him since February, and tonight was the seventeenth of June.

Just like Joy, Zak and Elodie, Alberto wasn't a senior, so he had no good reason to show up for prom in his Armani suit unless he was someone's plus one. But then it occurred to him he was the sort to wear designer clothes on any occasion, including PE. "I was passing by," he said quite lamely, "and I… heard music."

Mathias's forehead creased as Eric exploded in laughter, calling everyone's attention to himself. But Zak was not so easily fooled.

"Where were you? Nobody wanted to tell us anything. Only Madame Paquin said you'd left school and wouldn't be coming back."

"I was…" Alberto paused to study everyone's expressions. It seemed his appearance was so unexpected, nobody had noticed he had arrived with Mathias. They were all watching him eagerly, and he, too, felt he hadn't seen them in a long time — not only because of the months he'd spent away, but also because he had rarely been clearheaded enough to take a good look at their faces. "The truth is…" he said, ignoring Mathias's look of surprise. "I was unwell."

"Did something happen to you?" Joy asked, her voice laced with real concern.

"No." Alberto hesitated. "But I wasn't feeling myself, and I… I had to step away for a while."

The implications hovered in the air, and they all exchanged looks — except Xavier and Eric, who kept their eyes soberly on their feet.

"Are you better now?" Zak asked, his hand finding Eric's. "Will you take the exams with us?"

"Yes. And yes. I'll be back in September, if" — his mouth twisted — "*if* I pass the exams."

"Too bad I won't be back in September," Xavier said with a sigh. "I've already repeated a year. My dad would be furious if I repeated another."

"Oh," Alberto said, unsure how to react.

The conversation stirred toward the guys' post-Colette plans, to

Alberto's relief. Even better, Mathias leaned into his side, his hand finding his back again.

"You told them the truth," he whispered. "Are you okay?"

"Might as well," Alberto replied. "If I don't say anything, they'll make up their own version. And their version's always worse."

Mathias's hand gently stroked Alberto's back over his jacket. "It's not like you to care what other people think."

"But if I'm to see them more often now… I mean…" Alberto lowered his head. "If I'm to hang out with them, too, then I'd rather they understand me a minimum." He glanced up. "So I can take it easy, and you can take it easy, too."

Mathias was smiling. His smiles weren't so rare now, but the ones he reserved for Alberto were on another level. Alberto cast the others a nervous glance. "Will you stop smiling? They're going to notice."

Mathias stepped in front of him, a strange glow in his eyes. "You think?"

Alberto's heart gave a thump. Before he could reply, his vision filled, and his breath caught in his throat.

Mathias was kissing him. In front of everyone.

It was a soft kiss, of a tender nature rather than sensual. But it was so unexpected that it made Alberto stumble back into the wall with a sound of surprise. Still, he gripped Mathias's jacket for support and returned his kiss as collective gasps filled the air around them. Xavier shouted, "Gay kiss! Look! Gay kiss!" and someone stomped on his foot, stealing a curse from him. Alberto chuckled, and Mathias, in turn, smiled against his lips. Drawing back with a sigh, he gripped Alberto's hand and turned to the others.

"Yeah, so… here's the thing. Alberto and I are together. If any of you wants to comment, now's the fucking time."

No one said anything. They were all — save Eric and Xavier — staring at him with various degrees of shock. At last, Zak, looking particularly pale, blurted out, "That's from *Kill Bill*! I'm… I'm pretty sure. T-that line's from *Kill… Bill.*"

The others finally snapped out of it to shoot him a dark look.

Eric swung an arm over Zak's shoulder with an awkward laugh. "Don't mind him. My boyfriend's a cinephile."

Mathias cleverly took full advantage of their surprise. "No comment, then?" he asked. "Nothing? Then you can shut up about it forever." He drew Alberto to his side with a satisfied smile.

There were comments, but they were kept to an inaudible level for the most part, and Alberto didn't care. He glued himself to Mathias with a racing heart. "I wasn't expecting that."

"What?" Mathias looked amused. "You thought I would take you to prom only to hide you?" He frowned. "Wait… did you want—"

"No!" Alberto shook his head so fast, he became lightheaded. "I want what you want, I do! But I… I didn't want to… presume." Although now that he thought about it, Mathias's behaviour in the office made more sense. "I would never presume…"

"You should." Mathias kissed Alberto's cheek. "Now they know, so *we* can take it easy."

In response, Alberto buried his face in the crook of his neck. With a low hum, Mathias held him tight against him.

"So, you're gay, too?" Joy interrupted in a strangled voice. "And you couldn't say it before?"

Mathias tossed a vague look in her direction. "Why are you so obsessed with what people are all the time?" He turned his back to her. "I'm *his*, that's all you need to know."

Feeling naughty, Alberto swung both arms around Mathias's neck and enjoyed the look of envy on her face.

"You could just be upfront with it and save us some time," Joy said, her eyes narrowing at Alberto's guile. "It's not like anybody cares nowadays."

"If only we owed you anything," Alberto said, meeting her eyes. "If only."

Joy huffed, but she was cut off by Elodie. "Anyone else feeling like giving up on men?" she asked, letting her arms fall to her sides. "I feel like giving up."

Since Mathias's kiss and his unexpected announcement, Alberto had been floating again. Not in a fog as before, but like a balloon, hovering inches above the ground. Elodie's words yanked his string down. He released Mathias's neck to claim his hand, and he felt him squeeze back one, two, three times.

"You should speak to my mother," Alberto said. He was smiling. God, he felt *strong*. "She's giving up on men, too."

"When?" Xavier burst out, a hint of panic in his voice. "After tonight?"

Alberto's mother had been invited by the headmaster himself to be one of the chaperones at the dance tonight. She was inside with Mathias's father and a few other teachers. Xavier had apparently found out about it.

"Come here, angel."

Before Alberto could tell Xavier to get lost, Mathias caught his face for a kiss, and Alberto's anger disintegrated. Either out of consideration or awkwardness, the others turned their back to them — except for Eric, who watched them embrace with a smile. Just as Mathias, his eyes glowing like embers, was pushing Alberto against yet another wall, a squeaky voice spoke behind them, "Did nobody tell you the party's actually inside?"

Alberto recognised that voice and craned his neck toward the gymnasium. Dressed in the most astonishing black sequin tux with matching bowtie, Elisa was standing in the light of the doorframe with her camera. Alberto's lip curled fondly at the sight of her, but others did not welcome her with the same enthusiasm. Joy in particular gave her a condescending look. "It's that little girl from the paper again! What are you doing here?"

"She's right, you know," Mathias said, in a voice so low only Alberto could hear. His lips found the soft patch of skin behind Alberto's ear, causing him to shiver noticeably. "Why don't you all fuck off inside?"

"Mathias, behave," Alberto said, amazed at his own self-control. He waved at Elisa, who returned the favour before shaking her camera in front of her face with a haughty look.

"I'm press, I can be wherever I want."

"I don't think so." Joy approached Elisa with both hands on her hips. "How old are you anyway? Does your mother know you're here?"

Elisa also took a step forward. "Okay, bitch, will you back off?"

Mathias gave a loud sigh as Joy let out a cry of shock, but there was nothing she could do. Van Bergen himself appeared in a grey suit with matching vest and put his hand over Elisa's shoulder. "There you are." Looking at her as though she were a national treasure, he pulled her inside, ignoring Joy's pointed glares.

"How is he never punishing this horrible child?" she asked, fuming.

Xavier sniggered. "Didn't she slam you in the Summer Edition of the *Candy Guide*?"

Standing behind Joy, Elodie lifted her finger in front of her mouth to silence him. Zak saw it and smirked.

"Oh yes," he said slyly. "She gave Joy the award for *Gossip Girl, or most likely to start unfounded rumours*. Well deserved, I'd say." His eyes found Alberto's. This time, they exchanged a proper smile.

"Whatever," Joy said, vexed. "She's the worst."

Enough was enough. Alberto needed to intervene. "That's my sister you're talking about," he said, pushing Mathias's face away. The bastard had been nipping his neck *and* groping him in the shadows for a full minute now. Alberto was already half-hard, and this stupid party hadn't even started.

"That, I can believe," Joy said. "She's just as rude as you."

Alberto couldn't help but chortle. With a low sound of frustration, Mathias slipped his hand under Alberto's jacket and turned to face her.

"Actually, she's *my* sister," he said, "and I'm sorry. She knows you're not a bitch. She just really hates people calling her a little child or making comments about our mother, and she really, really likes saying the word *bitch*."

"All right," Joy said, her expression softening. "But only because she's *your* sister."

"The *Colette Times'* editor-in-chief is Mathias's sister?" Charles-Henry looked shocked. "Why am I the last one to know anything?"

"I'm on the same boat as you, brother," Xavier said with a shrug. "Come on, let's get inside." He held out his hand to Elodie, who pulled a frown.

"Joy's your date, not me. Remember?"

"Oh, crap!"

"I'm not his date!" Joy proudly tossed her hair back. "I only came here with him to get access. And" — she lowered her voice — "to dance with a certain man."

"I'm telling you, Van Bergen's gay!" Xavier retorted, all serious. "I saw him and his boyfriend at the Gay Pride last year." He gave the group a strange look. "His boyfriend's, like, our age. It's really weird."

"What?" Mathias unglued his face from Alberto's neck. "No, he's not."

Before Alberto could ask, Eric said, "Hang on!" His eyebrows shot up to his hairline, he approached Xavier. "What the hell were you doing at the Gay Pride?"

"I live nearby?" Xavier said hesitantly. "I thought it was a carnival at first, but the outfits were all wrong…"

"And you *stayed*?"

"Yeah? People there were really nice. They kept saying how proud they were of me."

Eric slapped Xavier around the back. "Oh, Xavier, I love you." He pulled him into a hug. "I just love you."

Alberto inadvertently let out a little laugh, which earned him a kiss from Mathias.

"Let's get inside, Eric," Zak said, taking his boyfriend's hand. "I want to dance."

Eric immediately dashed toward the building, dragging Zak behind him. Charles-Henry and Elodie went after them, followed by the still bickering Joy and Xavier. Alberto and Mathias remained outside a little bit longer, seemingly unable to take their hands off the other.

"Mati…" Alberto called between two particularly sweltering kisses. "Mati, do you know the headmaster's boyfriend?"

Still seeking his lips, Mathias gave him a dazed look. "Uh? What?"

"Do you know the headmaster's boyfriend?"

Mathias's lip curled into the deadliest little smirk. "Say that word again?"

"What, *boyfriend*?" Alberto rolled his eyes, but he was amused.

"*You* really shouldn't be allowed to pronounce the letters *b* and *p*." Mathias grunted. "Christ's sake…" He fidgeted with the front of his trousers. "How am I going to make it tonight? I'm half-hard already, and this fucking party hasn't even started." His eyes widened in surprise when Alberto burst into a laugh. "What? What did I say?"

"Nothing. Sometimes, it hits me hard, that's all."

"What does?"

"How we were meant to be."

Still smiling, Alberto led Mathias toward the building, his stomach filled with butterflies. Inside, they were assailed by the stifling heat, and the sight of countless balloons hovering a few inches from the ceiling, all of them in the colours of the rainbow. The dance floor was packed with the Colette seniors and their dates. Scattered around the court, tables covered with paper cloths were waiting for them to return. As for the decor, it couldn't be more eighties if it tried. With the playlist to match, Alberto thought for a second that he had travelled through time.

When Joy saw all this, she stopped dead in her tracks, and Alberto would have walked straight into her if not for Mathias, who pulled him to his side.

"Doesn't this look really kitsch for Colette?" Joy asked. "I mean… where did the budget go?" She turned to Eric. "This looks like it was paid for by Xavier's parents."

"They're known to be cheap," Charles-Henry informed Alberto, leaning into him with a complicit smile.

Mathias threw him a look so cold, Charles-Henry actually jumped to the side, knocking into Xavier.

"Ah," Eric said, sounding apologetic, "that would be my fault. I didn't want a stuffy party in a hotel, where people would be so worried about looking good that they wouldn't have fun. I wanted prom in the school's gymnasium, with fruit punch and retro music. That's what I told my dad, and the headmaster was into it."

"V.B.'s got no shortage of retro music, that's for sure," Mathias mumbled.

"Do you think he'll play Cher?" Alberto asked, turning to him excitedly.

Mathias replied by hugging him so close, Alberto felt his

burning fingers through his clothes. He swung his arm over Mathias's shoulder and pressed a kiss to his cheek.

"You told them to choose this music?" Joy was beside herself. "Are you insane?"

Eric didn't reply at first, his gaze falling on Zak, who was already dancing with Elodie. Alberto knew from the way Eric swiped his tongue over his lips exactly what part of Zak he was staring at. "I'm smarter than you think."

"I don't care about the music," Xavier said. "I came here to have fun, I'm gonna have fun." He swept a look around the room. "Alberto, where's your mum?"

With a strangled cry of protest, Alberto stomped forward, but Xavier was already hurrying toward the bar, where Mamma was serving the fruit punch. Despite her sober dress with long sleeves, the line for drinks was suspiciously long, and made mostly of boys. As he and Mathias made their way toward her, the others tailing after them, something caught Alberto's attention. At the edge of the dance floor, the headmaster, Elisa, and another young man Alberto didn't know, were dancing completely in synch to "Let's All Chant."

"The headmaster and your sister are *weirdly* close," Alberto said, frowning. "What's up with that?"

"About that…" Mathias's grip on his hand tightened. "*Pollito*, I think it's time I—"

"Look!" Xavier made a sudden U-turn, his eyes wide. "Guys, look!"

"Fuck's sake…" Mathias said, burying his nose in Alberto's shoulder.

"The headmaster's boyfriend is here!"

"That's him?" Eric asked, with a quick look at Mathias. "The one you saw at the Gay Pride?"

"Yeah, that's him!"

Eric started cackling, but when he glimpsed at the guy in question, his laughter died in his throat. Zak noticed, his eyebrows shooting up.

"Van Bergen's also gay?" Joy asked, sounding heartbroken. "And his boyfriend's my age. What a waste!"

"*Husband,*" Mathias corrected. "And he's not."

Alberto slipped him a curious glance.

"He's definitely not a student here," Eric said, breathless. "I'd have noticed." Zak ground his heel into his toes, making him yelp. "What did I say?"

"Stop, all of you!" Mathias burst out. "Stop making assumptions about people; you're driving me nuts." Everyone looked at him in surprise. "You don't know shit, so stop talking."

"Explain to us, then?" Elodie asked. "Please?"

Alberto gave a small nod. He didn't want to pressure Mathias, but he had grown as curious as the rest of them.

"He's not our age at all; he's closer to forty. And despite the grey hair, so's Van Bergen." Mathias was about to add something, but the headmaster himself appeared right in front of them.

"Why are you clustered here?" he boomed, squinting at them. "Remember the rules." He pointed at a handwritten sign nailed under the Prom 2011 banner which said: *No alcohol, no drugs, no cheating.*

"Now I immediately want to start cheating," Xavier said, pouting.

The way Van Bergen grinned at his badly put together sign made Alberto suspect he had no intention of actually enforcing it.

"Alex!" Mathias suddenly called, his face serious.

To everyone's shock, the headmaster replied, "What?"

"I want to tell people about you."

There was a silence. For the first time ever, Van Bergen seemed to lose some of his formidable countenance. "Very well," he said, sounding pleased.

"Oh my God!" Xavier pointed a shaky finger at them. "Are you guys also… a couple?"

Van Bergen gave him a look of pure resignation. "And *that*, kiddos, is the reason why you should never marry your cousin."

"We're not a couple!" Mathias shot Xavier a venomous look. "We're… family." He motioned toward the headmaster with a sigh. "Everyone, this is Alexander. Alexander, these are my friends, Eric, Zak, and Elodie. And you already know the others."

Xavier guffawed. "We're also his friends."

"No you're not." Mathias's ruthlessness sent a delicious shiver up Alberto's spine.

"Hello, friends and others." Alex raised his hand in a vague salute sign, his gaze lingering on Alberto. "And hello, Mathias's… friend?"

Alberto blinked at him.

"They know," Mathias said.

"Thank the gods." Alex gave a sigh of relief. "So, how's it going? Anyone tried the fruit punch yet?"

"Not yet, no!" Xavier held out his hand. "Can I call you Xander?"

The headmaster shook his hand with a frightening smile. "Why don't you try, see what happens?"

Xavier retrieved his hand with a yelp of pain. "That's okay," he squeaked. "Headmaster works just fine."

All this while, Alberto had been listening politely, surprised he was able to understand what was happening for once. But Mathias misinterpreted his silence as something else, because when he turned to him, his handsome face was twisted with worry.

"Alex is married to my mother's best friend, my godfather," he explained, his hand finding Alberto's. "So, I kinda grew up around him."

"We grew up around each other," Van Bergen corrected. "We were just kids when we had you."

"He's *not* my dad," Mathias said when Xavier's mouth fell open. "My dad's the maths teacher, Mr Rodin. He and Alex met at Colette a century ago—"

"Thanks," Van Bergen interrupted. "Real nice."

"Alberto, listen." Mathias held Alberto's hand between his own. "I didn't tell you because Alex asked me not to tell anyone. But school's over now, so who cares what these people know about me, about us." He ignored Zak's snort and Joy's frustrated sigh. "I'm sorry I didn't tell you. I was waiting for the right time…"

"Don't worry." Alberto dipped his head to kiss the back of Mathias's hand. "So, you know the headmaster. Big deal. Who doesn't have a few secrets?" His gaze fell on the wolf ring glinting on his finger. "This is nothing at all."

Joy suddenly let out a cry of triumph. "So, that explains why you like that little girl! Oh, it finally makes sense! You'd have to be family to stand someone like her."

Van Bergen ignored her better than Alberto could have ever done. "Mathias, since the cat's out of the bag—" He interrupted himself, an eyebrow quirked. "Never mind. Since everyone knows, don't forget to say hello to Simon." With a vague look of disgust at Xavier, who grinned cluelessly at him, the headmaster walked away, muttering, "*Xander…*"

As soon as he was gone, Elodie pulled a flask from her purse and took a giant swig from it. "If anyone asks… I'll be out here, looking for straight men to make out with."

"Me too!" Joy said, and they left arm in arm.

Charles-Henry immediately hurried after them, but it took Xavier a moment to follow. "Oh shit, wait for me!"

When he was gone, Mathias, Alberto, Eric, and Zak all burst into a laugh.

"I think he's sort of adorable now. I can't help it," Zak said.

"I agree," Alberto said softly. "I like him."

"And he likes *you*." Eric waggled his eyebrows suggestively.

Mathias stopped him with a dark look. "I hope he does get into Oxford or Cambridge or whatever. I hope he stays there forever."

Zak and Alberto exchanged a smile.

"Well…" Eric gave Mathias's back an affectionate pat. "Not that I don't appreciate not having to keep Mattou's *many* secrets anymore, but… couldn't you have done this before and saved me some trouble?" He pointed at his scalp, his lips pursed. "I think my hair was starting to turn grey!"

"You knew?" Zak asked. "You knew and didn't tell me?"

Mathias immediately stepped in. "I made him promise. Don't blame him for being a good friend."

"I'm not," Zak said. "I'm just amazed he's so good at it."

"Baby…" Eric spread open his arms, a smug look on his face. "I'm good at so many things, as you well know…"

"Except modesty." Zak shook his head.

Eric gave a resounding laugh. Alberto watched him, his forehead creasing. When their eyes met, Eric's ears turned bright pink, and he looked away with an awkward grin.

"So, Mathias, your dad really works here?" Zak asked, changing the subject. "That explains why you can do whatever you want and Van Bergen never goes medieval on you."

Eric wrapped his arms around his boyfriend with a thoughtful look. "This Simon must be a truly scary person if he can handle the headmaster."

Mathias laughed. A real laugh, which set his eyes alight and made Alberto want to curl into his side and melt into him. "Come and see."

From up close, Simon didn't look so like a student at all, but he still appeared younger than he was. He barely reached Alberto's chest, which made him wonder how he would look next to his husband, the only person taller than him. Clad in a white tuxedo, his skin was like snow, and his face so charming that Alberto was stricken, for once. Apparently, he wasn't the only one to think so; he could practically feel Eric shake next to him.

"Twink fetish," Alberto whispered by his ear.

"I don't know what you're talking about."

"Even worse… Asian twink fetish. Such a cliché."

"Shut up!"

"Eric?" Zak's face split into a dangerous smile. "Do you want to make out with me in one of the supply closets, or should I just dump you now so you can ask him out?" He waited, his arms folded over his chest.

"Let's go," Eric said, the gorgeous Simon immediately forgotten. "I'll catch you later, Matt."

"Take your time!" Mathias replied. He waited a moment before taking Alberto's hand. "Okay, let's do this."

Mathias approached his godfather, his palm feeling sweaty in Alberto's hand. "Simon," he said, his voice barely audible over the music, "this is Alberto."

Simon left Elisa on her own to dance to "Under Pressure." His lips stretched into the kindest, warmest smile Alberto had ever seen, adorned with two adorable little dimples. Alberto suddenly grew shy for no reason. He shook Simon's hand when he offered it and was surprised how strong his grip was.

"I've heard so much about you," Simon said.

"Oh, great," Alberto replied, nervous. He had the feeling that meeting this guy was as close to meeting Mathias's mother as he would get. Mathias ran his thumb across the skin of his hand, soothing him.

"I've met your mother already," Simon said. "She's lovely."

"I know, she's great." Alberto swallowed, unable to meet the man's eyes.

"Has Mathias asked you to dance yet?"

"No." Alberto gazed at Mathias, who was shaking his head. "No, he hasn't asked me."

"Too bad. He's a great dancer."

"*Really?*" Alberto's lip curled. "Is that so?"

"Only on special occasions," Mathias muttered.

"Today is a special occasion," Simon argued.

"No," Mathias said, and he dragged Alberto away.

Surprised, Alberto tossed a look over his shoulder. Simon was waving at him, but the headmaster returned and said something in his ear, and they both vanished into the crowd. Mathias took him to the end of the fruit punch line, his expression too innocent to be genuine.

"Dragging me away from your godfather so soon?" Alberto teased.

Mathias snorted. "Before he can do more damage to my reputation."

"What is it? You only dance at weddings?"

"Something like that."

"I *knew* your mother would have taught you. I knew it!" Alberto brought his lips near Mathias's ear. "Do you know a bit of Taek-wondo as well?"

"What if I do?"

"Mmm…" With the tip of his tongue, Alberto poked Mathias's earlobe. "Next time, you'll show me *your* moves."

"Keep talking, see what happens…" Mathias sounded all

choked up. When his hand reached down to fidget with the front of his trousers again, Alberto smirked with pride.

"Is it me, or is it getting hotter in here?" he taunted.

In lieu of an answer, Mathias gave him a wounded look. They eventually made it close enough to the bar that Alberto could see his mother. "Mamma!" he called, lifting his hand over his head.

"*Tesoro*! Come, come to me!"

The guys standing in front of them sniggered, but Alberto didn't care. Mathias rudely cut in front of them and snarled at the only one who dared to complain. It was Xavier, already carrying two cups of punch, his forehead glistening with sweat.

"Are you sure you don't want to dance?" he was asking Mamma.

"Oh no, thank you," she replied politely. "*Again.*"

"Go, Xavier, please!" Mathias's father tried to shoo him away. "He's unbelievable, this one."

"How are you doing, Mamma?" Alberto asked, as Mathias was kicking Xavier out of sight. "Are you having fun?"

"A ton!" She smiled at Cyril, who took over for her, and wiped her hands on a towel. "Alexander and Simon have invited us to spend a weekend with them at their home near the forest. Would you like to go?"

"I hope you like animals," Mathias muttered. "And getting dirty."

Alberto chortled. "You know I do." He turned to his mother. "We'll go. Are you still coming to lunch at Mathias's on Sunday?"

Mamma turned to Cyril, who gave a solemn nod and said, "I'm cooking."

"You are?" Mathias sounded surprised. "That's awesome…" He reached for the ladle and served Alberto a cup of punch. "Let me know if you need help."

Alberto thanked him for the cup and took a careful sip. "Heavens." He stuck out his tongue, his eyes watering. "This is absolutely vile."

"Okay!" Mathias clapped his hands and ushered him away from the bar. "We met my family, we had *absolutely vile* punch, and we made sure Xavier wouldn't become your next stepfather." He pushed himself into Alberto's space and placed his hand on his stomach. "Let's go home and free that tummy of yours."

"No!" Alberto laughed when Mathias's fingertips tickled him. "You'll see it later, if you're good."

"But…" Mathias cocked his head. "I'll see it sooner if I'm bad."

Alberto swatted him. "You *are* bad." He abruptly joined their lips together and pushed his tongue inside his mouth until Mathias was forced to take a step back with a needy sound.

They stayed an hour at most. The lights and the music, the carefree laughter of their friends, Alberto enjoyed it all, and yet, he longed for the quiet of Mathias's room, for his full attention. Their talks, their *domestic* ways, how they slept entangled at night. In the end it was him who called it a night, who whispered to Mathias his desire to return to the comfort of his home.

Overjoyed at the prospect of leaving, Mathias only requested to make a quick stop to the bathroom. As he waited for him to return, Alberto watched the others dance, an easy smile on his lips. A tinkle of laughter caught his attention. Van Bergen was half-perched on the bar, feeding his mother nonsense, which seemed to fill her with delight. Simon eventually intervened, taking her away for a dance. There was colour and life in her cheeks. Mamma would be all right.

And he… he would also be all right. Probably. If only he weren't so much in love, he thought he'd combust at times. If he didn't have that fear to lose Mathias to the darkness that would never truly leave him. He would be all right.

A faint shiver alerted Alberto to a presence by his side. He turned his head, his lips parting in surprise. Eric's suit was all wrinkled from all his dancing and bouncing around. Still, he looked pretty nice. Alberto was no longer angry at him. He was no longer angry at all.

"Can I ask you something?" he dared, because why not? He might not get another chance.

"Hm?" Eric's gaze fell on him, devoid of animosity. "Sure, go ahead."

"Why do you always act like a bumbling idiot in front of Mathias? I know you're smarter than that."

Eric chuckled, a slow smile spreading across his handsome face. "Why?" He met Alberto's eyes. "Because he likes it, why else?" His gaze slid toward the bathroom door. "It makes him smile."

"I see." It was the first time Alberto looked into Eric's eyes. Those blue, shimmering things. Then his own eyes annoyingly started to tickle and burn. "Thank you," he said, his voice thick, "for taking care of him."

"You're welcome." Eric's gaze grew distant. "When I met Mathias, I was really unhappy. He was there for me. He wouldn't admit it, but he was there for me." He scratched his chin with a sigh. "He's a good guy."

Alberto didn't know what to say. He knew too well why Eric was unhappy at that time. "It was my fault if you—"

"Let's not talk about that. You hurt me, I hurt you, all that." Eric hung his head. "I wish I could take it back, sometimes. I wish I—"

"I know. Me too."

"I love Mathias, that's all that matters." Eric abruptly reached toward his shoulder. "Do you love him?"

Alberto averted his touch as well as his eyes, keeping his head low.

"Well?" Eric insisted. "Do you?"

"Do I have to say it out loud?"

Eric was silent for a moment. "No, Alberto," he finally said. "You're okay." He extended his hand. "We're okay."

Alberto stared at it for a moment before he shook it. He wanted to say something, apologise maybe, but Eric was already gone.

When Mathias came out of the bathroom, an invigorated Alberto fell on him like a curse. "How's that half-mast?" he asked, his fingertips digging in inappropriate places. "Have we fully risen yet?"

"Feel that." Mathias caught his hand and placed it on his crotch. "It's almost like you're driving me insane."

"I very much hope so."

"Can we please go now?"

Alberto nodded. Their arms swung over each other, they hurried across the court toward the exit. There were looks here and there; Alberto faced them with pride. His man was so handsome, everyone should stare and be burned by the sight. He gave Mathias a languorous look. "You know the feeling's mutual, right?"

"Oh, yeah?"

"Yes."

Mathias kissed his cheek. "Good to know."

"Let's go home, Mati. Quickly. We'll remove our clothes and tell each other stupid, sappy things, and tomorrow—" Mathias opened the door for him. The cool, summer night air bathed their faces, and Alberto sighed in relief.

"Tomorrow, we're going to the park, remember?"

"Oh?"

"I got you that book you wanted to read."

"Oh, that's right…"

"Do you remember?"

"I do now. So… you'll read it to me?"

"Of course. And we'll have a picnic. I got tomatoes from Alex's garden, and I'll make you those maki you like…"

"With cucumber?"

"*And* avocado."

"And for dessert?"

"For dessert, it's a surprise…"

Alberto and Mathias exchanged a loving smile. Into the dimly lit streets of Paris, they walked, hand in hand, toward their future together.

Famous last words

Once again, my deepest thanks to Silvia and Monica for everything Italian, as well as Leugim and Ana Valeria for translating Mathias and Elisa's Spanish.

Once upon a time, in the distant land of first drafts, Alberto was an expendable villain, nothing more than an obstacle to Zak and Eric's love. Little by little, he grew into one of my favourite characters. I wish we could all be so lucky as to turn real life antagonists into beloved friends.

SPECIAL THANKS

To those who have made this duology from hell (known to me as *The Great Box of Knives*) possible, but especially:

To Ralf & Michael, Alba, Ira, Urban, Pilar, Ritchie, Theresa, Bertie, Theo, Josh, Strigo, Alexander, Michael, Cris, Nick and Maja.

Your support was more than appreciated.

To Liz, for putting me back together so I could get back to doing what I love. And for reminding me that I was strong. To Hannah and Siyah, for giving me the tools to resume a normal life.

To Cheyenne. Where do I start? You have been there for me in a way nobody has ever before, and so were your idioms! Not to forget the cat pictures. Thank you for giving me the confidence to keep pushing.

To Natalie, for her inextinguishable wells of patience and understanding. My horror fan buddies are, in my experience, a model of compassion.

To Travis, Rose, Maya, Silvia and Monica. Yours is my idea of the cool kids' table.

To Mariëlle, for her unwavering kindness throughout the dark times, as well as her constant generosity. You truly are one of a kind.

To Oscar and to Leugim, thank you for all our lengthy talks, and for accepting me for who I am without mockery or judgment.

Thank you to those who have stayed, but also to those who have left. Unnamed here, but present in my memory. Your contribution, no matter how small, was appreciated.

To my best friend and partner, who showed me some people truly are worth the effort, and who embodies the only logical answer to my pervasive existential dread.

And to every one of you who ever wrote a kind message when I was doubting myself: Thank you. Time and time again, you have proven yourself the kindest, most compassionate and open-minded readers. It's an honour to be able to entertain you.

***

COLETTE INTERNATIONAL IS CLOSING ITS DOORS UNTIL FURTHER NOTICE.

***

Thank you for having selected and read this book. I sincerely hope you have enjoyed it.

And if you did, would you please consider **leaving a review?** **It's an easy and sure way to support an indie author.**

I'm aware that your time is precious; writing a single line or using the star rating can truly make a difference.

Keep on reading if you want to get **free access to bonus content** about Alberto and Mathias, and many other Colette International freebies.

With Love,

Zelda

CHAPTER LIST

WINTER

Arc Four: Dreamers

Arc Five: Stalkers

Arc Six: Keepers

*Chapters in **bold** are written from Mathias's POV.*

ABOUT THE AUTHOR

ZELDA FRENCH (THEY/THEM) LIVES IN LONDON, LIKES CATS, SWEARING, GOOD WINE AND ROCK MUSIC, AND REALLY ENJOYS ANGSTY STORIES WITH HAPPY ENDINGS.

YOU CAN FIND MORE INFORMATION AT:
WWW.ZELDAFRENCH.COM

amazon.com/author/zeldafrench

goodreads.com/zeldafrench

bookbub.com/authors/zelda-french

instagram.com/zelda_french

tiktok.com/@zeldafrench

·

CONTENT WARNINGS

For the reasons listed below, this story isn't intended for readers under the age of 18. In addition to profanity and underage drinking, *Part Two* DEPICTS ACTS OR **MENTIONS** ACTS OF:

> Abuse (physical, mental, emotional, verbal, sexual), depression, grieving, harassment, homophobia, nervous collapse, sexism, suicidal thoughts, suicide, violence, and explicit sexual acts between two eighteen-year-olds.

TREAT YOURSELF WITH CARE AND PROCEED WITH CAUTION.

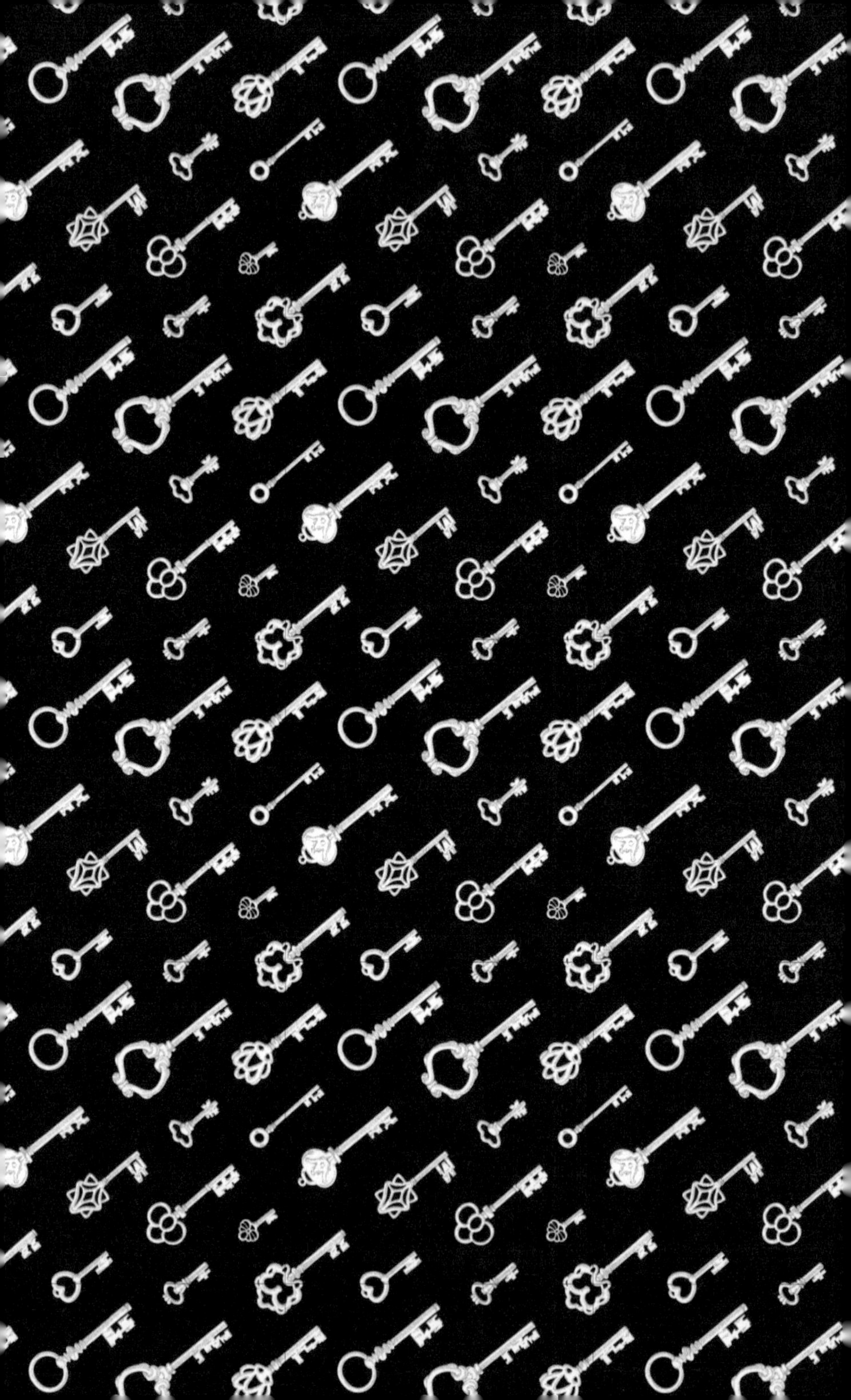